PINO

ANGEL IN HIS ARMS

Jared bit back a groan at the touch of her lips on his. Tessa was proving to be his agony and his ecstasy.

This was Tessa Sinclair—he told himself it was crazy to feel this way about her. This was the woman who was constantly causing him so much trouble. But all the logic in the world was lost in the ecstasy of her kiss.

This was Tessa, all right—this was the woman who wanted only to help other people. This was the woman who cared more about strangers than she did about herself. This was 'the Angel' as they called her affectionately in town.

And she was an angel to him.

Her kiss was heavenly, and just having her here, in his arms and knowing that she was safe, filled him with a sense of joy he couldn't explain. Jared wouldn't have thought it possible to feel this way about her a few weeks before, but now, everything about holding Tessa close and kissing her seemed right.

Jared tried to keep the kiss innocent, but when Tessa shifted on his lap, moving closer to him, he lost the battle. He tightened his arms around her, and deepened the kiss, parting her lips and seeking out her sweetness. . . .

BRIDES OF DURANGO:
TESSA

BOBBI SMITH

LEISURE BOOKS NEW YORK CITY

A LEISURE BOOK®

February 2000

Published by

Dorchester Publishing Co., Inc.
276 Fifth Avenue
New York, NY 10001

ISBN 0-8439-4678-4

The name "Leisure Books" and the stylized "L" with design are trademarks of Dorchester Publishing Co., Inc.

Printed in the United States of America.

This book is dedicated to the renowned, talented artist Pino Daeni. I have been honored and privileged to have his artwork grace my book covers, and my career has prospered because of it.
Thank you Pino! You're wonderful!

ACKNOWLEDGMENTS

I would like to thank the world's best book sales reps! The wonderful gang at HDG—Hearst Distribution Group—are responsible for getting my books out, and they are fabulous!

Nolan Bennett, Bill DeRuiter, Stephanie Lupo, Jennifer Marek, Mary Elder, Mabel Anguah, Christine Ouellette, Jim Curll, Bill Longo, Paul Pearce, Donna Loepp, Paul Kilber, Barry Kravac, Kathy Turpin, Terry White, Terry Bastuba, Virlee Neal, Renee Oldham, Chris Dunham, Peter Stephenson and Skip Marines—you are fantastic! Thanks!

I'd also like to thank Dr. Ed Schertzer, Dr. Richard Murray, and Dr. David McCollister for all their help, and to say 'Hi' to Charlotte Talbott and Suzanne Underwood, my two walking buddies, and to my friend Irene Hardy in Texas. Matt Ogles—you were a great PSR student last year! Charles DiFerdinando of the La Plata County, Animas History Museum was a big help with research! And I couldn't get everything done without Pam, Jocelyn, and Vonzell, my local postal employees. You're wonderful!

TESSA

Prologue

The wizened old woman gazed at the minister, her expression one of heartfelt emotion. "Reverend Trent, you are the answer to my prayers!"

"I'm just glad I could help, Mrs. Andrews," he told her, and he meant it. There was nothing John Trent liked to do more than bring joy to the lives of the less fortunate.

Lola Andrews clasped the package of direly needed food close to her breast as she smiled up at him. "You're a living saint."

John chuckled and blushed a bit. "I'm no saint, Mrs. Andrews. I'm just a man trying to do God's work."

"Well, you're doing a fine job, and I'm going to tell Him so," she said as she pressed a kiss to his cheek.

"Thank you."

In the sea of sadness that Lola's life had become, Reverend Trent was an island of comfort. Her husband had died earlier that spring, and since then her own health had been failing. She had no relatives to help her through these difficult times. She had only her friends from the church to rely on, and Reverend Trent was always there for her. It never ceased to amaze her how hard he worked to take care of those in need. He visited her regularly and always brought his young son, Jared, with him.

"And you, young man, it's so good to see you again, too," Lola told Jared, smiling warmly at the tall, sturdy, dark-haired youth who stood slightly behind his father.

He nodded and smiled in return.

"Men don't come any better than your father, Jared. Always remember that."

"Yes, ma'am," he answered respectfully.

"And you're going to grow up just like him, I'm sure of it," she stated firmly. She could already see the goodness in him, and the strength.

"I hope so."

The old woman looked back up at the reverend. "He's going to do you proud."

"Yes, he will," John agreed as he cast a warm smile at his son. "Now, you take care of yourself, Mrs. Andrews, and if you need anything else or an emergency comes up, you just send word. I'll get help to you as fast as I can."

"I'll do that, Reverend," she promised. "God bless you!"

"God bless you, too," he responded. "Good night."

John started off down the walk from her small,

run-down house, his son by his side. They had quite a distance to travel back to their own home on the other side of town, but they were in no rush to return. As they drove away in their carriage, he kept their pace leisurely. John was always on the lookout for people needing help, and if he traveled too quickly he feared he might miss someone.

"You've gotten awfully quiet, Jared," he remarked.

Jared glanced over at his father. "Mrs. Andrews really appreciates your visits, doesn't she?"

"She appreciates *our* visits, son" he answered gently.

Jared smiled, pleased with his answer.

"You'll find there are some folks who seem to be forgotten by everyone else," John explained. "They're the ones who need our help the most. We have to seek them out. It's our duty in life to bring joy to others whenever we can."

"She's very nice."

"Yes, she is," he agreed. "We'll check in on her again next week and make sure she's doing all right."

"Good."

John stayed off the main streets, choosing instead to use the less traveled roads. It was not the safest route, especially in the evening, but it afforded him the opportunity to see if there was anyone else in need this night. They were just coming up on an alleyway in one of the least respectable areas of town when John saw two men fighting. One was viciously pummeling the other as he dragged him into the darkened passageway.

"Wait here!" John ordered. He reined in and jumped out of the carriage to go to the man's aid.

"But Pa!" Jared knew a moment of fear.

"The man's in trouble. I have to help him."

John ran after the two, following them into the alley. He was intent on stopping the assault. As he entered the alley, the attacker came running at him. The man said nothing, but shoved John roughly aside as he passed.

"Stop!" John called out, but the assailant had already disappeared into the night.

John peered down into the darkness and spotted the other man lying facedown in the mud and filth. He ran to him, fearful that he'd been grievously wounded. Reaching his side, he knelt down and carefully started to turn him over. The stench of alcohol almost gagged John, but it didn't deter him. He was only concerned that the man might have been seriously hurt.

"Are you all right?"

"Get your hands off of me!" the man bellowed in a slurred voice, fighting against him. Drunk beyond all reason, he knew only rage at having been beaten and robbed.

John could see that the man was bleeding, and he knew he needed to get him to a doctor.

The drunk, thinking John was the assailant, wanted only to protect himself. He drew his gun and fired point-blank at the man laying hands on him.

Jared had remained in the carriage, intent on obeying his father, but when he heard him shout and saw the other man run out of the passageway, he feared his father was in danger, Jared jumped down from the carriage and ran after him to try to help. He had just entered the alley when the drunk fired his gun.

"Pa!" Jared's scream rent the night as he watched the horror unfolding before him.

The blast of the gunshot hit his father in the chest. John collapsed and lay still.

"Pa?" the drunk repeated dully, as he staggered to his feet and looked from the boy to the man lying in the mud.

"You killed him!" Jared cried as he ran to his father. He dropped to his knees beside him and saw just how terrible the wound was.

The drunk sobered, realizing what he'd done. He threw his gun aside and charged off as fast as he could go in his inebriated state.

For a moment Jared considered chasing him, but he knew he couldn't leave his father, not like this.

"Pa," Jared said softly, reverently, as he reached out to touch him. He had never seen anyone shot before, and it was something he would never forget. "Pa . . . don't die, Pa!"

As if from a great distance, John could hear the sound of his son's frantic call. He dragged himself back to reality by sheer force of will and opened his eyes to look up at his son one last time.

"Jared. I love you, Jared." It took all of his energy to reach inside his coat pocket and pull out the small Bible he carried with him at all times. "Here, son. Take this." He pressed the holy book into his hands.

"But Pa . . ." Jared stared down at the bloodied

17

Bible staining his hands now with the proof of his father's passing life.

"Tell your mother that I love her," John whispered, blood seeping from the corner of his mouth as his eyes drifted shut.

People who lived nearby had heard the gunshot and were coming at a run to help, but it was too late. When they reached Jared, John was already dead.

Jared stood apart from the crowd of people who'd come to the house to offer their sympathies on his father's death. The funeral had been that afternoon, and now, as the darkness of night claimed the land, it also claimed his heart.

"We're so sorry about John, Elizabeth," Audrey Taylor was saying to Jared's mother. "If there's anything we can do for you—anything at all—just let us know."

Cecelia Burnhart added, "John was such a good man. He was always helping others. It's horrible that something like this would happen to him."

"Have they found the one who did it yet?" Margaret Rollins asked.

"No," Elizabeth Trent responded tightly. "The sheriff hasn't learned anything yet."

"That's terrible! I hope they find the man soon! The world won't be the same without John," Audrey insisted.

"He's in a better place now." Cecelia tried to be reassuring.

"He's happy with God," Margaret added.

"He was such a wonderful man. No one cared about others more than John. He was always kind and so generous." Audrey couldn't praise him enough.

As Jared listened to their remarks and the talk of others gathered around, fury slowly filled him. They were wrong! They were all wrong! His father might have been a kind and generous man, but he had also been a fool! Jared was nearly shaking from the power of the emotions surging through him. Sure, his father had cared about others, but look what it had gotten him! He was dead. He'd been killed because of all his kindness and generosity. He'd been shot down in cold blood by a ruthless, stupid drunk!

Jared's hands began to shake as the power of his emotions gripped him. He silently quit the room, seeking solace away from the crowd of well-meaning but maddening visitors. He didn't want to hear any more of their comments about his father. He didn't want to hear how much everyone was going to miss him. He didn't want to know that the world was going to be a sadder place without him.

There was only one thing he wanted, and that was justice.

He wanted to catch the man who'd shot and killed his father. He wanted him locked up behind bars or swinging from a noose. He'd committed murder and should pay the price.

Jared left the house and went outside. He needed to be alone, to be away from all the noise and confusion. He found no peace in the night, though, only more turmoil and anger as he replayed in his mind the horror of the scene in the alley.

For the first time, then, Jared allowed himself

to grieve. Tortured sobs racked him as he mourned the loss of the father he had so loved and admired.

When at last the storm of his tormented emotions had passed, Jared drew a ragged breath. An undying, savage need for revenge began to burn within him, searing away his sorrow and hardening him against gentler emotions. It branded him forever with its power. He would not waste his time helping those who might shoot him for his efforts. Instead, he was going to concentrate on seeking justice and revenge. He was going to become the best lawman ever. He was going to hunt down killers and criminals and see that they paid for their crimes. Instead of relying on the Bible to save people, he was going to use a gun. He wanted to make certain that no one was ever gunned down again the way his father had been.

Any innocence in Jared's soul had been killed by the same bullet that had taken his father's life.

When Jared returned to his mother's side sometime later, he was no longer a boy.

He had become a man.

He knew what he had to do.

Chapter One

The church was aglow with candlelight, and the heavenly scent of flowers filled the air as Tessa slowly made her way down the aisle. The full skirt of her lace and satin bridal gown swayed gracefully about her hips as she moved ever forward.

She was getting married.

At last, she was getting married.

All around her were her friends and family. They were smiling as she passed them, their gazes warm and approving upon her as they whispered among themselves.

"She looks so lovely."

"I always knew she'd make a beautiful bride."

Tessa lifted her gaze to the altar. She could see the reverend waiting for her, Bible in hand, at the end of the aisle. Off to the side, with his back to her, stood her future husband.

Tessa smiled. Her mother had been urging her

to *find a good man and settle down for several years now, and it seemed the time had finally come. Getting married to the man she loved was every woman's dream, and her groom was her dream man. He was tall and dark and handsome and . . .*

Her heartbeat quickened as she reached the end of the aisle. Anticipation quivered through her.

This was her wedding day. She was going to live happily ever after.

Tessa stopped before the minister, who was gazing down at her, his expression serious. The moment had come. She was to be married.

The minister began the ceremony. "Dearly beloved, we are gathered here today . . ."

Tessa started to turn, to look up at her future husband as the minister went on. She wanted to gaze into her beloved's eyes and let him know without words just how much she loved him.

". . . to join in holy matrimony . . ."

This was the man she had dreamed of. This was the man she'd been waiting for. This was the man she wanted to spend the rest of her life with.

"Tessa Sinclair and—"

Tessa let out a cry of alarm as she stared up at her future husband. The man she was to marry loomed over her, tall, broad shouldered, and powerfully built, but he had no face! His features were a blur. They were completely indistinct. She didn't know who he was. There was no way to tell.

Horror overwhelmed her. In abject terror, she panicked and backed away. Turning, she ran back down the aisle. All thoughts of happiness and love were banished as she fled the scene, desperate to escape.

Tessa's heart was pounding a frantic rhythm, and her pulse was racing as she jerked awake. She struggled to catch her breath, as she slowly came to realize that she was riding in a stagecoach. The elderly woman sitting across from her was staring at her with an almost frightened look on her face.

"Tessa, dear, are you all right?" Doris Peters asked.

Tessa managed a tight smile—she wasn't really getting married. There had been no church, no altar, no faceless groom. "I'm fine," she answered a bit breathlessly. "It was only a dream."

"That must have been some dream," Doris told her. "You were talking and restless. In fact, you seemed so agitated that I almost woke you once or twice, but I knew you were tired and needed the sleep."

Before she'd fallen asleep, Tessa had been telling Doris how she'd just spent a week working at the new orphanage in Canyon Creek.

"I am tired, that's for sure," Tessa admitted.

"Just the fact that you could fall asleep on this stage is proof enough of that," Doris said as they hit another bump in the road and were jostled roughly about. "You must have worked really hard last week."

"I did, but it was a labor of love," she told her, smiling as she thought of the children she'd helped.

"You are so special, Tessa. Both you and your mother are so kind and giving."

"Thank you, but there is such joy in giving to

23

others this way. Years ago, after my father died, my mother was left alone with me and my brother to raise. We were poor and homeless, and someone helped us out. I swore then that I would do the same thing when I was old enough."

"And you have," the older woman said. She knew how generous Tessa was with the poor around Durango. Tessa owned and ran the boarding-house and was always feeding those in need and grubstaking down-on-their-luck miners.

"I'm just glad I'm able to help." She fell silent, and when she did, the image of her faceless dream husband drifted into her thoughts again. She shivered as she turned to gaze out the window.

"Thinking about your dream again?" Doris asked perceptively. "What was so terrible about it?"

"Oh, I don't know. I don't really remember," she answered quickly.

As troubling as the dream-turned-nightmare had been, Tessa wasn't going to discuss it with Doris. Doris was a very nice lady, but she was also a bit of a gossip. Tessa could just imagine who might hear tales of her faceless fiancé.

It was bad enough that her mother was always talking about her getting married. She was twenty-two and, in her mother's opinion, well on her way to becoming an old maid. She wasn't about to let anyone know that she was having nightmares about her unwed state.

"Are you sure you're all right now?" Doris pressed, still a bit concerned as she studied the slender, auburn-haired beauty sitting across from her. She could see the high color staining Tessa's cheeks and the slightly troubled look in her eyes. She couldn't help wondering what had upset her so.

"I'm all right."

"Well, good. I wouldn't want anything to be worrying you," she said with motherly warmth. She thought Tessa a darling girl and didn't want to think that she had any trouble in her life. Seeing that Tessa seemed relaxed again, Doris closed her eyes to seek some rest of her own.

Who were you? Tessa whispered to herself as she stared out the window, a vision of her faceless man before her.

She scowled, wondering why she'd even dreamed of getting married. She hadn't ever seriously thought about it. She was too caught up in taking care of the boardinghouse. And, she supposed, she'd never really been in love.

Were you Will? she asked herself silently.

The question left Tessa frowning as she tried to match Will's image with that of her phantom groom. Will was certainly her mother's choice for her, but somehow he didn't fit. Not that there was anything particularly wrong with Will Kenner. He was nice enough, she supposed. Her brother Michael had hired him on at their mine, and Will had proven himself to be honest and hardworking. He had come into town with Michael a time or two, but she'd had little time to think about courting and such.

Her mother, on the other hand, thought about her marrying a lot. Tessa knew her mother was going to be thrilled the day she finally settled down. But she had made up her mind that she wouldn't marry just for the sake of being married. She was happy the way she was.

Tessa's thoughts returned to her dream then, and she wondered again, *Who were you?*

It was then as she was lost in her musings that the shots rang out. Tessa and Doris were both jarred back to reality.

"Were those shots?" Doris asked, terrified, sitting up straight and clutching her reticule to her breast.

"Yes!" Tessa had become instantly alert at the sound. She tried to lean farther out the window to get a look at what was going on outside, but the ride was too rough. She was forced to sit back and hold on for dear life as the stage jolted to a faster pace.

The sound of the driver returning fire chilled them both.

"Oh, my God! They're going to kill us all!" Doris shrieked.

Tessa didn't say anything. She just kept a tight hold on the strap by the door and prayed silently that they could outrun the robbers.

Her prayer was not answered, though. More shots were fired at them, and she heard the driver scream. Then the stage started slowing. It finally came to a halt in a narrow canyon far from any civilization. Tessa heard horses riding up at a gallop. She was not surprised when a gruff male voice ordered them to get down out of the stage.

"You passengers! Your driver's been shot, and the same thing's going to happen to you if you don't get down out of there and keep your hands up!" The man's tone was harsh.

Doris was crying hysterically. Tessa reached out and touched her arm to try to calm her.

"We have to get out now, Doris."

"No! My life savings are in my purse! I can't lose my money! I won't lose it!"

"Shhh. They can hear you. Be quiet and just do what they say."

"No!"

"You! In the stage! Get out now, or we'll start shooting!" The order came again.

"We're coming!" Tessa answered, opening the door. She looked back at Doris. "We have to get out, Doris. Now! Come on."

Tessa climbed down first and turned to offer the older woman a helping hand. Doris's face went completely ashen as she saw the masked outlaws for the first time. Tessa, too, was intimidated by the gang. They wore gunnysacks over their heads with holes cut out for the eyes and mouth. The masks hid any clue to their identity. She had been hoping she would see something that would help her identify them later, but disguised as they were, their identities were a complete mystery.

"What do you want?" Tessa asked in the bravest voice she could muster as she glared up at the three.

Two of them had their guns trained on Tessa and Doris, while the third outlaw backed his horse away to slightly higher ground. He appeared to be the leader of the gang.

"Get their money!" the leader ordered in a gruff voice.

One of the outlaws chuckled evilly as he dismounted and came toward the two women. The other gunman climbed up into the driver's box, shoved the injured driver aside, and wrestled the strongbox to the ground.

The outlaw going after the women grabbed Tessa's reticule from her. His presence was frightening, but Tessa managed not to give in to her panic. She stood straight and proud before him as he opened her reticule and rifled through the contents. After stuffing what little money she had into his pockets, he threw the reticule aside and advanced on Doris.

"No!" the old woman cried, backing away, desperate to keep her hard-earned savings.

"I ain't got time for this, lady!" the outlaw snarled as he grabbed her purse.

But Doris was determined not to lose her money. She clung to the purse, refusing to give it up. It was then that the outlaw struck her full-force, and the old woman collapsed to the ground. Blood was dripping from her mouth, and she was sobbing.

"Doris!" Tessa dropped to her knees beside the woman and tried to comfort her.

"The stupid bitch shoulda given it up without a fight," the man said as he opened her purse. He looked inside and laughed loudly. "Oooeee! Lookee here what I found!"

He held up the wad of money for the other men to see.

"Damn! That's almost as much as I got here in the strongbox!" the other man crowed, stuffing the spoils from the strongbox into the saddlebags they'd brought with them.

"You can't take my savings! You can't!" Doris shouted, trying to get to her feet.

The outlaw wasn't in the mood to put up with a crazy woman, and he roughly pushed her back down.

"Why, you . . . !" Tessa had had all she could stand of his brutality. It was one thing to take their money. It was another altogether to abuse an old lady.

Furious beyond reason, Tessa charged at the man. Her assault was unexpected, and she managed to hit him once. She grabbed his mask, ripping a part of it. He reacted instinctively, fearful his identity would be discovered. He hit Tessa and turned his gun on her.

"It wouldn't take much for me to shoot you!" he threatened as he stood over her.

Tessa lay in the dirt at his feet. Her cheek was bruised and bloodied from the force of his blow, but she was glaring up at him defiantly. She only wished that she'd been able to tear the whole mask off him instead of just one little piece.

"In fact, I think I will," the outlaw went on, looking down the bore of his gun at her.

"No," came the shout from the leader. "Let's ride! Now!"

"But . . ." The gunman was furious. He was ready to shoot her point-blank.

"I said no!" the other man ordered again.

With that, the leader spun his horse around and started to ride off, leaving the other two to follow.

The frustrated outlaw cursed viciously as he slowly backed away from Tessa and Doris. He didn't holster his gun again until he had mounted up and was ready to follow the others.

Tessa was trembling as the three of them disappeared from sight. Terrified beyond reason, she somehow managed to make her way to Doris's side.

"Are you all right?" she asked.

Doris looked up at her with wide, frightened eyes. "Are they gone?"

"Yes."

"Oh, my God! We could have been killed!" She began to cry even harder. "And they took all of my savings! I have nothing left!"

Tessa's cheek was throbbing, but she gave no thought to her own injury. "Can you get up? I need to check on the driver. He's been shot."

"I—I think I can," Doris answered weakly.

Tessa slipped an arm about her and helped her to her feet. She then walked with her to a shady spot nearby and settled her on a large, flat rock.

"I've got to see how Butch is. I'll be right back."

It was difficult climbing up into the driver's box in her skirts, but she managed. To her horror, she discovered that Butch had been seriously wounded.

"He's still alive, Doris! Come help me get him down, so we can take him into town to the doctor!"

Doris felt light-headed and weak, but she knew it was an emergency. Forcing herself to calm down, she helped Tessa lower the injured man from the driver's box. It wasn't easy, but they finally got him inside the stagecoach.

"I'll tend to him. Can you drive?" Doris asked.

"I've never driven anything this big before, but

there's always a first time for everything," Tessa said with bravado she wasn't feeling.

Hoisting herself into the driver's seat, Tessa took up the reins. She prayed she could control the team as she slapped the reins on their backs and urged them to a gallop. They had to get to town fast. Butch's life depended upon it!

Will Kenner was angry as he rode at top speed from the scene of the robbery with his men following close behind. He yanked off his mask and cast a quick glance back at Zeke and Bob. He had a few things he wanted to say to Zeke, but knew he would have to wait until they'd gotten far away from the stagecoach.

The robbery had gone smoothly, but they couldn't afford to get overconfident because of their success. Overconfidence would result in mistakes, and mistakes often proved deadly in this business.

Almost an hour passed before Will finally reined in to rest the horses.

"Damn, we're good," Bob boasted.

"Yeah! How much do you think we got today? We made quite a haul with that old lady's money!" Zeke said, feeling cocky as he turned to Bob and Will. One look at Will's expression, though, sobered his mood. "What's the matter?"

"You dumb son of a bitch!" Will swore. "What the hell did you think you were doing pulling your gun on the woman like that? Don't you know who she was?"

"What woman?" Zeke was confused. "The old lady?"

"Hell, no! The young one—"

"That stupid, interfering bitch? She's lucky I didn't shoot her!" he snarled.

"That 'stupid, interfering bitch', was Michael's sister!"

"Are you serious?" Bob was shocked.

"What was she doing on the stage?" Zeke demanded defensively.

"How the hell am I supposed to know? All I know is that you'd better never do anything like that again!"

"Don't order me around," Zeke warned.

"When you act stupid, I sure as hell am going to order you around! Now, let's ride."

Will headed off again. He was still furious at Zeke for what had almost happened and needed more time to calm down. If anything had happened to Tessa—

Will gritted his teeth and kept riding. He had big plans for what he wanted to accomplish in Colorado, and he didn't want anything or anyone to ruin them.

When they had been working the Arizona Territory the year before, there had been four in their gang. Pete Howard had been riding with them then. They had robbed at will for months, easily avoiding capture and taking no chances. Pete, Bob and Zeke had even gone so far as to frame another fast gun for one of their robberies near Tucson. That had distracted the authorities for a while, but then the law had almost trapped them near Phoenix. The three of them had managed to escape, but Pete had been shot and arrested. With the law closing in, Will had decided it was time to leave Arizona. They had taken on new aliases then—Will, Bob and Zeke were not their real names—and headed for Colorado. Judging by the way things had gone so far, it had been a good decision.

Will had come to Durango ahead of Zeke and Bob to scout out the area. He'd taken a job working for Michael Sinclair at his gold mine, the Ace High. The Ace High was a small undertaking, and there had been only two other men working there when he'd hired on. Since then, those two had quit, so when Bob and Zeke showed up, Will had met with them and told them how to get hired. As he'd hoped, Michael had taken them on, and now they were the only workers, at the mine, along with Michael. From the very beginning, they'd made certain that Michael did not know they were friends.

The arrangement was perfect. Whenever Michael went into town to take care of business or to see his family, they knew he'd be gone for several days. It gave them the time they needed to sneak away from the mine, pull off a robbery, and get back before he returned. There was one shaft in the mine that had played out and was boarded up. They hid the loot there, knowing it would never be discovered.

This had been their second robbery, and no one seemed to have any idea who they were. That was good. Will knew they would have to keep striking at odd times and places to keep the authorities guessing about their identities. He'd heard how good the marshal of Durango was, and he didn't want to mess with Trent—No one wanted to mess with that arrogant bastard.

The biggest problem Will had right now was Zeke. Zeke had a violent streak. He wasn't too smart, which sometimes made him hard to control. That could be a dangerous combination, and Will knew he was going to have to keep a close eye on him.

Will led the way into the mountains. They would be forced to camp for the night and then make the last leg of the ride to the mine at sunup. They didn't want to risk Michael's returning ahead of them and discovering that they were gone.

Chapter Two

"Marshal Trent" shouted one of the townsfolk in the street. "Get out here fast! The stage is coming in at a run, and they're screamin' something about being robbed!"

Jared had been sitting at his desk, enjoying the quiet of the moment, but now that was over. He charged from his office, ready for trouble.

Glancing down the street, he stared in disbelief at the sight of what looked like a slender, auburn-haired woman driving the stage. As it came closer he could make out that it was Tessa Sinclair, and he could see that she was having trouble stopping the team. In a daring move, he stepped out into the street and grabbed the lead horse's bridle as the team slowed before him. The horses dragged Jared a short distance before they came to a ragged stop.

"What happened?" Jared demanded, still keeping a tight hold on the bridle.

"Three masked gunmen robbed us about four miles out of town. Our driver was shot, but he's still alive. He's in the stage," she quickly explained as she sawed back on the reins, struggling to keep control over the animals. She'd been glad when she'd seen Marshal Trent come running out of his office to meet them. She'd deliberately driven down this street in the hope that he'd be there, and she was impressed by the way he'd helped stop the team. He had a reputation as a fine lawman, and she hoped he could go after the outlaws right away.

Jared rushed to throw open the stage door. He stared into the cramped interior of the stage to find Doris Peters bent over Butch.

"How is he?"

"He's still breathing," Doris answered, glancing back at the marshal over her shoulder.

"Thank God." Jared got one good look at Butch's wound and turned toward the crowd of people who were gathering around. "I need help getting him out of here!"

Two men came forward, anxious to help Jared in any way they could. The three of them lifted the grievously injured driver from the confines of the stage.

"Take Butch down to Dr. Murray's office," he ordered. "Tell the doc I'll be down to check on him shortly."

"Yes, Marshal."

They hurried off, carrying the injured man to the office less than a block away.

Jared turned to the two women. It took a lot to

impress him, but Tessa Sinclair had just done it. In spite of the horror of the robbery, she'd kept her wits about her and had not only saved the driver's life, but had brought the stage in single-handedly. She was one hell of a woman, and darned pretty, too. He went to assist Tessa, who was now helping the older woman climb out of the stagecoach. Jared had been so caught up in the drama of stopping the team and getting Butch to the doctor that he hadn't paid a lot of attention to the two women. As they turned to speak to him, he went still.

"What happened to you?" Jared demanded at the sight of their bruised faces.

"One of the robbers did it!" Doris declared tearfully. "He hit me, and when Tessa tried to help me, he hit her, too! He was going to shoot her."

Jared's expression turned stony at her tale. He was outraged over the robbery, but even more furious that the robbers would hurt defenseless women. "Are you all right?"

"I don't know," Doris said, near hysteria again now that she no longer had to concentrate on helping Butch. "It was all so terrible, and they stole my money!"

"I need to talk with both of you about the robbery, but first I want Dr. Murray to take a look at you. Do you need any help getting over to his office or can you make it on your own?"

"I'll help Doris," Tessa told him.

"Should we come back to the jail to talk to you after we see him?" Doris asked, clinging to Tessa's arm for support.

"No, I'll come find you."

The women moved off, leaving Jared staring

after them. He'd been hard put to control his anger when he'd seen their injuries. But when Doris had told him that Tessa had been hurt coming to her aid, he'd almost lost his temper and said something to the young woman that he knew he would later regret. He couldn't imagine what she'd been thinking, putting herself in harm's way like that.

That was how innocent people got killed—just like his father.

A muscle worked in Jared's jaw. He turned away from the stagecoach and strode back toward the office. He had to get a posse ready to ride—and fast.

It was nearly an hour later when Jared knocked on the door at the Sinclair house. He had organized the posse, and arranged for Deputy Wells to take over for him while he was away. The posse was waiting for him at the jail, ready to ride out as soon as he returned. He had stopped to talk to Doris first at her home and was now ready to speak with Tessa. He needed to learn all he could about the gang of outlaws before he went after them. This was their second robbery in the area, and he was bound and determined to catch them.

Maggie Sinclair heard the knock at the door and hurried to answer it. She was thrilled to find that it was the lawman. She thought highly of him and knew that if anyone could catch the robbers, it would be Marshal Trent. The tall, dark-haired marshal had an aura of power and command about him that garnered respect from all who met him.

"Hello, Mrs. Sinclair. I need to speak with

Tessa, if she's able." His expression was serious as he spoke.

"Come in, Marshal Trent, and, please, just call me Miss Maggie, like everybody else does."

"Yes, ma'am."

"Tessa is right here in the parlor," she said, leading the way down the hall.

"Thank you." He followed her, taking off his hat as he came inside.

Maggie showed him into the parlor, where Tessa was sitting on the sofa. She sat down beside her daughter as he took a chair opposite them.

"Miss Sinclair," Jared said, taking care not to show any emotion as he saw the vivid mark on her cheek. It was testimony to the terror she'd been forced to endure, but it did nothing to mar her natural beauty. Tessa was a lovely woman, and he was impressed by how calm and in control she seemed. She had to be a very strong woman to be so composed after what she'd been through. He had just left Doris, and the older woman had been nearly hysterical as she'd related the details of what had happened during the robbery.

"Please call me Tessa," she invited. Jared Trent was a compellingly handsome man, and she found his presence reassuring. She started to smile in welcome, but the effort failed when the pain in her cheek reminded her of her injury.

"And I'm Jared," he returned. "Did everything go all right at the doctor's?"

"Yes. Dr. Murray said it was just a bad bruise, and that it will go away in a week or so."

His dark-eyed gaze was so intent upon her that she reached up self-consciously to touch her cheek. She attributed her sudden nervousness to all that had happened that day.

"I'm glad it was nothing more serious," he told her, and he meant it. He knew from what Doris had told him that Tessa was very lucky that she hadn't ended up dead.

"Did you speak with Doris already?"

"Yes, I just came from her house."

"How is she feeling?"

"She's still shaken and badly bruised, but I'm sure she'll be fine in time."

"Good. What can I help you with?"

"Tell me everything you remember about the men who robbed you. How many were there? What did they look like? What were they wearing? Did anything about them seem familiar?"

Tessa related what little she could, but it was nothing substantial. The outlaws had been smart and careful. And Jared was frustrated.

"So there was nothing distinguishing about them? Nothing at all?"

"No," Tessa answered slowly, thoughtfully. "If they had just been wearing bandannas, I might have been able to tell you more, but with the hood-type masks they had on I couldn't see their faces. I grabbed one outlaw's mask and did manage to tear it a little, but not enough to get a look at him."

"What about their horses? Was there anything about them that would make them stand out? Did you happen to notice any of their brands?"

"No. There was nothing unusual or different about their mounts," Tessa told him. "I wish there had been, but it all happened so fast. . . ."

"All right. You said the robbery happened about four miles out of town?"

"Yes, right where the road narrows. We were trapped. Poor Butch. Did you hear anything more about his condition from Dr. Murray? When Doris and I were there at the office, he told us that he'd managed to get the bullet out, but he still didn't know if Butch was going to make it or not."

"I haven't heard anything new. I'll check with the doc again before I ride out with the posse."

"So you *are* going after them," she said with satisfaction.

"The posse's waiting for me at the jail right now. If I can find the gang's trail and bring them in, I will," Jared promised her. He'd given chase after the first robbery the month before, but had lost their trail in the mountains. From the description of the masks Doris and Tessa had given him, he was certain it was the same gang.

"Good," Tessa said with heartfelt emotion. "I'll feel much better when I know they're locked up."

"So will I. These are vicious men, and they shouldn't be on the loose." He rose to go, and then knew he couldn't leave without cautioning her about her reckless behavior. "Doris told me how you tried to help her."

She nodded, looking up at him. "I couldn't believe that they were going to steal from an old lady."

"The men you were dealing with were not gentlemen—they were criminals. You could very easily have been killed today for your effort," he told her critically. "In the future, be more careful."

"But I couldn't just stand there and let that man hurt Doris!"

"All your good intentions could have gotten you shot. You wouldn't have been much help to her dead!"

The thought of someone as vibrant and beautiful as Tessa Sinclair dying senselessly over money infuriated Jared. His gaze went over her, seeing the fire of defiance in her eyes—and the mark of her injury. He realized then just how delicate she really was—and how vulnerable she had been to the outlaws' attack. She'd been unarmed and defenseless, and yet she'd tried to face down brutal bandits alone! If he hadn't been so angry with her, he might have admired her spirit.

Tessa saw the cold anger in the lawman's gaze, but though Marshal Trent was the intimidating sort, she didn't cower before him. She wouldn't have been able to live with herself if she hadn't tried to help her friend. "I had to do something" she countered. "They'd already shot Butch. What if they'd shot Doris, too?"

"You were no match for an armed stage robber." Jared lectured sternly. "Anytime you're dealing with criminals, take the path of least resistance. Give them what they want. What did you think you were doing, putting yourself in danger that way?"

"I know exactly what I was doing," she replied with cool dignity as she gave a stubborn lift of her chin. "I was helping a friend."

"Moral superiority is no defense against savage force," he countered.

"I know that," Tessa replied, her own anger returning at his harsh criticism. "But it was up to us to defend ourselves. It wasn't as if there were any brave lawmen riding up in the nick of time to save us!"

Her words were a slap in the face to Jared. He prided himself on keeping Durango safe from trouble. A muscle worked in his jaw as he struggled to control his temper.

"I'll be in touch."

With that, he strode from the room and the house. He didn't look back.

Tessa was glad when he left. His dictatorial manner had irritated her, and she decided that she didn't think he was quite so handsome, after all. No, in fact, she thought he was rather arrogant.

Will, Zeke, and Bob arrived at the Ace High by midmorning. They were pleased and relieved to find that Michael had not yet returned. Everything had gone according to plan. Life was good. After quickly tending to their mounts, they got a lantern and went to hide the money in the abandoned shaft. They had to get back to work again right away for it was important to convince Michael that they'd been hard at work the whole time he'd been gone.

"Not too bad for just two jobs," Zeke said as he stared down at the money they had stashed away.

"How long do you think it will be safe for us to keep this up? Do you think they'll catch up with us faster here than they did in Arizona?" Bob asked.

"No," Will answered. "I know Marshal Trent has a good reputation, but we'll just make sure we don't give him anything to go on. Who would suspect that we're the robbers and that we're hiding the money in a working mine?"

"I don't know about you, but I don't want to work here for too damned long," Zeke said, looking around the mine shaft. "This work is too hard."

Will shook his head in disgust. "You think any work is too hard, Zeke. No one will ever think to look for the money here."

"What money?"

The sound of Michael's voice coming from just behind them shocked all three.

"Michael? You're back early," Will said quickly, unsure of just how much their boss had overheard.

Will started walking back toward him, but Michael had already come near enough to see what they were doing.

"What money, Will?" Michael looked from Will to the others and then down to the saddlebags and small chest on the floor. "What are you doing in this shaft? Did you find something in here?"

Michael had returned from town early, knowing that there was a lot of work to be done at the mine and that his men worked a lot harder when he was there keeping track of things. And judging from what he'd just found, it was a good thing he had come back early. It didn't look as though they'd done much of anything in the three days he'd been away.

Michael started around the three men to see what it was they were talking about, and it was then that Will struck.

Will knew he had no choice. As Michael passed him, Will drew his gun from his holster and hit him full-force on the back of the head. Michael had been totally unsuspecting of any possible danger. He collapsed to the rocky ground and lay unmoving.

"Damn! What did you do that for?" Bob asked nervously as he stared down at Michael's prone figure.

"What was I going to do? Let him find out what we're doing here?"

"But he's going to be real mad when he comes around." Bob was scared.

"We ain't going to let him come back around," Zeke spoke up. "We've got to kill him."

"Couldn't we just tie him up and leave him here? Nobody would be coming to check for days, and it would give us time to get away!" Bob looked at Will, waiting to see what he would say.

Will smiled thinly. He'd had a plan about what he wanted to do here, but if Michael were dead . . . that changed things, and, as he thought about it now, it changed things for the better. This was definitely an opportunity for him. The mine would need someone to run it, and he could be that someone. He was Michael's friend, and he was ready and willing to take over running the Ace High for Tessa Sinclair and her mother. He knew the mother liked him already, and if he played things right, he might end up not only with the mine but with Michael's good-looking sister, too. "It seems such a tragedy that we had the cave-in this morning," he said in a cold voice.

"Cave-in?" Bob asked, confused. "What cave-in?"

"That's how Michael was killed, you know. We were checking out the abandoned shaft, and one of the support timbers gave way. It took all three of us over an hour to dig Michael out, and by the time we did, it was too late."

The three outlaws shared a look as they began to make Will's plan a reality.

It was much later that afternoon when Will mounted up, ready to ride for town. He was leading the horse that was carrying Michael's body. Will had had Zeke hit him several times so that Will looked like he'd been injured by the cave-in, too. He wanted all the sympathy he could get when he reached town with the tragic news.

"What do you want us to do while you're gone?" Bob asked. He was nervous.

"I want you to work the mine. That's what you were hired for, and that's what you should be doing."

"How long are you going to be?" Zeke asked.

"As long as it takes to set this up the way I want it—probably a few days."

They watched him ride off. Zeke was pleased by the way things were turning out, but Bob was worried and more than a little scared that the truth of their crime would be discovered.

Tessa stood beside her mother, her arm supportively around her shoulders, listening to Reverend Ford's final prayers over her brother's grave. The past week had been hellish for them. The stage robbery had been terrible enough to deal with, but her brother's tragic death had been devastating. Michael had been only twenty-eight years old, and now he was gone forever. Her heart ached, and she knew how totally lost her mother was feeling. It seemed her mother had aged ten years before her very eyes.

"Amen." The preacher concluded the final prayer, then turned to them. He took Maggie Sinclair's hands in his as he spoke. "Mrs. Sinclair."

He looked at Tessa. "Tessa. You both have my deepest sympathy in your loss. Michael was a fine young man. He will be sorely missed."

"Thank you, Reverend," Maggie managed in a voice choked with painful emotion.

"If you need anything, anything at all, just let me know," he said.

Tessa nodded, but didn't speak. She wasn't sure at that particular moment if she would be able to. Memories of her brother were overwhelming her. She had loved him dearly and wondered if she'd ever get over losing him.

Those who had come to the cemetery with them gathered around to speak with them.

"Tessa, I am so sorry." Julie Stevens, her closest girlfriend, hugged her.

"Me, too," Tessa answered raggedly. "Michael wasn't only my brother. He was my friend. I'm going to miss him."

"I know."

Adele and Lyle Stevens, Julie's parents, came up then to talk with Tessa and her mother as others offered their condolences, too.

Clad in the suit he'd bought just for the funeral, Will stood off to the side, slightly apart from the rest of the mourners. He was waiting for just the right moment to approach the two women. He had remained in town for the funeral and planned to stay on one more day to discuss what to do about the mine. He planned to offer to take over running it for them and hoped they would go along with the idea. It would be the perfect setup for him and the boys.

Will smiled to himself as he thought of how smoothly everything was going. Things couldn't have turned out any better if he'd planned it this way. He'd gone to a saloon the night before to have a few drinks and relax, and he'd heard all the talk of how the marshal and his posse still hadn't returned from trying to track down the outlaws who'd robbed the stage. The news had made him smile. This had been their second robbery, and they had successfully managed to elude the lawman. Life was good—especially now that they didn't have to worry about Michael. They could come and go as they pleased, and no one would ever be any the wiser about their activities.

"Will, we're going back to the house now. Would you care to join us?" Maggie Sinclair saw him standing by himself and invited him along. Michael had liked him, and she had always trusted her son's opinion of people.

"Thank you, Mrs. Sinclair. I'd like that." He made sure his manner was properly respectful. He offered her his arm, and he was pleased when she took it. Glancing up, he found Tessa's gaze upon him, so he gave her what he hoped passed for a reassuring smile as he led her mother from the graveside.

Chapter Three

Jared's mood was black. He was not a man who handled frustration well. They had been tracking the outlaws for days, but once again had lost their trail in the rocky, mountainous terrain. He prided himself on being thorough, but he feared that he'd missed something where these robbers were concerned. The only clue he'd been able to find was a small scrap of cloth near the actual scene of the robbery. Tessa had said that she'd managed to rip the robber's mask, and he hoped that this was the part she'd torn off. As far as clues went, it wasn't much, but it was better than coming back completely empty-handed.

It had been Jared's experience that men who resorted to robbery for a living weren't very smart. This gang, however, was proving to be a challenge—and this was the kind of challenge Jared didn't want in or around his town.

The posse was riding back into Durango now after almost a week on the trail—hot, tired and irritated by their lack of success.

"Any luck?" asked Nathan Wells, the deputy Jared had left in charge, as he came out of the jail to greet them.

"Luck? What's that?" Jared answered in sarcastic disgust as he dismounted. He dismissed the rest of his men, then entered the office with Nathan. He quickly explained to him what had happened while they were on the outlaws' trail. "How have things been around here?"

"It's been quiet. There was one thing, though."

"What happened?"

"Michael Sinclair was killed up at his mine," the deputy told him.

"Damn." He immediately thought of Tessa and her mother, and he could well imagine their pain. "How?"

"Will Kenner, one of the men who works at the Ace High with Michael, brought his body in. He said they were checking out an abandoned shaft, and one of the timbers gave way. Will was injured, too, but with the help of the other miners, he managed to dig Michael out."

"How's the family?"

"They're doing as well as can be expected, I guess. I went to the funeral yesterday."

Jared's expression was grim. He'd known and liked Michael. "I'd better go over today and extend my sympathies. I need to ask Tessa a few more questions about the robbery, too."

"It sounds like these boys are pretty slick," Nathan said.

"They aren't as slick as they think they are. They're going to make a mistake, and when they do, I'm going to be ready and waiting for them," he vowed.

Nathan nodded. He knew that anything Jared Trent set his mind to, he did. He had learned a lot during the time that he'd been working for him.

"How's Butch doing?" Jared asked.

"He's coming along. Dr. Murray says he'll make it, but it's going to take a while."

"I'm just glad he's going to be all right. It didn't look good the other day."

"What are you going to do about the robberies?"

"If we had any kind of physical description of the robbers, we'd stand a better chance of catching them. The way things are, though, we're going to have to sit tight and see what they try next." Jared didn't like being made a fool of. "I can be a very patient man when I have to be."

"Maybe we'll get lucky, and they'll move on."

"Somehow, I don't think that's going to happen." Jared gave him a sardonic grin as he started from the office. "I'm going to get cleaned up and then head over to the Sinclairs' to pay my respects. I'll see you in the morning."

With that, Jared returned to the small house he rented in town. It was less than half an hour later when he approached the Sinclair home. He wasn't looking forward to this interview, for he knew this had to be a terrible time for both Tessa and her mother. He knocked on the door and waited, hat in hand, to be let in.

"Marshal Trent." Jim Russell, gray-haired man

who lived at the boardinghouse, greeted him and held the door wide so he could enter. "Come in."

"Thank you," he said as he stepped inside. "How are things going?"

"Not too good," Jim said sadly. "Michael was much too young to die."

"Yes, he was," Jared agreed. "Nathan Wells told me what happened. I'm sorry."

"We all are. Maggie and Tessa are in here." He directed him down the hall and into the parlor. "Your visit is most timely. Tessa and I were just getting ready to ride up to the Ace High with Will and pay a visit to the men there."

Jared entered the parlor to find Tessa seated on the sofa next to her mother. She was wearing a day gown and had her thick hair tied back with just a simple ribbon. She looked ladylike and delicate; then, as she looked over toward him, he saw the bruise on her cheek. The mark was fading, but still visible, and the sight of the bruise, even now, had the power to trouble Jared.

"Tessa." He said her name as he moved toward her, acknowledging her mother, too. "Miss Maggie."

"Marshal Trent," she responded quickly, as if surprised to see him. Then she quickly corrected herself: "I mean Jared. I hadn't heard that you'd returned."

"We got back to town less than an hour ago, and I heard the terrible news about Michael. I'm sorry about your loss."

"So are we—but thank you," Tessa replied quietly, still struggling to come to grips with what had happened.

"He was a good boy," Maggie put in sadly. "I don't know what I'm going to do without him."

"You know Will and I are going to help you as much as we can," Jim said in a reassuring tone as he went to stand by Maggie.

"Will Kenner?" Jared asked.

"Yes," Tessa said. "He should be arriving any moment. He's agreed to stay on at the mine and take over running things for us. He had worked for Michael for some months and knows how my brother wanted things done."

"We're very fortunate to have Will working for us," Maggie said. "Why don't you take a seat, Marshal."

"Thank you, ma'am."

Another knock sounded at the door just then.

"That's probably Will now," Jim said as he went to answer it.

When Jim returned, Will was with him.

"Will, have you met Marshal Trent yet?" Tessa asked, smiling in welcome when the tall, blond, sturdily built miner appeared in the parlor doorway.

"No, I haven't," Will said. He went to Jared and shook hands.

"It's good to meet you. I understand you're the one who tried to save Michael," Jared said, noting Will's injuries—a few small cuts and abrasions and bruises. He definitely had fared better in the cave-in than Michael had.

Will looked up at the lawman, taking care to keep his expression solemn. "I just wish I could live that day all over again. I'd make sure we never went down in that shaft."

There was silence at his statement. There was nothing anyone could say. They all knew there was no changing the past.

"Tessa, there was another reason for my visit. If you have a moment?"

"Of course. Did you find something that will help us catch the robbers?" She was hopeful.

"As a matter of fact, I did want you to look at this and see if you recognize it." He went to her and handed her the small piece of cloth he'd found.

Will went still at the sight of the material, but no one noticed. They were all too busy watching Tessa and waiting for her answer.

"Oh, yes," she said softly as she handled the bit of material. "That's what I tore from the robber's mask!"

"You're sure?"

"I'm positive." Tessa looked up at him, the expression in her eyes suddenly brighter as she handed the scrap back to him. "Will this help you in any way?"

"I'm not sure, but I'm working on it."

"So you still don't know where they went to hide out or who they are?" Will asked casually.

"No. We lost the trail up in the mountains again," Jared answered, looking over at Will. "Whoever they are, they certainly know the area."

"I just wish you'd caught them," Tessa said quietly.

"So do I," he agreed in a flat tone, irritated by his lack of success. "And we will catch them—eventually."

"I hope so." Tessa sounded less than convinced. "If you'll excuse me, I have to get ready to go up to the mine with Will and Jim. Will you be need-ing me for anything else over the next few days?"

"No, not unless something unusual comes up."

"Fine. I'll check in with you when we get back, then." Tessa rose and left the room.

"Marshal Trent, thank you so much for coming by," Maggie said with heartfelt sincerity. "It was very thoughtful of you."

"I really am sorry about Michael. He was a good man."

"You're very kind," she said, looking at him with a tear-filled gaze. "It's just such a tragedy. No one should ever die that young."

"Miss Maggie, are you going to be all right if I make this trip with Tessa?" Jim asked solicitously.

The older woman looked at her longtime boarder and smiled sadly. "I'll be all right. Sludge will be here, and Henry, too. Besides, you and Tessa won't be gone that long, will you?"

"No. We should be back in less than a week."

Jared rose and said his good-byes to Miss Maggie, Jim, and Will. He left the parlor and headed down the hall, showing himself out. Tessa had just started back downstairs when he caught sight of her on the stairs. She had pulled her hair back and had styled it into a long braid. She was wearing pants, a blouse, a vest, and riding boots, and the vision caused him to stop. She had said she had to go change, and this was quite a change.

"Are you leaving?" Tessa asked when she saw him standing there.

"Yes, ma'am." Jared had seen her dressed this way before, but it had always been from a dis-tance around town. He'd never been this close to her, and he had to admit that she was quite an attractive sight in pants. He was immediately irritated with himself for having the thought. He hadn't come here to ogle Tessa Sinclair's legs. "You have a safe trip to the mine."

"Thanks."

Jared was scowling as he left the house.

The trek to the Ace High was not an easy one, but Tessa, Will, and Jim planned to make it in little over a day. They camped out about halfway for the night and were up at dawn and ready to ride.

Tessa knew some of the ladies in town criticized her because she occasionally made these trips, but she ignored their remarks. The one good thing was that there had never been any questioning of her virtue. Not that she would have wasted time defending herself. She had work to do and couldn't be bothered worrying about other people's pettiness. She knew she had nothing to be ashamed of, and that was all that mattered.

"We're almost there," Will remarked as he led the way up the last mile of the winding trail to the mine site.

"It's going to seem strange not to see Michael," she said softly, girding herself for what was to come. It was going to be painful, but she knew it was important that she speak to the miners about the changes that were taking place.

Will's expression was troubled and his tone regretful as he said, "If there had been any way I could have saved him—"

"I know, Will. You did everything you could," Tessa said. She could imagine how difficult it must have been for him to have survived while her brother had died.

"Mines can be dangerous places. You always have to be careful," Jim said. "One mistake can—"

"Prove deadly," Tessa finished sadly, then looked at Will.

Will had been very supportive, and she appreciated his willingness to help them run the mine. She had done some mining of her own and could have taken charge, but it was better to have Will there supervising things. That way she could still concentrate on the boardinghouse, for her mother wasn't able to run it by herself.

"I want to tell the men that nothing is more important than their welfare," she went on. "I don't want you to take any risks. Hitting a mother lode would be a wonderful thing, but all the riches in the world aren't worth one man's life."

"They'll appreciate your concern," Will answered, knowing full well that Zeke would. It would be just the excuse he needed not to work very hard.

Tessa fell silent as the Ace High came into view. The few small buildings that served as the office and housing for the men, and the mine's reinforced entrance, were all that marked its location. On past trips, Michael had always come rushing out to meet her. He'd been eager to see her and to tell her the progress they'd been making. Now only silence greeted her. Those wonderful days she'd spent with her brother were gone forever.

They reined in and dismounted. Will came to walk by Tessa's side as she headed for the office, while Jim tended the horses for them.

Will was quite satisfied with the way everything was going, though he was having a difficult time not watching Tessa every minute. He'd always thought her attractive, but dressed as she was now, he wanted her in a bad way. He would have to control his desire for her until the time was right, though, and it wasn't going to be easy if every time she came up to the mine to speak with him about business, she looked like this. He fought to keep from touching her as he opened the door for her and let her enter the office ahead of him. His baser needs urged him to take her, but he controlled himself. It wasn't often in life that things came easily to him, and he wasn't about to ruin this—not when he finally had everything set up so perfectly. He would have Tessa Sinclair. There was no doubt in his mind about that. One day in the not-too-distant future, she would be his—in all ways.

Will fought back a smug smile as he watched her move about the deserted office. He could tell that she was looking for signs of her brother. He remained quiet for a while to let her come to grips with the reality of the situation.

"Do you want me to call the men now? I'm sure Zeke and Bob will be glad to see you."

"That'll be fine—and before I leave, I want to go into the mine. I want to see where Michael . . ."

"Are you sure about that?" Will asked. "It's probably not all that safe in there. I told the boys to seal up the shaft good and tight."

"It's something I have to do," she answered simply. "But get the men first."

Will left her there in the office and went to call

the miners. It took a few minutes for Zeke and Bob to emerge from the mine.

"You're back," Zeke remarked with a nasty smile. "How did things go in town?"

"Keep your voice down," Will ordered. "Miss Tessa and Jim Russell rode up with me. She wants to talk to you two."

"Us? Why?" Bob asked fearfully.

Will pinned him with a cold-eyed, deadly glare as he said with a snarl, "You take care what you say, Bob. I'd hate for you to have a mining accident, too!"

Bob swallowed nervously and nodded. "I will, I will."

"Good. Things went fine in town." He turned back to Zeke and answered his question. "I'm going to be in charge of running the mine now. Miss Tessa's here just to talk with you about everything that went on, that's all."

"Where is she?" Zeke asked. He was annoyed that he had to act like he cared about Michael.

"She's up in the office waiting for you, so come on," Will said, not looking forward to this at all.

Jim was there with Tessa when Will returned with the two miners.

"Tessa, you've met Bob and Zeke before, haven't you?"

"Yes," she said softly, looking up at the three men who she'd heard had tried so hard to rescue her brother. "And I just wanted to thank you for what you did," she told them earnestly.

"What we did?" Bob's voice was almost a squeak.

"She gave him a gentle smile. "Will told me how hard you worked trying to save Michael after the cave-in. I want you to know how very grateful my mother and I are for your courage and bravery. Thank you so much for trying to help him."

Zeke nodded toward her. "It's just a shame we couldn't get him out in time."

"I know. Michael loved the Ace High," Tessa said softly. "And I want to keep things running as close to normal as we can. I already told Will that I don't want you to take any risks with this mine. All the money in the world isn't worth one person's life. So please be careful."

"We will, ma'am," Bob promised.

She graced him with a smile. "Will? Can you show me where it happened?"

"Come with me."

"Jim, do you want to come?"

"No. I'll wait here for you."

Will escorted Tessa from the house to the mine entrance. They picked up a lantern and started into the darkened interior. It didn't take long to reach the barricaded opening to the abandoned shaft.

"This is it," Will told her in a strained voice, looking sorrowful.

Tessa stood before the boarded-up shaft, staring at the newly devised blockade. A part of her wanted to see the exact spot of the cave-in, but she knew it was best to stay where she was. She lifted one hand to touch the barrier, and a rush of emotion swept over her, sending a chill down her spine. Her imagination played terrible scenes of Michael's death before her. Tears filled her eyes, and she bit her lip to keep from crying. After a long moment she looked up at Will. He was standing nearby.

"Thank you. I've seen enough."

Relief washed through Will as he walked with her from the mine. "Is there anything else you can think of that we haven't discussed? Anything else you're concerned about?"

"No. I'll make sure the payroll gets to you on time, the first of the month. If you find that you need anything, just send word to us."

"I will."

They emerged from the mine's cool darkness into the brightness of the late afternoon sun.

"Will you be starting back now or do you want to spend the night and ride back first thing in the morning?"

"Seeing as how it's so late, I think it'll be best if we ride out at sunup," she told him.

Will left her with Jim then, and went to straighten up the room that Michael had used as his own. She needed a private place to spend the night.

It was much later, well after midnight in fact, when Will lay in his own bed, awake and restless. As tired as he was, he figured he should have fallen asleep long ago, but rest was proving elusive as his mind conjured up image after image of Tessa. Tessa as she'd looked at the funeral . . . Tessa clad in pants walking before him . . . Tessa, even now, sleeping in the room behind the office not so very far away from him.

Will gave a low, frustrated growl and rolled

over. There was no denying that he desired her, and he wondered how long he would have to wait before he could make her his. He hoped it wasn't too long. He wasn't the kind of man who liked to wait for his pleasure, and he knew he was going to find much pleasure in her arms.

Chapter Four

Sarah Wilson lay huddled under the covers, pretending to be asleep as her husband, Boyd, climbed into bed with her. He had been in town drinking for most of the day, and she didn't want anything to do with him. Liquor turned him into a cruel, savage man. She hoped that if he thought she was sleeping he would ignore her and eventually pass out.

"Woman!" Boyd bellowed in a slurred, drunken voice. "I'm needin' a ride! Get over here so I can mount you!" He laughed at his own crudity.

She stiffened, but didn't respond to him. She silently prayed that the liquor he'd drunk would render him senseless very soon. Only then would she be able to relax.

But it wasn't to be.

"Damn it, woman! When I tell you I want somethin', you damned well better see that I get it!" he roared, grabbing her shoulder and dragging her toward him.

His grip was bruising, and she immediately struggled against him. She knew what was coming and she couldn't bear it again. "Don't!"

"You tellin' me no, woman?" Boyd snarled as he rose up above her on the bed and pinned her to the mattress.

"Let me go, Boyd! Don't!"

With all his strength, he backhanded her, bloodying her lip and snapping her head sideways. She continued to fight against his domination, but he wasn't about to let her up. His touch was punishing as he tore her gown from her body and took what he wanted without preamble or gentleness. The fact that her body was not ready to accept him didn't stop him. With force bordering on violence, he took what he believed was his to do with as he pleased—and he pleased to take her right now. She was his wife. It was her duty to submit to him. He pounded into her, battering her with the power of his drunken need. He wouldn't stop until he was satisfied.

"You love it and you know it." He panted as he bit at her neck and pawed at her breasts.

Sarah tried to squirm away, to escape his touch. Angered by her efforts, he hit her again and put his hands at her throat to choke her into submission.

"Don't fight me, Sarah. It might be the last damn thing you ever do!" he told her as he continued to thrust into her.

Sarah could taste blood in her mouth from his blows, and tears traced forlorn paths down her cheeks. She was helpless before his drunken strength. In silence, she began to pray that it would soon be over. She vowed to herself then and there that she would never suffer another beating at Boyd's hands again. He was her husband, but the vows they'd exchanged had been pledges to love and cherish one another. This wasn't love. Boyd had never loved her. She knew that now.

Sarah lay still. She forced her thoughts away from the present. She suffered his assertion of his conjugal rights without any more resistance. Her cheek ached, and every inch of her body cried out from the pain he was inflicting. When at last he finished and rolled off her, she did not move. She feared that it would rouse him again. She knew from past experience that if he came at her another time, he would be even crueler. Long minutes passed. She waited until she heard him snoring before she slipped from the bed.

Ten minutes later, Sarah escaped from the house with only one bag of her belongings. She knew what she had to do, and she was going to do it. It didn't matter anymore what the preacherman had told her when she'd gone to him desperate for help—that she was Boyd's wife, and if he was beating her, then she wasn't doing what she was supposed to do to keep her husband happy. He'd sent her back to Boyd telling her to work harder at pleasing him. When Boyd had learned what she'd done, he'd beaten her even more severely.

Now there would be no more. Sarah had made up her mind. She was leaving and she was never going back. She couldn't. Not now. Not with her child growing inside her. She wanted a new life, and she was going to have one. She was going to have a life filled with love and gentleness, not one of terrifying drunken abuse.

Sarah was frightened. She knew it wouldn't be easy to make it on her own. But she was going to do it for the sake of her unborn child.

There was only one person in town who could help her get away unnoticed, and that was Tessa Sinclair. Sarah was going to her now in the middle of the night. She'd heard about all the kind things Tessa did for people, and she hoped she could help her. Everyone was always talking about how Tessa was an angel in their midst. She worked with the orphans, and she helped down-on-their-luck miners. She helped homeless people find places to stay, and she never judged or criticized anyone. And right now, Sarah knew she needed all the help she could get. It wouldn't be easy getting out of Durango, but she was going to do it. She had no other choice but to flee for her own life and that of her child.

Tessa had been grateful that the weeks following Michael's death passed quickly and quietly. Things seemed to be running smoothly enough at the mine, and she kept herself and her mother busy running the boardinghouse.

It was past midnight when Tessa was awakened by someone knocking softly on the door that opened to the back alley. Tessa was surprised that anyone would come to the house at this time of night, but she also realized that it must be important for someone to come to see her now.

Tessa got up and pulled on her wrapper. Taking

her bedside lamp with her, she made her way quietly to the back door. No one else in the house was stirring, and she was glad. Whoever this was, she was certain her visitor wanted privacy.

Opening the door, Tessa found a young woman standing before her. Her face was battered, one eye swollen completely shut and her lip swollen to twice its normal size. It took only one look for Tessa to realize that this was serious.

"Come in, please."

"Thank you," Sarah said in a voice barely above a whisper as she hurried indoors and out of sight. Only when Tessa had closed and locked the door behind her did she breathe a bit easier. She'd been in terror ever since she'd crept from the house, fearing that Boyd would awaken and come after her in a drunken rage. She never wanted to face that again.

"My name's Sarah Wilson, and I need your help," she said quickly. "I have to get away. I have to . . ."

Sarah's tears started then, and she couldn't stop them. When Tessa slipped a supportive arm around her, she sagged wearily against her and gave in to her misery. It was long moments before she was able to pull herself together.

"Are you all right?" Tessa asked, truly worried about the young woman.

"Now that I'm with you, I am," Sarah said, managing to give her a smile.

Tessa smiled gently at her as she took her hand. "What happened? Should I call for Marshal Trent?"

"No!" Sarah trembled at the thought of having

Boyd arrested. She knew he'd be released right away and come after her again. "I just want to get out of town. I have to get away."

"Who did this to you?"

"My . . . my husband," she whispered in humiliation.

"Have you tried to get help from your minister?" Tessa knew that sometimes when a minister talked to a husband he began to understand how precious his wife was.

Sarah quickly told her everything she'd done since marrying Boyd a few months ago. She told her, too, about her unborn child. "I knew he drank when I married him, but I never dreamed he'd beat me. I never thought he'd be so cruel to me. I didn't tell him about the baby. I was afraid of what he might do."

Tessa patted her arm reassuringly. "Don't worry. If you don't want to go back to him, you don't have to. Do you have family anywhere? Someone who can take you in and help you?"

"My brother is in Denver. I can go to him. I think he'll help me," she said, clinging to her only hope.

"Let me see what I can do. You come with me."

She led Sarah up to an unoccupied bedroom on the second floor.

"Stay here for tonight. Try to get some sleep. In the morning I'll check both the stage schedules and the train schedules. I'll arrange the quickest passage out of town for you. Is that all right?"

"Bless you, Miss Tessa. It's no wonder everyone calls you 'the angel,'" Sarah said.

"They do?" Tessa had not heard that before, and she gave the other woman a surprised look.

"You didn't know that?"

"No, but I'm honored by it."

"There's nobody else like you, Miss Tessa. There's nobody else who will help out the way you do. That's why I came to you. I knew you would understand. I knew you would help me."

Tears burned in Tessa's eyes at her kind words. "I'm just glad I *can* help you. Now, you try to rest for a little while. Would you like something to eat or drink?"

"No. I'm too nervous to think about food."

"Well, let me get you a basin and some water. Maybe a cool compress will help with that swelling," she said, concerned. She remembered how badly her own cheek had ached after the stage robbery.

"Thanks. That would feel good."

"I'll be right back."

She hurried off to get the water and a cloth for Sarah. After she'd brought it to her and made her comfortable, she turned to leave.

"Miss Tessa?"

Tessa glanced back at the young woman.

"Please . . . I want you to be careful—real careful. If Boyd ever finds out that you're the one who helped me, he might come after you, and he's one mean man."

"We'll just make sure he never finds out where you've gone or who helped you get there," Tessa said confidently, not wanting Sarah to worry any more than she already was.

"Thank you."

* * *

When Tessa had gone, Sarah sat alone in silence, cherishing the quiet and the feeling of peace and security that surrounded her there. Before she finally dozed off, she offered up a prayer that she would be able to get out of town safely. Her rest didn't last long, though, for Tessa came back for her shortly after sunup. The knock at the door jarred her from her troubled sleep, and Sarah opened the door to find Tessa and her mother standing there, Tessa with a tray full of hot, steaming breakfast food.

"Good morning, Sarah. This is my mother," Tessa said as she entered the room and set the tray on the bedside table.

"It's nice to meet you, Mrs. Sinclair."

"Maggie will do, dear," she said warmly.

"Yes, ma'am."

"You can leave on the eight o'clock stage," Tessa told her. "Do you think you can be ready in time? That's barely an hour."

"Oh, yes. I can be ready. I want to be out of town before Boyd wakes up. He's mean when he's drunk, but when he's hungover, he's even worse. I don't ever want to see that man again."

"I can understand why," Maggie said, seeing how badly she'd been beaten. "Tessa tells me you're going to have a baby."

"Yes." Some of the fear that had shown in Sarah's face disappeared at the mention of her unborn child. She seemed more in control, more mature suddenly. "That's why I came here, Miss Maggie. That's why I've got to do this."

"I understand, child. From this day on, you take care of yourself. Don't let anyone treat you badly ever again. You don't deserve that. You seem to be a wonderful person, and you're going to be a wonderful mother."

Her kind words bolstered Sarah's tormented soul. "I'm going to try."

"Well, right now, eat some breakfast. We have to get you to the stage depot by eight. I'll go over now and buy the ticket. That way all you have to do is show up and get on the stage."

Just a few minutes before eight, Tessa accompanied Sarah, disguised as a widow, from her house. She was wearing a black dress and a heavy veil so no one would be able to recognize her. Tessa escorted her to the stage depot and pressed an envelope into her hand.

"What's this?"

"Some money to help you get settled," Tessa told her.

"But . . ." Sarah realized she had no way to pay Tessa back for all the expenses of her ticket and the extra cash.

"Don't worry about it."

"But I will worry. How can I ever repay you?"

"Don't even think about repaying me. Just pass along the kindness. That's all I ask of you—that, and a promise you'll take care of yourself and your child."

Sarah impulsively hugged her close. "You are my angel—my guardian angel," she whispered in her ear. "Bless you."

With that, she climbed into the stage and the driver closed the door.

Tessa remained at the depot, watching until the stagecoach had traveled out of sight. Knowing

that she'd done everything she could to help
Sarah, she started back home. She prayed that
the young woman would find safety and happiness. She deserved it after what she'd been
through.

Boyd woke up late in the morning. His mood was
ugly and his head was pounding.

"Sarah!" he bellowed.

When no response came, he rolled himself to a
sitting position and looked around the bedroom
with bleary eyes. There was no sign of her there,
so he got up and staggered into the front room.
Finding that empty, too, he headed for the
kitchen.

"Damn it, woman, where are you?" he shouted.

Boyd wanted her there right that minute, waiting on him hand and foot. But there was no
answer to his calls. The house was silent.

"When I find the bitch, I'm going to beat her
within an inch of her life!" he swore out loud as
he stumbled back into the bedroom and sat back
down on the bed.

Boyd groped on the nightstand for the open
bottle of whiskey that he'd left there, and, finding
it, he took a deep swallow. There was only one
thing that helped his hangovers, and that was
another drink. He chugged down a few more
gulps and then lay back to wait for the liquor to
take effect. Once his head stopped pounding, he
was going to get up and find his useless wife. He
didn't know where she'd gone, but once she came
back—and he knew she would be back; she
always came back—he was going to make sure
she never went anywhere without him again.

It was midafternoon before Boyd actually started looking for Sarah. It wasn't like her to stay away this long. She'd hidden from him in the past, but she'd always come back eventually. Trouble was, she hadn't shown up, and he was getting madder by the minute. It angered him that he had to get up and go look for her. When he did find her, she was going to get another taste of his temper for putting him out this way.

The pounding on the door took Tessa by surprise. She was home alone and wondered who could be so frantic to get in.

"I'm coming!" she called, hurrying down the hallway.

Tessa would never know how she managed to keep her expression calm as she opened the door and found herself face-to-face with Boyd Wilson. Her breath caught in her throat as she forced a smile.

"Why, hello, Mr. Wilson. What can I do for you?" She deliberately stepped outside, not wanting to be alone in the house with him.

"I came for my wife!" he said angrily, trying to look past her into the house. "Where the hell is she? I know she's here somewhere!"

"You're wife? Sarah?" Tessa wondered how he'd found out that Sarah had come to her. Someone on the street must have seen her coming into the house last night and told him.

"Yes, my wife, Sarah! I heard tell she came here and talked to you last night. I want to know where she is!" He towered over Tessa, a big, ugly, powerfully built man. His features were contorted by his fury, making him look even uglier.

73

Tessa studied him for a moment and understood why Sarah had fled. She could see no trace of kindness or gentleness in this man. She didn't know what had happened to him to make him so vicious, and she didn't want to know. Each and every person made the choice of how he was going to behave, and Boyd Wilson liked beating up other people. Tessa was sure it made him feel powerful and in control. Sarah had been right to leave when she had.

"I don't know where she is," she answered with dignity.

"You're lying!" he challenged, taking a threatening step toward her.

"I don't lie," she answered, looking him straight in the eye. And it wasn't a lie. At that particular moment she did not know where Sarah was.

"Miss Tessa? Is something wrong?"

Tessa had never in her life been so glad to see her boarder Sludge Phenning coming home from work. Sludge was not a very bright man, but he was big and strong and gentle of spirit. He worked for David Forsyth at the stables, and Tessa liked him a lot.

"Well, Sludge, you're home right on time tonight. Mr. Wilson stopped by for a visit, but he was just leaving," Tessa said as Sludge came to stand with her. "Good-bye, Mr. Wilson." It was a dismissal.

Boyd was a big man, but Sludge was at least three inches taller than he was. Sludge stood protectively by Tessa's side like a guardian angel.

"You ain't seen the last of me!" Boyd said in a low, threatening voice as he turned away, cursing.

Chapter Five

Tessa went inside and Sludge followed her in. She closed the door behind them and was tempted to lock it, but, with Sludge back and the others due home soon, she reasoned she was safe.

"Thank you," she told her boarder.

"For what?" Sludge asked innocently.

"There's something about that man I don't like—and you know I don't say that very often."

"He's mean," he answered simply. "I've seen him with his horses. I don't like him."

She smiled up at Sludge, seeing the complete truth of what he was feeling in his expression. "You're a very good judge of character, Sludge Phenning."

He blushed at her praise. "I'll be in my room."

Tessa watched him disappear up the steps and smiled to herself. Sludge was a very special man.

He'd lived at their house for almost a year now, and in all that time he had never caused them one problem. Sludge had always been helpful and courteous, and paid his room and board right on time. Other than the fact that he had no relatives, they knew little about him. He was a quiet giant of a man who kept to himself. The one thing they did know about him was that he loved animals. Certainly David Forsyth, down at the stable, was pleased to have him working for him, for Sludge had a way with horses that was rare.

Heading back into the kitchen, Tessa tried to put all thoughts of Boyd Wilson out of her mind. It was time to start cooking dinner. She hoped her mother and the other boarders, Jim and Henry, returned soon. She needed happy people around her tonight.

Dinner was enjoyable. Tessa did not mention Boyd Wilson's visit, and she was relieved when Sludge didn't either. She didn't want her mother to worry.

Bedtime came too early as far as Tessa was concerned. She tried to tell herself that she wasn't worried about Boyd, but the man did make her flesh crawl. She knew what he was capable of and would be just delighted if she never saw him again. She was glad, too, that Sarah was far away from him now. The young woman didn't deserve the torment of being married to someone like him.

When sleep finally claimed Tessa, it was near midnight. Her rest was troubled. Her dreams were jumbled and confusing. She saw visions of Sarah, beaten and desperate, and of Boyd, dominating and cruel.

Tessa frowned in her sleep, wanting to change things, wanting to make things better, yet feeling helpless. Their images faded, and her dream of her own wedding returned. This time, though, it was different. Instead of feeling excited about getting married, Tessa was frightened. Sarah's story of how Boyd had changed after their wedding haunted her as she walked down the aisle toward the altar and her unseen fiancé. She wondered if the same fate would befall her.

It was that thought that jarred her awake. She got out of bed, her heart pounding. She stood there, staring around the room for a moment, trying to calm herself. When at last she realized it had all just been a dream, she wandered to the window and looked out. The night was dark and peaceful. A gentle, cool breeze stirred the curtains.

"It was just a dream," she whispered to herself, and then she managed a smile.

Sarah was safe. She had helped her escape a dangerous situation, and by now the young woman was far away from the man who would do her harm. Sarah would be protected by her family in Denver. Sarah would start a new life, and Boyd would never find her. Everything would turn out all right.

Reassured by those thoughts, Tessa went back to bed and curled up under the covers. It was some time later before she finally drifted off again, but when she did, her sleep was deep and dreamless.

"I'm going to kill that bitch!" Boyd Wilson swore violently as he downed another shot of whiskey.

He had been in a bad mood when he'd first come into the High Time Saloon, and with each passing drink his mood had worsened. He slammed the empty glass down on the counter and watched as Dan, the bartender, refilled it.

"Calm down, Boyd," Dan said as he set the whiskey bottle aside and went back to polishing the bar in front of him. "Women are like that. They just like to make men crazy. There's no reason for you to get so worked up about things."

"What the hell do you know about any of this? You ain't never been married!" Boyd snarled, his temper about to explode. His anger and outrage were so great that he was ready to fight anybody—even Dan.

"You don't have to be married to know women," Dan told him with a confident smile. He wanted to distract Boyd and keep him from getting violent. He knew, along with everyone else in the High Time, just how nasty things might get if Boyd got out of hand.

Boyd could be one mean bastard, and the last thing they wanted in the saloon was trouble.

Boyd snorted in disgust. "Hell, you don't know nothing about them until you're married to them. They ain't nothing but trouble—always whining and complaining. It's a miracle I ain't killed her yet, but I may just do that when I get my hands on her again—and that stupid Sinclair bitch, too!"

Dan stiffened. "Get control of yourself, Wilson. I don't like it when you make threats. Miss Sinclair is a fine lady. She deserves your respect."

"Like hell she does! The way she runs around

this town, wearing pants and looking like a man? Why, she ain't nothing but an interfering slut!"

Dan grew even angrier at his insults. "Miss Sinclair's reputation is spotless. She dresses that way because she owns a mine and has to go inspect it. I don't know a living soul who has anything but praise for Tessa Sinclair and all the kind things she does to help people out around town."

"Kind things!" he shouted, on the brink of losing control. "That bitch helped my wife leave town! I'm going to make her pay for that! I'm gonna see to it that she never meddles in anybody else's life ever again! You just wait and see if I don't!" He lifted his glass and took a deep drink.

Dan was glad when another customer farther down the bar called out to him. He took his time waiting on the other man, for he was worried and trying to figure out what to do about Boyd. Shorty Dawson, one of his regular customers, came in then, and Dan was relieved. He made his way to the end of the bar to speak with him. When they'd finished talking, Shorty nodded and left. No one paid any attention to his departure, not even Boyd, and that was exactly what Dan had hoped would happen. Dan went back to waiting on his customers, but he kept an eye on Boyd.

Jared was enjoying another quiet evening in town. Sitting at his desk, he was reading the new issue of the Durango *Weekly Star* and feeling quite satisfied. Things had been so quiet in Durango this week that even Elise Jackson didn't have an exciting lead story for the paper. He grinned at her piece on the Ladies' Solidarity and their fundraising efforts. He liked dull—no shooting, no fights, no more stage robberies. The last thought stung, though, for although there had been no new robberies by the gang, he had not been able to learn anything more about them except that the material used for the masks was from bags that some miners used for transporting their ore. It was a clue, but with so many miners in the area, it didn't narrow down his area of search. The gang was still out there. He was certain of that.

Thoughts of the robbery brought Tessa to mind, and Jared's easygoing expression turned to a frown. He hadn't spoken to her since that day at her house, but it seemed she was never far from his thoughts, whether he wanted her to be or not. Certainly the vision of how she'd looked coming down the stairs wearing pants was seared into his memory. Sometimes when he was out around town, checking on stores and businesses, he would hear people talking about her. He never heard anyone say an unkind thing. Those who knew her had nothing but high praise for her acts of kindness and charity. In fact, listening to the gossip was the only way he'd found out what she'd been doing on the stage from Canyon Creek—working at the orphanage. There she'd been, donating her time and, knowing her, no doubt some of her own money, only to be robbed on the way back home. It infuriated him.

"Marshal Trent!"

The man's shout startled Jared. He was just rising from his desk to see what the trouble was when Shorty Dawson came charging into the office.

"Dan Lesseg needs you down at the High Time!" Shorty told him.

"What's happening?" Jared asked as he strapped on his gun belt.

"It's Boyd Wilson. He's all drunked up and threatening to kill people."

Jared was disgusted. He'd had run-ins before with Wilson and knew the man was a violent drunk. "Who does he want dead this week?"

"It's bad, Marshal. His wife left him, and he's wanting to kill her and Miss Tessa!"

Jared stopped and stared at him. "Tessa Sinclair? Why would he want to hurt her?"

"All Dan told me was that Wilson's wife had left him and he was blaming Miss Tessa. We gotta get back there right away. We can't let anything happen to her!"

"You're right about that." Jared growled in frustration. He had warned her to stay out of harm's way, and here she was in trouble again. He gave a disgusted shake of his head and led the way from the jail, his expression grim. There was no way Boyd Wilson was going to get anywhere near Tessa.

The more Boyd drank, the more frustrated he became. He slammed his empty glass down on the bar again and demanded in a loud, slurred voice, "Gimme another one."

"Don't you think you've had enough for one night?" Dan asked. He kept his tone mild. He didn't want to rile Boyd any more than he already was, but he also didn't want the man tearing up the saloon when he got too drunk to control himself.

Boyd was mean when he was sober, but he was even meaner when he was drunk. In a quick, violent move, Boyd surged across the bar and grabbed Dan by the front of his shirt. He jerked the bartender forcefully to him, smiling evilly at his startled expression.

Silence suddenly reigned in the saloon.

"Look, you stupid son of a bitch," Boyd said to Dan in a growl. "I said I want another drink! Get it for me or I'll—"

"Or you'll what?"

At the sound of Marshal Trent's voice, Boyd went still.

"What the . . . ?" Boyd didn't ease his fierce grip on Dan's shirt. He just looked over his shoulder. He was shocked to see the tall, powerful lawman standing right behind him. Marshal Trent's stance was determined, his expression fierce.

"What the hell are you doing here, Trent?" he said with a sneer.

"I heard you were stirring things up here at the High Time, so I thought I'd drop in and see what was going on. Looks like I didn't get here any too soon. Let Dan go, Boyd, *now.*" Jared's tone was commanding and brooked no argument.

"I don't think so," Boyd answered, giving the lawman a sarcastic half grin. He wasn't in the mood to have anyone tell him what to do. He was too furious with all that had happened in his life. He wanted to get his hands on his slut of a wife and that Sinclair bitch. He would start with Dan just because Dan was there, and he would work his way through town until he got to Tessa Sinclair. He was going to make her real sorry that she'd crossed him—real sorry. "I kinda like seeing him so scared, don't you?"

"I don't like anybody being scared in *my* town," Jared said. "Let him go."

Boyd released Dan, and the bartender backed quickly out of reach. Boyd still didn't turn around to face the marshal. Instead, he ignored him and picked up his glass. He took another drink, acting as if nothing had happened.

"Let's get you out of here and sober you up," Jared told him, not trusting Boyd's quiet manner. He knew too much about him to believe he would give up that easily.

"I'm not botherin' anybody, marshal. I'm just enjoyin' a drink here at the bar." He was fighting to keep his anger at the lawman's interference from showing. He didn't need Jared Trent sticking his nose in his business.

"That isn't what I heard, Boyd. I heard you've been threatening to kill people—like your wife and Miss Sinclair."

"I don't know what you're talking about," he ground out, looking up at Dan with hate-filled eyes, knowing the bartender had been the one to send for the law.

"Well, let's just take a walk outside and talk about it," Jared ordered.

"There ain't nothing to talk about. I didn't mean nothing by it."

"I don't like that kind of talk. Threats are serious business. Now, come on outside with me, and there won't be any trouble."

Boyd had been growing angrier and angrier with every passing minute. It had been bad enough to have been frustrated at every turn trying to find out where Sarah had gone, but having Marshal Trent trying to boss him around was just too much. When the lawman clamped a hand down on his shoulder to turn him around, Boyd exploded. He pivoted and attacked full-force, swinging out at the marshal in fury.

Jared knew all about Boyd's temper, and he was ready when the drunk came at him. He dodged Boyd's fist and landed a solid hit to the other man's jaw. Boyd was stunned by the force of his blow, and, for an instant, he let his defenses down. That hesitation allowed Jared to hit him twice more, knocking him to the floor.

Jared drew his gun and stood over Boyd. Jared's manner was deceptively calm as he looked over at the others standing at the bar.

"I could use a little help getting him to the jail."

"Yes, sir, Marshal Trent!"

Two men quickly came to his aid. Each man grabbed Boyd by an arm and together they dragged him out of the saloon.

Jared looked up at Dan. "Thanks for letting me know about this. I've had too much experience with him in the past to let things go. When he starts making threats, it's time to do something."

"I know. I've seen him in action too many times, too," Dan agreed. In fact, there was a time some months ago, when the saloon's owners had thrown him out. "Sam and Fernanda have told him to stay away."

"Why did you let him back?"

"He managed to convince Sam and Fernanda that he could control himself, and they liked the color of his money," Dan explained with a pained smile.

"What got him so fired up about Tessa Sinclair?"

"Evidently Sarah went to Miss Tessa after Boyd beat her up the last time, and Miss Tessa helped her get out of town."

Jared's eyes hardened at the news. "I see," he said tightly. "So his wife finally got smart and left, and he's blaming it on Tessa."

"That's right."

Jared nodded. "Thanks for your help."

"I appreciate your coming so fast. Drinks are on the house for you whenever you've got time to stop in."

"I'll be taking you up on that real soon, Dan."

With that, Jared quit the High Time. His mood was black as he followed the two men who were dragging Boyd to the jail. It wouldn't be pretty when the drunk came around, but he didn't care. At least for the time being, Boyd would be safely locked up where he couldn't hurt anybody. That was all that mattered for now.

"Thanks, boys," Jared told the two men after they'd deposited Boyd in the cell and he'd locked the door.

"Glad we could help out," they replied as they headed back to the saloon to finish their drinks.

When they'd gone, Jared settled back in at his desk. His expression was dark as he thought about Tessa Sinclair. A vision of the auburn-haired beauty danced before him, and he scowled even more. *Damn that woman!* Didn't she know what was good for her? He understood that she felt it was her duty to help the less fortunate, but now she'd gone and put herself in danger again. It was time he had another long talk with Miss Tessa.

Jared paused as vivid memories of his father's death besieged him. He knew firsthand what happened to people when they tried to help those in need. His father had been shot dead, murdered for trying to go to a beaten and injured drunk's aid.

Jared feared a similar fate would befall Tessa if she kept up the way she was going. A surge of protectiveness filled him. He could not, would not, stand idly by and let anything happen to her. He'd made a vow to himself a long time ago to stop men like Boyd, and he meant to keep it.

Swearing under his breath, too agitated to sit still, Jared got up and began to pace the room. He'd stopped Boyd for tonight, but what about in the morning, when he had to let him go? How could he be sure Boyd wouldn't go after Tessa? How could he protect Tessa from Boyd every minute of every day? The thought of Boyd's hands on Tessa filled him with fury. She was a lady and deserved to be treated as such. He hoped that once Boyd sobered up, he would see reason. Knowing Boyd the way he did, though, Jared doubted it.

Jared raked a hand through his hair as he stared out the office window at the dark, deserted street. He liked it deserted. Deserted meant it was a quiet night in town, and that suited him just fine right now. Boyd had been trouble enough for one night.

Chapter Six

Jared glared at Boyd Wilson as the man stood arrogantly and defiantly before him in the marshal's office the next morning. Since Boyd had sobered up, Jared had no legal reason to keep him locked up any longer, and Boyd knew it.

"I don't want to hear any more about you threatening people, Boyd." Jared's harsh tone left no doubt about the seriousness of his words.

"Don't worry, you won't," Boyd answered, meeting his gaze and fighting to keep from smirking. There would be no more threats and no more talk. It was time for him to do something about what had happened. It was time for action.

"Good. Now get out of here."

Boyd left the office, smiling to himself as he went. He wondered where the Sinclair bitch was and what she was doing. He was tempted to go after her right away, but decided to hold off and wait for just the right moment to have his revenge.

And he would claim his revenge.

There was no doubt about that.

Jared shook his head in disgust as he watched Boyd walk away. Boyd Wilson was trouble—he always had been and he always would be. Jared didn't believe for one minute that Boyd was through with Tessa or his wife. He knew from past experience that he was one dangerous man, and he was going to have to keep a close watch on him.

Turning back to his desk, Jared settled in and tried to clear off some of the paperwork that had piled up there. For all his efforts, though, he accomplished little. His thoughts were on Boyd and the threat he represented to Tessa. He knew he'd better speak with her, and the sooner, the better, though it was still relatively early in the day.

Jared got up from his desk and quit the office. His mood was not pleasant as he strode through the streets of Durango. He would rather have confronted a bunch of drunks in a barroom brawl than deal with Tessa, but there could be no avoiding it. He had to warn her about what had happened last night with Boyd.

"Mornin', Marshal Trent," one shopkeeper greeted him as he passed by.

Jared merely nodded tersely in response and kept going. He was a man on a mission. He had to speak to Tessa. He grimaced inwardly at the thought. Last night was just another example of how she had the knack for getting herself into trouble. Not that she had planned it that way. He was certain her intentions were good. They didn't call her "the angel" around town for nothing, but he also knew what the road to hell was paved with.

Jared thought of the stage robbery and the injuries she'd suffered trying to save Doris Peters's money. Even now, the memory had the power to irritate him. It had frustrated him because she'd put herself at risk, and because his efforts to bring in the outlaw gang had failed. Jared prided himself on getting his man, and it tested his temper sorely to know that he'd failed. The only good news was that Butch had recovered from his bullet wound. Otherwise the whole incident was still a sore spot with him.

In the weeks since the robbery, it seemed that almost everyone in town had something kind to say about Tessa. And now, to find out that she'd helped Sarah Wilson get away from Boyd, knowing how savage he could be, really tried Jared's patience.

He was scowling as he glanced down the street and saw the Sinclair boardinghouse just ahead. He was not looking forward to the upcoming conversation with Tessa. He had hoped that she would have heeded his warning to stay out of harm's way, but obviously she hadn't listened to anything he'd told her. He could almost predict what she was going to say to him when he confronted her about Boyd's wife. Girding himself for what he was certain would be a frustrating confrontation, he started up the path to the front door.

* * *

Tessa was tired when she awakened that morning. She felt as if she'd hardly gotten any sleep at all. Thoughts of Boyd and Sarah stayed with her, and she had to keep reassuring herself that the girl was safely away and would be fine. Tessa hoped if she kept telling herself that, eventually she would come to believe it.

She wanted to keep busy, so she set about doing her chores around the house. As she worked, the memory of her "dream wedding" taunted her. She told herself that it had all been just a nightmare. That there had been no reality in that dream at all—not in the mysterious groom or in her fears of marrying someone like Boyd. She had no intention of marrying anyone, and she found that a very pleasant, calming thought this morning.

Tessa was busy cleaning up the kitchen when she heard a knock at the front door. It was unusual for anyone to stop by for a visit at this time of day for most of their boarders had already left for their jobs and the house was usually quiet until dinnertime. Wiping her hands on a towel, she started from the kitchen into the hall to see who was at the door.

Tessa looked up as she walked down the hallway. It was going to be a warm day, so she had left the door open to admit a cooling breeze. She went still at the sight before her. There, standing in the open doorway, was the tall, broad-shouldered form of a man—and silhouetted as he was by the brightness of the sunshine, she couldn't see his face. The man looked like the groom in her dream.

A shiver of awareness trembled through her in spite of the warmth of the day. She told herself she was crazy, that it had been only a dream, but the man's visage was shadowed, while his body was visible. She paused for a moment, caught off guard by the sensation that she'd experienced this moment before. It was disorienting and confusing.

"Tessa?" Jared had been watching for her. When she'd stepped out into the hallway, he once again noticed how pretty she was. She was so strong-willed it always amazed him that she should seem so delicate. With a will like hers, she should have been about six feet, four inches tall and weighed in at over two hundred pounds so she could match him toe-to-toe for determination. Instead she was fragile-looking, her complexion flawless. There was no trace of the bruise left to mar the pale beauty of her cheek. Her auburn hair was thick and lustrous, her figure enticing. She was wearing a dress today, but even so, his gaze was appreciatively going over her slender curves as she stood before him in the hallway. When Jared realized the direction of his thoughts, he gave himself a fierce mental shake and reminded himself just why he was there.

"Miss Sinclair?"

The sound of Jared's voice effectively ended Tessa's fantasy and forced her back to reality.

This wasn't any dream man. It was only Marshal Trent.

She sighed slightly as disappointment swept through her—along with a bit of annoyance. Jared Trent definitely wasn't the man of her dreams. She thought him rude and arrogant, and the less she saw of him, the better. She knew the talk around town had it that he was a wonderful lawman, but she was beginning to have her doubts. After all, he hadn't been able to bring in the gang that had robbed the stage that day.

"Jared, this is an unexpected pleasure. What brings you here so early?"

Starting forward again, Tessa couldn't imagine why he'd come to see her, unless, possibly, he'd learned something new about the outlaw gang. Certainly they had nothing else to discuss.

Tessa's tone was so sweet that Jared knew she hadn't meant a word of her greeting.

"I need to talk with you." He kept his tone stern, for he wanted her to know he was serious.

"Oh? Did you finally arrest the men who robbed the stage? Do you need me to identify them?" She was hopeful.

"No, this has nothing to do with the robbery."

"So you still haven't found them?"

"No," he said curtly, not appreciating her reminder of his lack of success. "Do you mind if I come in?"

When she hesitated, he grew even more annoyed. He wondered why this one woman had the power to irritate him so.

"This is important," he insisted.

"Of course."

Tessa finally stepped back to let Jared enter. As he moved past her into the hallway, she was once again impressed by the sheer size of him. He towered over her, his very presence seeming to fill the hallway. Everything about him spoke of power and control, from the erect way he carried himself to the way his gun rode easily on his hip. She had to admit that Jared was an intimidating man, and he was handsome, too, in a rugged sort of way, though it irked her to acknowledge that. His eyes were dark and somehow knowing. It was almost as if he had the power to look right through her—and that bothered Tessa a lot.

"There was some trouble in town last night." Jared began, taking off his Stetson as he came inside.

"What does that have to do with me?"

"It was Boyd Wilson," he announced flatly.

She went still, suddenly concerned about Sarah's safety. She looked up at him, her eyes wide and questioning. "What happened? Is Sarah all right?"

"You tell me," he countered. "All I know is that Boyd got drunk at the High Time Saloon last night and started threatening to kill his wife—and you."

"Oh." The news chilled her, but she was relieved to learn that Boyd hadn't found Sarah.

Jared was pleased when Tessa looked a bit disconcerted. At least that proved to him that she did realize the seriousness of the situation. "I locked him up for the night, but I had to let him out this morning once he'd sobered up."

"I see." Fear edged through her.

"I hope you do see, Tessa," he said in a growl. "I know how mean Boyd can be. You'll have to be very careful for a while. I don't trust the man."

"Neither do I."

"Didn't you realize what you were getting yourself into when you started messing with Boyd?"

She took his comment as more criticism, and her anger rescued her from her worry about Boyd's threats. "I wasn't 'messing' with Boyd, as you put it. I was helping Sarah!"

"I warned you about putting yourself in danger!"

"No one else would help her," she countered. "What was I supposed to do? Stand by and let him keep beating her? Maybe kill her? She'd just found out she was with child. I had to do something to help her."

"Damn it, woman, this isn't your problem!"

"I made it my problem. She came to me a couple nights ago, battered and bloody. Boyd had come home drunk and had beaten her before he'd . . ." She paused, not knowing what to call Boyd's asserting his husbandly rights. He certainly hadn't been making love to Sarah.

"I understand." Jared swore under his breath at the man's brutality. "You should have sent Sarah to a minister for help."

"She'd gone to one once, and he'd told her it was her wifely duty to stay with Boyd and to please him, that *she* had to work at making their marriage a happy one. That was why she stayed with Boyd for as long as she did. He'd started beating her just after the wedding." For an instant, Tessa thought she saw a flicker of some fierce emotion in the lawman's expression, but it was so quickly masked that she wondered if she'd really seen it at all. "Sarah probably would have stayed with him, believing the minister's advice, if it hadn't been for the baby. I think realizing she had another life growing within her made her understand that nothing was ever going to change and that she really had to get away—if not for her own sake, then for her child's."

Jared had never had any use for Boyd, and Tessa's story just reinforced his feelings about the man. "Well, it isn't just Sarah we've got to worry about right now. It's you, too. He's holding you responsible for her leaving, so take care. Make sure you don't go anywhere alone, and keep an eye out for him."

"Don't worry. I will. I don't want anything to do with the man. He came by here yesterday, and he said I hadn't seen the last of him when he left."

"And I'd be willing to bet that you haven't. I want you to keep your doors locked, and from now on, start giving some thought to the consequences of your actions," he ordered tersely.

Tessa lifted her chin defiantly as she answered, "I did give it some thought. I know that Sarah is safely away from Boyd. I know the man isn't going to hurt her or her child ever again. *Those are the consequences of my actions.*"

Jared was tempted to shake her, to try to put some sense into her, but he controlled the urge with an effort. "Those might not be the only consequences. Don't you realize—"

He didn't get any farther before Maggie Sinclair appeared on the porch and started inside, followed closely by Will Kenner. Their arrival abruptly ended Jared and Tessa's heated conversation.

Tessa was amazed at how pleased she was to see them—even Will. She hadn't known he was going to be in town this week, but she was delighted that he'd shown up now.

"Why, Marshal Trent! What a wonderful surprise!" Maggie thought him a nice man, and most handsome, too. "You know Will Kenner, don't you?"

"Yes, ma'am." He nodded toward the other man.

"Jared was just leaving," Tessa said quickly, wanting him to go.

She spoke so determinedly that her mother looked at her in surprise. "You're leaving already? What a shame. It would have been nice to visit with you for a while. We never get to see you. Will you be attending the big dance Saturday night?"

"I'll be around."

"Working or having fun?" Maggie asked. She knew his job was a never-ending one.

"Probably both," he answered, managing a grin at her. "It just depends on how well the boys in town hold their liquor."

"I hope for your sake that they're all very well behaved."

"I appreciate the thought."

"Thank you for coming by, Marshal," Tessa said with a benign smile. She just wanted him to go away now that her mother was home. She didn't want her mother to hear about Boyd's threats and start worrying.

Jared deliberately ignored Tessa as he turned to her mother. "I was just telling your daughter that Boyd Wilson found out that she helped Sarah get out of town, and he's been making threats."

"No!" Maggie paled as she looked at Tessa.

"It'll be all right, Mother. Nothing's going to happen. Sarah's safe now, and that's all that matters."

"Yes, dear, but that man is such a brute."

"He's not going to do anything to me."

"We do still have your father's pistol in the house," Maggie said.

"Do you know how to use it?" Jared asked Tessa, his gaze upon her piercing.

"Yes, if I have to," she told him.

"Good." He was satisfied with that news.

"Surely you don't think Boyd would . . . ?" Will began in concern.

"No. Nothing's going to happen," Tessa reassured him. "Everything's fine now that Sarah is free of him."

"I'll be going now," Jared said. "If you need anything or if anything happens, you know where to find me."

"Thank you, Marshal." Maggie appreciated his taking the time to warn them. "Let's hope that by Saturday night everything will have calmed down."

"Yes, ma'am," he answered. "Tessa, Will."

Jared left the house, hoping he'd made some impression on Tessa about the possible danger she was facing. Judging from the way she'd acted, though, he doubted she'd taken his warning seriously. He frowned as he stopped to look around the area. There were any number of places for Boyd to hide near the house, should the man decide to come after her. His frown deepened. It was hard to protect someone like Tessa, someone who believed the best of people and never prepared for the worst. He'd have to ride by several times during the night to make sure all was quiet, and he'd have to try to keep track of Boyd. He shook his head in frustration and started back toward his office.

Chapter Seven

Once Marshal Trent had gone, Tessa was relieved. She didn't know what it was about the man that irritated her so, but she found him almost insufferable with his high-handed lawman's ways.

"Why are you in town, Will? Is something wrong at the mine?" Tessa asked as she led the way into the parlor and sat down on the sofa.

Her mother joined her there, while Will took the chair facing them.

"We were running short on some supplies. I'd planned to be heading back early tomorrow, but now I'm glad I ran into you, Miss Maggie," he said, looking at the older woman. "After what Marshal Trent just told us, I'm wondering if I should stay in town at least through the weekend to keep an eye on things." His blue-eyed gaze was warm upon Tessa.

The last thing Tessa wanted was Will hovering around her. "That's very kind of you, but—"

"That's a wonderful idea," Maggie put in before her daughter could say more. His offer had just raised him even higher in her estimation.

"Good. I'll do it."

"Do you have a place to stay?" Maggie asked.

"I've already taken a room at the hotel."

"What about the supplies you needed for the mine? Can you afford to stay away that long?" Tessa asked. It wasn't that she didn't want him to remain in town, she told herself. It was that he was responsible for their mine, and it was no small job.

"I'm sure the boys can handle things without me for an extra day or two. It'll be fine," he said confidently. He was looking forward to the dance on Saturday night.

"Then you've done a fine job of getting things in order up there," Maggie said.

"Thank you. The men are serious about their work and more careful than ever after what happened," he explained.

"Michael was always concerned about the quality of the workers," Tessa said, remembering how hard her brother had worked at making the mine pay. "That's why he spent so much time at the site supervising."

"Michael was doing a fine job. I still can't believe what happened."

Maggie's expression grew as she thought of her beloved son. The tragic accident was still devastatingly painful for her. "I miss him. I suppose I always will," she said softly. "Nothing will ever be the same now that he's gone."

"I know," Will sympathized. "And I'm glad I'm staying close this weekend. Michael would have wanted me to do it, and I would have worried if I'd gone back, knowing that Boyd is threatening you."

"Everything is going to be fine. I don't think Boyd's going to try anything," Tessa said.

"I hope you're right," Maggie said, "but I'm still going to get your father's revolver out before we go to bed tonight. I want to make sure it's loaded and close at hand—just in case."

"All right." Tessa didn't want to think that they might need it, but she understood her mother's concern.

"And I'll be here, too," Jim Russell announced as he came to stand in the parlor doorway. He'd been out back when he'd seen Marshal Trent leaving, and had come inside to find out why the lawman had stopped by. "What kind of trouble are we expecting?"

Tessa quickly explained all that had happened with Boyd.

"If Marshal Trent says be careful, then I'd listen to him," Jim advised. "He's a good lawman. He knows what he's talking about. They don't come any better than Jared."

Tessa had always respected Jim's opinion on things, but this time she wondered. "Let's just hope we see no sign of Boyd Wilson ever again." She was sick of talking about the man who seemed to have caused only pain in people's lives. "Maybe one day Boyd will come to his senses and understand the terrible things he's done. Maybe someday he'll change his ways."

"It would be wonderful if it were that simple," Jim said, "but I don't think men like him ever change."

"Then let's pray that Sarah's far away and Boyd never finds her. That's the best we can hope for," Tessa said.

Jim went on upstairs as talk turned to the mine. Once Will had related the latest news, he left to take care of his own business.

"It's wonderful that Will cares enough to stay on in town," Maggie remarked.

Tessa didn't necessarily think so, but she wasn't going to argue with her mother. "I'm just sorry we're in this situation at all, but there was no way I could turn Sarah away when she came to me. I had to help her. She had no one else she could go to."

"I know that, darling. Sarah is a lovely girl. She didn't deserve what happened to her. It was terrible. The sad thing is that there are so many others just like her. You were right to help her. I'm glad we were able to get her away from that brute. You're a very special, very caring person, Tessa," Maggie said as she went to hug her.

"I just want to help out whenever I can. I remember what it was like for us right after Papa died, and—"

"You were so young," Maggie said sadly, remembering the hard times they'd had. "But you learned a lot from Frances, didn't you?"

Tessa smiled. "Frances was an extraordinary woman."

Maggie kissed her on the cheek, then hurried off to tend to her cooking.

Tessa walked to the parlor window and stared out at the quiet street. Thoughts of all the people she'd helped through the years came to her then, and she smiled bittersweetly. Jared Trent obviously had no idea what it was like to be desperate and alone in the world, to be without family or friends. Why, if it hadn't been for Frances Roland—or Saint Frances, as Tessa thought of her—she doubted that she and her mother would be where they were today.

Memories of that terrible time so many years ago swept over her. Her father had just died, leaving her mother nearly destitute, with two small children to raise and no family to help out. They'd managed to eke out a living for a short time, struggling constantly just to make ends meet. When her mother had taken seriously ill, though, their situation had become desperate.

It had been then that Frances Roland had learned of their plight and stepped in to help. Without any thought except how she could help them, she had nursed Maggie and taken care of Tessa and Michael until Maggie had recovered. Once her mother was back on her feet, Frances was the one who'd suggested Maggie open a restaurant. She had heard about what a wonderful cook she was. Frances had helped them establish their first restaurant, and they had all been thrilled when it proved a success.

Tessa had gone back to find Frances some years later and had offered to repay her for all her help. To Tessa's amazement, Frances had refused to take any money from her. To this very day, Tessa remembered their conversation.

"My helping your family wasn't about money or getting paid back," Frances had explained gently, love shining in her eyes. "If you want to repay me, then do so by helping others. Pass along the kindness I've shown you. Do unto others as you would have them do unto you."

"But you've helped us so much," Tessa had argued, confused. "Surely you'll let me pay back some of what we owe you?"

Frances had only smiled serenely at her. "You don't owe me a thing, child. It was my pleasure to help you. Just be happy. That's all the reward I need."

Even now the memory of her kind words had the power to bring tears to Tessa's eyes. She had never known anyone else as generous as Frances. She'd learned a lot from her, and she had tried to live her life as the other woman had taught her—helping others every chance she got.

The reward of knowing she'd made a positive difference in someone else's life was enormous. Helping Sarah had been the right thing to do—no matter what Jared Trent said. She knew that she would do the same thing again if presented with the same problem.

Thoughts of the marshal and his arrogant ways erased Tessa's smile. Why he thought he could tell her what to do mystified her. She was her own woman. She could take care of herself. She did not need or want his opinion. And she would not stop helping others, no matter what Jared Trent said.

At that thought, Tessa found herself smiling once more, and she was glad. If she never saw the interfering lawman again, it would be fine with her.

Jared returned to his office and worked at clearing off his desk. Time passed slowly, for he kept expecting trouble. Finally, near midafternoon, he left the office and made his way slowly through town. He wouldn't admit it to himself openly, but he was looking for Boyd. He felt compelled to do everything in his power to make sure Tessa was safe.

Stops at local saloons found no trace of the man. No one had seen or heard from him that day, but Jared knew that didn't mean a lot. Lowlife that Boyd was, he could have been anywhere, doing anything, with anybody. Jared would keep a careful watch. This was his town. It was his duty to make sure all the people in it were protected from harm.

"What are you planning to wear to the dance Saturday night?" Julie Stevens asked Tessa as they made their way toward George Lansing's mercantile later that afternoon.

"I think my blue dress," Tessa answered, though she had not really given it much thought yet.

"You do look pretty in it, that's for sure. My mother ordered me a pale pink gown from Philadelphia, and it just got here this week, so I'll be wearing that," Julie bragged. She did love to dress up and flirt.

"I bet Clint will like you in that," Tessa teased,

smiling at her friend. Clint had been trying to court Julie for some time now. He seemed quite smitten with her.

Julie made a face. "You know how I feel about Clint."

"You've certainly told me often enough!" She laughed.

"I'm not going to marry a cowboy. I made up my mind about that long ago."

"That's a shame. There are quite a few of them who would love to court you."

Petite and blond as Julie was, men were drawn to her like bees to honey.

"Sorry, I'm just not interested. I know who I want to marry. I want to marry an educated gentleman who will take me back east to live, and no cowboy around here can do that."

"I can't believe you're serious. Are you really that determined to leave Durango?"

"I want to live in New York or Philadelphia. Someplace exciting and sophisticated."

"Durango can be exciting," Tessa argued. "Didn't we have all that excitement with Preacher Farnsworth not so very long ago? And what about the bank robbery and that terrible Harris gang?"

Julie gave an unladylike snort. "That's not the kind of excitement I'm talking about, and you know it! I want soirees and fancy teas and trips to the theater and—"

"I know, I know," Tessa responded. "I guess we'll just have to keep looking for the perfect man for you."

"I'm beginning to wonder if he even exists," Julie said sadly. "I mean, first I thought I was in love with Ben, and then, Trace had me so fooled when he was disguised as Gabe West." She gave a slow shake of her head. "What about you? What kind of man are you looking for? Haven't you ever fallen in love?"

Tessa looked thoughtful for a moment as she seriously considered the question. "No, I don't think I've ever been in love. I guess I've been too busy with the boardinghouse and the mine."

"One of these days you'll meet the right man and you will, just wait. You'll see."

"Maybe, maybe not."

"Don't you want to get married?"

Tessa shrugged. "I don't know."

"Your dream man is out there. You just haven't found him yet."

"I suppose." Her friend's use of the term *dream man* surprised Tessa and brought back memories of her troubling dreams. She didn't reveal anything about them to Julie, though. They were too confusing. Who dreamed about a man with no face?

"Your mother seems very fond of Will, but what about you?" Julie was watching her friend carefully, trying to judge her reaction.

"I like Will," she answered hesitantly. "He's nice, and he is good-looking."

"Very," Julie agreed, thinking of the tall, blond-haired miner.

"He has been a big help to us since Michael died."

"It was wonderful the way he stepped in and took over like that."

"You almost sound like you're interested in him." Tessa cast her a sidelong glance.

"No, thanks! No miners for me, either! I'm after

a man who is truly a gentleman. I want a man who's well-read. A man who can quote the classics. I want a man who knows which fork to use at dinner. I want a man who—"

"I understand." Tessa grinned.

"Well, what about Marshal Trent?" Julie said with just the hint of a smile, wanting to get a reaction out of her. She knew how the lawman got on Tessa's nerves.

"No, thanks! He's arrogant and annoying and—"

"I get the picture, but you know there are some females in town who think he's wonderful husband material—Melissa Davenport for one. You should hear her talking about how she plans to marry him."

"I wish her luck. She can have him."

Tessa glanced up just then as a rider moved past them down the street. The animal was a fine piece of horseflesh, but it was the stranger riding him that caught and held Tessa's attention. The darkly handsome cowboy rode as if he were one with his mount. He held the reins with easy power, looking neither left nor right. His hat rode low over his forehead, and his jaw was hard and lean and darkened by several days' growth of beard. His shoulders were broad, his waist trim. For all that he was just another cowboy, there was something about him that spoke of danger.

"Are you sure you don't want a cowboy?" Tessa said to Julie as she let her gaze follow the man's slow, steady progress down the street. "What about him?"

Julie looked up, and though for a moment she did watch the man, she shook her head in refusal.

"As far as cowboys go, I suppose he's all right, but he's not the kind of man I want."

"Somehow I knew you were going to say that."

"Well, what about you? If you think he's so handsome, follow him, see where he goes, and invite him to the dance Saturday night," Julie challenged.

"No, thanks. I've got enough men to worry about. Between Boyd's threats and Will staying in town to keep an eye on me, I don't have time for any more men or excitement in my life."

"I do have the time, and I'd like some excitement in my life. The trouble is, the man has got to be the right one."

"And that's not him?" Tessa nodded toward the stranger again.

Julie cast one last glance in the stranger's direction. "No. That's not him," she said with certainty. She could tell just by looking at him that he was no gentleman.

They entered the store to do their shopping.

Steve Madison made his way slowly through the streets of Durango. At last he'd reached his goal. Now if only everything else he'd planned went as smoothly.

Reining in before a quiet-looking saloon, he dismounted and tied up his horse. If there was one thing he needed right now, it was a drink. This day had been long in coming, and he deserved a celebration. He strode inside and stepped up to the bar.

"Whiskey," he ordered.

Liam, the bartender, hurried to splash a healthy portion of the potent liquor in a tumbler for him. "You're new in town, aren't you?" He knew just about everybody in Durango, and he'd never seen this man before. He certainly would have remembered him, because he had the look of a gunfighter about him. He looked like a man who expected trouble.

"Just rode in," Steve answered as he took a deep drink.

"Staying long?"

"A few days." He was evasive.

"Well, welcome to Durango, friend. Where's home?" Business was slow, so Liam had time to talk.

"Arizona," Steve offered, but he doubted he would ever be going back—not after all that had happened to him there.

"What brings you to our fair town?"

"I heard good things about Durango, so I thought I'd take a look around. Where's a decent place to stay?"

"Any of the hotels will take care of you, but if you're wanting the best food in town, then you'll want to stay at the Sinclair boardinghouse. Miss Maggie's cooking is the best, and Miss Tessa ain't too hard on the eyes, either."

"Who's Miss Tessa?"

"She and her mother own and run the place. They are some fine ladies. Miss Tessa is known around here as 'the angel,' but we don't call her that to her face," he explained.

"Why?"

"I think it might embarrass her. She's always doing kind things for people, taking care of everyone, helping out whenever she can. There aren't many women like Miss Tessa. Why, just a little while ago she was on a stage that got robbed, and she was hurt trying to help a little old lady keep her life savings."

Steve smiled slightly at the news. "Sounds like you're kinda fond of her."

"Oh, we all love her, and her mother, too. But she's a quality lady."

"Where's their boardinghouse?"

"Just up the street a ways." Liam gave him the directions. "You won't be sorry, especially after you've had one of Miss Maggie's dinners."

"I'm looking forward to it."

It was neither the promise of a hot meal nor the presence of a pretty woman that helped Steve make his decision to stay at the Sinclair place. It was the news that this Tessa had been on a stage that had been robbed. He had come to Durango because he'd seen a copy of the Durango *Weekly Star* with an article in it about a stage robbery that had taken place near the town. To learn that he might be able to talk to someone who had actually been on that stage encouraged him.

Steve didn't know how long it would take him to find out what he needed to know and to exact his revenge for the wrongs that had been done to him, but he wasn't going to quit until he had. He'd vowed to get even when he'd been locked up in prison, and he was going to keep that pledge.

Once Steve finished his whiskey, he paid for the drink and left. It was getting late in the afternoon, and he needed to get settled for the night. He wondered how much he could learn about the stage robbers from this woman Tessa Sinclair.

* * *

Liam worried as he watched the stranger leave the saloon. The man had a hard look about him. In fact, there was something about him that seemed downright dangerous. Liam hoped he hadn't done the wrong thing by sending him to Miss Tessa's place.

Chapter Eight

"I think I'll go up to the mine at the end of the month. That will be payday, and I can also take a look around and see how things are going," Tessa told her mother as they sat in the dining room finishing up dinner that evening.

Since Tessa had returned from shopping with Julie, the rest of her day had passed uneventfully, and she'd been glad. It was good to be distracted from worries about Boyd by the real business of running the boardinghouse. There were things that needed to be taken care of, and they wouldn't get done unless she did them.

"Do you think it will be safe for you to go with all this trouble?" Maggie asked.

"I can't live my life worrying about Boyd Wilson," she declared, telling herself it was the truth.

"So you didn't hear anything more from

Marshal Trent today?" Jim asked in between bites of Maggie's delicious stew. He and the two other boarders—Henry Crawford and Sludge—had been too busy enjoying the delicious, plentiful fare to talk much before now, but he was still concerned about Tessa's safety.

"Not a word," Tessa told him.

"I wonder if that's good or bad?" Maggie said thoughtfully.

"In this case, Mother, no news is definitely good news."

At that moment a knock came at the front door. The boardinghouse was usually quiet at dinnertime, so Tessa hoped it wasn't the marshal returning for some reason. She didn't want the rest of her night ruined.

"I'll get it," Tessa said, rising from the table to see who was there.

She girded herself for another confrontation with Jared. She was relieved to find that it wasn't the marshal at all. Instead she found a tall, dark-haired stranger waiting at the door—the same stranger she'd seen riding into town earlier that afternoon while she'd been with Julie.

"Can I help you?" she asked, surprised and curious.

"Yes, ma'am," Steve said, politely. Taking a good look at the young woman standing before him, he decided this had to be the Tessa the bartender had been talking about. He understood now exactly what the man had meant when he'd said that Miss Tessa was easy on the eyes. She was one good-looking woman. "I need a place to stay while I'm in Durango, and your place was recommended to me."

"Of course, Mr. . . . ?" She eyed him critically. He had met her gaze forthrightly as he spoke, and she always judged a man by whether he looked her in the eye or not. She didn't trust a man with a shifty-eyed gaze.

"My name's Madison, ma'am. Steve Madison."

"Well, it's nice to meet you, Mr. Madison. We were just finishing up dinner. Would you care to join us?" she invited.

Steve could smell the delicious aroma of home cooking and wasn't about to turn down such an invitation. "I'd like that, ma'am, thank you. I was told the meals here were the best in town."

"Well, my mother will be glad to hear that. Come on in. I'm Tessa Sinclair."

"It's a pleasure to meet you." Steve took off his hat as he entered the house and followed her the short distance down the hallway to the dining room.

"Everybody," Tessa announced, drawing the attention of those seated at the dinner table, "this is Steve Madison. He'll be taking a room with us for a while."

"Good evening, Mr. Madison," Maggie said. "I'm Maggie Sinclair. Welcome to our home."

"Evening, ma'am."

The older woman grinned at his gentlemanly greeting. "You don't have to call me 'ma'am'. I'm just Maggie. Have a seat, and I'll fix you a plate of food."

The other introductions were made as Steve sat down. In short order, Maggie set a heaping plate of food before him.

Steve quickly dove in and immediately determined that the bartender had been right on two counts: Tessa was mighty pretty and her mother was a fine cook. The food tasted as good as it smelled.

"What brings you to Durango?" Jim asked as he leaned back in his chair after finishing his dessert.

"I'd been hearing good things about the area, so I thought I'd come take a look around. It certainly is friendly here."

"We like to make folks feel welcome," Maggie said, giving him a genuine smile as she sat back down at the table.

"I do feel welcome, thank you," Steve said in between bites. "This is the best meal I've had in years."

Maggie was genuinely pleased with his praise. "I wouldn't go that far."

"I would," he answered as he thought of the miserable prison fare he'd suffered.

Tessa found the seriousness of his remark puzzling. She'd known many miners and railroad workers who'd truly enjoyed her mother's meals, but none of them had ever seemed quite as serious about their praise as this man.

"Well, eat up. There's more where that came from, if you've a mind for seconds," Maggie encouraged.

"What do you do for a living?" Jim asked, curious about the new boarder. He could tell Steve was an intense young man.

Steve looked up at him, taking care to keep his expression unreadable. "A little bit of everything."

"How long do you plan to stay?" Tessa asked as she stood up and began to clear the table.

"I'm not sure right now. It depends on how

everything goes, but I'm sure I'll be here at least a few weeks."

"Well, we're delighted to have you," Maggie said, and then she went on to tell him the basic rules of the house. "We all have keys to the house, and you'll have a key to your room. We respect each other's privacy. We don't allow any smoking. If you have to smoke, do it at one of the saloons, not here."

"I don't smoke, so that won't be a problem," he told her.

"We can arrange to have your laundry done for you. Meals are served at the same time every day—six A.M., noon, and six P.M."

"If they're all as good as this one was, I won't be missing any of your mealtimes."

"They are," Sludge said, and Henry nodded in agreement.

"Welcome to Sinclair House, Mr. Madison," Tessa said.

"Please, call me Steve," he said. "When I was talking to the bartender about where to stay, he was telling me about how you were on the stage that got robbed not too long ago. That must have been very frightening for you."

"That happened a while ago, and it was scary," she said, not really wanting to talk or think about it.

"It was very brave of you to try to help the old woman the way you did," Steve told her.

"They still got her money."

"But you tried to help her. That's more than most folks would do."

Tessa shrugged. "I would have felt better if I'd

stopped them. What's troubling is that they're still on the loose."

"So they got away with it?" Steve was trying to sound conversational. He did not want to reveal his real reason for being there.

"So far, yes. Marshal Trent did try to track them down, but he lost their trail up in the mountains. It bothers me that they were able to get away with it."

"They may have gotten the money, but at least you're still alive," Sludge put in. "You know it's just plain lucky that they didn't kill you."

"You're right, Sludge," she agreed reluctantly, "but it still doesn't make it any easier to accept that good, honest, hardworking people can be hurt by men like that."

"Did you get a look at them?" Steve asked.

"No," she said regretfully. "They were all wearing masks, so I couldn't give the marshal much to go on."

"If Marshal Trent could have found them, he would have," Jim said, coming to Jared's defense.

"I suppose," she agreed unenthusiastically.

"You don't sound like you have much confidence in your lawman," Steve remarked.

Tessa shrugged and answered evasively, "Jim thinks the world of him."

"Marshal Trent's as good as they come," Jim said.

"But he couldn't track the gang?"

Jim frowned. "It wasn't for lack of trying. He rode out with a posse as soon as he learned of the robbery, but by then the trail was cold. He tracked them as far as he could, but it gets rocky up in the mountains."

"Let's hope they're long gone and never bother another stage again," Maggie said.

"I'd just like to see them get what's coming to them," Tessa said fiercely, remembering the horror of that terrible day.

"Someday they will," Jim told her. "Give Marshal Trent a chance. He'll bring them in."

"I hope so. The day they're behind bars can't come soon enough for me."

"Steve, would you like me to show you to your room?" Maggie asked when he'd finally finished eating.

"Yes, ma'am."

"It's upstairs at the far end of the hall," she said, leading the way from the dining room. "I'll see the rest of you gentlemen at breakfast," she told Jim, Sludge, and Henry.

They all called out a polite goodnight to her.

"Here you are," Maggie said, handing Steve a set of keys as she opened the door to the room for him.

The bedroom was sparsely furnished with only a double bed, dresser, washstand, and night table.

"It's very basic, but if there's anything else you need, all you have to do is ask," she explained. "There's a room for bathing three doors down the hall on the left."

Steve nodded, pleased with the arrangements. The bed with its fresh, clean sheets looked most inviting. He could hardly wait to stretch out on its welcoming softness. "It looks fine, Miss Maggie. Thank you."

"We charge three dollars a week, and that includes your meals."

"Here." He reached in his pocket to take out the first week's rent, and handed it over to her.

"Thank you."

"It's worth every penny, believe me."

"Is there anything else we can do for you? Anything else you need right now?"

"No, I'll just have to take care of my horse and get my things. I saw a stable down the street. Is that a good one?"

"Yes. David Forsyth is the owner, and Sludge works there. They're very good with horses. Also, in case you hadn't heard, there's going to be a big dance in town this Saturday night. It's quite an event. Everyone in town is excited about it, so you might want to plan on going."

"I'll keep it in mind."

"Good night, Steve. I hope you're comfortable here."

"I will be, Miss Maggie, and thanks again."

Steve followed her back downstairs and then went out to take care of his horse. It was some time later when he was stretched out on the bed, actually relaxing for the first time in months. He'd considered going back to the bar for another drink, but the lure of the comfort of lying in bed undisturbed dissuaded him. He needed a good night's sleep more than he needed another shot of whiskey.

It had been a long time since Steve had been able to take it easy and do nothing. Not that he didn't have a lot to think about. He did, but things seemed to have been going his way today, and he just wanted to enjoy the moment while he could. Past experience had proven to him that it wouldn't last—not after what he'd been through this year.

Memories of all that had happened to him played in Steve's mind as he stared into the darkness. It had all started in a saloon in Tucson. He had been drinking heavily and playing high-stakes poker with three men named Howard, Clark and Roberts. He had won a considerable amount of money from them and had been feeling quite good when he'd called it a night. The very next day, however, he had been arrested for robbing a stagecoach just outside of town. When the lawman had searched his saddlebags, he'd found his poker winnings along with a mask that resembled the ones worn by the robbers. Steve had protested his innocence, but the lawman had known of his reputation as a fast gun and had believed him to be part of the gang that had pulled off the job. His trial had been a farce, and before he'd known what to do, he'd been convicted and sent to prison. While he'd been locked up, he'd had a lot of time to think about it, and he'd finally figured out who'd framed him. It had been Howard, Clark and Roberts. That night while he'd slept, they must have put the mask in his saddlebag.

It had been purely by accident that he'd finally been set free. The gang had struck again, outside Phoenix this time, and one of the members had been wounded and caught. During the questioning, the robber had laughed at the lawmen for arresting and convicting the wrong man—Steve. A telegram to the prison from the lawman there in Phoenix had set him free, but Steve was still furious over being falsely convicted in the first place. He'd lost months of his life, convicted of a crime he hadn't committed. As he'd ridden away from the prison, he'd been determined to find the rest of the gang and put an end to their lawless ways.

That was when he'd decided to make the trip to Phoenix. He had managed to convince the lawman there to let him speak with the captured gunman for a few minutes in private. He'd had only to threaten the weasel with instant death to be told that the rest of the gang—Dave Turner, Al Clark and Chuck Roberts had been planning to leave Arizona until things quieted down. As far as he knew, they were headed for Colorado.

Steve never considered mentioning what he'd learned to the lawmen there in Arizona—not after what they'd done to him. He would never trust another lawman again. If he wanted justice he would have to mete it out on his own.

So here he was in Durango. He'd read about the recent robberies in the Durango *Weekly Star,* and realized they were the gang's work. He was going to find the men who'd set him up, and when he did, the payback was going to be hell— and he was going to enjoy every minute of it.

Steve closed his eyes, ready for a good night's sleep. It would be his first in a long time.

Tessa wasn't sure what had awakened her, but she woke up abruptly from a sound sleep. She'd had no trouble falling asleep tonight. It had been a long, stressful day, and she'd been ready for some peace and quiet.

Now, though, Tessa sat upright in her bed, her

heart pounding a nervous rhythm. She frowned into the darkness, remaining silent, listening, not moving, trying to discern what had disturbed her sleep. Immediate and frightening thoughts of Boyd haunted her, but she refused to panic. Her mother had insisted she keep the loaded revolver in her room with her, and Tessa reached for it on her nightstand.

Tessa had never liked guns, but tonight she was glad that she had one. Slipping from her bed, she pulled on her night wrapper and belted it. Then she cautiously, silently made her way to the door. She opened it a bit and waited, listening, trying to hear if there was anyone moving about downstairs. It could very well be that one of the boarders had made the noise that had awakened her, so she knew she'd have to be careful as she ventured forth to investigate.

Her tread was silent as she left her bedroom. She paused in the heavy shadows at the top of the steps to wait and listen, but she heard nothing. All seemed quiet and undisturbed. Still, she knew something had to have made the noise that had awakened her. She took the steps slowly, pausing to look in all directions as she descended, but nothing seemed out of order.

A shiver trembled through Tessa as she finally acknowledged that she really was scared. Her father's gun was heavy in her hand, and she prayed she wouldn't have to use it. She'd never shot anyone in her life, and she certainly didn't want to start now—not even that miserable excuse for a man, Boyd Wilson. She almost wished Jared was there, but not quite. Swallowing tightly, she continued on, determined to reassure herself that the house was undisturbed.

Jared had tried to sleep, but it had proven pointless. During the day Boyd's threats had troubled him, but now that it was night, he was even more worried. He knew everything was probably all right, but just to reassure himself, he got up, dressed, and saddled his horse. He was feeling so uneasy, he decided to ride past the Sinclair place one more time. Something was bothering him, and he wanted to make sure that Tessa and her mother were all right.

Keeping his horse moving at a slow pace, he rode past the front of the building. There were no lights on. All seemed quiet. It was as he glanced in the parlor window one last time that he saw what looked like a shadowy figure moving around inside.

Jared reined in abruptly. He feared that someone had broken into the house—and that it might be Boyd. He dismounted and stealthily made his way toward the front door. Jared was tense as he tried to decide the best thing to do. He wanted to be sure Tessa was safe. That was most important to him.

Taking great care to make sure he wasn't seen, Jared drew his gun and moved forward. He was ready for the trouble he was sure was to come. There was someone sneaking around inside the Sinclair house, and he was going to capture the culprit right now.

Jared stayed low as he moved nearer. He needed the element of surprise on his side if he was going up against Boyd. As he reached the front door, he grew tense. Sweat beaded his brow and he tightened his grip on his gun. There was no time left to wonder what he should do, though. He had to act to save Tessa. He just prayed he wasn't too late.

With all his might, Jared kicked in the front door. He surged through the open doorway, gun in hand.

Chapter Nine

Tessa had been just about ready to go back upstairs to bed, when she thought she heard someone moving around outside, near the front of the house. She crept down the hall toward the door, listening, waiting, not sure what to expect.

It was then that the front door crashed open and a tall, dark figure came charging inside.

Tessa could see the intruder was armed, and she lifted her gun, ready to fire. Before she could even think about pulling the trigger, the man knocked the revolver from her grip. Hard, unyielding arms came around her, and she was held pinned against the broad expanse of her attacker's chest. It had all happened so fast that she had no time to react.

"Let me go!" Tessa cried out, fighting frantically against the man's overwhelming strength.

Jared went completely still.

Bobbi Smith

"Tessa?" Jared said her name in complete shock as he realized just what had happened.

"You?" She gasped in outrage, twisting around to look up at him in the darkness.

Jared was so stunned to find it was Tessa that he stood unmoving with her still held clasped tightly to him. He was suddenly very aware of her womanly curves pressed against him. Her gown and wrapper offered little in the way of barriers between them.

"Good God, woman! What the hell were you thinking, sneaking around in the dark like that? You could have been killed just now."

"*I* could have been killed?" she countered angrily. Jared's harsh words stung, and any fear she'd been feeling was replaced by fury. She glared up at him, her eyes sparkling with the power of her emotion. "This is my house!"

"I saw you moving around in the dark and thought someone had broken in. I was ready to shoot you!"

Tessa was all too aware of being held so close against the hard, lean length of him, and in one defiant gesture, she shoved against his chest with all her might. Jared immediately released her. His anger was as real as hers. He might have killed her.

"You were just lucky *I* didn't shoot *you!*" she challenged.

"What were you doing sneaking around in the dark?" he demanded, shaken by the realization that he might have been the one to harm her—when all he'd been trying to do was save her.

Just then Steve came running down the steps,

gun at the ready, followed by the others. He peered into the darkened hallway, prepared for trouble.

Tessa saw him and quickly called out, "It's all right, Steve!"

She moved away from Jared to light a lamp. Her hands were trembling as she struck the match, but she refused to let any of them see just how frightened she'd been.

"Are you sure?" Steve asked, his gaze narrowing as he looked from her to the man standing nearby.

"I'm fine. It's just Marshal Trent," Tessa told him, as if that explained everything.

Steve looked over at Jared and with the help of the lamplight made out the badge on his chest. He slowly lowered his gun as Maggie came to his side.

"What happened? Tessa? What's going on? What was that terrible noise?" Maggie was terrified.

Jared spoke up first. "I was riding by, and I thought I saw someone sneaking around in the parlor. I was expecting trouble from Boyd, so I broke in the door."

"And it was Tessa?" Steve asked.

"It was Tessa," he confirmed.

"Darling, are you sure you're all right?" Maggie asked, hurrying past Steve and down the rest of the stairs to rush to her daughter's side.

"Yes, Mother, but I don't think our door is," Tessa replied as she glanced at the badly damaged door. It was hanging crazily on its hinges.

"Oh, my," Maggie said softly. The crash that

had awakened her had been a loud one, and now she understood. Jared must have used quite a bit of force breaking the door open.

"Why were you downstairs?" Jared asked again.

"Something woke me from a sound sleep, and I had to find out what it was."

"If it had been Boyd, you would have been no match for him" Jared said angrily. He was very aware of how her silken wrapper clung to her shapely figure. She looked beautiful, and he wanted her out of the other men's sight as quickly as possible. He concentrated on keeping his gaze focused on her face, to keep from being distracted himself, but it wasn't easy.

"I had my father's gun. I wasn't helpless," she countered. "Besides, I couldn't just sit up in my room waiting for him to come upstairs and attack me! If I'd found Boyd in the house, I would have shot him. You're just lucky I didn't shoot you."

"I'm very lucky," Jared ground out, not wanting to argue any further with her. He'd disarmed her easily. She hadn't had a chance against him. He was very aware, even if she wasn't, of what would have happened to her if it had been Boyd coming through that door or if Boyd had been waiting for her at the bottom of the steps. "Since you think you heard something down here, I'm going to take a look around. I suggest you go back up to your room and stay there."

"This is my house. I'll do whatever I want," she returned.

"Marshal Trent is right, dear," Maggie told her sensibly, only now aware of her daughter's state of undress. "Let's get you upstairs and let the marshal take care of things down here."

It irked Tessa to be so dismissed, but she abided by her mother's wisdom and allowed her to lead her back upstairs.

Jared started to go outside. Steve stopped him.

"Would you like some help?" he offered.

"Sure," Jared said. "We haven't met before."

"No, I'm Steve Madison. I just got into town today."

Jared nodded, though he frowned slightly. There was something familiar about the name, but he couldn't say quite what. "Good to meet you. I'm Jared Trent, as you've probably already figured out."

"Do you want me to take a look around back?"

"Yes."

"We'll help, too!" Jim offered, and Sludge and Henry nodded.

"Sludge and Henry, why don't you two go with Steve, and Jim can come with me while I check over here," Jared directed. He doubted they would find anything, though, for even if there had been an intruder earlier, he certainly would be long gone by now.

It was nearly half an hour later when the men decided to give up the search. They hadn't found any indication that there had been anyone around, and so they relaxed a little bit.

"I'll send someone over to fix the door in the morning," Jared told Maggie when they went back inside to find her waiting for them in the kitchen. He was both relieved and disappointed that Tessa was nowhere in sight. His conflicting emotions where she was concerned irritated him. He didn't need to see her again. He didn't know why he wanted to—but a part of him did. "Until then, I think we can tie it shut."

"I'll take care of it for you," Steve said. "If that's all right with you, Miss Maggie?"

"Thank you, Steve."

"Is Tessa all right?" Jared asked.

"She's fine now."

"Good. I'll check back with you in the morning."

As Jared rode away into the night, he didn't look back. If he had, he would have seen Tessa watching him from her bedroom window.

"Are you sure you're all right, darling?" Maggie asked when she went to Tessa after Steve had secured the door and everything had quieted down.

Tessa was still up, pacing the bedroom, her mood tense and distracted. "I'm fine. It's just that I can't believe what happened downstairs!"

"It's good to know that Marshal Trent is keeping such a close eye on things. He really must be worried about Boyd to do what he just did," she remarked thoughtfully.

"We were just lucky that no one got hurt. Did they find any sign that someone had been around the house?"

"They didn't find a thing."

Tessa frowned, still wondering what had awakened her. "I guess that's good."

"Are you going to be able to get back to sleep?"

"I'm going to try, now that I know everything's safe."

"Well, good night, sweetheart," her mother said, pressing a kiss to her cheek. "I'm glad everything turned out the way it did."

When her mother had gone, Tessa turned down her lamp and climbed back into bed. She closed her eyes, wanting to sleep, but images of Jared as he'd looked when he'd come through the door haunted her. He had been fierce and dangerous like some avenging angel coming to her defense, except that she was the one he'd been attacking. The tnought might have made her smile, if she hadn't been so angry.

Boyd sat in the darkness in his own house very much aware that the marshal had just ridden by another time. Hate filled him. He had been drinking since midday, and each succeeding drink had left him more enraged.

He hated Sarah and he hated Tessa Sinclair.

He lifted the liquor bottle to his lips. Some of the whiskey dribbled down his chin, but he didn't care. He smiled drunkenly to himself. He had almost gotten to Tessa Sinclair tonight, but the damned marshal had shown up and ruined everything. He'd been forced to sneak away. He'd get another chance, though, and soon. There was no way he would let that woman get away with what she'd done. She needed to be taught a lesson, and he was going to be the one to do it!

Getting to his feet, Boyd staggered into the bedroom. There were still some of Sarah's clothes hanging in the wardrobe. The very sight of them infuriated him. He tore them from the wardrobe and ripped them to shreds. The action eased some of his violent anger, but didn't erase it. Only getting his hands on Tessa and Sarah would do that.

Boyd didn't like being patient, but with the lawman keeping such a close watch on him, he'd have to be careful. Nothing was going to stop him, though. He was going to do whatever was necessary to get his revenge.

When Tessa came downstairs the following morning, it was easy for her to see the damage Jared had done to the front door. Jared certainly must have hit it hard. She frowned as she thought of how angry he'd been over the incident. Tessa knew she should have been pleased that he'd broken down the door to save her, but his arrogant attitude when he'd found out she wasn't in trouble had been most irritating.

Tessa supposed Jared was just doing his job. She knew he wasn't hounding her because he cared anything about her. As the marshal, it was his duty to make sure everything stayed quiet in town, and she supposed that was what he'd been doing. Still, she had never given him a reason to think that she needed his guidance or protection in any way, shape, or form.

Tessa shook her head as she untied the door and opened it a bit. Steve had managed to secure it for the balance of the night, but it was going to need some major repairs right away. She'd already spoken to him about working on it today.

"What happened to the door?"

The sound of Will's voice caught her off guard. She hadn't expected him to show up so early.

"Will! You startled me, and after last night . . ."

"What happened last night?" he asked worriedly.

"Nothing happened, really. Marshal Trent thought there was an intruder in the house, but the person he'd seen through the window was me." She quickly explained everything that had happened.

"You should have sent word to me. I would have come to help you right away," he told her, immediately concerned. "Do you want me to move in here with you, so I can help protect you?"

"I don't have any rooms left. We took on a new boarder yesterday."

"I don't mind sleeping on the sofa. I want to make sure that you're safe."

"It's very kind of you to offer, but I'll be all right. Why don't you come on in and join us for breakfast?"

He followed her to the dining room, where her mother was serving the morning meal.

"Good morning, Will," Maggie greeted him. "I guess Tessa told you all about our excitement last night."

"She did, and I'm worried about it. What if there had been an intruder? There would have been no one here to help you."

"I was here," Steve said from where he sat at the far end of the table.

Will glanced at the newcomer for the first time and took an immediate dislike to him. The rest of the men who boarded with Tessa were no threat to his plans, but this man was young and good-looking, and Will didn't like the way Tessa

133

was smiling at him. "You must be the new boarder."

She quickly introduced them. "Steve's going to be staying on with us for a while, and I hired him this morning to do all the odd jobs around the house."

She had appreciated his help the night before, and after speaking to him about repairing the door this morning, she'd proposed the arrangement. He needed money, and she needed a handyman.

Will noticed Tessa's expression as she looked at Steve, and it irked him. He didn't want her to show interest in any other man.

"That's good," Will said, gritting his teeth against his real desire to tell the man to get out of the boardinghouse and never come back. He sat down at the table and accepted the plate of food Maggie held out to him.

"On a happier note, there's only one more day until the big dance," Maggie said, changing the subject once they'd settled in to eat. "Are you going to go, Steve? Everyone always has a good time."

"I hadn't given it much thought, ma'am," he replied. He had never been much of a dancer, but it would give him an opportunity to see more of the townsfolk.

"It's quite a big celebration," Tessa explained. "You should plan on it."

"Well, if you and your mother will each save me a dance, I'll go," he promised with a grin.

The other men laughed except for Will. He didn't want anyone else dancing with Tessa.

"It will be our pleasure to save you a dance," Maggie said. "What about you, Sludge? Are you going to dance with us Saturday night? And Henry?"

Sludge blushed at being put on the spot. He adored the two women, but rarely went to any social functions. "I don't know, Miss Maggie. I guess if you want me to, I could."

"I would love to dance with you, Sludge," she told him, and she meant it. He was a dear man, for all that he wasn't the fastest at catching on to things, but he was always honest and caring. In all the time he'd lived with them, he had always been a perfect gentleman.

"What about you, Henry? Are you going?" Tessa challenged him good-naturedly. Henry had lived with them for only four months. He'd always been well mannered, but very quiet, staying to himself quite a bit. "I won't have a dance card, but I promise to save a dance for you, if you'll come."

"Oh, no, Miss Tessa. I couldn't do that."

"Are you sure?"

"I'm sure," he finally admitted nervously.

"Well, why not?" Maggie asked.

He looked very uncomfortable. "Well, Miss Maggie . . . I, uh, I can't dance."

"That's all right, Henry," Tessa reassured him. "If that's all that's bothering you, Mother and I can teach you. We've still got time."

Henry went still. No one had ever wanted to dance with him before, and certainly no one had ever cared enough to make such a kind offer. He had had his eye on one lady in town, but had been too shy even to think of speaking with her. If he knew how to dance, though, he could ask her on Saturday night. "Well, are you sure?"

Jim smiled at him. "I can tell you from experience that both Miss Maggie and Miss Tessa are very good dancers. If you're going to learn from anyone, they're the ones to teach you."

Henry looked up at them and smiled. "I reckon I'd like that, if you don't mind."

"We don't have a lot of time, so let's have our first lesson tonight, right after dinner," Tessa said.

"Oh, yes, ma'am," Henry said, delighted at the prospect. He came from a long line of hardworking people who barely eked out a living. There had never been any time in his life for social skills, but now he was going to get the chance to learn to dance. "I'll be here."

"Me, too," Jim said, grinning at Maggie. "I'll play my fiddle for you, and maybe take a refresher course, too."

Maggie blushed a little. "Why, Jim Russell, you know very well you can dance!"

His smile broadened. "But I can always use some practice with a pretty woman."

Tessa laughed in delight, while Maggie just smiled and blushed even more.

"We should have enough time to teach you the basics," Tessa told Henry. "You'll be fine. It'll give the girls in Durango a thrill to have a new man to dance with."

This time it was Henry's turn to blush.

Will had to fight to keep what he was really feeling from showing. Instead, he managed a tight smile. He didn't like the idea of any other man's hands on Tessa.

"If the lessons are open to everyone, I'd like to come, too. I'm like Jim. I never want to pass up the chance to dance with a pretty woman," Will complimented, and he was pleased when Tessa smiled at him.

"With so many men wanting lessons, I think I'd better invite Julie over to help us," she said to her mother, a twinkle shining in her eyes as she thought that Steve might just show up, too.

"That'd be wonderful."

Chapter Ten

Jared was standing at the bar in the High Time Saloon, downing his second drink. It was only nine o'clock in the morning, but he'd already told Nathan he wouldn't be in until late in the afternoon. He had been up all night and was still too tense even to think about sleep. That was why he'd resorted to liquor. On days like this, nothing else would work.

Dan sensed that the marshal needed to be left alone, so he'd stayed at the far end of the bar, giving him his peace. But now that he saw his glass was empty again, he knew it was time to approach him. "Another one?"

Jared nodded and shoved the glass back across the bar toward Dan.

"Long night?" Dan asked.

"Real long," Jared ground out, not offering any

more than that. He was still shaken by what might have happened at the Sinclair house. He just thanked God that he'd had sense enough not to go in shooting. He gave a disgusted shake of his head at the thought that Tessa might have come to harm at his hands.

It had taken him only an instant to realize his mistake, and then the awareness had come to him—the sweet heat of her gentle curves pressed tightly to him. He didn't want to think about Tessa this way, but images of her wearing only her nightgown and wrapper stayed with him and wouldn't be dismissed.

Jared took another drink.

Damn, but she was good-looking.

He conceded that much. Tessa was a beautiful young woman.

Damn, but it felt wonderful to hold her that way.

He growled at himself, trying to deny his desire.

Tessa Sinclair is nothing but trouble.

He knew that.

He wanted nothing to do with her.

He tried to convince himself.

Jared told himself that it was his job that kept throwing them together, and, good lawman that he was, he would do his job. He would keep her safe from Boyd Wilson and from anyone or anything else she got herself involved in, but he was not going to let her mean anything more than that to him. She was a responsibility. That was all.

Jared drained his glass.

"You want one more?" Dan asked. He noticed

that the marshal's expression was still dark and that he hadn't really relaxed since he'd come into the saloon.

Jared shook his head.

"They're on the house, you know," Dan added.

"Thanks, but no," Jared said. "I've had enough. I'll see you later."

Jared strode from the saloon, out into the brightness of the day. There had still been no sign of Boyd Wilson, and he doubted there would be in the daylight. Evil men like Boyd seemed to do their dirty work in the dark.

Jared headed home. He needed some sleep.

Julie's heart was quite light as she made her way to Tessa's house that night. A letter had come from Ellen Prescott, a friend she'd made when she'd been back east at school, and as far as Julie was concerned, the news was the best ever. Ellen and her older brother, Roderick, were coming west on an excursion, and Ellen wanted to stop in Durango for a visit with Julie and her parents.

Julie was excited, and her parents were thrilled. The Prescotts were very well received back east, and she remembered Roderick Prescott well. He'd been six years older than she and Ellen, very mature and very good-looking. By the time she had returned home, he had already graduated from the university and had taken a position teaching literature there. Julie had kept in touch with Ellen, and, through her letters, Julie had learned that Roderick had since published several literary works and had written some poetry.

Julie sighed dreamily and smiled to herself at

the thought of debonair Roderick Prescott coming to town. He was tall and blond and, oh, so very handsome. He'd always been a gentleman when she'd been around him, though, of course, he'd thought her a mere child—a friend to his little sister, and nothing more. But that would all be changed now. That had been some time ago. Now she was a woman fully grown.

As she started up the front walk to Tessa's house, Julie's mood was ebullient. Ellen and Roderick would be arriving in less than a week. Ellen had asked in her letter if there was any kind of literary society in Durango that might want to have Roderick read selected passages from his works while they were in town. Julie was going to discuss it with Tessa tonight and see what they could arrange. The short notice meant nothing. She was just delighted that they were coming and couldn't wait to tell her best friend.

The sound of Jim playing his fiddle came to her as she drew near, and it surprised her. She wondered what was going on inside. When Tessa had stopped by her house that afternoon and invited her to come over for a visit, she hadn't said anything about a celebration of any sort tonight. Julie supposed the older man was just in the mood to play his instrument. It didn't matter. Nothing mattered to Julie tonight except the news that Roderick Prescott would soon be coming to Durango. That knowledge alone left her walking on air.

Julie finally took notice of the repairs to the front door when she knocked on it, and she realized how terrible last night must have been for

Tessa. She'd been so caught up in her thoughts of Roderick that she'd forgotten what Tessa had told her during their earlier visit.

The door was opened almost as soon as Julie knocked.

"You came! I am so glad!" Tessa said in delight as she ushered her friend inside.

"You are?" She was surprised by Tessa's reaction and wondered what was going on. "Why?"

"Because . . ." Tessa glanced over her shoulder toward the parlor. "*We* need you."

"*We*, who? And for what?"

"You'll see."

Tessa took Julie by the arm and led her down the hall. As they entered the parlor, Jim stopped playing.

Julie stared around herself in amazement. The furniture had all been shoved back against the walls, and the carpet had been rolled up. Jim was standing in the corner with his fiddle poised, ready to start playing again. Sludge and Henry were both standing off to the side with Maggie, looking a bit uncomfortable and nervous. Will was there, too.

"What's going on?" Julie asked, puzzled.

"Welcome to Julie and Tessa's School of Dance," Tessa announced, giving her friend a quick pleading look she hoped the men didn't see. "Henry wants to go to the dance Saturday night, but he's never learned how to dance, and Sludge wants to polish up his skills, too. I volunteered. I told them we'd help them."

"You did?" There had been no missing the look her friend had given her, so Julie managed a slight smile.

"Mother will help, too, when we need a rest, and Will came to help demonstrate the steps. Are you ready?"

"Whenever you are," Julie responded, but she was wondering what Tessa had been thinking to do this to her. Tessa knew what she wanted in a man, and Sludge and Henry were about as far as you could get from her ideal—from Roderick.

The arrogance of that thought bothered Julie. She had never considered herself a mean-spirited person. It was just that she knew what she wanted in a man—and what she didn't want. Sludge and Henry were nice men, but she had no interest in either one of them. Roderick was coming to town! That was the most important thing, and now she wouldn't even have time to tell Tessa. She would have to spend the night teaching these two how to dance. She girded herself for the evening to come and prayed she didn't get trod upon too heavily.

As Julie surrendered gracefully to Tessa's urgings, she realized that this was very much like Tessa. Her friend always helped out everyone she could, and the minute she'd found out that Henry needed dancing lessons, she'd arranged for that to happen. Julie's smile became real as she thought of how tenderhearted Tessa was.

Tessa saw the change in Julie and was pleased. She always knew she could count on Julie to help her.

"Will?" Tessa looked at him. "Why don't you dance me around the room a few times so Sludge and Henry can see the steps?"

Will didn't need any further encouragement.

He'd been waiting for the chance to hold Tessa. He went to her and took her in his arms.

"Boys, this is the best part," he told Sludge and Henry with a grin. "You get to hold your girl."

Jim started up a tune, and they circled the room.

Tessa was a bit irritated by Will's remark. She wasn't Will's anything, but she held her tongue. This wasn't the time for a disagreement. This was a time for helping Sludge and Henry. She glanced toward the parlor doorway one last time as Will whisked her past it, wondering where Steve was. He'd told her that morning that he would be there in time for the lessons, but she hadn't seen him for several hours. She moved easily to Will's lead, and when Jim ended the tune, she was ready to take on Henry.

"Did you both watch what Will was doing?" Tessa asked Sludge and Henry.

"Yes, ma'am, but Will made it look easy," Henry remarked.

"It is easy," Will said confidently. He was feeling quite superior to the other two, and he'd enjoyed having Tessa rubbing up against him as they'd danced. He couldn't wait to start courting her. He was certain she was desperate for a man in her life now that her brother was dead, so he figured it probably wouldn't be too much longer before he could approach her. The thought of having her sent a shaft of heat through his body, and he was forced to fight his need. This wasn't the time.

"Henry, if you would do me the honor?" Tessa approached him and took his hand to draw him out on the makeshift dance floor. "Sludge, will you dance with Julie?"

"Yes, ma'am." Sludge bobbed his head nervously and blushed as Julie approached him.

Julie wasn't sure that Tessa's attempt to teach these two would work, but she would do her best. "All right, Sludge, let's give it a whirl."

It didn't take long for Tessa to realize that teaching the two men to dance was going to be a little more difficult than she'd originally anticipated. She and Julie practiced each step with them, changing partners occasionally just for fun and to keep the mood of the evening light. Jim started his tunes over and over again to help them, but neither man showed any natural talent or rhythm or ability. The women realized it was going to be a long night.

"Shall we give them another demonstration?" Will offered after the two women had suffered through many awkward attempts by their unskilled partners to circle the room. He knew this meant nothing, that this was only practice, but he still didn't like seeing Tessa in the other men's arms. "Tessa?"

"I think I need a minute's rest," she said. "But I'm sure Julie would love to allow you to squire her around and show the boys another time how it's done."

Anger flashed for an instant in Will's eyes at being so rejected, but was quickly disguised. "Julie?"

Will danced her around the floor, demonstrating the steps once again. Julie was a good dancer and pretty, but she wasn't Tessa. He made it a point to keep an eye on Tessa the whole time he was dancing with Julie. He frowned when she disappeared into the hallway. He couldn't imagine where she'd gone, and he wanted the dance to end so he could go after her and check.

As Jim finished the tune, Will looked up to see that Tessa had returned. She was standing in the doorway with Steve. She was looking up at him, obviously laughing at something he'd said. It took all Will's control not to scowl.

"Steve's finally showed up," Tessa announced when Jim had stopped playing. "Julie, this is Steve. He's our new boarder."

Julie had been standing with her back to the doorway when the dance ended. When Will released her, she turned and grew still. There before her was the cowboy she and Tessa had seen riding into town the day before.

"Steve . . . ?" she said tentatively.

"Steve Madison, ma'am," Steve told her, nodding courteously in her direction.

"And I'm Julie Stevens." Julie realized that Steve was even better-looking up close than he had been from a distance, and that was saying something. He's just a cowboy! she told herself. "Do you need dance lessons, too?"

"If you're offering," he said, slanting her a grin. It had been a long time since he'd had the pleasure of dancing with a lady.

His grin and the dimple it revealed in his cheek were so rakish that Julie's heart beat a bit faster than normal. She remained standing where she was as Jim struck up another tune.

Steve took her in his arms as Tessa grabbed Sludge's hand and Maggie cornered Henry. Will stood alone, resentfully watching the others. He couldn't believe that Tessa had chosen Sludge over him.

Julie had no time to think as Steve whirled her about the room. His steps were infinitely more polished than either of the other two boarders, but he was not as skilled as Will had been. Somehow that didn't matter to her. The warm pressure of his hand at the small of her back was sending shivers up her spine, and the power of his shoulder beneath her hand revealed to her that he was strong and muscular. The rhythm he set for them seemed perfect, and they moved smoothly about the room, caught up in the moment.

Steve was staring down at the lovely blonde in his arms. She was beautiful. Tessa had mentioned that her friend Julie might come by and help with the dance lessons, but he'd had no idea that Julie would look like this. Her hair was the color of sunlight. Her complexion was flawless. She moved with graceful rhythm, never missing a step even when he faltered. The hint of her womanly curves pressed ever so lightly against him was heavenly.

The sudden sensual awareness of their innocent contact jarred Steve. He hadn't expected to feel anything like this. They were dancing. That was all. It had been a very long time since he'd had any dealings with good women, and he was surprised by the power of the attraction he felt for Julie.

Steve forced his thoughts away from her. He had no time for women or any of the complications that went with them. He was in Durango for one reason and one reason only, and that was to find the gang that had been responsible for his being sent to prison. He couldn't let anything distract him.

The music ended. The others discussed what they'd done wrong, while Julie stood awkwardly beside Steve. She wasn't quite certain what to do or say, and that bothered her, for it definitely wasn't like her to be so discomfited.

"Thank you, Julie," Steve said, deliberately taking a step away from her. The sweet scent of her perfume and the memory their dance were too disturbing.

"You're a good dancer. You didn't need any lessons," she returned, troubled by the unexpected and unmistakable attraction she felt for him.

"It's been a while since I danced last, and I knew I could use some practice."

Wanting to distance herself from his overpowering nearness, Julie smiled faintly at him and moved off to talk to Jim. She was going to make sure that she did not dance with Steve again. She would leave that to Tessa and Miss Maggie.

Julie was slightly surprised when Steve disappeared upstairs after dancing only one more dance with each of the other women. She found herself wondering why he hadn't come back, even though she told herself that it didn't matter what the cowboy did, because she didn't care. Steve had been adequate on the dance floor and nothing more. Julie convinced herself that she was glad he hadn't asked her to dance again.

The lessons continued for almost another hour, until everyone finally agreed to call it a night. Sludge and Henry went upstairs to bed, while Will lingered in the parlor to talk a little longer with Jim and Maggie.

Julie was glad she finally was going to have a

moment alone with Tessa. She all but dragged her friend out onto the front porch so they could speak privately.

"I've got something so exciting to tell you!"

"What? That you loved dancing with Sludge and Henry tonight and you want to open a real School of Dance right here in Durango?"

"Be serious. I've been waiting for hours to tell you this, and it has nothing to do with dancing!"

"Tell me what?"

"I got the most exciting letter today!"

"From whom?"

"I've told you about my friend Ellen from back east at school, haven't I?"

"Yes, you've mentioned her before. What happened?" Tessa saw that Julie's excitement was real, and she smiled at her delight.

"It's not what happened. It's what's going to happen! Ellen's coming to Durango for a visit, and . . ."

Tessa could tell that it was the rest of what she had to tell her that had Julie so excited. "And?"

"And she's bringing her older brother Roderick with her!"

"Why are you so excited about this Roderick?" Tessa asked, seeing the animation in her friend's expression. She had rarely seen Julie so thrilled about anything.

Julie quickly told her everything about him. "Roderick is such a wonderful man." She sighed. "I can't wait to see him again. He's nothing like the men around here."

"He sounds interesting."

"Oh, he's more than interesting. He's fascinating! Tessa, do you suppose the Women's Solidarity might want to invite Roderick to be a featured guest? He could read from his works. It would be so . . . so cultural."

"We can ask them tomorrow. You say Ellen and Roderick are going to arrive next week?"

"That's what Ellen's letter said."

Tessa understood her friend's excitement. This Roderick sounded like the perfect man for Julie. From what she'd just said, he was sophisticated and handsome and cultured. He was Julie's dream man.

Tessa was reminded of her own dream man. She wondered why it was so simple for Julie to know who her ideal man was, while she had no idea. "I'm looking forward to meeting Roderick. He sounds wonderful."

"Oh, he is. Seeing him again is going to be so . . ." She paused, at a loss for words. "Oh, Tessa, you know what I mean. Roderick is perfect, just perfect." She smiled ecstatically. "It's just too bad that he won't be here in time for the dance on Saturday night."

"Well, I don't think you have too much to worry about there. You won't be lacking for dance partners. Sludge and Henry are quite taken with you, and Will and Steve will be there, too."

The mention of Steve brought a hint of color to her cheeks. "Why didn't you tell me that he was your new boarder?"

"I didn't think of it, with everything that had happened the night before."

"That was exciting. I suppose we're lucky that Marshal Trent didn't show up and try to break down the door tonight," she said with a laugh.

"It was very scary last night, Julie." Tessa grew

serious as she remembered the terror of the encounter. "Someone could have been hurt."

"I'm sure it was, but you have to admit that it's good to know Marshal Trent is keeping such a close eye on you. That threat from Boyd sounds serious."

"I know," Tessa said vaguely. A shiver trembled through her at the memory she'd denied all day. Suddenly she recalled in vivid detail what it had been like to be held in Jared's arms and she wondered how it would have felt to dance with him tonight. As quickly as the thought came, she banished it. She didn't want to dance with Jared. She didn't want anything to do with the arrogant, overbearing lawman.

"You know," Julie went on, her mood lightening again, "if Marshal Trent had broken in tonight, we could have given him dancing lessons, too."

This time Julie did manage to make Tessa laugh. "Good night, Julie!"

"I guess I had better start home," Julie said, realizing that it was starting to get dark.

"Let me go get Jim for you. He promised he would escort you home."

"There's no need," Will said from the doorway. "I'll be glad to see you home, Julie."

"Why, thank you, Will," Tessa replied.

"Make sure you lock the door once we're gone," Will ordered Tessa.

"I will," she answered, somehow resenting the fact that Will was telling her what to do.

Tessa remained on the porch, watching the two of them until they'd disappeared from sight. She was not aware that Jared had already passed by the house twice on horseback that evening. He was on his way back up the street once more as she went back inside.

In spite of her resentment of Will's unasked-for advice, she did lock the door.

Chapter Eleven

"Nathan, who the hell is Steve Madison? Where do I know that name from?" Jared asked his deputy when he saw him in the office the following morning. He'd been trying to remember ever since he'd met the man at the Sinclairs', and he'd had no luck.

Nathan was sitting at Jared's desk reading the latest issue of the Durango *Weekly Star*. He looked up and frowned.

"Madison . . . Madison . . ." Nathan paused thoughtfully. "Wasn't Steve Madison a fast gun from the Arizona Territory?"

"That's right," Jared said, growing serious as he finally recalled what little he'd heard about the gunman.

"He was locked up for something a while back. I haven't heard any more recently. Why are you worrying about him?"

"Because Steve Madison is right here in Durango," he answered tightly.

"Doing what?"

"That's what I'd like to know."

"This doesn't sound good. We don't need his kind of trouble in town."

"Do you remember what he was arrested for?"

"No. I never heard. I just know that talk had it he was one to keep an eye on."

"I plan to do just that." Jared started out of the office again. "I'll be back in a little while."

Jared headed straight for the Sinclair boardinghouse. He wanted to have a few words with Steve Madison. He didn't like his being there in his town, and he really didn't like his staying with Tessa. There wasn't anything Jared could do about that, but he could certainly let the man know that he knew who he was and that he would be watching him and wouldn't tolerate any trouble.

"Miss Maggie, I was wondering if Steve is around?" Jared asked when the older woman answered the door.

"I'm sorry, Marshal Trent, but he's not. He left a while ago and didn't say where he was going or when he'd be back."

"Will you let him know I was looking for him?"

"I sure will."

"Everything was quiet for you last night? You didn't have any trouble?"

"No, thank heaven, and I like it this way. You should have stopped by for a visit earlier last evening, though. Tessa and Julie Stevens were giving some of the boys dancing lessons. Jim was playing his fiddle, and we had quite a time."

"Sorry I missed it," he answered. He'd heard the music when he'd ridden by to check on them and had wondered at it.

"Are you still planning on coming to the dance tonight?"

"I'll be there."

"Good. I'll look forward to seeing you."

Jared was frustrated as he left the house. He wouldn't admit it to himself, but he had hoped to see Tessa. He hadn't caught sight of her inside, so he figured she wasn't home. The thought immediately left him worrying about where she was and if she was watching for Boyd. Just because things had been quiet so far, that didn't mean the man had gone away or changed his mind about taking revenge. Boyd was as mean and nasty as they came.

Walking back through town, Jared decided to stop in at a few places just to see what was going on. He was pleased when he found Steve at the bar in the High Time Saloon.

"Little early to be drinking, don't you think, Madison?" Jared remarked as he went to stand beside him.

Steve had seen the lawman checking out the saloon from outside the swinging doors. He'd known Trent was after him when he'd caught sight of him and had come straight inside.

"What can I do for you, Marshal?" He looked at him, meeting his gaze steadily, without fear.

"I just wanted you to know that I know who you are, and I'll be watching you."

Steve heard the cold edge to his voice and knew his reputation had preceded him. He nodded and slowly turned his attention back to his drink.

"I won't tolerate any trouble in my town," Jared went on.

"I don't plan on giving you any," Steve answered, fighting to keep his anger under control. He didn't have much use for lawmen anymore after the way he'd been treated in Arizona. Trent had seemed decent enough that night at the house, but now there was an unspoken threat in his voice that Steve didn't like.

"Then we understand each other."

"We do."

"Good." Jared looked over at Dan, who'd been pretending not to be listening as he busily worked at drying a glass. "Dan."

"See you later, Marshal Trent."

Jared left the saloon.

Dan looked over at the man Marshal Trent had called Steve Madison. "What was that all about?"

"Nothing important," Steve answered, shrugging off his question.

"Marshal Trent's one hell of a lawman. He keeps things good and safe here in Durango."

"What about those stage robberies you had not too long ago? I was reading about them in your paper. He hasn't caught those outlaws yet, has he?"

Dan looked troubled. "No, not yet, but the marshal's doing what he can. He rode out with a posse after each robbery, and they tracked them quite a ways, but they lost their trail up in the mountains both times. With any luck, the gang's long gone and won't try anything else around here again."

Steve wanted to tell him that he didn't want the

gang to be gone, that he wanted the outlaws to try to pull off another job so he could catch up with them, but he said nothing. He would wait, and listen, and hope that he could find out what he needed to know. He'd waited this long; he could wait a little longer.

Boyd smiled as he stared at his own reflection in the mirror. He was wearing his best clothes and looked quite presentable. Tonight was the dance—and tonight was the night. His plan was going to work, and he was going to enjoy every minute of it.

As ready as he would ever be to set his plan in motion, Boyd left the house. He checked to make sure his horses were saddled, ready and waiting. When the time came, he would have to move quickly and quietly.

The raised dance floor was crowded with dancing couples as music filled the night air. Brightly colored lanterns and some torches had been positioned around the area to provide lighting. Tessa stood with her mother and Jim, watching Sludge and Henry dancing with the young ladies of their choice.

"I can't believe Henry is doing so well," Tessa whispered to her mother as she watched him successfully circle the dance floor. "I was worried about him."

"So was I. He didn't seem to be the most graceful of men last night," she said kindly, "but he's doing fine with Sylvie Johnson."

"Sludge is doing wonderfully, too," Tessa

added, glancing toward where the big man was squiring a tall, willowy young woman. "I don't know her. Do you?"

"No, but she's certainly keeping up with him."

"Good evening, ladies, Jim," Will said as he appeared by Tessa's side. He had been waiting anxiously for this moment. It had been pleasant enough dancing with Tessa at the house last night, but tonight was going to be even better.

"Good evening, Will." Maggie smiled at him, pleased to see him.

"Will," Jim responded.

"Hello, Will," Tessa said, looking up at him. He looked handsome, dressed up as he was, and she smiled in welcome.

"Tessa? May I have this dance?" Will invited, his gaze warm upon her.

"Of course."

He led her out among the dancers.

"You look lovely tonight," he told her. The blue gown she was wearing was modestly cut, but the bodice was low enough to entice his imagination. She had styled her hair up away from her face, with a few errant curls escaping down her back. The style emphasized the slender line of her throat, and Will knew a driving urge to press kisses down the sweet curve of her neck to her shoulder. Later, he told himself. He had the sudden unwelcome thought that maybe some of the other men there were having the same thoughts about her, and jealousy filled him. She was his, and nobody else's.

"Thank you."

"I take it your day was uneventful?"

"Yes, and I enjoyed every minute of it."

"Since things seem to be quiet around here, I'll head back up to the mine tomorrow."

"That will be good. I'm sure the men are wondering what's happened to you."

"I was detained by urgent business," he said seriously. "I couldn't leave you, knowing about Boyd's threats."

"That was thoughtful of you, and I appreciate it. But with Marshal Trent keeping an eye on things, I think everything will be fine now," she told him.

"I hope so. I don't want anything to happen to you."

Something about his tone bothered her. It seemed almost too intimate. When the dance concluded, Tessa was glad to be returned to her mother's side.

"You two make such a handsome couple," Maggie said to Tessa in a soft tone, for only her to hear.

Tessa smiled at her mother and nodded. Henry appeared before her to ask her for the next dance, and she quickly accepted.

The music started, and Will was left to watch her move off in Henry's arms.

Jared stood in the shadows, just outside the circle of light from the lanterns, quietly observing all the festivities. The only trouble so far had been a couple of drunken cowboys he'd had to haul off to jail to sober up; otherwise, the evening was going smoothly. Everyone seemed to be having a good time.

"You hiding back here to surprise any trouble-makers or are you hiding from young ladies who are trying to force you to dance?" Trace Jackson asked as he brought his wife, Elise, to join Jared. They had seen him standing there alone and decided that he needed some company.

"I haven't seen you two out there dancing," Jared returned with a laugh, but he knew Trace was very astute about some things. Melissa Davenport would be looking for him, as she always did at social occasions, but he didn't have time for her tonight. Lovely though Melissa was, Jared was on the lookout for Boyd, and he didn't want to be distracted.

"We haven't danced yet because we just arrived," Elise explained. "We had to finish getting the paper out first."

"What's your lead story this week?"

"Don't worry. It's not about the robberies again," she told him. "I know you've done everything you can to solve the crimes. Until there's a new lead or a new angle on the gang, I'm not going to run anything else on them."

Jared slanted her a wry half smile. "The townsfolk may think you're going too easy on me."

Elise shrugged. She was a professional when it came to her reporting, and she knew when to run with a story and when to sit tight.

"I don't bow to public opinion," she said with dignity. "But I do love to sell newspapers." She smiled as she finished, thinking of how well the *Weekly Star* was doing.

"I've heard that about you," Jared said, grinning even more broadly as he remembered his first escapade with Elise. She'd posed as a bride to entrap a phony preacher. The "reverend" had a gang that went out and robbed the houses of those attending his services. Elise's trouble had started when her would-be groom hadn't shown up, and she'd been forced to recruit Trace—a complete stranger to her then—to take the groom's place. Who would have thought after that beginning that these two would end up happily married?

"Our lead story this week is about the upcoming visit of a noted university professor from back east. One Mr. Roderick Prescott is coming to town for a visit. It seems he's friends with Julie Stevens and her family. Julie says there are plans in the works for him to read from selected passages of his own literary works for the Ladies' Solidarity."

"It was a slow news week?" Jared asked perceptively.

"Very, and we thank you for that, Marshal Trent," Trace said. As an ex-lawman himself, he enjoyed living in a peaceful town.

The music ended, and another tune started up. Jared glanced at Elise.

"May I have this dance, ma'am?"

"Why, Marshal Trent, I thought you'd never ask. Excuse me, darling, I'm running off with this good-looking lawman."

"But you'll be back?"

"And you'd better be ready to dance with me yourself," she said as Jared whisked her away.

Melissa Davenport had been standing to the side of the dance floor watching for some sign of Jared Trent.

"Why isn't he here yet?" she demanded of her close friend Dena Kaye. She had been anxiously anticipating this night. She could hardly wait to dance with Jared again. "There hasn't been any trouble in town tonight. Jared should be here by now."

"Maybe something's going on we haven't heard about," Dena offered.

"I doubt it. If anything had happened, we'd know it."

"I suppose you're right," she agreed, knowing that news did travel fast around town when there was a social event going on. She glanced up just then and caught sight of the marshal dancing with Elise Jackson. "Look! There he is now!"

Melissa's mood brightened immediately. "I knew he'd show up. I just knew he would."

"And he's dancing with Elise. That's good. A married woman is no competition for you."

"I'll say. I'll see you later. Right now I want to get over there by him so I can talk to him as soon as the dance is over."

"Good luck," Dena teased.

Melissa just flashed her a triumphant look as she made her way casually in Jared's direction. Her careful planning worked. Just as the music stopped, she was by his side. It all looked very accidental, but Melissa knew how important careful planning was to a successful outcome— and she did have a definite outcome in mind where Jared was concerned.

"Why, Jared," Melissa said sweetly. "I was hoping to see you tonight. Hello, Elise."

"Hello, Melissa," Jared greeted her. He told himself he'd known this moment was inevitable tonight, but he'd somehow hoped to avoid it.

True, the petite, dark-haired woman was pretty enough, but she was far too serious for his liking.

"Melissa, it's good to see you again," Elise told her. Then giving Jared an innocent look, she added, "Are you claiming Jared for the next dance? Trace is coming after me, and I'd hate for Jared to have to sit this one out."

"I'd love to dance with Jared," Melissa answered as the next tune began.

Jared was trapped and he had Elise to thank for it. He glared at her as he took Melissa in his arms.

"My pleasure," he assured Melissa.

Melissa was in heaven as Jared guided her around the dance floor. She attempted to make small talk with him, but for some reason he seemed distracted. She thought she was looking quite her best tonight and had hoped to have his undivided attention.

"Is something bothering you?" she asked.

Jared glanced down at her then, realizing that he was being less than attentive. He was worrying about Boyd, though, and couldn't allow himself to relax completely. "I'm sorry, Melissa. There has been some trouble, but nothing too exciting. I just want to make sure nothing else happens tonight."

"You are so serious about your job," she said, gazing up at him adoringly. She had yet to get him to kiss her, but she was working on it. These things took time, she knew. "We're very blessed to have you here in Durango."

Jared smiled down at her. "I appreciate your kind words, Melissa."

"They're the truth," she said, sliding her hand up his shoulder a bit, loving having the freedom to actually be able to touch him for this moment.

Jared looked up again, and it was then that he spotted Tessa dancing with Will. For some reason, the sight of her with the other man bothered him, though he wasn't sure why. And that made him frown.

Melissa saw the change in his expression. She cast a surreptitious glance in the direction he was looking and saw Tessa Sinclair dancing with a tall, blond-haired man. Jealousy ate at Melissa at the thought that Jared was more interested in the other woman than he was in her. It seemed everybody in town loved Tessa, and it annoyed Melissa to no end. All she ever heard was how wonderful Tessa Sinclair was, and she was getting very tired of it. She knew she was just going to have to work that much harder to make Jared hers.

Tessa found herself in Will's arms again. It seemed the minute Henry was gone, Will appeared.

"Are you having a good time tonight?" he asked.

"Yes, it's wonderful to see Sludge and Henry doing so well. I don't think they've missed a dance yet."

"But what about you? Are you having a good time?" Will was hoping to hear her say that she was thrilled to be with him and that she was enjoying their time together.

"It's always nice to have the chance to get out and visit with friends." Tessa was very aware of what Will wanted to hear, but she couldn't say it. He was an attractive man, but something about him bothered her.

Her answer frustrated Will. He'd hoped she'd tell him that she was glad he'd stayed in town to help protect her and to be with her tonight. He'd been ready to broach the subject of truly courting her, but the coolness of her reply put him off. He remained silent as they finished the dance.

As the music came to an end, Will and Tessa found themselves standing near Jared and Melissa.

"Why, good evening, Tessa," Jared said. His gaze went over her, and he found himself thinking that she looked lovely in her blue gown. "Will." He added the other man as an after-thought. "You know Melissa, don't you?"

They exchanged greetings, and as the music began again, Jared took the opportunity to claim Tessa for the next dance.

Melissa managed to disguise the jealousy that surged through her, and when a ranch hand approached her and invited her to dance, she quickly took him up on his offer.

Will retreated to the side of the dance floor to look on in carefully disguised irritation. Even though the lawman had taken Tessa away from him, Will still felt superior. He figured Trent wasn't much of a lawman when you got down to it. Here they were, attending the same social function, and yet the marshal had no idea that he was the leader of the gang that had robbed two stagecoaches so close to town. A sense of smugness filled Will. The other man could have his dance with Tessa. In the end, he was going to win. He was going to have all the money from the holdups, and he was going to have Tessa for his own. He was sure of it.

Chapter Twelve

Tessa had been dancing with a variety of men all night, and she'd enjoyed each and every dance. She was caught completely off guard, though, by the feelings that swept over her when Jared Trent swept her out onto the dance floor. His strong, powerful arms sent shivers of awareness rippling through her in a sensual assault unlike anything she'd known before. The heat of his body pressed to hers was a firebrand that evoked memories of just how it had felt the other night when he'd broken down the door to save her. They moved in unison to the rhythm of the melody, and she was spellbound.

This was Jared, she tried to tell herself. She could barely tolerate the man. She wasn't even sure why he'd asked her to dance, except to be polite, and she'd accepted only so as not to cause a scene. She had never dreamed it would feel this way to dance with him.

Tessa looked up at Jared from beneath lowered lashes, studying the hard line of his jaw and the firm set of his mouth. She had to admit that he was a handsome man, in a rugged sort of way. He had an aura of control and authority about him that she found compelling, and the way he carried himself spoke of power and self-confidence. All along, she had thought him arrogant, but maybe . . .

Jared glanced down at her then, to find her gazing up at him, her expression thoughtful.

"You look like you're worrying about something. Were you afraid that I needed dancing lessons, too?" he asked, smiling at her.

His smile so transformed him that for a moment Tessa could only stare up at him. It was then that she realized she had never seen him smile before. He had a beautiful smile.

"Oh, no! I saw how good you were with Elise and Melissa, and I knew I was safe." She was glad she'd had a quick response to cover her sudden, unexpected nervousness.

"I'll always make sure you're safe," he said, turning serious.

Tessa instinctively knew he meant it. "Thank you."

"My pleasure," he told her, slanting her a wry grin. "Especially the 'saving you from rough dancers' part. Watch out for Clint Parker, though. He's here tonight, and I heard talk that he can be one tough cowboy on a lady's feet."

"I've had enough personal experience with him to tell you everything you heard is true. He hasn't asked me to dance yet, but if he comes near me, I'll expect you to miraculously appear by my side and rescue me."

It was then, as he spun her around in a graceful move, that Jared thought he caught a glimpse of Boyd standing in the crowd watching them. Jared scowled, then quickly disguised his concern. He didn't want to worry Tessa. He couldn't be sure it had been Boyd, and the man had already disappeared from sight.

Tessa had almost relaxed and started to enjoy the dance, when she felt Jared suddenly tense. She looked up, wondering what was bothering him, and found his gaze upon her. His expression was closed, unreadable. She gave him a tentative smile just as the music ended.

Jared escorted her back to stand with her mother. He would have preferred to stay there with her for the rest of the night, but he didn't trust Boyd one bit. If the man was brazen enough to show up here, he was going to watch his every move.

"Thank you for the dance," he said distractedly. He walked away from her without a backward glance.

Tessa was a bit startled by his sudden indifference. She watched him stride off into the crowd. He'd left her so abruptly that she was puzzled—and a bit hurt.

It surprised Tessa to find that she cared what the man did. For a moment there, something about being in Jared Trent's arms had felt right—very right. Her gaze swept over those gathered around the sides of the dance floor, but she could see no sign of him. Jared had gone.

In a fit of irritation with herself, Tessa stiffened her back and looked around to see who wasn't dancing. She spotted Steve standing alone nearby and started his way. She had no intention of being a wallflower right now.

Julie hadn't been eager to attend the dance. True, it did give her the opportunity to wear the new gown her mother had bought for her, but tonight she honestly had wanted to stay home and think about Roderick and make plans for his upcoming visit.

"This is going to be so much fun," Adele Stevens was saying as her husband, Lyle, escorted them to the festivities.

"Indeed, we haven't danced in quite a while, my dear," Lyle said, his eyes aglow as he looked down at his wife.

"I'm looking forward to it."

"Julie, I meant to tell you before we left the house that you look very pretty in your new dress."

"Thank you, Papa."

They neared the crowd and were immediately welcomed by friends.

Will had been biding his time, looking on as the other couples moved about the dance floor. He'd wanted to spend more time with Tessa, but it appeared he wasn't going to get the chance. She was a very popular woman. Every time a tune ended, she was claimed by another eager male before he could reach her side.

Will smiled to himself when he saw Julie arrive

and knew this was a golden opportunity. Listening to Tessa and Julie talking the other night, he had realized that Julie's father was a banker in town. Will knew this was his chance to be introduced to Mr. Stevens and learn some information that would help him and the boys with their next job. It was certainly worth a try.

"Evening, Julie," Will said as he approached them.

"Hello, Will." She greeted him with a smile. She knew that Miss Maggie liked and trusted him, and she thought him a nice man. "Have you ever met my parents?"

"No, I've never had the pleasure."

Julie quickly made the introductions. They made small talk for a few minutes, and then Will invited Julie to dance. He felt quite proud of himself as he whisked her around the floor. He had just made a vital connection, and he was going to see if he could make it pay off.

Steve had told himself that he was going to the dance to check out the townsfolk and see if he recognized anyone who'd been a part of the gang. He didn't care about the dancing, and he didn't care if he saw Julie again. As he stood there watching Julie in Will's arms, though, Steve knew he'd been lying to himself. He had wanted to see her again, and he definitely wanted to dance with her one more time.

All day, the memory of their dance the night before had haunted him. He had deliberately left the parlor and had gone upstairs to his room before the lessons had ended. He had been lying

171

down trying to fall asleep when he'd heard Julie and Tessa go out on the front porch to talk after Jim had stopped playing.

Steve hadn't meant to eavesdrop, but it had been a quiet night and he'd heard their every word. It was obvious from that conversation that Julie knew exactly what she wanted in a man, and it wasn't a man like him.

Steve had tried to sleep, but thoughts of how wonderful it had felt to hold her had kept him awake and restless. He lay long into the night, thinking about his life and his future—and wondering if he even had a future.

Now here he was at the dance. When the music stopped, Steve walked straight up to where Julie was standing with Will. He hadn't meant to do it. He'd told himself it was ridiculous, that he knew exactly how Julie felt, but that didn't stop him.

"Evening, Julie, Will," he said, then looked at Julie. "Julie? May I have the next dance?"

The music started up again, and she nodded in response. Julie hoped the hesitancy she was feeling didn't show as she allowed Steve to guide her out onto the dance floor. She had not been able to forget her reaction to him last night. She told herself now that it was good that they were dancing again, so she could see that she'd blown everything out of proportion in her own mind. But when he took her in his arms, her breath caught in her throat.

"You look beautiful tonight," Steve said as he led her smoothly among the dancers.

"Why, thank you," she answered, gazing up at him. She was hoping she could find some flaw in his chiseled features, but he seemed even more handsome tonight than before.

Their rhythm was perfect together as they circled the floor. Steve had hoped his reaction to Julie the previous evening had been his imagination working overtime, but looking down at her now, he knew it had been real—very real. She was one of the most beautiful women he'd ever seen, and it seemed she was meant to be in his arms. She fit perfectly against him. It was almost as if they were one as they moved to the music. Julie was delicate and lovely, the picture of innocence and beauty—she was everything Steve had ever dreamed of in a woman, but he knew with painful clarity that she could never be his.

Nothing could ever come of what he was feeling for her, but he decided to enjoy the moment while he could. It would all be over soon enough. She would have the man named Roderick whom she'd sounded so excited about, and he would be gone—or dead. Steve inhaled deeply the sweet scent of her perfume, and for just that moment in time, he allowed himself to believe that his life could be this wonderful.

Boyd was laughing as he made his way down a back alley. He'd deliberately let Marshal Trent see him to draw him away from Tessa Sinclair's side. It was just a matter of time now. Everything had been set in motion. Everything was going to turn out right. He was certain of it. With Tessa unguarded, his plan would work.

* * *

173

Tessa finished dancing with Sludge, only to be claimed by Clint. She'd remembered Jared's promise to protect her, but she could see no sign of him anywhere. Smiling, she danced with the awkward cowboy, never more grateful for her innate sense of timing so she could avoid being trod upon. When the dance ended, she thanked him and left the dance floor to get a cup of punch from the nearby refreshment table. As she passed by, she was greeted by many of the townsfolk. She stopped to speak with them, enjoying the easy camaraderie of the night. It wasn't often that she truly got to have fun, but tonight was proving to be delightful. With so many people around, she gave little thought to Boyd. He couldn't harm her here. She was safe. It felt good after the last few, tense days of worrying, and she finally allowed herself to relax.

Tessa took up a cup and drank thirstily of the cooling punch. It was just what she needed after having danced so many dances. She let her gaze drift around the townsfolk, but saw no sign of Jared anywhere. She hadn't seen him since he'd left her so abruptly. She told herself that it didn't matter if he was there or not, because she didn't care anyway.

Lifting the cup to her lips, Tessa was about to take another sip when she heard someone call her name.

"Miss Tessa!" a small boy cried in a pleading tone.

Tessa looked over to see him standing in an alleyway nearby. She was surprised that a child so young would be up at this time of night, let alone be all by himself. He surely couldn't be older than four or five.

"Yes? What is it?" She hurried to the boy and knelt down to talk to him.

"My name's Rusty—Rusty Lucas! You gotta come with me!" he said, sounding frantic as he grabbed her arm. "It's my ma!"

"What's wrong with your mother, Rusty?" Tessa was instantly worried. Obviously the boy was poor and frightened and in dire need of help.

"She's sick, ma'am, real sick. She told me to come find you. She said you would help her— that you would know what to do." He looked her straight in the eye as he tugged on her arm.

"Let me see if I can find Dr. Murray."

"There ain't no time, Miss Tessa. My ma wanted you. Now. We gotta hurry! Come with me, please," he begged.

"Tessa? Is something wrong?" Julie had been making her way to the refreshment table when she saw her friend talking to the child.

"His mother's very ill, and she sent him to find me. I have to go to her," she told Julie.

"Do you want me to come with you?"

"No, we'll be fine. Just let my mother know where I've gone. Where do you live, Rusty?"

He told her an address that was in an unsavory part of town.

"Tell my mother for me, Julie, will you? I'll be back just as soon as I'm sure his mother is going to be all right."

"I'll go find her right now, so she won't worry," Julie promised. "You be careful."

"I will."

"C'mon, Miss Tessa. My ma needs you!" He hurried off down the alley.

Tessa knew no fear as she followed the little

boy. She was only concerned about the sick woman who sounded so desperately ill. When Rusty crossed the railroad tracks and then started down another alley, Tessa wondered where he was going.

"Rusty? Why are you going this way?" She hesitated at the entrance to the darkened passageway.

"It's a shortcut, Miss Tessa. Ma needs you now! We gotta hurry!"

His desperation seemed so real, his fear for his mother so honest, that she cast aside the uneasiness she was feeling and started down the pathway.

Boyd almost laughed out loud when he saw Tessa coming. He'd known she would come. He'd known she wouldn't be able to resist helping somebody. Well, she was helping somebody, all right. She was helping him.

Boyd smiled as he watched the little boy in action. Rusty Lucas might be only five years old, but he was already one hell of a con man—the kid had earned every penny of the dollar he'd paid him.

Waiting in the shadows, Boyd was ready to take his revenge. Tessa Sinclair was going to pay for all the trouble she'd caused him. He was going to make sure she never, ever interfered in anyone else's marriage again.

As Tessa passed before him, Boyd made his move. He grabbed her from behind and clamped a meaty hand over her mouth before she could even utter a cry of surprise.

"I knew you'd come if I sent a little kid to get

you," Boyd said in her ear as he gave a lascivious laugh.

Tessa went still for an instant, then realized what had happened—she'd been tricked by Boyd! She began to fight, knowing what her fate would be at his hands and refusing to go with him quietly. If she could just break free, she was certain she could run for help and save herself.

Boyd was shocked by her resistance. Sarah had fought him once in a while, but not with nearly as much strength as this one, and after a while Sarah had always cowered before his dominant strength. He had expected the same reaction from Tessa, but she was kicking and twisting, biting and fighting him with all her might. He tightened his grip on her, wanting to stop her struggles against him. They had a ride ahead of them, and he couldn't be fighting with her while they were on the trail.

Tessa was desperate to get free of Boyd's punishing hold. Frantic, she fought him with all her might. She knew what he was capable of, and knew she had to escape him. Her hopes faded, though, as he crushed her back against him, his hands painful upon her. As she continued to struggle, he dropped his hand to her throat, choking her.

"You stupid bitch!" Boyd snarled in her ear as she continued to fight him. "I've a mind to kill you right here, right now!" He tightened his hand even more.

Tessa tried to scream, but he was cutting off her air. She could only gasp. When she finally fainted, she slumped against Boyd, and he deliberately let her drop unconscious to the ground.

"You killed her!" Rusty charged, frightened by what he'd just witnessed.

"Shut up, kid," Boyd snapped. He peered down at Tessa and could still see the slow rise and fall of her chest. "She ain't dead."

"Is she gonna be all right?" Rusty asked as he stared at Tessa's still form.

"Go away."

"You didn't tell me you were going to hurt her!" Rusty looked up at him condemningly.

"I'll hurt you if you don't get the hell out of here!" he said in a snarl.

Rusty's eyes filled with tears. "I'm gonna tell!"

"You say a word, and I'll come after you and hurt you just like I hurt her! You understand me, boy?" Boyd grabbed Rusty by the shirtfront, wanting to scare him. "I paid you for a job, and you did it. I expect you to keep your mouth shut!"

"But—"

"If I hear that you told anybody, I'm going to come looking for you." His threat was real. "You understand me?"

Rusty nodded in mute obedience. When Boyd released him, he ran away into the night, terrified of the evil he'd just witnessed.

Jared was tense and growing angry. His expression was black as he stood apart from the others, watching and waiting. He was looking for some sign of Boyd, but it seemed the man had disappeared into thin air. His instincts were telling him that something wasn't right, but if he couldn't track Boyd down, the only alternative was to stay by Tessa and make sure she got home safely. He might even insist that she let him go through the house tonight and check everything before he left her. Something just wasn't right.

Jared made his way slowly back toward the dance floor. He was alert, looking for trouble, aware that all was not as it seemed. He saw Miss Maggie with Jim and Julie Stevens, and moved toward them.

"So she went to take care of a woman named Lucas?" Maggie was asking Julie, her expression worried.

"The boy was crying and insisting she come with him. He said his ma needed her right away," Julie explained.

"She did what?" Jared asked harshly. "How long ago?"

Both women were taken aback by the sharp anger of his tone.

"Just a few minutes. Why? Do you think something's wrong?"

"Which way did she go?" he demanded. There was no time to discuss anything. He had to find her—and fast.

"Why, it was over here," Julie explained as she led him toward the refreshment area and pointed out the alleyway where the boy had stood.

"And what address did he give her?"

As she was repeating it, Jared had already started down the alley. "Find Deputy Wells. Tell him what happened and tell him to get my horse and follow me there."

"Marshall Trent!" Maggie was suddenly frightened. "You don't think—"

"I'll be back." He ran off down the alley and out of sight.

Maggie looked up at Julie, terror in her eyes. "Tessa's got to be all right. She's got to be!"

Julie slipped an arm about her shoulders in a supportive gesture. "She will be. Tessa's just fine. You know how she is when someone needs her help. That little boy was really scared about his mother being sick, and Tessa could no more have refused to help him than she could have stopped breathing."

Maggie looked a bit relieved at her words. "I hope you're right, dear. I hope you're right."

"Let's go find Deputy Wells, shall we?" Julie offered, wanting to distract her. As she led Maggie away from the alley, though, Julie couldn't looking back and wondering why Marshal Trent had been so concerned.

It took Julie a few minutes to locate the deputy, but she finally found him and told him what had happened.

Nathan immediately left the dance to do as he'd been ordered. He raced back to the office and got both their mounts before heading for the address he'd been given.

Jared's instincts were screaming a warning that all was not what it seemed as he neared the address he'd been given for the sick woman. It proved to be as he'd feared—there was no house at that address and no sign of Tessa. He looked around the dark street, hoping for some clue to her whereabouts, but saw nothing. All was quiet—almost too quiet.

Memories of his father's death haunted him,

but he fought them down. He had to find Tessa. He couldn't let his own fears immobilize him.

It was then that Jared saw a slight, furtive movement farther down the block. He took off at a run in that direction, gun drawn, ready for trouble.

Chapter Thirteen

Jared stopped before the place where he'd seen someone moving and peered into the darkness.

"Come out of there now!" he demanded, and then he waited, nerves on edge, to see who would emerge.

The sound of crying surprised him.

"What the . . . ?"

Jared moved in closer, and bent down to try to see under the porch. It was then that he made out the boy cowering there, trying to hide from him.

"What are you doing hiding under there, boy? I'm Marshal Trent. You come out of there now, unless you want me to crawl in after you!"

The crying stopped, and he heard rustling as the child slowly emerged from his hiding place. He looked up at the tall lawman, his expression fearful.

"What's your name?"

"My name's Rusty—Rusty Lucas, but I didn't mean nothing by it, Marshal Trent. I just needed the money." Rusty sobbed. He'd been hiding ever since Boyd had ridden away with Miss Tessa.

"Needed the money? What money? What are you talking about?" Jared hunkered down in front of the child so he could get a better look at him. He was young. Jared figured he wasn't much older than six. He was dirty, and his face was tearstained.

"That man . . . he made me do it!"

"What man? What did he make you do?"

"He made me tell Miss Tessa a story—that my ma was sick," he sputtered in between his sobs. "I didn't know—"

"You didn't know what?" Jared asked tersely, running desperately short of patience.

"I didn't know he was going to hurt her!" Rusty blurted out miserably.

"Oh, God." His instincts had been right! It *had* been Boyd in the crowd. Jared swore under his breath as he realized that it had all been a trap. Boyd had deliberately revealed himself to lure him away from Tessa's side, just so he could get to her while she was alone. "What did he do with Miss Tessa?"

"He hurt her."

"How?" He went still at this news.

"I don't know," Rusty cried. "He was holding her real tight, and then she fell down, and she was just lying there. He took her away on a horse. He told me if I told anybody about her, he'd come back and hurt me, too! But Miss Tessa is a nice lady. He shouldn't have hurt her."

"Son, I need to know where he went with Miss

Tessa. Did he mention where he was going?" Jared said. He was barely in control. He wanted to leave that instant, but realized the child might have heard something more, something that would help him find her.

"No, but they rode out that way." Rusty pointed in the direction Boyd had gone.

"How long ago?"

"I dunno."

"Ten minutes?"

Rusty nodded.

Jared heard the sound of horses coming. He looked up to see Nathan riding up, leading Jared's horse. He was pleased the deputy had followed his orders. Jared stood up, his posture rigid. His expression was dangerous, his eyes glittering with the power of his fury.

"Did you find her?" Nathan asked.

"Boyd's got her," Jared told him, and he quickly explained all that had happened.

"What do you want to do?"

"You take care of the boy, then get a posse together and come after me. I'm riding out right now," he said as he strode to his horse and swung up into the saddle. "And I'm not coming back until I've found her."

Jared put his heels to his mount's sides and galloped off in the direction Rusty had indicated. He was glad there was a full moon tonight. He was going to need all the help he could get to track them down.

Julie and her parents had gathered supportively around Maggie as they waited to hear what had happened to Tessa. Jim and Will were there, too.

"Do you think we should go back to the house and wait for them there?" Jim suggested.

"No!" Maggie said fiercely. "I'm not going anywhere until I know my Tessa is all right."

More than half an hour had passed before Deputy Wells finally returned.

"Mrs. Sinclair?" Nathan said gently. "I need to speak with you privately."

Maggie pierced him with a feverish, emotional look. "No. Tell me here," she said.

Jim took her hand, and she gripped it tightly. Deputy Wells looked uncomfortable.

"Where's Marshal Trent?" she asked before he could begin.

"He's gone after your daughter, ma'am," Nathan began to explain. "It appears she's been abducted by Boyd Wilson."

"Oh, my God, no!" Maggie turned to Jim, her tears falling freely as her worst fears were realized.

Will stepped forward, furious that this could have happened in the midst of such a crowd of people.

"How did Boyd get her? What are you and your marshal doing about it?" he demanded.

"Marshal Trent's already gone after her. He rode out immediately," Nathan said. "I'm rounding up a posse right now. You want to ride with me?"

"I'll get my horse."

"We'll leave from here in twenty minutes."

Will turned to Maggie. "We'll find her," he said solemnly.

"Please, Will," she said, looking up at him as if he were the most wonderful man in the world.

Will hurried off to get ready. Tessa was going to be his. If he found Boyd Wilson before Marshal Trent did, the man wouldn't live to see the light of day.

"What should I do?" Maggie looked at Nathan. "I just lost my Michael. If anything happens to Tessa I don't think I could go on."

She was sobbing as she clung to Jim, needing his strength and support.

Julie realized someone had to take charge, and she did just that.

"Let's get you back home, Miss Maggie," Julie said in a gentle tone. "We'll wait for Tessa there."

Maggie looked at the younger woman, needing reassurance. "You really think she'll be back? That she'll be all right?"

"I have no doubt whatsoever that Marshal Trent will find her and bring her home safely," Julie said with certainty.

The older woman suddenly looked frail and helpless. "I hope you're right."

Julie stepped forward and took her arm, leading her away from the curious onlookers who were gathering around, wondering what had happened.

"I'm going to stay with Miss Maggie for as long as she needs me," she told her parents as she passed them.

"Do you want us to come with you?" Adele offered, worried about Maggie, too.

"I think we'll be all right."

"If you need anything, just send word," her father told her.

"I will."

Shepherded by Jim, Julie walked Miss Maggie home.

Steve had gone to the High Time after his one and only dance with Julie. He had seen no sign of anyone involved with the gang at the dance, so he'd gone off to try to relax for a while. A few drinks and a few poker hands later, he still wasn't feeling any better about things—and he knew why.

It was Julie.

Steve didn't want to be attracted to her. He didn't want to care about her. He had no business even thinking about her. He was an ex-con gunman, and she was a banker's daughter. Despite his best arguments with himself, though, Steve still found himself drawn to Julie's beauty and innocence.

Even the liquor didn't have the power to erase the memory of how it had felt to hold her close. It was almost with disgust that he folded his losing poker hand, drained the last of his drink, and started back to the boardinghouse. Tonight he hoped to get some sleep, but right now he doubted that was going to happen.

Steve was surprised to see that the house was brightly lit as he walked up the street. He'd thought everyone would still be at the dance, and he wondered who had come home so early.

As Steve let himself in, the sound of crying and hushed conversation greeted him. He was immediately concerned. He went straight to the parlor doorway.

"Miss Maggie?"

He looked in the parlor to see Miss Maggie

seated on the sofa with Jim and Julie hovering over her. They all looked up when he spoke.

"Steve. You surprised us," Jim said.

At the sight of Steve standing in the doorway, a sense of relief filled Julie. He appeared so strong, so solid. Instinctively she started toward him.

"What's wrong?" he asked, frowning as he saw the older woman's obvious distress.

"Let's go outside," Julie said softly, nodding to Jim to take care of Miss Maggie. She stepped out into the hall and Steve followed her lead.

"It's Tessa," she said when they were finally on the porch, out of earshot.

"What happened?" He went still. "Was it Boyd?"

Julie looked up at him, her wide eyes revealing the terror she was fighting so hard to control.

"Yes, it was Boyd. He set the whole thing up. He lured her away from the dance, and I was right there." She gave a small sob as she remembered her friend's determination to help the little boy. "I should never have let her go. I should have made her let me go with her, but she said—"

"How did he do it?" Steve demanded.

She explained what had happened. "Tessa always helps those in need. She never turns down any request for help, and Boyd knew that. Why didn't I realize—"

"It's not your fault, Julie," Steve told her, understanding the guilt she was feeling. "There was no way you could have known that Boyd was behind it. Did the posse ride out yet? I want to go with them."

"They left over an hour ago."

"Damn," he swore softly. He wanted to help

them find Tessa before it was too late. He'd known men like Boyd, and he knew how vicious they could be. "I should be with them."

Julie looked up at him. In the pale moonlight, he appeared fierce and powerful, and she felt a primeval need to be close to him. His nearness, the manly strength of him, somehow comforted her.

"I'm glad you're not," she said softly. It was then that her tears came, and she buried her face in her hands, overcome with worry for her friend.

"Julie." Steve said her name softly, and an ache grew within him.

He wanted to ease her pain, to take her in his arms and hold her to his heart. He wanted to erase the torment he'd seen in her eyes, but he held himself back.

When Steve said her name, Julie's will to be strong shattered. She turned to him, needing the comfort and reassurance his strength could give her.

Steve hadn't meant for this to happen. He'd meant to keep his distance from her. It was safer for both of them that way, but when she turned to him, he was lost. His arms surrounded her in a protective embrace. He wanted to shield her from pain, to ease the anguish he knew was tearing her apart. She felt small and fragile in his arms, and his protective instincts surged to life. He'd never felt this way about a woman before, and the fierceness of his need to keep her safe surprised him.

"Marshal Trent will find her. You'll see," he promised in a low voice.

"He has to. He just has to." She lifted tear-filled eyes to gaze up at Steve.

Their gazes met and locked. For an instant, time stood still. It was only the two of them, alone in the sweet heat of the starlit summer night.

Steve tried to resist his need to kiss her. He tried to put the desire from him, but Julie was too beautiful. He could no more deny himself her kiss than he could stop breathing. He bent to her, capturing her lips in a gentle, cherishing exploration.

Julie's eyes slowly drifted shut as Steve's lips moved over hers. Every fiber of her being was aware of him—of the heat of him, of the iron strength of him. She shifted closer, desperate to be nearer to him, needing to be nearer to him.

At her unspoken invitation, Steve deepened the kiss. Julie responded, lifting her arms to encircle his neck. It was enchantment for them both.

Only the sound of a horse coming down the street tore them apart. They stood in the darkness, panting for breath, staring at each other.

Julie had been spellbound by the feelings that had been surging through her. She'd been kissed by several men, but she'd never experienced anything like Steve's embrace. All she wanted to do was go back into his arms and stay there forever.

"I'm sorry," Steve said, his voice low and gruff. The last thing he'd wanted to do was let her go, but he'd known it wouldn't do for anyone to happen upon them kissing that way. "That shouldn't have happened."

His words were a slap in the face to Julie. She had just been thinking about how wonderful he was, and now he was regretting he'd ever kissed her. Somehow she managed not to betray the hurt she felt at his statement.

"I know," she answered tightly. "You're absolutely right—it shouldn't have happened. I'm sorry, too. We'd better get back inside."

Turning her back on him, Julie went indoors. She kept her head held high. Once she was inside, she paused for a moment in the hallway to gather her wits; then, after taking a deep breath, she returned to sit with Miss Maggie.

Steve remained where he was on the porch, standing alone in the darkness.

Boyd had never been so full of himself as he rode at top speed toward the line cabin where he planned to hide out. His plan had worked! Tessa Sinclair was his!

He glanced back over his shoulder. Tessa was tied across the horse with a blanket over her, so no one would be able to see her if he happened upon anyone on the trail. It hadn't bothered him that she'd passed out. In fact, he was glad that she had. She was less trouble to him this way. He planned to stop and check on her in another hour or so, and if he found that she'd regained consciousness, then he'd let her ride normally. Until then, he was going to keep running. He wanted to put some distance between them and the town.

Once someone noticed she was gone, Boyd knew Marshal Trent would try to find them, but he would never find them where he was going. No one would think to look for them in an old abandoned line shack. It was far enough away from everything and everyone that if the bitch started screaming, it wouldn't matter. There wouldn't be a living soul around to hear her.

The thought of Tessa screaming broadened his smile. He was going to love every minute of teaching her a few things. She was a pretty woman, prettier than Sarah even, so he would easily find his comfort between her thighs. In his mind he saw himself forcefully spreading her legs, and he shifted in the saddle. He spurred his horse to a faster gait, wanting to get to the line shack all that much sooner.

Tessa regained consciousness slowly—and painfully. It took her only an instant to realize how perilous her situation was. Bound hand and foot, she was helpless on the jarring horse. Her throat was sore from Boyd's assault, and she ached all over. She realized she should be glad she was still alive, but the thought was not particularly comforting, considering that her future was in Boyd's hands.

Swearing to be brave and fight him every inch of the way, Tessa prepared herself for the terror to come. It wasn't going to be easy, but she would not give in to his brutality. She offered up a silent prayer that someone had realized she was in trouble and was pursuing Boyd right now.

Thoughts of Jared came to her then, and she remembered how he'd broken down the front door the other night in his misguided attempt to rescue her. With all her heart, she hoped he would find some way to save her before it was too late.

Tessa remembered all the tales of horror that Sarah had told her. She knew just how savage

A Special Offer For Leisure Historical Romance Readers Only!

Get Four FREE* Romance Novels

A $21.96 Value!

Travel to exotic worlds filled with passion
and adventure—without leaving your home!

**Plus, you'll save at least $5.00
every time you buy!**

Thrill to the most sensual, adventure-filled Historical Romances on the market today...

FROM 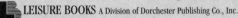 LEISURE BOOKS

As a home subscriber to the Leisure Historical Romance Book Club, you'll enjoy the best in today's BRAND-NEW Historical Romance fiction. For over twenty-five years, Leisure Books has brought you the award-winning, high-quality authors you know and love to read. Each Leisure Historical Romance will sweep you away to a world of high adventure...and intimate romance. Discover for yourself all the passion and excitement millions of readers thrill to each and every month.

SAVE AT LEAST *$5.00* EACH TIME YOU BUY!

Each month, the Leisure Historical Romance Book Club brings you four brand-new titles from Leisure Books, America's foremost publisher of Historical Romances. EACH PACKAGE WILL SAVE YOU AT LEAST $5.00 FROM THE BOOKSTORE PRICE! And you'll never miss a new title with our convenient home delivery service.

Here's how we do it. Each package will carry a 10-DAY EXAMINATION privilege. At the end of that time, if you decide to keep your books, simply pay the low invoice price of $16.96 ($17.75 US in Canada), no shipping or handling charges added*. HOME DELIVERY IS ALWAYS FREE*. With today's top Historical Romance novels selling for $5.99 and higher, our price SAVES YOU AT LEAST $5.00 with each shipment.

AND YOUR FIRST FOUR-BOOK SHIPMENT IS TOTALLY FREE!*

IT'S A BARGAIN YOU CAN'T BEAT! A Super $21.96 Value!

LEISURE BOOKS A Division of Dorchester Publishing Co., Inc.

GET YOUR 4 FREE* BOOKS NOW—
A $21.96 VALUE!

Mail the Free* Book
Certificate
Today!

Get Four Books Totally
F R E E* —
A $21.96 Value!

(Tear Here and Mail Your FREE* Book Card Today!)

PLEASE RUSH
MY FOUR FREE*
BOOKS TO ME
RIGHT AWAY!

Leisure Historical Romance Book Club
P.O. Box 6613
Edison, NJ 08818-6613

AFFIX
STAMP
HERE

Boyd could be. What she was facing would take all of her courage and wits to survive.

Just then the horse stopped.

Tessa began to tremble.

Chapter Fourteen

Boyd dismounted and went back to check on Tessa. He threw the blanket off of her and saw that she was conscious. He smiled, quite satisfied with himself.

"Well, honey, it looks like you're back among the living. How'd you like to sit up and ride normal-like?" he asked with a menacing chuckle.

Tessa nodded, not trusting her voice. She suffered in silence as he untied the ropes that had held her bound on the horse's back and then dragged her off the mount. Boyd knelt down and untied her legs. He ran a hand familiarly up her calf, toying with her, then stood up and loomed threateningly over her.

"I got a lot I want to teach you, woman, but this ain't the time right now. Though, I tell you, I am tempted to take the time." He leered down at her.

Tessa looked up at him without flinching. She was careful to keep her expression blank.

"Why ain't you talking? A cat got your tongue?" She only stared at him in defiant silence.

"Get on the horse. We got some miles to go yet, before I can get my enjoyment outta you."

Tessa turned to her horse. Though her hands were still bound, she managed to mount up astride. It wasn't easy because she was wearing a dress, but she did it.

Boyd came to stand next to her. He lifted her skirt and ran a hand up underneath it, kneading her thigh. He smiled when he felt her tense against his touch.

"Yeah, we got a lot to look forward to tonight. We should be at the line shack in another hour or two, so I want you to start thinking about how you're going to pleasure me. I can almost feel your hands on me. . . ."

She almost gagged as he continued his explicit talk, telling in detail what he wanted her to do. Of all the men in the world she'd ever longed to touch or kiss, Boyd would be dead last on the list. Tessa listened to his rantings, and she wondered how Sarah had managed to stay with him for as long as she had. Her heart went out to the other woman—wherever she was—and more than ever, even in spite of her own dangerous situation, Tessa was glad that she'd helped her to get away.

Boyd left her, then took up her reins and mounted his own horse. He started off again, leading her horse.

Tessa looked back the way they'd come, desperately hoping to see some sign that someone was tracking them, but she saw only the dark emptiness of the night.

They rode on for what seemed like endless miles. Boyd fell silent only a few times during the trek. Mostly he entertained Tessa with stories of what he was going to do to Sarah once he finally got his hands on her. It wasn't pretty.

With every passing mile and threat, Tessa's conviction to fight him tooth and nail hardened. She would not—could not— give in to this man without a fight. Boyd was basically a coward. He only picked on women he could overpower. Sarah hadn't put up much of a fight, but he'd never dealt with Tessa Sinclair before. She was girding herself, preparing for the horrible confrontation she knew was to come.

"Here we are, sweetheart," Boyd called back to Tessa as he turned his horse up a narrow, rocky path. "There ain't nobody ever gonna find us up here, and that's just the way I want it. I want to be all alone with you."

Tessa had no idea where they were as they started up the road. When the trail ended, she could see in the moonlight a small shack that must have been a line cabin.

"Where are we?" she finally asked.

"Don't you worry about that none. There ain't a soul within miles of this place. I made sure of that when I decided to bring you here. I got us supplies in and everything. We ain't going anywhere until I get tired of you." He reined in and dismounted. He dropped the reins to her horse as he walked toward her.

It was then that Tessa made her first daring

move. The moment she realized Boyd was no longer holding her reins, she kneed her horse with all her might and leaned low over its neck to try to grab the reins herself.

"You little bitch!" Boyd roared as the horse half reared and threatened to bolt.

Tessa tried to turn her mount using only her knees. She was desperate to make her escape on horseback, but Boyd moved too quickly for her. He snared her still-dangling reins and brought the horse quickly under control. Angered by her escape attempt, he pulled her from her horse's back.

"I'd hate like hell for anything to happen to you just yet!"

"Don't touch me!" Tessa jerked free of his hold.

Boyd only laughed as he pulled her back against him. He lifted one hand to touch her cheek. "Pretty soon you're going to be begging me to touch you. Just wait."

"I can wait, believe me!" She squirmed against him, hating being this close to him. He reeked of body odor and liquor, and she almost gagged.

Her words made him even angrier. He took her arm in a viselike grip and started toward the cabin.

"If you hadn't helped Sarah, you wouldn't be here right now!" he said in a snarl as he forced her along with him. "Maybe by the time I'm done with you, you'll have learned to mind your own business!"

Tessa dug her heels in and refused to move.

Cursing, Boyd was forced to bodily drag her along with him.

"Come on, honey. We're going to have us some fun!"

"No!" she screamed.

The forlorn sound of her cry echoed through the night.

Tessa knew that once he got her inside the cabin, any chance of escape would be gone. She continued to try to tear herself away from him, but he only laughed at her struggles.

"I do love feisty women. Sarah wasn't like you. She'd fight me a little bit, but then she'd just lie there and let me hit her. You're going to be much more fun," he said, his breath hot on her neck as he leaned toward her.

Boyd opened the door and shoved her inside the shack ahead of him. He quickly lit a lamp and stood back to look at her as she stood before him.

"You know, missy, you and me—we could have fun tonight. What do you say? This can be easy or this can be a fight. Either way I'm going to have you, so you might as well lie down on that bed and spread your legs. I've waited about as long as I can. I've been thinking about this and planning this, and I'm ready for you now."

Boyd advanced on her.

Tessa backed away. She nervously let her gaze dart about the small one-room cabin, searching for an escape route or some kind of weapon she could use to defend herself. Her hands were still bound, but she knew that if she could get hold of a revolver or a knife she might be able to stop him. The shack was sparsely furnished, though, with only the cot and a table and chairs. There was nothing she could use to save herself.

"Stay away from me, Boyd Wilson. Marshal Trent is coming after us, and it won't be pretty once he catches up with you."

Boyd only laughed again. "Trent doesn't even know you're gone yet. I sent him on a wild-goose chase while I was trapping you. It'll be dawn before he can even get out of town with a posse, and by then I'll have had my fill of you."

His statement terrified her. She remembered how Jared had left her side so quickly at the dance, and she feared that what Boyd was saying was true. Jared hadn't even been there when she'd been kidnapped; it was possible no one would even notice she was missing until morning.

"You're wrong!" she argued. "Jared knows all about you! He'll come after me!"

"Oh, it's 'Jared,' is it?" he said in a sneer, closing in on her. "You know him real good, do you?"

"Yes, and when he gets here, he's going to—"

"Give up your dreaming, bitch. There ain't nobody who knows where we are. It's just you and me, alone in this here line shack. I planned it this way, so we wouldn't be interrupted."

He advanced on her threateningly, his eyes aglow with his lecherous intent.

"Stay away from me, Boyd Wilson! Don't you even think about touching me!"

"Oh, I'm more than thinking about it. I'm looking forward to it!" He came even nearer.

Tessa made her move. In a last, frantic, desperate attempt to flee, she shoved a chair at him and made a run for the door. She managed to throw the door wide, but she never made it outside. Boyd caught up with her and grabbed her from behind. He slammed her back against his chest.

Tessa cried out in true horror and pain. Her worst nightmare was coming true. She twisted in his arms, trying to break free. She couldn't get away, but in a stroke of pure luck, her struggles allowed her to grab his sidearm.

Boyd realized instantly what she'd done, and he snared her wrist, trying to strip the gun from her hand. He was shocked by the strength and fury of her fight. Sarah had never resisted him this much. It only made him madder and even more determined to force her to obey him and to submit to him.

They continued the savage battle over the gun. He finally managed to force Tessa's hand up so the revolver was pointed away from them both.

The sound of a gunshot exploded the stillness.

Jared was growing frustrated. He had stayed on Boyd's trail for hours now, but the going had been slow, even with the brightness of the nearly full moon. Its muted light had helped him with the tracking, but he still felt he wasn't gaining on them fast enough. He feared he wouldn't catch up with them in time to save Tessa from whatever torture Boyd had planned for her.

Reining his mount in, Jared sat in silence and studied the rocky landscape around him. They had to be somewhere close—but where? He dismounted to check the tracks. They had passed this way. He climbed back in the saddle and urged his horse on at a slow, measured gait.

Jared hoped Boyd didn't realize that he was this close on his trail. If the man felt overconfident, he might make a mistake.

It was then, in the silence of the night, that the sound of Tessa's cry came to Jared.

"No!"

The desperate sound pierced him to the very

depths of his soul. He tensed, waiting, listening, hoping for another clue to her whereabouts. Her cry had been distant, but had not seemed too far off. When all remained quiet, he kneed his mount forward again.

Jared knew Boyd had worked for the Rocking K Ranch for a while and that this was Rocking K land. There had to be a good reason he'd come this way, and Jared was convinced that the man believed he had a safe hideout somewhere close by. He planned on proving him wrong very shortly.

Jared hadn't ridden too much farther when the sound of a gunshot rent the night. The explosion sent a chill through his very soul. Drawing his sidearm, he urged his horse to a gallop. There had been no mistaking the direction the shot had come from, and he feared for Tessa's life.

The low glow of the lamplight from the run-down line shack's window was a beacon. Jared knew he'd finally found them. Reining in a short distance away, he dismounted and, staying low, cautiously approached the cabin. He could see no movement inside the shack and feared he was too late.

Silently Jared offered up a prayer that the gunshot hadn't harmed Tessa. Jared was reliving his worst nightmare as he moved ever nearer the cabin. He knew that if anything had happened to her he would never be able to forgive himself. He had watched his father die. He would not let it happen to Tessa.

Jared knew Tessa was everything that was good about people. She was generous and kind and loving, not to mention beautiful and intelligent.

She didn't deserve the savagery Boyd was trying to wreak upon her. He had to save her—now.

Reaching the side of the shack, Jared pressed himself close against it. He slowly rose to take a look in the window.

Tessa struggled against Boyd's overwhelming strength as he dragged her across the cabin toward the bed.

"Get your hands off me, Boyd!"

"Hell, no, woman. I want my hands all over you!" he told her, laughing at her efforts to free herself.

He was able to control her, but he had to admit that she was a feisty female. Sarah had been easy to dominate. This one was going to be harder, but he knew that ultimately having her would be worth the fight. Just feeling her struggling against him as he forced her toward the bed was arousing him. He was on fire with wanting her, and it wouldn't be long now.

"I'd rather die than let you touch me!" she swore.

"Don't tempt me, sweetheart!" he said hotly in her ear as he pawed at her.

The heat of his breath on her neck made Tessa's flesh crawl, and she could just imagine how horrible it was going to be to be forced to submit to him. Determined to save herself, she fought him even harder, twisting and turning with all her might.

To her misery, Boyd only laughed at her efforts. He lifted her and bodily threw her upon the bed. Tessa tried to get back up and get away, but he grabbed her by the bodice of her gown and shoved her back down. The material ripped in his hand, and he grinned evilly as her lacy chemise was revealed to him.

Boyd went still. Drool was gathering in the corner of his mouth as he stared down at her. She was his. Nothing was going to stop him from having her now—nothing.

Flaming heat settled low in his loins. This was the time. Boyd laid the revolver on the floor next to the bed and fell heavily upon Tessa, ready for her.

Tessa kicked at Boyd and tried to push him off her, but he was too heavy. He tried to kiss her, but she turned her head to avoid him.

Boyd gripped her chin and forced her to look at him. He could see the fear in her eyes, and he liked it. He felt a rush of power.

"You know what's gonna happen next?" he asked as he leaned down to cover her mouth with his.

"No!" Tessa's cry was smothered by his sloppy attack. She almost gagged as he thrust his tongue crudely into her mouth. She tried to tear herself free of him, but succeeded only in exciting him more with her movements.

"Yeah, darling. That's how I like it. You move for me now." He was growling as he pressed wet, disgusting kisses down her throat toward her breasts.

"Stop it! You're an animal! Get off of me!"

"I ain't getting off of you until I'm through!"

He pushed her skirts up and was reaching down to open his pants. He was not about to be deterred.

Tessa was experiencing true, helpless terror for the very first time in her life. In her heart, she'd been holding fast to the hope that Jared would rescue her. She'd believed that this couldn't really be happening to her—that Jared would somehow find a way to get there in time, but now she realized that there would be no escaping Boyd. She was his prisoner, and helpless before his brute strength. She closed her eyes to the sight of him exposing himself, and she emotionally girded herself for the torment to come. There would be no escape now. There would be no—

In that instant the door of the cabin seemed to explode inward.

The resounding crash startled Boyd. He froze and looked back over his shoulder to see the lawman coming through the door, his gun in hand. The sight of Jared charging into the cabin spurred him to action. Boyd threw himself off the bed and made a grab for the revolver where he'd left it on the floor.

Chapter Fifteen

Everything seemed to happen in an instant. Boyd took aim at Jared. Tessa saw what he was about to do, and she kicked out at him just in time. Her blow jarred him enough that his shot went wide, missing Jared. Boyd leaped to his feet in a roar of frustration.

Boyd's move gave Jared just the target he needed for he'd feared shooting wildly with Tessa in the room. He turned and fired, his aim true and deadly. The bullet took Boyd square in the chest, and the force of the shot sent him crashing back against the wall. He collapsed and lay unmoving, dead before he hit the floor.

Jared glanced toward the bed. From where he was standing, he could see only Tessa's legs, but it seemed she wasn't moving.

"Tessa?" Jared said her name cautiously, fearing she'd been injured in some way.

"Oh, Jared!" Tessa's voice was barely a whisper as she ran straight to him.

Jared opened his arms to her and enfolded her in his protective embrace.

"Thank God I got here in time," he said hoarsely as he held her close.

"I was praying you'd come."

"You're all right? You're not hurt?" he asked, holding her away from him a bit so he could look down at her and make sure she really hadn't been harmed in any way.

"I knew you'd save me," Tessa told him in a soft voice as she gazed up at him. Jared looked so fiercely protective that she almost smiled at him. She knew she was safe now.

At her words, wild, chaotic emotions charged through Jared.

I knew you'd save me.

He struggled to control himself, swallowing tightly against the powerful feelings that filled him. He lifted one hand to gently touch her cheek. "I told you I would always keep you safe. Sometimes angels need protecting, too."

The look in her eyes was so open and inviting that Jared couldn't help himself. He bent to her and kissed her. It was a cherishing kiss, an adoring kiss, a fragile expression of the wild emotions they were both feeling. Jared wanted to lose himself in her embrace, but he was still too aware of what had just happened to her. Without ending the kiss, he bent to lift her into his arms and carried her away from the scene of the attack.

At his gesture, Tessa looped her arms about his neck. She held on to him, relishing his power and control. When at last his lips left hers, she rested her head trustingly on his shoulder.

Jared found a small clearing near the front of the cabin, and he sat down there. He kept Tessa on his lap, cradling her against him, and offered up a silent prayer of thanks that he had reached her in time—that she was safe. They remained that way for a time, sitting in silence, wrapped in each other's arms, slowly coming to grips with the reality of her rescue and the joy of her safety.

"You really are all right?" Jared asked some time later as he drew a ragged breath.

She nodded. "You got here just in time," she said quietly. "How did you know where to find me?"

"When I heard that you'd gone with the little boy at the dance, I suspected all wasn't what it seemed—especially since I'd seen Boyd just a short time before."

"You did?" She was surprised by this revelation.

"That was why I left you after our dance. I caught a glimpse of him in the crowd and wanted to keep an eye on him to make sure he didn't get near you. He got away from me, though. When I realized I'd lost him, I came back to keep watch over you, and that was when I heard Julie telling your mother where you'd gone. I found the boy and he told me what had happened, so I was able to get on your trail right away."

Tessa lifted her head to look up at him. "Thank you," she whispered, drawing him down to her for another kiss.

Jared bit back a groan at the touch of her lips

on his. Tessa was proving to be his agony and his ecstasy.

This was Tessa Sinclair. He told himself it was crazy to feel this way about her. This was the woman who was constantly causing him so much trouble. But all the logic in the world was lost in the ecstasy of her kiss.

This was Tessa, all right. This was the woman who wanted only to help other people. This was the woman who cared more about strangers than she did about herself. This was "the angel," as they called her affectionately in town.

And she was an angel to him.

Her kiss was heavenly, and just having her here in his arms and knowing that she was safe filled him with a sense of joy he couldn't explain. Jared wouldn't have thought it possible to feel this way about her a few weeks before, but now, everything about holding Tessa close and kissing her seemed right.

Jared tried to keep the kiss innocent, but when Tessa shifted on his lap, moving closer to him, he lost the battle. He tightened his arms around her and deepened the kiss, parting her lips and seeking out her sweetness.

Tessa was momentarily surprised by Jared's unexpected show of ardor. But after Boyd's disgusting pawing and slobbering, Jared's kiss was perfect. He had saved her from a fate worse than death. He had rescued her from certain abasement and rape. She gloried in his honor and in his strength.

Jared finally ended the embrace to save his own sanity. With Tessa pressed so intimately against him, he could not deny that he wanted her, but as much as he would have loved to continue kissing her, he knew what was best. Tessa had just been through hell. She was vulnerable and in no condition to make love to him. He held her near, waiting for his own breathing to calm, but it didn't happen. Just having her this close to him aroused him. Jared knew that he had to get up and move away from her for a few moments.

"I'd better take a look around and check on things. Do you want to spend the night in the cabin or—" He didn't get any farther.

"No!" she answered quickly, shuddering visibly at the thought. She never wanted to go inside that line shack again as long as she lived.

"All right, then I'm going build a fire and see what we can use to camp out for the night."

She nodded, but was reluctant to let him go. Right now she felt safe only when he was holding her; still, she knew Jared was right. He did need to build a campfire. Reluctantly she moved off his lap.

Jared wanted to pull her back, to hold her to him and never let her go, but he had a duty to perform. Unable to resist, he pressed one last, quick kiss to her lips, then got up and started the fire.

"There's a posse coming after us, but I don't know how far behind me they are," he told her as he returned to her side carrying his bedroll. He'd tended to his horse and had checked around the area to make sure everything seemed safe. As he stood over her, he began to unbutton his shirt.

"What are you doing?" she asked a bit nervously as he stripped the shirt off and stood naked to the waist. She stared up at him, realizing suddenly that he was a beautiful specimen of manhood. He was long and lean. His shoulders were broad, his chest wide and powerful. He was bronzed from the sun, and she knew a sudden desire to run her hands over that hard-muscled strength.

"You need something to cover yourself with. The posse could ride in at any time."

Tessa had been so caught up in all that had happened that she hadn't even thought about her torn bodice. She glanced down, seeing how much of her bosom was revealed by the torn dress.

"Thank you," she said softly, blushing slightly as she took the proffered garment and quickly put it on.

The shirt was still warm from his body and held a hint of Jared's scent. Tessa breathed deeply of it, feeling safe and protected.

Jared spread out the bedroll for her to sit on, then glanced toward the shack.

"I need to go see about Boyd. Will you be all right out here alone for a few minutes?" he asked, still worrying about her.

"I'll be fine. You're here with me, so I know nothing bad is going to happen."

Her words touched him deeply. He left her without saying anything more and went into the line shack. It was a gruesome job, but he had to tend to it. He wrapped Boyd's body in one of the blankets from the bed and then put out the single lamp that was still burning. He closed the damaged door as best he could as he left the cabin. He didn't want Tessa to accidentally get a glimpse of the body where it lay on the floor. She'd been through enough for one night. She didn't need to see that.

Jared brought the extra blanket from the bed with him when he returned to her side. He sat down beside Tessa as she huddled before the fire. He could see that she was trembling now, and he realized that reaction was finally setting in. He did not attempt to touch her, not wanting to frighten her in any way.

"Here, you'll need this tonight," he said as he handed her the blanket.

"What about you? I even have your shirt."

"I'll be all right," he said.

"Thanks."

She took the cover and wrapped it around herself. They sat quietly together awhile longer.

"You were right, you know," Tessa finally admitted in a low voice.

"About what?" he asked.

"I should have been more careful. I shouldn't have taken such a risk with Sarah, but she was frantic and needed help so badly," she explained. "I knew Boyd was a miserable excuse for a man, but I understand even more clearly now why she was so desperate to get away from him."

"You're too kind for your own good."

She shrugged slightly. "I care. I like making things better for people, but now I know that sometimes trying to make things better can end up getting you hurt."

"You're right. I've seen what putting yourself in danger that way can do."

Tessa heard the bitterness in his voice and wondered at it. "What happened to you to make you feel this way?"

"Nothing happened to me," he replied brusquely.

She looked over at him, seeing his taut expression and realizing that there was something bothering him deep inside.

"Who, then?" she asked perceptively.

Jared hadn't spoken of his father's death in years. Despite all the time that had passed, it was still painful for him to remember that night.

"You can't talk about it?"

A muscle worked in his jaw as he glanced at her. He held himself rigidly, and, for the first time in a long time, he spoke of his father and all that had happened that fateful, terrible night.

"My father was a minister," he began, and continued telling her of his father's efforts with the poor and hungry and homeless. "And then there was that night. . . . I was with him, helping him take food to an old widow woman." Jared paused and drew a harsh breath. "It was late when we finally started home, and my father saw a man being attacked. He went to help him, but by the time my father reached him, the attacker had already fled. The beaten man was so drunk he pulled his gun and shot my father."

Tessa gasped at this revelation.

"And you saw it all," she said slowly, solemnly.

"I saw it all," he confirmed, his emotions under tight control. "That was when I vowed I was going to grow up to be the best damned lawman around."

With his revelation came understanding for

Tessa. Tessa thought of their first encounter after the stage robbery and how harsh he had been with her. She remembered, too, how he'd spoken to her after hearing about Boyd's threats. She stared at Jared, seeing him in a whole new light. In his compellingly handsome features, she no longer saw arrogance and anger. Now she could see the hidden torment he carried with him every minute of every day. Reaching out with a gentle hand, she touched his arm.

"You are the best damned lawman around," she told him softly. "You saved me."

He looked at her then, and her words touched his heart. In the moonlight she was beautiful, and she was looking at him with such yearning that he knew he had to kiss her again, to seek solace in her embrace. He leaned toward her, seeking and finding her lips in a sweet, soft kiss that spoke of pain and need and emptiness.

Tessa turned into Jared's arms and held him close. She wanted to somehow erase the pain that had scarred him so, but she knew it couldn't be. He had learned to live with his father's tragic death as best he could, and he had turned his terrible loss into a way of living that had helped others as much in his own way as his father had in his. Jared Trent was a very special man.

When Jared finally broke off the kiss, he smiled gently down at her. "I think you'd better try to get some rest now. I'll be right here in case you need me."

She nodded mutely, then asked, "What happened to the man who shot your father?"

"The sheriff caught him. I identified him and he went to prison."

"Good. I'm glad."

"So was I, but it didn't bring my father back."

They sat quietly, reflectively, for a long moment.

"Will you hold me tonight?" Tessa asked in all innocence, just wanting to be close to him again.

Jared bit back a groan at her request. He knew it would be a true test of his honor. "All right."

She gave him a tentative smile and lay down. Jared stretched out next to her. Even with the slight padding of the bedroll, the ground was hard and unforgiving.

When Tessa shifted nearer to Jared, pressing herself slightly against him, seeking the comfort of his strength, all thoughts of the hardness of the makeshift bed were forgotten. He lay still, cherishing her closeness. He wanted her, there was no doubt about that, but he knew he wouldn't act upon his desire for her—not after the terrible ordeal she'd been through at Boyd's hands. He would prove to her that not all men were animals.

And so Jared lay sleepless on the hard ground, with Tessa curled up trustingly against him.

Chapter Sixteen

Boyd's hands were harsh upon her, tearing at her clothes. She was twisting and turning, trying to get away, desperate to escape him. He rose up over her and laughed at her pitiful efforts.

"You're gonna be mine, bitch!"

"No!" Tessa let out a cry.

At her cry, Jared rose up, reaching for his gun. He had not really been asleep—holding her in his arms had made that impossible for him. When she had drifted off, she'd moved slightly away from him. He had started to relax then as the long, dark hours of the night slowly passed. When Tessa had begun to move restlessly in her sleep, though, he'd sensed that her rest was troubled.

"Tessa?" He was instantly alert, ready for trouble. His gaze swept over the area, looking for some sign of danger, but there was nothing. It was quiet. He glanced at her and saw that she was trembling and crying.

"Oh, Jared." She breathed his name in obvious relief as she became more fully aware of her surroundings. "I'm sorry. It was terrible. It was Boyd, and . . . Hold me. Just hold me."

The last request was so desperate that he immediately holstered his gun and took her in his arms. He cradled her gently and could feel her trembling slowly subside and her breathing calm as he held her. He started to let her go, but she clung to him.

"No—please, hold me tighter. Don't let me go," she whispered, trying to banish the last remnants of her nightmare of Boyd.

Jared bit back a groan as she pressed herself more tightly to his chest. He did as she'd asked, enfolding her in his embrace, but he paid the price for it. His body ached at her nearness. There was no ignoring the sweetness of her curves. He was tremendously grateful when she stopped moving and just rested against him.

"Are you going to be all right?" he finally asked, and he was thankful, too, that his voice didn't give away any of the sensual torture he was enduring.

Tessa nodded, but didn't speak. She prided herself on being strong, but that last vision of Boyd coming at her had been so real, it had unnerved her.

"Let's lie down again," Jared suggested. He thought if they did, she might move a little away from him and give him some peace.

"All right," Tessa answered.

Jared let her go, and she did lie down. When he

stretched back out, rolling on his side to watch over her, she shifted closer to him, pressing her back against his chest, getting as near to him as she could. He knew without her saying so what she needed, and he put his arm around her.

It wasn't easy for Jared to remain still and just hold her, but he did it. He wondered sleeplessly if there was any kind of reward in heaven for this kind of self-control. He knew that if she tried to move any closer to him, all might be lost. So he silently prayed that she would fall asleep—and soon.

Morning couldn't come quickly enough for him.

Next to Jared, Nathan was one of the best trackers around, and he was furious because he knew they had to give it up for the night. The sky had become cloudy, blocking the moonlight and making the trail too difficult to follow over the rocky terrain.

"We'll bed down here until sunup," he ordered in disgust.

"What do you mean?" Will demanded as he rode to his side.

"I mean the trail's too difficult here. We have to wait for daylight."

"No. We've got to keep going. Wilson's got Tessa. We can't leave her at that man's mercy."

"I know you're personally involved, what with Miss Tessa being your boss and all, but we're stopping here for the rest of the night." Nathan was annoyed enough at the situation without Will giving him any trouble. "I don't like it any better than you do."

217

"Then let's keep trying," Will insisted.

"You can't track 'em if you can't find the trail."

"Deputy Wells is right, Kenner. We're going to have to stop till dawn," Deputy Tom Colvin told him.

Will barely managed to control his temper as he glared at the other members of the posse, who had already started to dismount. He wheeled his horse around and rode a short distance away. He was too angry to want to have anything to do with them. He was angry with Tessa, too, for putting herself in this situation. She'd known Boyd was looking for her. She'd known he was threatening to hurt her, and yet she'd allowed herself to be drawn away from the dance by a little boy claiming to have a sick mother. Once he had her back, he was going to make sure she never did anything so ridiculous again. Once she was his wife, she would curtail her "helpful" activities. He was going to see to it. First, though, they had to find her.

He did not sleep, but lay a distance from the other men, mulling over exactly what he was going to do to Boyd when he got his hands on him.

Dawn was long in coming for Jared. There were moments when Tessa stirred against him in her sleep that he thought it would never come. The night had been torturous for him, and he was greatly relieved at first light.

Ready to wake Tessa so they could be on their way, he gazed down at her. She looked so lovely in the pale light of the morning that he could only stare at her for a moment, memorizing the beauty of her features as she nestled quietly, trustingly against him.

"Tessa." He said her name gently, not wanting to startle her.

"Ummm," was her reply, but she did not awaken.

She stirred slightly, but remained asleep, torturing Jared even more.

Jared had thought he had his wayward desires under control, but just that simple motion aroused him. He knew he had to get away from her. "Tessa, it's sun up. We need to get back to town. Everyone is worrying about you." He spoke a little more loudly than he'd meant to, but he had to wake her so he could escape her tempting nearness.

"It's morning already?" Tessa asked sleepily as she opened her eyes. She started to stretch and found herself moving against the hard, muscular width of his chest. The discovery was both startling and comforting. She went still for a moment as she looked up at him. "Thank you," she told him.

He nodded, but didn't say anything. Carefully, he put her from him and got up, moving quickly away.

Tessa was an innocent, and so she had no idea of her effect on Jared. She only thought he was in a hurry to return to town. She got up and tried to straighten her clothing. When she realized the futility of her efforts, she merely buttoned Jared's shirt. It covered the torn bodice and gave her a modicum of modesty.

"I'll check in the house and see if Boyd had any supplies up here," Jared called to her. He was deliberately keeping distance between them.

It was the first time Tessa had thought about food. She had to admit she was a bit hungry. She stoked the campfire while she waited for Jared to return. She had no desire whatsoever to go back into that cabin. It was going to be difficult enough for her, taking Boyd's body with them on the ride back to town, but she knew it had to be done.

Jared emerged from the cabin a few minutes later with a small wrapped bundle. "Cheese and bread were all I could find."

"It sounds like the best of breakfasts to me right now," she told him.

He spread the wrapping out on the ground and pulled out his knife to cut thick slices of cheese. They each tore off hunks of the bread and ate quickly without much discussion. When they'd finished, Jared spoke up first.

"It'll take me a few minutes to take care of Boyd. Once that's done, I'll be ready to head out."

"Do you think the posse's close?"

"Knowing Nathan, I'm sure of it. I was actually surprised he didn't catch up with us last night." He stood up and walked back to the cabin.

Tessa deliberately moved away, keeping her back to the cabin, not wanting to witness Jared's gruesome task. It was almost half an hour later when they rode away. Tessa could not bring herself to look back.

"There they are!" Nathan shouted to his men as he spurred his horse to a run to meet Jared and

Tessa. He saw the body tied to the horse, and immediately knew what had happened.

Jared raised an arm in greeting as he saw his deputy. They had been on the trail for less than an hour, and he was pleased to see the posse.

"You're all right?" Nathan asked Tessa as he reined in before them.

"I'm fine, thanks to Jared," Tessa told him. "He rescued me just in time."

"Tessa!" Will came charging up and stopped his horse close beside hers. His gaze went over her, searching for some sign that she'd been harmed. He noticed that she was wearing the marshal's shirt and that bothered him, knowing that her gown must have been damaged in some way.

"Will? You rode with the posse, too?"

"I had to come after you. I was so worried! Thank God, you're all right."

"I was just telling Deputy Wells that Jared saved me from Boyd. It was terrible."

"Thank you, Marshal Trent," Will said, looking up at the other man and hiding his resentment that he had been the one to save her.

Jared just nodded in his direction.

"And Boyd's dead?" Will saw the body tied to the horse.

"Yeah, he's dead," Jared answered.

"Good," Will said, pleased with the news.

"Jared—here," Tom called out to him, tossing him the jacket he'd had tied to the back of his saddle.

"Thanks." Jared was glad to have the garment. He shrugged into it as he looked at Nathan. "We'd better head back. I'm sure Miss Maggie is waiting for us."

"How is my mother?" Tessa looked at Will, knowing how upset her mother must be by all that had happened.

"She was worried and afraid, but I promised her we'd find you before I left," he said confidently.

"Let's hurry," Tessa said, glancing at Jared.

They rode on toward Durango. Will positioned himself near Tessa for the trek. When they stopped by a small stream to rest and water the horses an hour later, he dismounted quickly and hurried to help her down.

"Why, thank you, Will, but I'm fine, really." She tried to discourage him from hovering so close.

"I was worried about you, Tessa," he told her as he walked with her to the water's edge. He angled their path so they were a distance away from the others, and when they stopped by the stream, he boldly took her hand.

Tessa was completely taken by surprise at his move. She looked up at him, a bit troubled by his daring.

"Tessa, I just wanted you to know that I care about you—deeply. When I thought something had happened to you . . ."

"Everything is all right now." She tried to sound compassionate without being too cool, but she just didn't share his feelings—no matter what her mother had hoped for between them.

"I know, but I don't ever want anything to happen to you again. I want to be able to protect you and keep you safe. I—"

"Will, thank you, but I—"

"Tessa, are you rested enough to ride some

more?" Jared had already mounted up, and he rode over to where they were standing. He'd noticed something in the way she was holding herself with Will that bothered him. Then, when the man had taken her hand, she'd definitely stiffened. Jared wasn't certain she wanted him to interrupt, but he was taking a chance that his instincts were correct. Besides, he didn't really like seeing Will's hands on her.

She was glad of his interruption. "Yes, Jared. We need to get back—the sooner, the better. I can't wait to see my mother."

"I'm sure the feeling is mutual," he answered.

Tessa drew her hand away from Will's and started back toward her mount. Jared dismounted and walked beside her, leaving Will to follow. When they reached her horse, he helped her to mount. It wasn't easy to do, wearing a skirt as she was, but with Jared lifting her, she made it, just as she had earlier that morning when they'd left the line shack. He helped her arrange her skirts and then mounted his own horse again. He led the way toward town, and Tessa followed close behind him, giving Will no chance to dominate her again.

Will had remained back by the water's edge, glowering after them as they'd walked away. He didn't like the lawman at all, and he wasn't too pleased with Tessa either. How dared she just walk away from him after he'd been telling her how much he cared about her!

Mentally, he sneered at Jared. He might have saved Tessa from Boyd last night, but that had been only because Boyd had been so stupid.

Jared still had no idea that the leader of the gang that had been robbing the stagecoaches was riding as a member of his posse.

The thought almost brought a smile to Will's face, but he fought it down. He would gloat later, once they'd made off with the biggest prize of all. During the course of the dance, before all the trouble had started, he had spoken at length with Lyle Stevens and some of his business friends. It had become clear to Will during the course of the conversation that a big gold shipment would be passing through town very soon. If it was half the size he thought it was going to be, he and the boys could retire forever, and he was finding that prospect more and more pleasing. Once they got back to town and he was certain Tessa was safe with her mother, Will was going to ride for the Ace High. He and the boys had some planning to do.

Julie had seen Maggie to bed long after midnight. Steve and Jim had remained with her a little longer until she'd decided to seek what comfort she could on the parlor sofa. She hadn't thought she would fall asleep, but somehow she'd finally drifted off in the wee hours of the morning. She awoke at dawn, tormented by the knowledge that Tessa had still not returned.

Rising from the sofa, Julie went to the parlor window and brushed aside the curtain to watch the sunrise. The morning sky was cloudless. It promised to be a beautiful day, but Julie could see no beauty in it without word of Tessa's safety. She prayed Marshal Trent had found her in time. She knew just how vicious a man Boyd Wilson was.

The thought of Boyd sent a shiver of disgust through her, and she turned away from the window to find Steve standing in the parlor doorway, watching her. He looked so tall and powerful—his shoulders seemed to fill the entire doorway. He hadn't shaved yet, and the hint of a day's growth of beard gave him a more dangerous look. She shivered again, but not from thoughts of Boyd.

"Oh, good morning," she said a bit nervously. After the way they'd parted last night on the porch, she hadn't been sure he would even speak to her again. He had eventually followed her back inside, but when Miss Maggie had gone to bed, he had retired to his own room.

"There's been no word of Tessa yet?" he asked, trying not to notice how pretty she looked this morning. There was a slight flush to her cheeks, and her hair had come loose and tumbled about her shoulders in golden splendor.

"No," she answered, "nothing."

He nodded and left.

She stared at the empty doorway, not the least bit surprised that he hadn't wanted anything to do with her this morning. He'd made that clear enough last night after he'd kissed her. She regretted now that she'd been so weak around him. She would make sure it never happened again.

Unconsciously, Julie straightened her spine at the memory of Steve's rejection. That didn't matter. What mattered was Tessa's safety, and she hoped against hope that Jared Trent proved to be the fine lawman everyone believed him to be. He had to save her! He just had to.

Julie knew she couldn't go back to sleep, so she

went into the kitchen to see about making breakfast. She doubted Miss Maggie would want anything, but she was certain her boarders would still want their morning meal. Julie didn't pride herself on being much of a cook, but she would do her best. At least the cooking would keep her busy. She couldn't bear the thought of sitting idly by and waiting for word of Tessa's safety.

"Why, Julie, dear, I had no idea you were such a good cook," Maggie told her an hour later as she joined Julie and the others for breakfast.

"I didn't know you were going to get up," she said, surprised by the older woman's appearance in the dining room.

Maggie's expression was haunted and tired. "I only slept a little while all night. I guess I should have come down earlier to help you."

"I did just fine, didn't I?" she asked the men gathered around the table eating the scrambled eggs and fried ham slices she'd made for them.

"Yes, ma'am," Sludge answered as he dug eagerly into the hot fare. "And you look real pretty, too." When he realized what he'd said, he blushed and, looking down, quickly stuffed his mouth full of eggs so he wouldn't say anything more.

"Why, thank you, Sludge." Julie laughed, looking down at the gown she was still wearing and the apron she'd donned over it. "It is rather a different kind of outfit for a cook, isn't it?"

Maggie took a seat at the table and joined the meal. She ate sparingly. She was not hungry, but she knew she would need something to help her get through the day.

"Where's Steve this morning?" Maggie asked.

"He came down earlier and left, but he didn't say where he was going," Julie told her.

"I've just been down to the marshal's office," Steve announced as he came into the dining room.

No one had heard him return, and they were surprised by his appearance.

"Did you learn anything?" Maggie asked quickly, hopefully.

"No. There's been no word since they rode out last night."

"I see." Maggie nodded. She'd expected as much, but she'd hoped that somehow, some way, Jared had found Tessa quickly and had brought her back.

"Come and eat," Jim invited Steve, motioning to an empty chair. "We got us a new cook this morning."

"I'm no Miss Maggie, but at least nobody will be going hungry today," Julie said.

Steve didn't look at Julie but slid into the chair and helped himself to the eggs.

Julie sat down, too, taking a small portion for herself, though she honestly didn't feel much like eating. She kept watch over the table, making sure everyone had what he needed. She also found herself surreptitiously watching Steve as he ate. She expected him to be rough, and she was surprised when he was as mannerly as her own father.

After Henry and Sludge had left to go to work, Jim helped Julie clear the table.

"Miss Tessa wanted me to fix the back porch steps," Steve said. "So I'll start on them today."

227

"Thank you, Steve. She'll be glad you're working on them," Maggie told him. She was too weary to do anything else, so she remained at the table to sit and wait.

The day passed slowly. Each minute seemed an hour; each hour seemed endless. Both Jim and Steve made additional trips to the marshal's office to see if there was any news, but each time they returned with nothing to report.

Julie's parents came by for a visit and brought Julie a change of clothes. She'd already told them that she would be staying on with Maggie until word came.

At noon, Julie went out back to call Steve in to eat, and she found herself hard-pressed not to stare at him. He'd shed his shirt to do the manual labor, and she had never seen a man so unclothed before. His arms were thickly corded with muscle, and his chest was broad and tanned and lightly furred. She swallowed tightly against the strange feelings that filled her and hurried back inside after telling him the meal was ready. Julie found she was almost disappointed when he appeared in the dining room fully clothed. Her imagination gave her no rest, and she was glad when they finished eating and he went back outside to resume work.

It was midafternoon when Maggie heard the sound of horses coming up the street. She'd been sitting on the sofa and rose quickly to look out the window. Her expression was one of pure joy as she turned back to Julie and Jim.

"It's Tessa!" she cried as she started at a run for the front door.

Chapter Seventeen

Tessa heard her mother's cry and almost threw herself from her horse in her rush to get to her. They came together on the front porch, each enfolded in the other's loving embrace.

"You're back! You're back!" Maggie was sobbing.

Tessa couldn't speak. She just wanted to hold her mother and reassure her that everything was fine.

"Are you all right? He didn't hurt you, did he?" Maggie finally asked. She held Tessa slightly away from her so she could give her a good looking-over. She saw that she was wearing Jared's shirt and her expression darkened. "What happened to your—"

"Nothing happened, Mother. I'm fine. Jared found me and saved me just in time."

"And Boyd? Where is that no-good . . . ?" For

the first time in her life, Maggie was ready to swear and actually to do someone bodily harm.

"He's dead, Miss Maggie," Jared told her solemnly. He had come to stand on the porch with them.

"Oh, Marshal Trent." The old woman sighed his name, a look of pure adoration on her face as she turned to him. "Thank you for saving my girl. Thank you for being so wonderful. You're my hero."

She wasn't the least bit deterred by his only having the jacket on. She went to him and kissed his cheek. Jared actually blushed a bit at her praise.

"Will you be all right now?" Jared asked Tessa, seeing that she seemed relaxed and calm.

"I'm home and I'm safe, thanks to you."

"I'd better get on back to the office and take care of things. I'll check in on you later."

Tessa knew one of the first things he would have to take care of was leaving Boyd with the undertaker.

"Thank you, Jared." Her words were simple but heartfelt as her gaze met his.

"You're welcome," he answered, then returned to his horse and rode on with his men.

Will remained behind. He dismounted and joined the women on the porch. "It's a wonderful thing that the marshal got to you in time last night," he said, praising Jared because at the moment it was what was expected of him.

"Jared Trent is every bit as good as his reputation," Tessa confirmed, any doubts she'd had about his abilities as a lawman gone forever.

Julie and Jim had come out to see her, and they

crowded around her now, glad that she was home, giving her warm hugs of welcome.

"Thank God for Marshal Trent!" Julie exclaimed. "You should have seen him last night at the dance when he found out what had happened, Tessa. He went after you right away. Nothing was going to stop that man from finding you."

Tessa hugged her friend. "I'm just glad I'm back safe and sound."

"So are we!" Jim replied.

Steve came around the side of the house, having heard the commotion out front. He actually smiled when he saw Tessa.

"Welcome home," he greeted her.

She smiled at him warmly. "Thank you, Steve. I always knew coming home was special, but now I truly know how important home is."

"It's time for a celebration! Just think how excited Sludge and Henry are going to be when they find out you're safe!" Maggie declared. "Come on, Julie! Let's see what we can put together for dinner while Tessa gets cleaned up."

"That is a wonderful idea," Tessa said. She had been longing for a hot bath ever since Boyd had first touched her. Somehow just having his hands upon her had left her feeling soiled in some way, and she was going to enjoy scrubbing off every last trace of Boyd from her body and her soul. "And I guess I could use some clean clothes, too," she said with a grin as she looked down at her ruined skirt and Jared's shirt.

"Oh, I don't know," Julie teased. "That shirt is certainly attractive on you."

"Boyd tore my bodice, and Jared gave me his shirt to wear," she said quietly, looking down the street in the direction he'd gone, even though he was already out of sight.

"He is a gentleman, that one," Maggie said, ushering her daughter inside. "We're lucky to have him. Yes, we are."

Will was silently gnashing his teeth as he followed them inside. No one had thanked him for his help with the posse. No one had thought of how he'd gone after Tessa to save her. He was going to have to do something and fast. Tonight would be the night.

Steve watched as they all went back indoors; then he returned to making his repairs on the back porch. He was glad Tessa was back unharmed. Trent did seem to be one hell of a good lawman, but that didn't mean he was going to trust him. He'd had his fill of lawmen. He'd take care of his own problems himself.

When they were inside, Julie noticed that Steve had not followed them in.

"Where did Steve go?" she asked Maggie, though she wasn't sure why she cared.

"I don't know," Maggie answered. "Maybe he's still working out back. Want to take a look and see? Tell him that he's got the rest of the day off. We're celebrating! There's no time for working now that Tessa's home."

Julie went out the back door to find Steve hard at work finishing his repairs to the porch.

"Miss Maggie says you can take the rest of the day off," she announced.

Steve had not heard Julie come outside, and he glanced sharply her way at the sound of her voice. His reaction to the sight of her was always the same. He wanted her. He knew it wasn't to be, though, and he knew he had to stay away from her. He was not the man for her. He was a fast gun and an ex-con. She'd made no secret of what she wanted in a man, and he wasn't it. Even so, the memory of their dance and their kiss stayed with him. It had been hard all last night knowing she was sleeping on the sofa just downstairs, and yet realizing nothing was ever going to happen between them.

"That's all right. I'll just keep at it. It won't take that much longer to finish this job off." He turned his back to her and kept working.

For some reason she couldn't explain, it was important to her that he come inside and join in the fun. "You sure? Miss Maggie said—"

"I heard you, Julie," he cut her off sharply without even looking back at her. "I'll be in later, when I'm done."

Julie flushed with anger at being so rudely dismissed. Something about him was so infuriating! She had only been trying to be friendly. In a huff, she turned and stomped back inside.

Steve took a deep breath, glad that she was gone. He kept working.

After leaving the Sinclairs, Jared dismissed his posse and then took Boyd's body to Jehosephat Jones, the undertaker. Boyd would be buried in a simple grave at the local cemetery. Jared knew he would have to track Sarah down so he could notify her about her husband's death. Returning to the office, he found Trace waiting for him, along with two reporters from other newspapers.

"All right, Marshal! What's the story!" one of the reporters demanded as he walked in.

Jared's gaze met Trace's, but he gave them all a half smile. "We tracked down Boyd Wilson. He was shot and killed resisting arrest."

"And Miss Tessa? How is she?" the other man demanded.

"She's just fine."

"She wasn't—"

Jared silenced him with a look. "I said she was just fine," he ground out. "She was uninjured."

"Where did you find them? Was it rough tracking? How much of a fight did he put up?"

Jared answered all their questions patiently and was glad when they raced off to write their stories for their papers.

Only Trace remained behind. He'd sat quietly watching his friend handle the other two. He'd recognized the anger in Jared's expression when questioned too closely about Tessa, and he was waiting for the right time to ask him for the complete truth. He would never betray Jared's trust by printing it, but he knew there was more to the story.

"So what really happened?" he asked when they were alone.

"It was close—damn close—but I did get there in time." He sat down heavily at his desk and leaned back, weariness etched into his features.

"You look like you had a rough night."

Jared only nodded as he related what had happened during the gunfight. "If I'd been ten minutes later . . ." His expression was grim.

"But you weren't," Trace reassured him.

"What do you say I get cleaned up and meet you for a drink?"

"I'm buying."

"You're on."

Jared was tired and filthy when he finally got to his house. He made short order of bathing, and had just started to shave when he remembered in all too vivid detail what Boyd had almost done to Tessa. His hands began to shake and he was forced to stop shaving for a minute. That had been close—too close for his comfort.

Jared fought back a shudder as he finished shaving. He was tired, but glad that he'd agreed to meet Trace. Getting dressed again, he left the house. A strong drink with a friend was just what he needed.

Jared walked to the office of the Durango *Weekly Star*.

Trace was hard at work at his desk when he heard the sound of the front door opening.

"Jared, that you?"

"Last time I checked," Jared joked as he entered the office.

Trace opened his bottom drawer and took out the bottle of whiskey he kept there. "Grab us a couple of glasses," he directed as he opened the bottle.

Jared got two tumblers from the water tray nearby and set them before Trace on his desk. He smiled as his friend poured them each a healthy portion and then handed him his glass.

"Good job, Jared," Trace said, lifting his own tumbler in acknowledgment.

"I'm glad things worked out the way they did."

"It's a great story. We're going to sell a lot of papers with this one." Trace took a deep drink. "Sit down and relax."

"I'd like to, but I think it's going to take a while." He sat down in the chair and stretched his long legs out in front of him.

"Rough night?"

"Very." He let his thoughts slide back to the hours he'd spent by the campfire holding Tessa against him.

"Tessa give you a hard time?" Trace asked perceptively.

"She always gives me a hard time. That woman is nothing but trouble." He shook his head as he took a deep drink of the whiskey. He enjoyed the way it burned all the way down. He hadn't eaten in a long time, but didn't give food a thought.

"I used to think the same thing about Elise," Trace sympathized, but his statement drew a sharp look from Jared.

"That was different, you and Elise."

"Why?"

"Because you two were in love."

"And you're not?" he asked.

"No! I don't love Tessa. It seems all I do is save her. Every time I turn around she's got herself into more trouble—first with the stage robbery and then with Boyd. God only knows what she'll get involved with next."

"Whatever it is, you'll be there to help her."

"I don't remember anybody telling me that my job required me to keep Tessa Sinclair out of danger." He downed the rest of his whiskey and reached for the bottle to refill his glass. "I might have thought twice about taking it if I'd known that."

Trace just chuckled at how nervous his friend had become.

"What are you laughing at?" Jared sat back and took another drink.

"You. You're in love and you don't even recognize it."

"I am not in love," he denied.

"I thought the same thing with Elise. She was driving me to distraction. All I wanted to do was keep my identity a secret until I'd brought in Matt Harris and his gang, and then she printed that story revealing that Trace Jackson was still alive and well, not knowing it was me." He grinned at the memory. "She caused me no end of trouble, but heaven knows I couldn't live without her now."

"Thank you, darling," Elise said, appearing in the doorway to his office.

"I didn't hear you come in," Trace said, rising to go to her and press a kiss on her cheek.

"Obviously, but thank you for the sweet sentiment." She gazed up at her husband adoringly. "I feel the same way about you."

"I was just explaining to Jared how wonderful it is that he's finally in love," Trace told her.

"You're in love with Tessa?" she asked quickly, looking over at him.

"That's your husband talking. I never said I was in love!" he protested.

"He hasn't recognized it yet, but he will. He has all the classic symptoms," Trace confirmed.

"Obviously," Elise agreed as she watched Jared down another healthy swallow of the potent liquor and pour more into his glass. The reporter in her had already come to the correct conclusions. "I know you're not here drinking whiskey because Boyd Wilson's dead. If that was the case, your mood would be better. You look downright surly, so something is troubling you, and I'll just bet it's a woman."

"Be quiet, Elise," Jared said in a growl.

She laughed at his irritation. "Men are so adorable when they're trying to hide from the truth of their feelings. Does Tessa love you, Jared?"

"No," he replied. "Will Kenner's the man she cares about."

Jared remembered all too clearly how Will had taken her hand when they'd stopped to water the horses. Will had taken over running her mine for her, so he was sure that she had some kind of feelings for the man. It had irked him to ride away from her house while Will stayed on, but he couldn't linger there when he had other serious business to attend to—like taking care of Boyd. He lifted his glass and drained it.

"Oh, I don't know. If I had to choose between the two of you, there would be no contest," she said with an endearing smile. "You'd win hands down."

"I appreciate your approval, but I'm not in a contest with Will or any other man. Tessa Sinclair is not the woman for me. She's nothing but trouble."

He said it with such determination that Elise had to fight to keep from smiling too widely at him.

"If you say so, Jared."

"I do. Now, can we change the subject?" he asked, reaching once again for Trace's bottle.

It was over an hour later when Jared made his way slowly back home. He'd had too much to drink and he knew it. He was glad that he'd told Nathan he didn't know when he'd be at the office in the morning. Tired as he was, he hoped he could sleep late. A good night's sleep would do him a world of good right now. He was sure of it.

Tonight he wouldn't have Tessa curled up against him. Tonight he would sleep.

Peacefully.

Dreamlessly.

Alone.

Jared frowned at the thought. Holding Tessa had been his heaven and his hell last night. Damn, but it had felt so right to have her in his arms, even if he couldn't make love to her.

And he had wanted her. Seeing Boyd with his hands on her, hurting her that way, had left him in a rage. He had never felt that way about another woman. Tessa was beautiful. Her kisses had been wonderful.

And he—

The next thought that came to him shocked him, and he mentally pushed it aside.

Tessa meant trouble, plain and simple. That was all there was to it. He'd be lucky if she managed to stay out of harm's way for a while, so he wouldn't have to see her. The farther away from her he stayed, the better.

Reaching his house, Jared let himself in and didn't even bother to light a lamp. He'd definitely had too much to drink, and he didn't care. He went straight into his bedroom and, after taking off his boots and gun belt, fell across the bed.

Sleep claimed him almost instantly. Instead of the deep, dreamless rest he'd hoped for, though, his sleep was filled with images of Tessa. He saw her as she'd looked driving the stage into town single-handedly. He saw her coming down the steps at the boardinghouse wearing pants. He saw her in her gown the night of the dance. He saw her fighting off Boyd and then running straight into Jared's arms. He saw her as she'd been the night before, curled up against him, sleeping. Jared did not awaken, but slept on through the night. Whiskey was a wonderful potion.

Tessa stood alone on the back porch enjoying the quiet of the night and the bright moon in the star-studded sky. She was thrilled to be home and safe. The celebration tonight had been wonderful. She was truly blessed to be so loved. They had ended up with a houseful by the time Julie's parents joined them.

Tessa had found herself watching for Jared and hoping that he would come. When the celebration had started, she'd sent Sludge to Jared's house to invite him to join them. Sludge had returned a short time later with the news that the marshal was not at home. She'd been surprised how disappointed she felt. She had wanted to see him again.

There had been no mistaking that Will had seemed particularly pleased when Jared didn't show up. Will had stayed by her side most of the evening, dominating her, being solicitous of her every wish. It had nearly driven her crazy. She'd been glad when everyone had decided to call it an evening and go home. It had forced Will to leave, too, and she'd been relieved.

"Tessa?"

The sound of Will's voice startled her. "Will?"

"I was hoping you'd still be up. I started to go back to my room, but I wanted to see you one more time," he said as he appeared out of the shadows.

She had an eerie feeling about him, and she wondered how long he'd been hanging around the house. "I was just about ready to go in," she said.

He came up Steve's newly repaired steps to join her. "I know it's late and you must be exhausted after what you've just been through, but I wanted you to know how happy I am that you're safe. I was really worried about you."

She looked up at him in the moonlight. Will wasn't an unattractive man, yet she felt no physical attraction to him. If anything, the complete seriousness of his expression concerned her.

"Thank you, Will."

"Tessa." He moved nearer, lifting one hand to touch her cheek. "I've found that I care about you—deeply. When I thought you'd been harmed, well, wild horses couldn't have kept me from riding with that posse. I had to help find you. I had to make sure you came home safely."

"I know—"

"Tessa." Her name was almost a groan as Will took her in his arms and kissed her.

She'd instinctively sensed it was coming, but she didn't react quickly enough to avoid his embrace. She suffered his hungry kiss for a moment and then finally reached up to push him gently away. "Will, please don't."

"But Tessa, I care about you."

Tessa tried to be sympathetic as she answered, "I think of you as a friend, Will. I'm sorry, but I just don't feel that way about you."

Will stared down at her, fighting with all his might to control his temper. How dared she refuse him? He wanted to throttle her, to force her to his way of thinking, but he controlled the urge with an effort.

"I see." It was all he could say.

"I'd better go in now, Will. Good night."

Tessa moved away from him and went inside, closing and locking the door behind her.

Will stood rigidly on the porch for only a moment longer, then furiously stalked off into the night. He was going to have to rethink his plans.

Tessa stayed in the darkness of the hallway, waiting for Will to leave. When he finally walked off, she breathed a sigh of relief. She'd known that Will had feelings for her, but she'd never expected him to declare himself. She wasn't interested in him. He worked the mine for her and she did like him as a person, but she had no romantic interest in him whatsoever.

Tessa made her way upstairs and undressed. After donning her nightgown, she sought the soft comfort of her solitary bed. She'd hoped she would fall asleep easily, but it didn't happen. She lay in the dark, remembering how wonderful it felt to be lying in the safe haven of Jared's arms. Will intruded on her thoughts then, and she immediately wished that she'd had Jared there to protect her this evening on the porch. She'd missed him tonight at their little party, and she missed him now.

Tessa made up her mind to find Jared and thank him for all he'd done for her. If he hadn't ridden out ahead of the posse, God only knew what would have been her ultimate fate at Boyd's hands. He might have killed her. Jared had truly been her guardian angel. The thought of him with wings and a halo made her smile.

When she finally fell asleep, her sleep was dreamless and contented.

Chapter Eighteen

Tessa left the house late in the morning the following day. She was on her way to Jared's office to speak with him when she met Elise on the street.

"Tessa, it is so good to see you!" Elise said, giving her a quick, warm hug. "I'm glad Jared found you in time. That must have been terrifying for you."

"It was," Tessa responded. "I was very blessed that everything turned out as well as it did."

"It's wonderful that Jared was able to go after you and track you down so quickly. He came by the newspaper office late last night and was telling us about it. The world is well rid of Boyd Wilson."

"Speaking of Jared, I was just on my way to his office to see him. I wanted to thank him for what he did."

"Oh, well, I guess you don't know. . . ."

"Know what?"

"He hasn't shown up at work this morning," Elise said, making sure she sounded concerned, although she was sure she knew exactly why Jared hadn't shown up.

"He hasn't? Is something wrong?"

Elise shrugged. "I went over to ask a few follow-up questions for the article I'm writing for the paper and only Deputy Wells was there."

"That is unusual." Tessa was surprised and worried. She had really wanted to talk to Jared today. "Do you suppose something's wrong with him?"

"He's so dedicated, only illness would keep him home. If he is sick, he doesn't have anyone to help him. He lives alone," Elise said, trying not to smile. She knew Tessa would help anyone who needed aid. "Maybe you should check in on him at his house."

"You're right. I'll stop by and see how he is." She was frowning.

"I'll see you later then." Elise watched Tessa head off toward Jared's house, and she finally allowed herself to smile. She loved playing Cupid.

As was normal for him, Jared awakened at first light. He immediately regretted it. Jared couldn't remember a time in his life when he'd had such a bad headache, and he knew he had no one to blame but himself. He fleetingly thought about arresting Trace for supplying him with liquor, and then laughed. The laughter hurt, so he stopped laughing. He was very glad now that he'd told Nathan he might not be in early today. The way he felt, he had no intention of showing up until later—much later. He was even considering taking a day off, and that was very unusual for him. He got up long enough to close all the curtains, and then went back to bed.

Several hours passed before Jared finally forced himself to get up. He pulled on his boots, washed, and thought about eating, but decided against it. He was tempted to take another drink to ease the pain and was glad that he didn't keep any liquor in the house.

Thoughts of Tessa and his conversation with Trace and Elise last night intruded on his misery, and only made him more irritable. He'd seen the way she was with Will, but he remembered, too, the sweetness of the kisses they had shared before the campfire. Jared tried to convince himself that that had only happened because she'd been terrified and needed comforting, but something in his heart told him different.

He scowled.

The knock at the door surprised him. No one usually came by to see him, and he liked it that way. He was a man who valued his privacy. Jared was growling to himself as he made his way to open the door. He knew it had to be important if someone had bothered to come over. He wondered what could have gone wrong now.

When he saw Tessa standing there, he knew what had gone wrong.

"What are you doing here?" he demanded curtly, shielding his eyes a bit from the glare of the sun.

Tessa was taken aback by the coldness of his greeting. She was surprised, too, by his appearance. He looked totally disreputable this morning. He hadn't shaved and his clothes were rumpled. "I was going to your office when I heard you might be sick. I came by here to see if you needed anything."

"Who told you I was sick?" Jared snapped.

"I met Elise, and she said—"

"I can just imagine what she said," he broke in. Squinting at Tessa in the sunlight, he went on. "I thought I told you to stop helping people."

Tessa knew when she wasn't welcome, and she stiffened at his verbal attack. "You're in a bad mood today. All I wanted to do was thank you for everything you did for me. That was why I was going to the office in the first place."

"Fine," Jared said tersely, trying not to notice how beautiful she looked. He was staring at her lips and remembering how sweet they'd tasted. He remembered a lot more, too. In spite of his headache, he found he wanted to take her in his arms. Jared wondered miserably if Trace and Elise had been right, but in an act of pure self-defense, he bit out, "You're welcome. Now go away and leave me alone."

Tessa was surprised by the change in him. He had been so kind and thoughtful yesterday, and now he was so cold and rude. She wondered why. "Are you sure you want me to leave you alone? If you're really sick—"

"I'm not sick! I'm hungover! And, no, damn it, I don't want you to leave, but you'd better—if you know what's good for you." His last words sounded almost like a threat.

She was shocked. "I don't understand."

Jared was trapped as he stood there staring at

her. God, but she was beautiful. He wanted her so badly. His body was aching with the need to be one with her, but he knew it wouldn't work between them. He knew he should insist she leave now. He knew he should send her away from him.

But he didn't.

He took her by the arm and pulled her inside. Without saying a word, he shoved the door shut to give them privacy, and then he kissed her. It was a hot, passionate exchange that told her without words everything he was feeling.

Tessa melted against him, linking her arms around his neck and returning his kiss without reserve.

"I care about you, Tessa," Jared said in a hoarse voice when he ended the kiss and miserably put her from him. "But it'll never work between us."

She hadn't wanted to move away from him, and she stared up at Jared in confusion. "Why not?"

He shook his head and took a step back, deliberately putting more distance between them. He was too tempted by her nearness to think straight. "Because we're too different."

"Oh, no, we're not," she countered, closing on him. "Whether you'll admit it or not, we are just alike. We both help people in trouble."

"No, I—"

"You put yourself in danger coming after me," she challenged, interrupting him. "Boyd could have killed you!"

"That's because it's my job," he said.

"That's because you chose to make it your job. You want to help people. Everyone goes to you when they're in trouble and need help. They know they can count on you. They know they can trust you. How can you think that you don't help others?" She moved to stand right before him and, lifting one hand, she gently caressed his cheek. "You are just like your father."

Pain that had nothing to do with his hangover stabbed at Jared's heart. He stood there, staring down at Tessa, experiencing emotions he hadn't allowed himself to feel in years.

If he loved, he was vulnerable.

If he loved, he could be hurt.

"I love you, Tessa." The words were torn from him.

"I love you, Jared," she whispered, tears filling her eyes as she rose on tiptoe to press her lips to his.

His arms surrounded her in a fierce embrace. He crushed her to his chest as he deepened the kiss, and she gloried in his need. Jared lost himself in the wonder of Tessa's nearness. She fit against him perfectly, and he never wanted to let her go. Desire surged through him, and he stifled a groan as he ended the kiss and just stood there holding her.

"You should go now," he said hoarsely, savoring the feel of her, the scent of her.

"But I came here to make you feel better," Tessa said in a husky voice as she gazed up at him. She could see he was exerting rigid self-control, trying not to let things get out of hand, but the siren in her was lured on by the challenge of seeing if she could break his will.

"Oh, you've done that," Jared said with a half smile.

"I want to make sure," she said softly, reaching up to him and drawing him back down to her.

Tessa kissed him hungrily, needing to know that he wanted her. She had never been aggressive with a man before, but then she'd never felt this way about a man before. She'd felt nothing when Will had kissed her, but Jared's kisses left her breathless and excited. She knew only a driving need to get closer to him, to touch him and to hold him.

Jared meant to send her from him, but somehow at the willing touch of her lips, all logic fled. It was just the two of them, alone, and they would not be interrupted. He lifted his hands to frame her face as he pulled away from her one last time.

"If you stay . . ."

"What you trying to save me from, Marshal Trent?" she asked with a throaty laugh.

"From me."

But Tessa would have none of it. She had waited a lifetime for this man and this moment.

Tessa did not speak, but simply kissed him again, and in her kiss Jared found his answer. He groaned and surrendered to his need for her. He lifted her in his arms and carried her to his bed. He laid her gently upon the softness and then followed her down.

Kiss after passionate kiss roused their desire to a firestorm. Jared's lips left hers to explore the sweetness of her throat as his hand sought the curve of her breast.

Tessa tensed at his bold touch, then relaxed and gave herself over to his lovemaking. She wanted this. She wanted him. Tessa gave no thought to anything but the wonder of being with Jared.

When he began to unbutton the bodice of her day gown, she helped him, and then reached out to unfasten his shirt. She wanted to be close to him. With eager hands, she helped him take off his shirt, and she caressed the width of his chest and shoulders, marveling in the heat and strength of him. She'd wanted to do this when they'd lain before the campfire—and now she could.

Jared had to make sure she was willing, especially after what had almost happened with Boyd. She was an innocent—an angel.

"Tessa," he said seriously as he paused long enough to force her to look at him. He marveled at how beautiful she was. Her hair was spread about her in all its silken, burnished glory. High color stained her cheeks.

"What, Jared?" She, too, was studying him, memorizing the hard, lean lines of his face and the fiery passion in his gaze. He was the handsomest, most wonderful man she'd ever known.

"If you want to go . . ." Heaven knew he wanted her to stay, but he had to offer. It had to be her decision. He would not force her.

She lifted one hand to his lips to stop him from talking. "Shhh."

Taking her hand away, she looped her arms around his neck and drew him down to her.

It was her unspoken invitation that shattered his barely maintained control. Jared closed his eyes as he began to kiss her again.

Shouts outside the house shattered their temporary haven.

"Marshal Trent!" a man's voice yelled. "Marshal Trent! Hurry! It's an emergency!"

Jared was up off the bed immediately, swearing

under his breath. He began to pull on his shirt and button it.

"What is it?" Tessa asked, getting up quickly. She was startled by the interruption and suddenly very aware of where she was and what had almost happened. She quickly began to button her bodice and straighten her clothing.

"I don't know. Stay here. I'll be right back." He rushed from the room to answer the door, shutting the bedroom door behind him.

"Marshal Trent! We got trouble!" Harvey Landon was shouting as Jared opened the front door.

"What's happened?" Jared asked as he stepped outside to see what all the excitement was about.

"There's a fire!"

"Where?"

"About four blocks over!" Harvey was running in the direction of the fire to help out.

"I'll be right there!"

Jared ran back inside to find that Tessa had finished straightening her clothes. He quickly told her what had happened.

"Four blocks over?" she repeated. "That could be close to my house!"

"Let's hurry!"

They were almost out the door when Jared caught her by the arm and stopped her.

"What?" She looked up at him, wondering why he was hesitating.

Jared paused only long enough to kiss her one last time. "Now, let's go."

Tessa followed him from the house, and they ran in the direction of the smoke.

* * *

Elise was grinning broadly as she entered the newspaper office. Trace looked up from his desk, saw her expression, and knew she'd been up to something. He got up and came out front to find out what she'd done.

"You are too happy," he said. "What have you done now?"

"Me?" she asked with wide-eyed innocence. "Why, I haven't done a thing except . . ."

"Except?"

"Well," Elise began, "I saw Tessa this morning and mentioned to her that Jared might be a bit under the weather. I told her that I thought it would be good if she went to his house and checked on him, because he hadn't gone in to work today."

"Did she go?"

"Yes," she answered triumphantly.

In spite of himself, Trace started to grin, too. "It'll be interesting to see what happens, but you're not getting a story out of this—unless it will be a society-page announcement about their wedding."

"Yes, dear," she promised, knowing that that would be enough as long as their friends were happy.

"Fire!"

They both heard the shouts and immediately ran from the office. As they stood in the street, they could see the smoke billowing up over the buildings.

"That wasn't the kind of lead story I was hoping for," Elise said as they hurried to help.

Bobbi Smith

"Let's hope it's not too serious," Trace said.

They knew every volunteer would be needed to control the fire. As they neared the site of the fire, they stopped to stare at the mass confusion. The scene was chaotic. Everyone knew that if the fire spread, there might be no stopping it at all.

Chapter Nineteen

Jared approached the burning house from the rear with Tessa close behind him. The smoke was thick and acrid, but that didn't stop him. He knew how deadly fires could be, and he wanted to make sure no one was trapped inside.

"This doesn't look good," he told Tessa after quickly surveying the scene.

Some of the people from town were already there, trying to get a bucket brigade going. Their efforts weren't very organized, and there was no sign of the volunteer firefighters or the horse-drawn fire engine.

"We'd better get some buckets of our own and see if we can help them!" Tessa said, starting around to the front to join the others.

It was just then that Della Emerson appeared in an upstairs window, holding her youngest child, a toddler named Mark. She saw Jared and started to scream.

"Marshal Trent! Help me!" she cried. Smoke was billowing from behind her, choking her.

Jared and Tessa both looked up, and Jared immediately started toward the back door.

"Jared! No!" Tessa shouted at him, fearing for his life, knowing it was too dangerous for him to go inside the burning house. "Wait!"

He glanced back at her without pausing. "I have to go. I can't wait!"

Across the distance, their gazes met. Time seemed suspended for a moment and then he turned away. He kicked in the locked back door. The fierce heat blasted him, but it didn't stop him. He charged inside, determined to save the woman and her child.

"Jared!" Tessa called his name, but he had disappeared from sight.

"What is it?" Steve asked. He'd heard Tessa shouting and rushed to her side. "Where is Jared?"

"He just went inside!"

"Help!" Della cried again.

Steve looked up and saw the woman with the child. The smoke was about to overcome her, and the heat of the flames was threatening her. He knew she was in desperate circumstances.

Tessa gripped Steve's arm. She looked at him, her expression terrified. "Jared's trying to save her, but I don't know if he can! The fire is out of control!"

They both began to choke as the wind shifted directions and smoke billowed over them. It was then that they heard a resounding crash as part of the flooring collapsed inside.

"Oh, God!" Tessa stared in horror as the flames seemed to leap even higher. "Jared!" she called, and started toward the house, frantic to go to him and help him.

Steve had to grab her forcefully to stop her. "No! I'll do it! You wait here!"

Julie and her mother ran up just then, ready to help in any way they could.

"Here!" Steve said, putting Tessa into her care. "Watch her!"

Julie gave him a frightened look, wondering what he was planning to do. "Steve?"

Steve didn't respond. Without a thought for his own safety, he entered the fiery hell of the burning house. Jared had gone in there trying to save the woman and child, and he might be in trouble. Steve knew he couldn't stand by and do nothing.

Tessa, Julie, and Adele stood motionless, watching, waiting, terrified by what they feared was happening inside. The woman had disappeared from the window, but they didn't know what that signified. Out in front of the house, they could hear the arrival of the horse-drawn fire engine, and they prayed the blaze would soon be under control.

Tessa felt almost numb, as if the world around her wasn't real. She felt detached from reality. Everything around her seemed distant and otherworldly. All she could think about was that Jared had gone inside the inferno, and she didn't know if he would come out alive. She held her breath, fearing something horrendous might have happened to him.

"Where are they, Julie? Why haven't they come back out?" Tessa asked.

"I don't know." Julie had gone pale when Steve had rushed inside to try to help Jared. She told herself she didn't care about Steve. She told herself he didn't mean anything to her, but the fact that he had put himself in harm's way to help others surprised her. He was a cowboy—probably a gunslinger—but he was also a man who saw danger and did not run from it, who saw someone in need and went to help. She offered up a prayer that he and Jared and the others trapped inside would be safe.

"I've got to do something!" Tessa declared. She started forward, meaning to follow the two men inside. She couldn't wait any longer. She had to do something to help them.

"Tessa, no!" Julie called out. She chased her friend, grabbing her shoulder, trying to stop her. "You'll be killed if you go in there. You have to wait. Steve and Jared will be back. I know they will."

"But what if something's happened to Jared?" she asked in torment.

"He's fine. You'll see!" she said, trying to encourage her friend even as she held her back. "You have to trust them!"

They stood in silence amid the smoke and heat. Each minute seemed an hour, and their tension grew with every passing moment. Tessa clutched at Julie's hands, while their gazes were fixed on the gaping opening that had once been the back door. They could see no sign of movement. They heard no more cries for help. There was only the deadly crackling of the flames as they devoured all in their path.

More of the townsfolk gathered around them.

"Did Marshal Trent go in after Mrs. Emerson?" someone asked.

"Yes," Julie answered, knowing that Tessa was incapable of responding at that particular moment.

"Ain't that just like the man," another said, proud of their lawman.

They all stood together, paralyzed by fear, haunted by what might be happening inside. They were tormented by nightmarish visions of what the men could be facing in their efforts to save the woman and child.

Jared had entered the house and had raced through the smoke and flames, heading for the stairs to the second floor. He had just started up them when a wall collapsed and part of the floor gave way in the hall. A beam struck him, knocking him backward down the steps and leaving him stunned.

It had been the sound of Della Emerson's screams that had jarred him back to full awareness. The smoke was threatening to overwhelm him. He knew he had to get up and move or he was going to die. He lifted a hand to his forehead, and when he took it away his hand was covered with blood. Jared staggered to his feet and started up the steps again. Flames were all around him, but he knew he couldn't retreat. He could not leave the woman and child alone to die.

Jared reached the landing at the top of the

stairs and called out to her. The smoke was leaving him confused and disoriented. "Where are you?"

"Here! We're here, Marshal Trent!" Della called back.

Jared started toward the sound of her voice, staying low, praying that he found her in time.

Steve had entered the house after him and reached the stairs just as Jared moved off toward the woman. Steve took the steps two at a time, taking care to avoid the flames that seemed to be leaping at him.

"Trent? Where did you go?"

"Here!" Jared called back. He had already reached Della's side and was leading her toward the staircase.

Steve found them and took the child.

"Can we still make it down?" Jared asked, knowing how dangerously close the blaze was to the stairway.

"We have to hurry!"

"No! I can't go that way! No!" Della cried, terrified of the searing intensity of the flames.

Jared grabbed her and held her close to him to shield her as best he could. He looked back toward the window, wondering if they could somehow lower her down that way, but flames had started eating at the walls there. "There's no other way out. We have to try!"

She was screaming, but Jared didn't think about anything except getting back out the door before the rest of the building started to collapse. He'd been lucky that he'd escaped the force of the falling wall without serious injury.

He didn't want to test his luck any further right now.

Jared charged down the stairs, making sure Steve and the boy were close behind them. Della never stopped screaming, but Jared didn't pay any attention. He was too busy watching the leaping flames and trying to stay low so he could breathe and see better. He could hear Steve right behind him, and that gave him some measure of relief. Steve's showing up had been a godsend. Jared didn't know how he would have gotten both the woman and the child out of the house without his help.

"This way, Steve!" he shouted over his shoulder as he reached the downstairs hall.

He was forced to climb over the piles of debris from the collapsed wall, but he managed. He could make out the doorway ahead of them, and he headed for that light, knowing that outside was safety and fresh air and Tessa.

Jared and Steve came crashing out the back door, gasping for breath, stumbling to safety. Jared was half carrying Della as they staggered from the building. Steve was carrying Mark, who was clutching at him, knowing he was his savior.

"Thank God!" A cheer went up from the crowd.

Tessa and Julie raced forward to help. Tessa threw her arms around Jared and Della, guiding them away from the heat of the flames. Without thought, Julie went to Steve and, putting her arm around him, led him and the boy away from the inferno.

A roar of excitement and relief swept through those who had gathered to watch as the rescuers and victims were taken away to a quiet spot far from the danger.

"Mrs. Emerson? Are you all right?" Tessa asked as she helped the woman sit down upon the ground.

"Oh!" She coughed and choked as she tried to speak. "Oh, Marshal Trent, thank you! Thank you! What would I have done without you? Where is my baby? Where is Mark?"

"He's right here," Steve told her, coming to her side to hand over the toddler.

The boy went eagerly to his mother, secure in the circle of her arms, knowing that if she were holding him, no harm could come to him. He wrapped his little arms around her neck and hung on for dear life. "Mama!"

"Oh, darling, we're safe! We're safe!" Della said, crying as she held her son to her heart. "Has anybody seen Clara? Where's my Clara?"

Della suddenly realized that her daughter was missing. Della started to get up, realizing that she couldn't see her child anywhere. When she'd discovered that there was a fire in the parlor, she'd run back upstairs to get the baby, who'd been sleeping, while she'd sent her young daughter Clara outside to wait for her in safety. That was how she'd gotten trapped upstairs.

"Mama!" Clara came running to her mother's side, crying. "I'm sorry, Mama! I'm sorry! I didn't mean to knock the lamp over!" She was sobbing hysterically. "I tried to pick it up but I couldn't!"

"Oh, Clara." Della then realized how the terrible fire had started. She was heartsick over all they had lost, but relieved that no one had been harmed. Things could be replaced. Lives were lost forever. "It'll be all right. You and your brother are fine, and that's all that matters."

She held her two children to her bosom and rocked them as she let her own tears flow. Her face was stained and blackened, her hair and clothing singed, but she didn't care. She had her two most precious possessions. She had her children.

Tessa looked over at Jared and saw for the first time the blood on his forehead. Her heart lurched at the knowledge that he had been injured.

"You're hurt!" she said.

"It's nothing."

"Let me take a look at you," Dr. Murray offered.

When the news of the fire had reached the good doctor at his office, he had rushed over to see if he could be of any help. It took him only a minute to examine the cut.

"It's deep. Let's go over to the office, and I'll clean it up for you."

Jared was still worried about the fire spreading. "But I need to—"

"Go, Jared," Steve told him, coming to speak with him. "There are enough people here now to keep things under control."

Jared looked Steve in the eye, taking measure of the man. He hadn't expected him to help out the way he had. He was beginning to wonder if his original assessment of him had been wrong. He stuck out his hand to Steve in a gesture of friendship and trust.

"Thanks for your help."

Steve knew it had cost the lawman to say that. He couldn't prevent a half grin as he shook his hand. "You're welcome."

Jared looked up toward Tessa. She was standing by Della. As if sensing he was looking at her, she glanced up and met his gaze. She started toward him, meaning to accompany him to the doctor's office, but Della spoke up.

"Miss Tessa, we got no place to go, no place to stay now. Do you have any room left at your place? Could you take us in?" Della asked, still in shock. She was holding her children to her breast, trying to make sense of all that had happened.

"I'm sure we can find somewhere for you and the children to stay," Tessa told her.

She wanted to go with Jared and the doctor to make sure he was all right. Her terror had been real when she'd thought something had happened to him, but Della's request stopped her. She knew the woman and her children needed her, and she couldn't leave them. Della had no family of her own in town, and her husband worked for the railroad and was gone right now. She cast Jared a quick, apologetic look.

"You go on," he urged her.

"I'll see you later?"

He nodded and started to leave with the physician.

Della called out to him, "Thank you, Marshal Trent."

Jared paused to look back. "I'm glad you're all safe."

"We are, thanks to you."

When Jared and the doctor had gone, Tessa turned back to the newly homeless woman.

"Would you like to go to my house now? I don't think there's anything else we can do here."

As they looked at the burning house, one charred wall suddenly fell inward with a roar that left Tessa shuddering. The thought that Jared and the others had been inside just moments before was unnerving.

"Looks like you got out of there just in time," Tessa said, glancing over to where Steve was standing near Julie. She noticed that her friend looked decidedly pale. "Julie, are you feeling all right?"

"I've never watched a fire before. It's very frightening," she lied.

"And deadly," Steve added.

"You didn't get hurt, did you?" Julie found herself asking.

"No. I'm fine." He started off, back toward the boardinghouse.

"I don't know your name, mister," Della called out, "but thank you for helping rescue us."

Steve looked back and smiled at the beautiful sight of the mother and her children.

"My name's Steve Madison," he answered. "And I was glad to help."

In the crowd that had gathered, several of the men heard him say his name, and they exchanged troubled looks.

"Let's all walk over to the house together," Tessa suggested to Della. "Steve is staying with us, too. He's my new handyman."

They moved off.

Julie started to go look for her mother, who was somewhere in the crowd, but found herself glancing back in the direction Steve had gone. For all that he was walking with Tessa, Della, and the children, there was something about the way he

265

held himself that made him seem aloof and with-drawn—a solitary man. It puzzled her even as it intrigued her. He was a man with a lot of secrets.

Will had been so angry after he'd left Tessa that he'd headed straight for the mine that night. As he'd ridden mile after mile on the miserable roads, his mood had not improved. He'd made camp only when he'd been too exhausted to ride on, and then had slept only long enough to refresh himself. He'd headed out again, wanting to get back to Bob and Zeke as soon as possible.

Will's mood had remained ugly through the entire ride. He had had his future planned out, but now it seemed little Miss Sinclair was not going to cooperate.

So she thought of him as only a friend, did she?

Will actually laughed out loud as he wondered what she would say if she ever learned that her brother hadn't died in an accident—that he'd actually killed him. The thought pleased him now. He wanted Tessa to suffer for rejecting him, and he hoped that someday she would learn the truth about her brother's death.

Will had another plan formulated by the time he was near the mine. It was a lucky coincidence that he'd learned from Lyle Stevens about the gold shipment leaving town soon. He intended to make that the gang's last and most successful robbery. Once they'd stolen the gold, they would ride away from Durango and never look back.

And that would suit him just fine.

Chapter Twenty

Melissa Davenport had reached the burning house just as Jared had come running out the back doorway with Mrs. Emerson in his arms. Her heart had fluttered at the sight of him being so brave and daring. Melissa had long thought Jared was wonderful, and seeing him saving the woman from almost certain harm only enhanced her opinion of him.

Melissa had wanted to go to him and tell him what a hero he was. She'd wanted to praise him for his bravery, but Tessa had been right there with him, and there had been no way for her to approach him. Then she'd seen the blood on his face and had realized he'd been injured. She'd watched from a distance as he'd gone off with Dr. Murray, and she'd known what she would do. She followed quietly after him. She would be waiting

267

for him when he emerged from the doctor's office.

As Melissa made her way through town, she thought about Jared and Tessa. It had been bad enough that Jared had had to go rescue Tessa from her kidnapping ordeal, but something about the way they were acting with each other bothered her. She'd wished she had an excuse for Jared to come and rescue her, but the only thing she needed rescuing from was boredom.

"Melissa? What happened at the Emersons'?" Dena asked as she came hurrying up.

"I don't know how it started, but the house has burned. It looks like a total loss."

"That's terrible. Was anyone hurt?"

"Only Jared," she answered, and then told Dena what had happened. "I'm on my way to see if I can 'casually' run into him when he leaves the doctor's office."

"You are such a conniver."

"I'm not conniving. I'm just determined," she said. "It seems I never get to spend much time with Jared, no matter how well I plan things."

"Maybe he's just not interested in you," her friend blurted out.

Melissa made a face at her. "If he's not, then I've got to figure out a way to *make* him interested in me."

"You will. I have faith in you."

"Good, because I really want to marry him. He's so handsome. I'm sure he's the man for me."

"What about Tessa Sinclair, though? Do you think she has any romantic interest in him?"

"I'm not sure," Melissa said a bit frustrated. "I

was just watching them together at the fire. When Jared came running out of the house with Mrs. Emerson, Tessa was right there waiting for him."

"And they did dance together at the dance, you know."

"I know. I guess I'll just have to work that much harder to get his attention."

"Do you want me to go with you now?"

"No, I've got to do this on my own. I'll let you know how it goes later this evening."

"I'll be waiting to hear from you." Dena moved off.

Squaring her shoulders, Melissa marched on.

"That should take care of it," Dr. Murray told Jared as he finished putting a small bandage on his forehead.

Jared gingerly touched it. "Thanks. What do I owe you?"

"Nothing," he answered, and grinned at the lawman's surprised look. "It's my pleasure to help out the town hero. You did a fine job saving Mrs. Emerson."

"I appreciate it," Jared said, taking up his hat and starting from the office.

No sooner had he emerged onto the sidewalk than he saw Melissa coming toward him. Somehow he managed a smile.

"Hello, Melissa," he said.

"Jared, I heard that you were hurt, and I wanted to make sure you were all right." She gazed up at him, seeing the bandage. She was glad that things had turned out so well. He didn't look seriously injured.

"I'm going to be fine, thanks to the doc," he answered.

"Thank heaven. We can't let anything happen to you. We need you too much around here," Melissa declared.

"I was heading back to the office."

"Mind if I walk with you a ways?"

"Not at all." Jared didn't want to encourage her, but he did like her.

Jared made small talk with her as they walked along the streets of town. Even as he was speaking with Melissa, though, his thoughts were of Tessa—and what might have come to pass between them if they had not been interrupted. He fought down a grin as he realized there had been more than one fire in Durango that day. One fire had been put out, but the other was still burning. Jared longed to be with Tessa, but realized he had better check in with Nathan first and make sure that all was quiet in town now that everything was under control at the Emersons'. When they reached the office, he bid Melissa good-bye and went inside.

Melissa had been totally unaware of the direction of Jared's thoughts. She was feeling quite wonderful as she left him, and she was wondering how soon she could manage to see him again.

From the moment Tessa had returned home from the fire with Della and the two children, her life had become chaotic. Jared was constantly in her thoughts. Sweet memories of kissing him and touching him played in her mind distractingly as she'd helped the homeless family settle in.

Her mother had welcomed the Emersons with

open arms and had immediately set about making room for them. Maggie gave up her sewing room, and Steve moved a bed in for them. It would be crowded, but Della didn't care. She was just overwhelmed by their kindness and very grateful. Clara and Mark immediately made themselves at home, to Maggie's delight. She loved children, and having them in the house certainly brightened her day.

Several times Tessa found herself watching the street for some sign of Jared, but the hours passed and he did not come. Dinnertime found everyone crowded around the dining room table.

"I'd like to offer the prayer, if you don't mind?" Della asked, looking at Tessa and Maggie.

"Please."

"Dear Lord, we thank you for this bounty you have set before us and for the friends who do your good works here on Earth." Della looked up at Tessa, her mother, and Steve. "Bless us, Lord, and keep us safe. Amen."

"Amen," everyone echoed.

And then they dug in. The food was delicious and all ate heartily. They were just about finished eating when a knock came at the door.

Tessa hurried to answer it, thinking it was Jared. She was actually disappointed to see Julie standing there.

"Oh, it's you," she said.

"I'm sorry," Julie returned with a grin. "Should I be somebody else? Like maybe our illustrious marshal?"

"I was concerned about him. I haven't seen him since this morning."

"From the look you just gave me and from the

way you were acting this morning, I'd say you're more than just 'concerned' about Jared."

"He is a very special man," Tessa agreed without revealing too much of how she was feeling. It was all too new to her, and too exciting. "Come on in for a while."

Julie wanted to tease her more about Jared, but decided to wait when the two children came running out into the hallway, ending any attempt at adult conversation. As they entered the dining room, Sludge rose to pull up an extra chair for Julie, and she thanked him as she sat down. She found herself sitting almost directly across the table from Steve.

"Good evening, Steve," she said to him.

"Julie," he answered evenly. He hadn't thought to see her tonight, and reluctantly admitted to himself that he was glad she'd come by.

"Well, I just came over to see how everyone is doing. I spoke to the women's group at my church, and we're going to be collecting clothing and household items and taking donations for you, Della."

"Oh, thank you, Julie," Della said with heartfelt emotion. The people in Durango were truly special. "I know when my Neal gets home, he'll do everything he can to see that you're paid back."

Julie spoke up. "No one expects to be paid back for this. We just want to help you. The minister is hoping to find another house for you, too."

Tears welled up in the woman's eyes. "Your kindness won't be forgotten."

"You've been busy since this morning," Tessa remarked, proud of her friend's efforts.

"I wanted to help," Julie said simply.

The conversation shifted to other things for a while, and then Julie remembered the good news she had for Tessa.

"I almost forgot to tell you! I spoke with Kelly Nease and Jennifer Colvin, and the Women's Solidarity is all set to welcome Roderick as a guest lecturer on Thursday night."

"That's wonderful," Tessa said. "I'll be looking forward to it."

"Who's this Roderick fella?" Jim asked, curious, looking from Julie to Tessa.

"He's a professor from a university back east, and the brother of one of my friends from school. He's also a published author," she explained, her eyes aglow as she thought of the handsome, debonair Roderick.

"Impressive," Jim said with a nod.

"They'll be arriving in Durango tomorrow and are planning on spending a few days with us," Julie told them, her excitement obvious. "Their stop here is part of a western excursion they're taking."

"We'll all have to turn out and support him when he speaks," Maggie said, wanting their important visitor to have a good crowd at his lecture.

"Yes, ma'am," Sludge and Henry replied.

Steve hadn't said anything; he'd just been listening and watching Julie. When she spoke of Roderick her eyes lit up. It bothered him, though he couldn't deny that he'd always known the truth of how she felt. He was glad when Miss Maggie suggested they retire to the parlor, for it gave him the opportunity he needed to get away. He left the house and headed for the High Time to relax for a little while.

Jared had found himself virtually trapped at the office all day. Nathan had covered for him as best he could, but he'd had a lot of work waiting for him that had to be caught up. It was after dark when he finally managed to get away. And he knew right where he was going first—he was going to find Tessa. He'd already been away from her for too long.

All day he'd been distracted by the sweet memories of what had happened between them that morning. He smiled in the darkness now as he headed straight for Tessa's house.

"Marshal Trent! Come in! What a pleasure to see you!" Maggie said as she held the door wide for him.

"It's good to see you, too, Miss Maggie." He took off his hat as he entered the house and followed her to the parlor.

"Look who's here," Maggie announced as she showed Jared in.

Tessa looked up and her breath caught in her throat at the sight of him, standing so tall and darkly handsome in the doorway. The bandage on his forehead did not mar his good looks, but added a rakishness to his appeal. Heat flushed through her as she remembered his kiss and intimate touch. *He had come to her at last!*

"Hello, Jared," she said, rising and going to him. She wanted to throw herself in his arms and kiss him in welcome, but she managed to control the urge. She was very aware of Julie watching her as she crossed the room. "I'm glad you had the time to come over."

"I wanted to make sure Della and the children were doing all right."

"She just took them on up to bed a little while ago," Maggie offered. "But they're doing just fine. Julie's been out working for them all day."

"You have?" he asked, looking at her.

Julie quickly told him about the help she'd recruited for the family, and Jared grinned. He stayed for a while, enjoying the conversation. He had hoped for a few minutes alone with Tessa, but realized that it wasn't going to happen. She was sitting beside him on the sofa, and he could feel the light pressure of her thigh against his, but that was all the contact he could make with her. They would have no privacy tonight.

"I was telling everyone earlier that a friend of mine from back east will be lecturing at the Women's Solidarity on Thursday. Do you think you'll be able to attend?" Julie asked Jared.

"I'll make it a point to be there," he promised, glancing at Tessa. If nothing else, at least he would be able to see her then, and maybe they could steal a few minutes alone.

"We're looking forward to it," Tessa told him, her gaze meeting his.

When the evening drew to a close, Jared found himself escorting Julie home. Tessa gave him a slight smile as he started from the house, and he knew they were going to have to find some time to talk privately.

Tessa watched Jared leave and sighed as she went up to her own room. There had been so much she'd wanted to say to Jared, but there had been no chance tonight. She hoped she could find a way to spend some time with him tomorrow, but with the Emersons living with them, she had her doubts.

Patience had never been one of Tessa's virtues, but she had the feeling she was going to have to learn how to be patient, starting right now.

Steve was still savoring his first drink when he heard the sound of drunken voices raised at one of the poker tables.

"I'm tellin' ya, that's him!" one man was all but yelling.

"You're nuts, Avery."

"Like hell I am!" the drunk returned. "I think I'm going to call him out right now!"

The drunk knocked over his chair as he stood abruptly. He lurched toward the bar, his expression angry.

Dan knew trouble when he saw it.

"This don't look good," he muttered aloud as he stopped pouring a drink and reached under the bar to rest his hand on the trusty shotgun he'd started keeping there ever since the incident with Boyd Wilson.

Steve had heard the drunk's ramblings and went still. He didn't want any trouble. He'd come to the bar to get away from trouble—namely Julie. This other kind of trouble he didn't want either. He took another drink and tried to ignore what was going on behind them.

"Hey, you!" Avery called out in a loud voice as he stood a few feet behind Steve.

"You talking to me?" Steve asked, just glancing at him and keeping his hands on the bar.

"Your name's Madison, ain't it? Steve Madison?" he demanded.

"Yes."

"I told you!" Avery shouted to his friends. "I told you it was him!"

"Is there something I can do for you?" Steve asked, still not moving. He'd been in situations like this before and knew how one wrong move could result in a bloodbath, with a lot of innocent people getting killed.

"You're the fast gun, right?" Avery asked, his attitude challenging and hostile.

Steve shrugged. "I've seen faster."

"Look, you son of a bitch!" Avery had purposely insulted Steve, wanting to make a name for himself.

"Hold it right there, Avery," Dan ordered, pulling out his shotgun and laying it strategically on the bar.

"What the hell are you doing?" The drunk looked at the bartender in shock.

"I'm stopping trouble before it starts!" Dan said tersely. "Get the hell outta my saloon if you're thinking about stirring things up."

"But this is—"

"This is the man who saved a child from a burning building today," Dan said. "Now, go on! You're a young hothead who doesn't have a lick of sense. Get out!"

He gestured toward the door with the shotgun.

Avery was humiliated and furious, but he knew he'd lose in a showdown with Dan's shotgun. He glared at Steve, then turned and stalked from the saloon.

"Sorry about that," Dan apologized. "Sometimes these young kids get all riled up when they drink."

"That's how they end up dead," Steve said flatly. He'd wondered how long he could keep his reputation quiet, but he knew now that word was out.

"Let me get you another drink," Dan offered, shoving his weapon safely back under the bar.

Steve reached into his pocket to get the money to pay for his drink.

"No. Put your money away. This one's on me," Dan told him. "I know all about what you did today, helping to save the Emersons and all, and I appreciate it."

Steve was shocked by his kindness. He wasn't used to people being nice to him. "You sure?"

"Positive." Dan refilled his tumbler with the house's best whiskey.

Chapter Twenty-one

Julie could hardly contain her excitement as she saw the train approaching. This was it! The day had finally come! Roderick and Ellen would soon be there!

"Are you excited, dear?" Adele asked her daughter as she waited with her at the depot.

"You can't tell?" She looked over at her mother, her eyes aglow.

Adele smiled gently as she teased, "Only a little. It will be nice to see them again. It's been so long."

"Yes, it has, and now I'm a woman, Mother. Do you think Roderick will notice?"

It wasn't the first time that day that Julie had asked her mother about her appearance, and for yet another time, Adele reassured her that she looked fine.

"You are positively gorgeous, darling. I'm glad you decided to wear that dress. The teal color is very becoming, and wearing your hair up that way is perfect."

Her mother always seemed to know just the right thing to say to her to make her feel more confident. Julie hugged her impulsively and turned back to watch the train.

"Thank you, Mother."

"There's nothing to thank me for, dear. I always tell you the truth," she responded. "Are you sure they want to stay at the hotel? We certainly have enough room for them to stay with us at the house."

"I know, but Ellen said they would be taking rooms at the hotel when she wrote to me. Look! Here it is now!"

The train slowed to a stop before them.

Julie stood breathlessly waiting for her first glimpse of Roderick—and Ellen, too, of course.

The door opened, and a tall, burly cowboy stepped down first.

Julie's anticipation grew as she strained to catch a glimpse of those inside the cars.

The cowboy turned and reached up to help someone out.

Julie tried to see who was getting out next, hoping it was Ellen.

It turned out to be a little old lady.

When no one else appeared in the exit for a moment, Julie took a tentative step forward. Her spirits sank as she began to fear that something had changed Roderick and Ellen's plans and that they were not on the train.

Then Roderick appeared in the exit. He did not step down immediately, but stood poised in the doorway, looking around the station and town.

Julie gazed up at Roderick, her heart pounding a wild rhythm. He had not changed at all—except possibly to get even more good-looking. Tall and blond, he was lean and classically handsome. The suit he wore fit his trim, broad-shouldered physique perfectly. Roderick looked every bit the educated gentleman that he was, and Julie almost sighed aloud.

"Roderick?" she said.

He quickly looked her way.

"Julie?" For a moment, a slight frown creased his brow, as if he were trying to reconcile this lovely woman with the sixteen-year-old girl he'd last seen. Then he smiled, his gaze appreciative. "Julie, is that really you?"

"Yes." It was a rare day when Julie found herself speechless, but this was all she could say.

"Ellen, Julie's here to meet us," Roderick said as he stepped down and then helped his sister descend.

"Ellen!" Speechless no more, Julie all but shouted her delight at seeing her old friend. Without a thought for decorum, she threw herself into Ellen's arms.

Ellen was just as delighted to see Julie. The two women embraced, thrilled to be reunited.

"I cannot tell you how excited I am about your being here," Julie told them excitedly. "My mother came with me to meet you, too. You remember my mother, don't you?"

"Of course, Mrs. Stevens." Ellen turned to greet

the other woman. "And you've met my brother Roderick before, haven't you?"

"Oh, yes, although it has been a while." Adele smiled up at Roderick, completely understanding her daughter's attraction to him.

Roderick smiled at Julie's mother. "It's a pleasure to see you again."

"We are delighted that you've come to visit us. Let's go back to the house. I've got some refreshments ready for you."

"That would be wonderful," Ellen said as Roderick spoke to the stationmaster about tending to their baggage.

Roderick offered Julie his arm, and she felt as if she were floating on air as she took it and allowed him to escort her home. She was looking up at him, hanging on his every word as he regaled her with tales of their adventures on the trip so far.

Steve was on his way back to the boardinghouse from the general store when he saw Julie walking away from the depot, arm in arm with a man he'd never seen before. Just by looking at him, he immediately judged the man to be a dude, and knew he had to be the Roderick she'd been talking about for the last week. Julie seemed to be captivated by whatever the man was saying to her, and Steve felt a stab of jealousy.

Since they were all walking in the same direction and Steve didn't particularly want their paths to cross right then, he decided to take a different route back to the boardinghouse. He'd just started down a side street when he heard a shout ring out loudly behind him.

"You! Madison!"

Steve recognized the voice immediately and stopped. It was the kid from the High Time. He slowly turned to face him. He'd dealt with many young men like him in Arizona. They were young and stupid—little more than boys trying to earn a reputation for themselves as fast guns. Steve wanted nothing to do with him.

"What can I do for you?" Steve asked coolly, taking care to make no sudden moves.

"I'm beginning to think your reputation is all talk, Madison!" Avery said with a snarl

Steve didn't move. He just continued to stare at him. "I'm not looking for trouble."

"Don't matter whether you were looking for it or not! Trouble done found you! You were a coward last night in the High Time when you let Dan fight your fight for you. You gonna be a coward today?"

As Avery spoke, some of the townspeople came out onto the sidewalks to see what was going on.

Steve was furious and wondered where Jared was. If ever he'd wanted a lawman to show up, it was now, but he saw no sign of Jared anywhere.

"You're making a big mistake," Steve said slowly, his tone deadly serious.

"Put that bag you're carrying down, and let's just see how fast you really are, Madison!" Avery was confident he could take Steve Madison. He'd been practicing his draw for months now, and he wanted everyone to know how fast he was. He wanted to prove himself and get some respect.

"I've got no fight with you." Steve refused to be drawn into a gunfight. All he wanted to do was return to the boardinghouse and get to work. "I'm leaving."

Steve turned his back and started to walk away.

Behind him, Avery was shaking with the power of his fury. He was ready for this showdown, and he wasn't about to be denied.

"Madison!" Avery was all but screaming at him.

Steve kept walking, slowly, steadily.

The fact that the gunfighter ignored him completely set Avery off. He went for his gun.

"*Steve!*"

Steve heard Julie shout his name in warning. He didn't know where she'd come from, but he knew instinctively what he had to do. Steve dropped low and spun around, drawing his gun and firing just as Avery got his first shot off at him. Avery's shot went wide, but Steve's found its mark. Steve's bullet hit Avery in the wrist and sent his revolver flying from his fist.

Those who had witnessed the shoot-out were amazed by what they'd just seen.

"Oh, my God!" Julie said in a strangled voice as she stared in horror at the scene before her. If she hadn't shouted, Steve would have been dead right now! She swallowed tightly and began to tremble. She didn't know what trick of fate had put her at that particular corner at that particular moment in time, but she would forever be thankful. Steve had tried to walk away from the confrontation. He had tried to avoid the showdown with the other man, and the hotheaded kid hadn't let him. Even so, when Steve could have killed him, he had deliberately chosen *not* to. She was stunned.

"You know that man?" Roderick asked in

amazement. He'd been shocked when she'd called out the warning to him.

"Yes. I need to see . . ." She started toward Steve, but Roderick caught her by the arm and stopped her.

"That's no place for a lady like you. You might get hurt," Roderick said, disgusted by the violence they'd just witnessed. "We must move on."

"I can't believe I just saw a real Western gun-fight!" Ellen was saying to Adele as they continued on to the house. "Is it always this wild in Durango?"

"Actually, this is very unusual," Adele told her. "Durango is generally a very civilized town."

Adele noticed how upset her daughter was as Roderick drew her away from the scene. She watched as Julie looked back once more to where Steve was standing just as Marshal Trent came rushing through the crowd.

When Jared got word that there was trouble, he hurried immediately to the site of the shoot-out. It took him only an instant to figure out what had happened. Avery was hunched over, shaken and pale in the middle of the street, cradling his bloodied arm. Jared glanced toward Steve and saw him standing tall and straight, gun still in hand. Jared walked over to Avery.

"You're damned lucky you're still alive," Jared ground out, showing little sympathy. "Get over to the doc's right now!"

Avery stumbled off, blood dripping from his wound. He did not even bother to try to pick up his gun. His humiliation ran deep.

Jared went to Steve. He saw the wary look in the other man's eyes and knew that he was expecting trouble from him. He knew, too, that he was going to surprise him.

"Thanks," Jared said, looking Steve straight in the eye.

Steve was caught off guard by his remark and, for an instant, looked shocked.

"You could have killed him," Jared went on, "and you deliberately winged him instead. When Avery's had time to think about what almost happened here today, he's going to realize what a lucky man he is."

"If that kid keeps going the way he's going, he isn't going to be alive much longer to think about anything." Steve slowly holstered his gun, but he knew that he was really the lucky one. If Julie hadn't shouted a warning to him, he'd be lying dead in the middle of the street right now—shot in the back by a hotheaded young kid out to make a name for himself. He bent down to pick up the bag he'd dropped. "Do you need me to go back to the office with you?"

"No. You're free to go."

Again Steve was surprised, especially after what he'd been through with the law in Arizona. He was beginning to think that Jared Trent was a damned good lawman. He nodded and glanced once more in the direction Julie had gone, but she had already disappeared from sight with Roderick.

Jared watched him walk away, then turned back to disperse the crowd.

"What happened, Jared?" Elise asked as she

came hurrying up to speak to him. She'd been in the newspaper office when word had come about the gunfight.

"Avery Hanes tried to call Steve Madison out."

" 'Tried to?' "

"Steve didn't want any trouble and he started to walk away from it, but Avery drew on him. Steve only winged him."

"Avery's a lucky man."

"Very."

"Madison has quite a reputation as a gunman, doesn't he?"

"I'd heard as much, but he's not wanted anywhere. I let him know right away when he came into town that I wouldn't stand for any trouble. What Avery did today wasn't Steve's fault."

"So you like the man," Elise remarked.

Jared thought about it for a moment and realized that he did. "Yes. I wouldn't have been able to save the Emersons from the fire without his help."

"I think I can get a good story out of this," Elise told him, and she went back to the office to start writing her article.

"That wasn't quite what we had in mind for a welcome to town for you," Adele was saying as they sat in her parlor a short time later.

"It was quite a revelation and most interesting—especially the fact that you knew one of the gunfighters," Roderick said, his tone snobbish. He still couldn't believe that Julie had called out to the man the way she had.

"Steve Madison's a good man. He didn't deserve

to be shot in the back by the likes of Avery Hanes!" Julie found herself defending Steve.

"Back east, we hear about these things happening, but I never dreamed it was such a common occurrence," Ellen said, still a bit shaken by the display.

"It's not!" Julie protested, somehow irritated by their attitudes. "We were just lucky we got there when we did."

"Lucky?" Roderick looked at her askance.

"Yes, who knows what would have happened if I hadn't been there to warn Steve."

"So you know the *gunslinger?*" Roderick drawled the word. He was curious as to what kind of life she must lead to be acquainted with such men.

"He's relatively new in town. He's staying at my friend's boardinghouse. That's how I met him. He seems like a nice enough man."

"How did he become a fast draw?" Ellen asked, intrigued by the notion that she'd just seen a real, live Wild West gunman in action.

"To tell you the truth, I don't know anything about his past. All I know is that he's been in town for a few weeks and seems like a decent person. He just helped rescue a woman and her baby from a burning building."

"Fascinating," Roderick said, but he obviously had no real interest. "Enough about gunslingers now. What else is exciting in Durango?"

"Well, I've spoken to the Women's Solidarity, and if you'll do us the honor, we would love to have you as the guest speaker at our meeting Thursday night. Everyone was thrilled when I told them you were coming to town. They're very eager to hear you read from your works," Julie told him.

Roderick smiled brightly at the prospect of bringing some semblance of culture to this obviously quite uncivilized place. "What a wonderful idea. Thank you, Julie. It would be my pleasure."

"How long will you be staying?" Julie asked.

"We're due to leave on Saturday," Ellen told them.

"Well, at least that gives us a few days to show you the sights," Adele said, noticing the look of disappointment that appeared briefly on Julie's face, but was quickly disguised.

"We'll just have to make the most of each minute you're here," Julie said, trying to keep her tone light. Four days with Roderick was not enough.

"We're looking forward to it," Ellen said.

A short time later Adele and Julie showed them to their hotel. Ellen and Roderick wanted to rest for a while, so they made plans to come to the Stevens' home that night for dinner.

"What do you think, Mother?" Julie asked as she and her mother left the hotel. "Isn't he wonderful?"

"He's very much a gentleman, Julie," Adele answered a little elusively. She'd always considered herself a fine judge of character, and for all that Roderick did seem to be quite debonair and sophisticated, there was something about him that troubled her. What it was, she couldn't rightly say.

"Yes, he is." Julie sighed, remembering how it had felt to walk the streets of Durango on his arm. She smiled.

They returned to the house and went inside.

"There they are now," Lyle announced as he stood in the parlor doorway. "Julie, you have company."

"Oh?" Julie frowned.

As Julie went to his side, she could not imagine who had stopped by to see her at this time of the day. To her surprise, she found Steve sitting on the sofa in the exact same place where Roderick had been sitting. She could only stare at him, thinking how very different he was from Roderick, thinking of how stunned Roderick had been when he'd learned that she'd known someone like Steve.

"Hello, Julie," Steve said, his voice deep and husky. He stood up as she came into the room.

"Steve? Why are you here?" She stopped where she was.

Her welcome was about what Steve had expected. After all, she had just spent the better part of the day with Roderick. He'd figured she wouldn't want anything to do with him, so he decided to make his visit quick.

"I just came to thank you for what you did today," he explained. "If you hadn't called out to me when you did . . . Well, you saved my life. Thank you." He turned to reach behind him on the sofa then, and held out a small bouquet of wildflowers he'd picked for her. "Here. These are for you."

Steve went to her and handed her the flowers.

Surprised, Julie looked from the flowers to

Steve and back to the flowers again. She said nothing.

The moment was awkward for Steve, so he covered up by looking straight at Lyle.

"It's good to see you again. I'll be going now. Ma'am."

He nodded to her mother and, walking past Julie, let himself out of the house.

Chapter Twenty-two

"I want you to meet my good friend Tessa," Julie was saying as she walked toward the Sinclair home with Ellen and Roderick the following morning. She had met them at their hotel and had promised to give them the grand tour of town today.

"I think you've written to me about her several times," Ellen said. "Doesn't she run a boarding-house or something?"

"Yes, she does. She also owns a gold mine, but she has hired men who run it for her."

"She sounds quite interesting," Roderick said with hidden sarcasm. He had already conjured up a mental image of what this Tessa must look like. No doubt she was an ugly old maid who had to work to support herself. Why else would she be so involved in all the business dealings? It was very unbecoming for a female.

"Oh, she is. We call her 'the angel' behind her back."

"Why?" Ellen asked.

"Tessa and her mother love to help people in trouble. If they see anyone in need, they do what they can to help them."

At that story, Roderick was even more convinced she was unmarriageable, but he said nothing.

"Here we are," Julie announced as she led the way up the front porch steps and knocked on the door.

No one answered right away, and Julie was puzzled. There was always someone at home at the Sinclairs'.

"That's odd," Julie remarked more to herself than to her companions. "Let's take a look around back."

They started around the house, and heard the sound of children's laughter. She smiled over her shoulder at Ellen and Roderick.

"This is where they must be hiding."

"They?" Roderick repeated.

"The Emerson family lost their home in a fire a few days ago, and Tessa took them in. They'll be staying here until they can find suitable housing."

"I see."

They rounded the corner of the house then, and Julie stopped to stare at the scene before her. Steve was sitting on one of the porch steps holding Mark on his lap, while little Clara Emerson was sitting close beside him, gazing up at him adoringly.

Julie had been hoping to see Steve, especially after the way she'd acted the night before. She wasn't quite sure what had left her so speechless when he'd come to the house, but she'd felt sorry about it after he'd gone. She'd wanted to tell him that she was glad he hadn't been hurt in the shoot-out, but somehow she hadn't been able to find the words. Even her mother had remarked on the strange way she'd reacted to his visit and his gift of flowers.

Julie stood there watching Steve with the children for a moment. She was amazed at the ease with which he spoke to Clara and little Mark and how the children warmed to him.

"You got this for me, Mr. Steve?" Clara was asking him.

The child was holding something close to her that Julie couldn't quite make out.

"Yes, I did, Clara. I know you and your brother lost all your toys in the fire, and I wanted you to have something to play with."

"Thank you," she said in childish delight as she held out the small doll and gazed at it. "She's beautiful."

"You're welcome. And here, Mark, this is for you." He handed the boy a small wooden boat.

The toddler's eyes widened in surprise, and he squealed happily as he clutched it in his pudgy little hands.

"He can play with that when he takes his tubby!" Clara was thrilled for her brother, too.

"Maybe he'll grow up to be a ship's captain," Steve said with a grin.

"I don't think so, Mr. Steve," Clara said, suddenly serious. "There aren't many ships around Durango."

Steve laughed at her deduction, enjoying her

honest innocence. "You're right about that, Clara. Shall we go find your mother and see if she likes your presents?"

"Oh, yes!"

Steve stood, still holding Mark, and Clara quickly grabbed his free hand. It was then that he looked over and saw Julie coming his way with her visitors. He knew they'd already seen him, so there would be no escaping this encounter.

"Mornin'," he greeted them casually. "This is a pleasant surprise. Look, Clara and Mark, we've got company."

"Hello," Clara said, while Mark just clutched his boat tighter and stuck his thumb in his mouth.

"We came by to see Tessa, but no one answered the front door," Julie said, thinking how natural Steve looked holding the children. The children seemed to love him and be comfortable with him, and that puzzled her. He was an intimidating man, yet the little ones went to him freely and eagerly, with open affection. "Is she here?"

"I'm surprised Tessa didn't hear you knock. She's in the kitchen. Go ahead in," Steve answered, trying not to notice how pretty Julie looked this morning.

"Thanks. Steve, this is my friend Ellen and her brother Roderick. They're in town visiting for a few days."

"Nice to meet you," Steve responded.

"Aren't you the fellow from the gunfight yesterday?" Roderick asked, recognizing him.

"That was me," he answered flatly.

"That was a fine display of marksmanship. Do you get a lot of practice in that kind of situation?"

"Not if I can help it."

"Here's Tessa now," Julie said brightly, glad to see her friend coming to the door so they could go inside.

"Miss Tessa! Look! Mr. Steve bought us presents!" Clara went running to Tessa to show her the doll.

"That's wonderful, honey," Tessa said as she admired the gift.

"I'm gonna show my mama!" She ran inside.

"Steve, would you like me to take Mark?" Tessa offered.

"Yes, I'd better get back to work," he said, handing the child over. "Nice to have met you." He nodded to Ellen and Roderick before disappearing around the side of the house.

"Ellen, Roderick, it is so good to finally get to meet you."

Tessa came forward, Mark in arms. She had donned her pants today to have more freedom as she worked around the house. She was surprised by their unexpected visit, but pleased.

"How do you do?" Roderick was completely shocked to see her dressed in men's pants, but he quickly hid his reaction. He had never seen a woman so clad before.

"Hello, Tessa," Ellen said.

"I'm glad you came by. Julie has been telling me all about you, and she was so excited when she found out you were coming last week."

"We're excited about being here," Ellen told her.

"Come in, please," she invited, keeping Mark on her hip as she went back indoors.

Roderick followed the women inside, only half

listening to their idle female chatter. He had not been overly thrilled with Ellen's idea of making this excursion, but he'd agreed to go along to please her. He'd known that she'd wanted to see her friend Julie again and so he'd agreed to making Durango part of the trip. He remembered Julie quite well. She'd been a lovely, well-brought-up young lady when she'd been at school with Ellen. She had grown into a beauty, and her parents were very well-off, judging from their home and her father's job as a banker.

As an academic, Roderick never concerned himself with anything so common as money. He had loftier things to concern himself with—his writing career and his status as a professor. He knew, however, that money was important, and having a wealthy wife would certainly make life more pleasant.

Roderick had been looking forward to renewing his acquaintance with Julie, but now he was beginning to wonder about her and the type of life she led here in Durango. It seemed to be quite a different world from his. Never in Roderick's wildest imaginings could he fancy residing in a town where women wore pants and no one thought anything of it—where gunslingers could take up residence with impunity, and where parents of little children would allow their offspring to associate with men of that ilk. It had troubled him enough when he'd found out yesterday that Julie knew the gunman on a first-name basis, but these other revelations were still worse.

"Have a seat," Tessa invited, waving them toward the dining room table. "I'm sorry my mother's not here to meet you. I know she's looking forward to it, but she had a meeting with the ladies from church and probably won't be home until later this afternoon."

"She'll be attending Roderick's reading at the Solidarity, won't she?" Julie asked.

"She wouldn't miss it for the world," Tessa confirmed. "In fact, I think all her friends will show up, too. You should have quite a crowd tomorrow night. The ladies I've spoken with are all quite enthusiastic about it."

"That will be wonderful. I appreciate the support," Roderick acknowledged.

"It isn't often we get someone of your status here in town. We're delighted you came," Tessa told him.

Roderick was pleased by her compliments and by the news that there would be a good crowd for his reading. He loved being the center of attention, and perhaps bringing some culture to this untamed little village wouldn't be such a bad thing. Lord knew these people certainly needed it.

They had just settled in for what Roderick hoped would be an intelligent conversation, when Clara came running back into the room with Della following her.

"Tessa, you could have called me. You didn't have to take care of Mark," Della said, going to take her son from her.

"He's an angel, Della. He's no trouble at all."

"I'm glad he's behaving himself, but I can't help wondering just how long it's going to last."

Tessa laughed as she handed him over, then introduced Della to Ellen and Roderick.

No one noticed the sneering look that Roderick

quickly hid as he was introduced to her. He had no respect for her whatsoever. Her clothes were ill-fitting and gave her the look of a less-than-intelligent person from the very poorest section of town.

"Do you know where Steve went? I've got to thank him for the children's toys."

Her question only reaffirmed Roderick's already low opinion of her. How could she let her children associate with the likes of Steve?

"He had a few more things to take care of out back. I'd start looking for him there."

"Thanks. Nice to meet you," Della called as she left the dining room with Clara and Mark in tow.

Roderick was quite bored with the conversation and was looking forward to returning to his hotel room so he could have some time to himself. He had been in the middle of reading a scholarly treatise that morning and had had to tear himself away from it to accompany his sister on this visit. Forcing himself to be sociable, he turned his full attention to the conversation.

Jared was sitting with Nathan in his office late that afternoon when he heard the door open and looked up, expecting trouble. It stood there in the form of Melissa Davenport.

"Hello, Jared," she said with a sweet smile. "I was hoping you'd be in the office today. Hello, Deputy Wells." She didn't bother to look at the other man as she spoke, though. She had eyes only for Jared.

"Afternoon, Melissa," Jared returned. "What brings you in today?"

"I just wanted to check and see how you were

doing." Her gaze was on him, and she noted that he was still wearing the bandage. "Has it been bothering you?"

"No. I'm fine. Dr. Murray told me to keep the bandage on for four or five days, so I'm just following orders."

She smiled. "I'm glad it was nothing more serious. Everyone's been talking about how brave you were to go in that burning house and rescue Mrs. Emerson."

"I'm just relieved that everything turned out as well as it did."

"Yes. The ladies at church have taken up quite a collection for her, and I think the reverend has found a house for her to rent."

"That's good news, and I'm sure she could use some, after all she's been through this week. Have you told her yet?"

"No. There is a group planning to go visit her tomorrow. I was wondering if you would like to be there when we tell her?" No one else in her group of friends knew she was asking Jared, but that didn't matter. She'd needed an excuse to see him again, and this was as good as any.

"What time will you be going?"

"At two o'clock."

"If I can get away, I'll meet you there."

"That would be wonderful, and if not, I'll probably see you at the Women's Solidarity tomorrow night, won't I?"

Jared felt as if he were in a trap. "If things are quiet around town, I should be there."

"I'll see you then," Melissa said as she turned and started from the office. "Good-bye, Deputy Wells."

As she opened the door she found herself face-to-face with Tessa. She blinked in surprise, wondering what the other woman was doing there.

"Hello, Tessa," Melissa said.

"Melissa." Tessa smiled at her.

"Hello, Tessa," Jared greeted her, his voice warm and welcoming.

"Jared." She looked over at him, trying to keep her expression blank.

"I'll see you tomorrow, Jared," Melissa said, then flitted from the office feeling quite triumphant. She would be with him tomorrow afternoon.

A slow smile spread across Jared's handsome features as Tessa entered the office. She was wearing a simple skirt and blouse, but he thought she'd never looked lovelier.

Nathan was oblivious to any undercurrents between them. He was just glad to see her.

"Afternoon, Miss Tessa," Nathan said.

"Hello, Deputy Wells. Are you keeping things good and quiet around town?"

"Yes, ma'am. I'm working hard at it."

"Speaking of which, why don't you go see Lyle Stevens and ask him if he's had any news on that shipment we were discussing?" Jared suggested. They had been talking earlier about the gold shipment that would be passing through the area sometime in the next week.

"I'll do that. Miss Tessa, it was sure enough good to see you again."

"Why, thank you, Deputy. It's always nice to see you, too."

Jared waited barely a minute after Nathan had gone before he stood up. They shared a quick, excited look and he took her by the hand and drew her back to the cell area.

The moment they were out of sight of the front door, Tessa was in his arms. Jared's kiss was tinged with a hint of desperation as he crushed her to him. It seemed so long since he'd been able to hold her last, and there was much unfinished business between them. His lips moved over hers persuasively, evoking a wild response from her. She had wanted this kiss as much as he had, and when they finally broke apart she smiled up at him seductively.

"I like coming to the jail to talk to the marshal. Maybe I should do this more often. Or maybe, better yet, you can arrest me for something tonight," she said, glancing toward the cell and the single cot there.

Jared groaned at her teasing. "Don't tempt me. I can think of several reasons to lock you up right now."

"Name one," she said, looking up at him hungrily.

"Disturbing the peace," he said as he pulled her back into his arms. "My peace," he whispered as his lips sought hers again.

"Is that all? That wouldn't get me much time in jail, would it?" she asked when he ended the kiss.

"Ummm, let me see . . ." He pressed a kiss to the corner of her mouth, then shifted a little to forge a path down her throat to the buttons on her blouse. "There could be the matter of indecent exposure."

Tessa sighed as his lips traced the vee of her neckline. She arched slightly to him and slipped her hands up his back, drawing him closer. "What about trespassing?"

"That, too," he agreed, sounding more distracted as he did some trespassing of his own.

A sensual haze enveloped them. They both knew they could do no more than kiss. Their doings would be too easily discovered if they dared attempt any more, but their desire built to such heights that they had to force themselves apart. They knew that they just might reach the point where neither one of them could say no, and this definitely wasn't the time or place. Jared, however, was considering the merits of being locked away in solitary confinement with Tessa for a few endless days and nights. He found the prospect of no visitors or interruptions most intriguing.

"There was a reason I came to see you," Tessa said in a slightly breathless voice as she regretfully moved away from him.

"You didn't just come by for the tour of the back of the jail?" he asked with a wicked grin.

"That wasn't my original purpose, but it's proven to be so interesting, I may have to come back and take the tour again."

"I will be glad to serve as your guide whenever you feel the need."

She slanted him a wicked smile as they moved back toward the outer office area. They were both relieved to find that no one else had come in while they had been otherwise occupied.

"I came to see you to boldly ask you if you'd like to go to dinner tonight. Julie invited me to join her and her out-of-town guests, and she said if I wanted to ask you, that would be fine."

"Julie knows how we feel about each other?" He was surprised.

"She was with me when you went into the burning house. There was no way I could pretend I wasn't worried about you," she said, looking up at him, her heart shining in her eyes.

"What time should I come by for you?"

She gave him the details of what they'd arranged and then looked longingly over his shoulder toward the cell area again.

"Don't tempt me," Jared said in a low voice. "There's nothing I'd like more than to kiss you again right now."

Tessa looked at him and saw the flame of desire burning in his eyes. She smiled. "Maybe we can find a few minutes to be alone tonight."

Jared started to answer her when the door opened and Nathan returned.

"I've got all the information you need," Nathan announced.

"Good." Jared had known his return was inevitable, but he'd hoped for a few more minutes alone with Tessa. "I'll speak with you later."

"I'll be looking forward to it," she said.

As far as she was concerned, the rest of the day couldn't pass quickly enough.

Chapter Twenty-three

Julie was taking her time getting dressed; she wanted to look her best for Roderick. As she worked at styling her hair, though, she found herself frowning as she recalled a part of the conversation she'd had with Ellen and Roderick earlier that afternoon.

"Julie, I was wondering," Ellen had asked when they'd left Tessa's house.

"What?"

"Do you suppose we could invite that Steve to dine with us?" Ellen had glanced back toward the house, as if hoping to catch one last glimpse of him.

Julie had been shocked by her suggestion, and so had Roderick.

"Ellen, you can't be serious," Roderick had said, looking at his sister as if she were mad. His tone was condemning.

Ellen shrugged slightly. "There's something about him. He's so . . . manly. I find him very interesting, and I wanted to have the opportunity to talk with him more."

"I won't have you talking with him or any other man like him," Roderick had dictated.

"But I've never met anyone like Steve before," she'd said a bit dreamily. It was obvious she found Steve most attractive.

"And I pray to God you never do again," her brother declared.

"Oh, Roderick, we came out west to experience another part of the country, and this Steve Madison is part of that experience."

Julie had found herself growing angry at the way Ellen was speaking of Steve—as if he were some kind of experiment to be studied and analyzed.

"Steve is no 'experience,'" she'd found herself saying. "Steve is just a man. He's a good man, a kind man, a brave man."

Both Roderick and Ellen had looked at her strangely. Men who lived by the gun were completely foreign to life in their society.

"You sound as though you have feelings for him," Roderick had said, sounding a bit surprised.

Julie had quickly denied that. "I don't have feelings for him, but I do respect him."

"I see," Roderick had said a bit disapprovingly.

Julie thought now of how Ellen had hurried to change the topic. In a way, she was glad Steve hadn't been mentioned again. She hadn't wanted to include Steve in their plans. She wanted to be able to concentrate solely upon Roderick tonight. She wanted to impress him with her wittiness and intelligence. She wanted to make him notice her as a woman and think of her as more than a friend. She didn't want to be distracted by Steve.

Time was running out on her original plan. Ellen and Roderick would be leaving Durango in just a few days. Unless she could spark some kind of interest in Roderick, she was afraid he would leave and she would never see him again.

With one last touch to her hair, Julie decided she was ready. Her father had agreed to take her to the hotel in the family carriage and he was waiting for her now as she descended the staircase.

"Julie, I don't think I've ever seen you looking quite so lovely," Lyle told her as he came to kiss her cheek.

"Thank you, Papa," she said; then in a lower voice she said to him, "Let's just hope Roderick agrees."

"How could he not?" her father said proudly. "You are the prettiest girl in Durango."

"And you're prejudiced," she answered, laughing.

She bade her mother good-bye, and they were off to meet the others.

Jared arrived on time to pick Tessa up. He was surprised when Sludge, Henry, and Miss Maggie all were waiting for him with her. He felt much like a callow youth claiming a young lady for her first dance.

"Have a good time," Miss Maggie told them as they were leaving.

"We will, Mother," Tessa assured her. She waved to the others as she took Jared's arm, and they started down the walk.

"You look pretty tonight," Jared said.

The dress she'd worn was modestly cut, but its green color accentuated her fair complexion and burnished hair. She'd worn her hair down and had tied it back from her face with a matching green ribbon. The style was simple, yet elegant, and Jared had been hard-pressed not to kiss her on sight. In fact, he was wondering how he was going to keep his hands off her all night.

"Did you make any arrests after I left the office this afternoon?" Tessa asked, her lips curving into just the hint of a wicked smile as she slanted him a sidelong look.

Jared almost groaned at her sensual ploy. "No, but I thought about it."

She gave a soft laugh and squeezed his arm as they continued on their way toward the place where they were to meet the others.

The dinner was delicious. The conversation seemed to focus mainly on Roderick, and he enjoyed every minute of it.

"Jared, how did you become a lawman?" Roderick finally asked, just to give the man a chance to speak.

Jared had been sitting there observing as the others talked. He had met several other men like this Roderick and was glad that they eventually went back wherever they came from. He knew life was too short to be so caught up in oneself.

"It seemed like the thing to do at the time," he

answered easily, not particularly wanting to share his personal history. He recognized Roderick for what he was, and would tolerate him as long as he had to.

Tessa, however, was proud of Jared and what he did, and she wanted Roderick to have a better understanding of just who the marshal was and why he did what he did.

"Jared became a lawman because he likes to help people," Tessa told Roderick and Ellen. Her gaze was warm upon Jared as she spoke.

"Somehow I've never thought of a lawman as someone who 'helps' people," Roderick remarked.

"That's probably because you've never been in any real kind of trouble—and I don't mean 'breaking the law' kind of trouble," Tessa pointed out. "Jared's job is far more than just enforcing the law."

"Oh, really?"

"Jared's a very special man."

They were sitting beside one another at the table, and she slipped her hand onto his thigh as she spoke. She had needed to touch him, had been aching to do it ever since they'd been seated.

No one was aware of her move except Jared. His leg tensed beneath her hands for her touch stirred to life fires he was trying to keep safely banked.

"It's quite a thankless job, though, isn't it?" Roderick asked. "I mean, the quality of the people you're forced to deal with on a daily basis has to be less than desirable."

The easterner's attitude was starting to bother

Jared. He pinned him with a cold look. "People are people. Some are luckier than others in what life hands them. I just try to straighten things out and keep the peace."

"And you do a fine job," Julie said, praising him. "Why, the way you saved Mrs. Emerson from the burning house was amazing. You're a very brave man, Jared."

"I was lucky that day," he told her seriously, "and Steve was there to help me, too. I don't think I could have gotten both her and the boy out on my own."

"But you tried. How many men were there watching the blaze who didn't even try to help?" Julie pointed out. "And you were injured, too."

Jared self-consciously touched his forehead. "This was nothing. I'm just glad Mrs. Emerson and the boy weren't hurt."

"So your life isn't all chasing down outlaws and overseeing hangings?" Roderick stated.

"A lawman's work is never really done. Just when you think everything is quiet, something will happen."

His words seemed prophetic.

"Marshal Trent!" The call came from the front of the restaurant.

Jared looked up to see Nathan standing there in the entranceway, looking toward him. "Excuse me a minute," he said.

Tessa watched as he went to speak with his deputy. His expression was dark when he returned to the table a short time later. He didn't sit back down.

"I'd appreciate it if you could see Tessa home

for me. There's some trouble at one of the saloons, and I don't know how long it'll take to straighten things out."

"It will be my pleasure," Roderick replied.

Jared looked at Tessa, his expression serious and tinged with regret that he had to leave her. He had hoped they'd find a moment to be alone. He'd hoped for some time for just the two of them, but it wasn't going to happen tonight. "I'll speak with you soon."

"Be careful," Tessa said.

She watched him stride away, a tall and commanding man—a man in control. She noticed, too, how the gazes of the other diners in the restaurant followed him as he crossed the room. Jared Trent was a man whose very presence demanded attention and respect.

Roderick was secretly pleased that Jared had been called away. He had wearied of Julie singing his praises.

When they'd finished dinner, Ellen decided to retire for the evening. Roderick, Julie, and Tessa walked with her from the restaurant to the hotel. Then, after accompanying Tessa home, Roderick and Julie went on to her house. Julie was pleased to see that her parents had already gone to bed for the night. She and Roderick lingered on the front porch.

"I'm looking forward to your lecture and readings tomorrow night," Julie told him.

"I am, too," he answered. He did enjoy having a captive audience. "You will accompany us, won't you?"

"Of course. I'll have my father bring the carriage, and he can drive us to the meeting place. Are you enjoying your visit so far?"

"Very much so."

Roderick let his gaze roam over her in the moonlit darkness. He was not unaware of Julie as a woman. She was pretty and certainly seemed quite amenable. He had given some thought to courting her, and the fact of her wealth was certainly an added encouragement to do so. He knew Ellen was very fond of Julie and that he could certainly do far worse for a bride. His studies and career would always be the most important things in his life. He could never let anything as trivial as romance interfere with them, and whatever woman he married would have to learn to live with that truth.

Julie was standing beside him at the porch railing, staring up at the starry sky. She was unaware of his heated scrutiny. Her thoughts were a bit confused, and her mood was unclear. She had expected tonight to be one of the best nights of her whole life. She had dined out in a nice restaurant with Roderick. The conversation had been educated and cultured and intelligent, covering any number of timely topics. And yet, she'd found herself bored and actually a little distracted—even now. She had no idea why she was feeling this way, and that was what was bothering her.

Roderick was the man she'd thought she'd waited her whole life for.

Roderick was the man she could marry and move back east with.

Roderick was the man who knew which fork to use and could quote the classics to her.

Julie frowned.

"You look troubled," Roderick said, moving a step nearer as he saw her expression.

"Oh, no," she denied as she looked up at him. He did appear very handsome in the moonlight, but somehow she wasn't as affected by his good looks tonight as she had been previously.

"And you look very beautiful, Julie," he said softly.

It was then that he made his move, slipping an arm around her waist to draw her to him. He was pleased when she did not resist, but then he hadn't really expected her to. Bending to Julie, he captured her lips in a kiss.

Julie held her breath in anticipation. She had been hoping for days on end that Roderick would kiss her. She had been hoping he was attracted to her that way. She waited for the exciting sensations she was sure were going to come to rush through her with the first touch of his lips on hers.

And yet . . .

The burning memory of Steve's kiss surfaced from the depths of Julie's consciousness and overwhelmed Roderick's effort.

Roderick's kiss was sweet. Steve's kiss had been disturbing.

Roderick's kiss was as polite and well mannered as he was. Steve's kiss had been arousing.

Roderick's kiss was pleasant. Steve's kiss had spoken of untamed passion and flaming desire.

She had expected paradise in Roderick's arms.

She'd gotten nice.

The realization completely shocked Julie.

"I'll see you tomorrow?" Roderick asked with

confidence as he released her and moved away. She had fallen into his arms just as he'd expected her to. The evening had gone quite well.

"Oh, yes," she answered a bit breathlessly.

"Good night."

Roderick headed down the walk and back toward the hotel. He was swaggering a bit as he went. Julie was his for the asking, he was sure.

Julie watched him go, her heart beating a painful rhythm. She'd been left breathless after his kiss, all right, but only because of the shocking truth that had been revealed to her.

She wanted Steve—not Roderick.

"That's ridiculous," she said, denying aloud the wild idea that had come out of nowhere.

Julie went inside and went to bed, but sleep did not come easily to her that night.

To say that Jared was irritated would have been putting it mildly. The small riot that had broken out between the drunks at the Gold Dust Saloon had not been easily controlled, and it was late by the time he'd gotten everything settled. He'd left the jail in Nathan's capable hands and planned to go home. It was only the sight of the lamps still burning in the newspaper office that prompted him to stop in and see if Trace and Elise were working against their deadline.

"Going to press, are you?" Jared asked as he came through the door. He'd caught sight of Trace through the window.

"It's that time of the week," Trace answered, looking up at his friend. "What are you doing out now? Was there trouble tonight?"

"Nothing too exciting. Just a fight down at the Gold Dust. Nothing that Nathan and I couldn't handle."

"How are things going with Tessa?"

Jared almost snarled at him for asking. He'd had such high hopes for the evening, and the disappointment of having to leave her so early rode heavily on him.

"Fine."

"Fine?"

"Fine," he repeated.

Trace grinned. "Have you proposed yet?"

"No."

"Well, why not? What are you waiting for? You love Tessa, don't you?"

Jared hated admitting to his friend that he'd been right, and he knew how Elise was going to react when Trace told her. "Yes."

"Then what's holding you back?"

He was quiet, thoughtful. He didn't have an answer for Trace. He didn't know what was holding him back. There was nothing he wanted more than to be with Tessa. Lord knew, she haunted his thoughts morning, noon, and night.

"You know, you're right. I should ask her to marry me," he declared bravely. "I'll do it tomorrow night after that lecture at the Women's Solidarity meeting."

"Not a minute too soon, either, my friend. How about a drink to celebrate?" Trace reached for the bottle in the bottom drawer.

"All right, but just one this time. I've got some planning to do."

Chapter Twenty-four

The Women's Solidarity meetings were usually well attended, but were by no means crowded. Tonight, however, proved to be the exception. As Lyle drove his carriage up before the meeting hall, he was surprised by the number of people he saw going inside.

"It looks like you are a most popular young man, Roderick," Lyle told him, pleased with the turnout. He had feared that no one would care, but it looked as if the ladies had done a fine job of stirring up interest in the lecture.

Roderick was quite pleased. "I'm glad. It can be most disconcerting to speak at a function when the attendees have no interest in one's topic."

Lyle brought the carriage to a stop and waited as everyone climbed down.

"I'll find a place to leave the carriage, and I'll be back. Save a seat for me, Adele."

"Yes, dear."

"I have to show Roderick where to go, Mother. Can you take Ellen with you?"

"Of course, dear. Shall I save you a seat, too?"

"I don't think it's necessary. I'm not sure if they'll need me to help with any of the arrangements or not."

"We'll see you after Roderick's speech then."

Adele led Ellen off as Julie and Roderick made their way to the front of the hall to meet with Kelly Nease, the president of the group.

"Kelly, I'd like you to meet Roderick Prescott," Julie said. "Roderick, this is Kelly Nease. She's the president of the Women's Solidarity."

Dark-haired, green-eyed Kelly was the type of woman who never met a stranger. She had a happy, outgoing personality and was at ease with almost everyone, but one look at the sophisticated, cosmopolitan Roderick left her momentarily speechless. She felt a bit like a young girl at her first dance.

"Why, hello, Mr. Prescott," Kelly finally managed with a nervous half smile.

"Hello, Mrs. Nease. It's a pleasure to meet you. Thank you for inviting me here tonight."

"It's our pleasure, believe me," she returned. "We'll be ready to start in about five minutes. Why don't you have a seat and relax here by the podium?"

"Thanks. I'll do that."

"Julie, do you want to sit up here with him?" Kelly asked.

"There's no need. I'll sit in the audience." She looked at Roderick and smiled. "I'm looking forward to hearing you."

He smiled in return as Kelly showed him to his chair.

Julie made her way toward the entrance of the hall, greeting people she knew as she went. She was truly surprised and delighted by the number of townsfolk showing up tonight, and she hoped there was enough seating for everyone. She paused by the door to watch all that was transpiring and went still when she heard a voice behind her.

"Evening, Julie," Steve said as he entered the hall and found her standing right there before him. He had hoped to see her tonight, but had had no idea that she would be the first person he met. He thought she looked as lovely as ever.

A shiver went down Julie's spine at the deep sound of his voice.

"Why, Steve," she responded, turning to face him. "I didn't know you'd be coming to hear Roderick tonight."

"I heard it was the place to be, so I thought I'd better show up." He smiled at her.

Julie felt her heart flutter at his smile. He was such a serious man, and it was very rare to see him display any emotion at all. She swallowed nervously, but could think of nothing particularly witty to say to him—especially not after what she'd realized while she'd been kissing Roderick last night.

"I see a couple of empty chairs over there." Steve pointed out the seats to her. "Would you care to sit with me, or are you expected to join someone?"

"No."

At her refusal, Steve thought she meant she

didn't want to sit with him. For just an instant his disappointment showed in his expression. He quickly masked it, knowing he should have expected as much. He was no competition for Roderick. "Well, it was good to see to you—"

"No, Steve! I didn't mean that I don't want to sit with you," she quickly amended, touching his arm to stop him when he would have turned away. "I meant no—as in no one is expecting me."

"Oh." Steve really smiled at her then.

Julie had thought he was handsome before, but now she had to admit she'd never seen a better-looking man. His genuine smile transformed him. No longer did he seem forbidding and withdrawn. She stared up at him, amazed at the difference in him.

"Shall we sit down?" he asked.

"Oh, yes." Julie actually found herself blushing a bit, and she ducked her head as Steve ushered her to the two empty seats.

They settled in together to listen to Roderick.

Tessa arrived at the meeting with her mother, Sludge, Henry, and Jim. She had hoped that Jared would be able to attend with them, but she hadn't heard from him all day. She told herself that he must have been very busy, but it didn't lessen her disappointment. Tessa had convinced herself that she was looking forward to Roderick's readings. True, she was curious to see what kind of works he'd written, but she really was thinking of Jared and wondering how long it would be before she'd see him again.

* * *

319

"Good evening, everyone," Kelly Nease said loudly as she stood at the podium in the front of the room.

The crowd gathered there had been noisy in anticipation of the event to come, but when Kelly spoke they all quieted. They knew that if she had something to say, it was important.

"I'd like to welcome everyone and thank you for coming this evening. You're in for a treat tonight. We are honored to have as our guest speaker noted university professor and author Roderick Prescott. He will be reading from his own published works. Professor Prescott asks that if you have any questions, please do not interrupt him, but hold them until the end, at which time he will be more than happy to entertain any questions you might have," Kelly explained. Her excitement at having such a prestigious visitor in their midst was obvious. "Ladies and gentlemen, may I present to you Professor Prescott."

Kelly turned toward Roderick and began to applaud, and the audience followed suit.

Roderick rose and went to stand at the podium. He was so handsome and debonair that all the women were already impressed with him. The females looked on, enraptured, as he began to read.

Jared couldn't believe how badly his luck had been going the last few days. Every time he'd been about to get the chance to spend some time with Tessa, something had happened. Now here he was stuck at the jail when all he had wanted to do was accompany Tessa to the lecture.

After his talk with Trace the night before, Jared

had been ready to propose. He wasn't quite sure
how he was going to go about it yet. Just coming
out and asking her seemed the simplest way, but
he didn't want to blurt out his proposal in front of
her mother, Sludge, Henry, and Jim—not to mention the Emersons, too. He wanted the moment
to be special, private, something she would
remember forever.

But fate kept interfering with his plans. Things
had been peaceful most of the day; then Darren
and Curt Moore had come into town on ranch
business and had decided it was their night to stir
things up. They were now cooling their heels and
sobering up, safely locked in a cell in back.

It was Nathan's night off, and Deputy Tom
Colvin had come in to work with Jared. Tom had
gone to check around town and wouldn't be back
for a time. So Jared was forced to sit and wait
and hope that he would have the opportunity to
see Tessa for at least a little while sometime
tonight.

His eagerness to get out of the office and go to
the lecture surprised Jared. He truly loved his job,
but tonight sitting there at his desk was remind-
ing him of her visit and the kisses they'd shared in
the back.

Disturbing the peace.

Trespassing.

Indecent exposure.

Jared grinned and shook his head slightly. If it
wasn't for the Moore boys locked up in back, he
might have considered arresting Tessa tonight,
just to have her to himself for a while. The way
things were working out, it seemed that course of
action might be his only hope.

Jared chuckled to himself as he imagined the public outcry that would erupt if he arrested Durango's "angel," not to mention the headline Trace and Elise might come up with to go with the story. He supposed he'd better think of another way to get Tessa alone—although he had enjoyed helping her "disturb the peace."

"All's quiet," Tom Colvin announced as he returned to the office a short time later.

Jared was delighted to hear his news. "I like hearing that. Think you can handle things here for the rest of the night?"

"No problem," Tom assured him.

"The Moore boys aren't saying much in back. I don't think they'll give you any trouble."

"I'll see you in the morning."

"Good night." Jared tried not to look as if he was in too much of a hurry as he left the office.

Jared went straight to the meeting hall. The lecture had already begun, and he didn't know if he'd be able to get close to Tessa or not. He was surprised by the large number of people in attendance. He'd known more people than usual were going to show up to hear Roderick's readings, but he'd had no idea this many would turn out.

Making his way to the door, Jared stood there silently and listened to Roderick as he read from his books at the podium. He let his gaze sweep the room and caught sight of Tessa sitting with her mother and the others from the boarding-house on the far side. There were no empty seats near her, so he realized he was going to have to wait until the end of the lecture to speak with her.

"Jared!" Melissa said in an excited whisper. She

had seen him come to the doorway and had immediately jumped up to go to him. "I have an empty seat right by me."

Melissa brazenly took Jared's arm before he could say a word and drew him along with her.

Jared was trapped. There was no way to resist her without making a scene, so he was forced to accompany her.

At that moment Tessa noticed the movement by the doorway and looked up. It shocked her to see Jared entering the hall and making his way to the back of the room with Melissa clinging to his arm. *Melissa!* She could see the way the other woman was gazing up at him, and she felt the sting of jealousy that he was with her tonight.

Tessa's mind began to wander, and she remembered that the night she'd gone to the jail, Melissa had been there right before her. Now here Jared was with Melissa again. She didn't think he cared for the girl, but then why was he sitting with her? Had he kissed her at the jail, too? Disturbed by the images that thought brought to mind, Tessa turned her attention back to Roderick, but she found she couldn't concentrate at all.

Roderick read for over an hour, during which time several men in the back of the audience fell asleep. He didn't notice, he was caught up in the brilliance of his own work.

Julie noticed the sleeping men and was very glad they didn't snore. Julie knew Roderick certainly sounded intelligent, but most of the townsfolk didn't really care a whole lot about the obscure, esoteric ideas he was expounding on. They were mainly simple folk who were concerned with day-to-day living and making ends meet. She could tell that a large majority of the attendees had grown restless after the first half hour.

As far as deep thoughts went, Julie found herself ignoring Roderick as she pondered the mysterious reality of time. Why was it that there were moments in life when time passed very quickly, and then there were moments when it seemed to move so incredibly slowly? She was certain that the minutes were seeming like hours to everyone but her there at the lecture hall.

Here she was, sitting with Steve at her side, and she didn't want the speech to end. She was enjoying having Steve so near. Their chairs were close together, and so the hard strength of his thigh was pressed to hers. Roderick had worn a heavy cologne this evening that had nearly gagged her when he'd sat next to her in the carriage on the ride over. Steve, however, had only a clean, manly scent about him, and it was very refreshing—and, she had to admit, very sensual. Julie knew that when Roderick was finished speaking, she and Steve would part, but she wanted to enjoy every minute of having him close while she could.

"In closing, I'd like to thank the Women's Solidarity so much for inviting me here tonight," Roderick finally said.

Applause sounded, not raucous, as it would have been at a saloon after a performance by dancing girls, but polite and energetic. Roderick was beaming, convinced that he'd impressed everyone with his brilliant writings and deep thoughts. He held court as reporters from the newspaper hurried to the front to talk with him, and numerous females closed in, wanting to speak with him privately.

Those seated all rose and started to exit the hall. Tessa had been determined to be one of the first out the doors, and she made it. She'd already told her mother that she was going to leave as quickly as she could, so Maggie wasn't surprised.

Jared found himself trapped with Melissa. It took him a good ten minutes to extricate himself from her possessive grip, and by then Tessa had already disappeared. Puzzled by her sudden departure, he left the hall and went in search of her.

Lyle, Adele, and Ellen sought Julie out as soon as Roderick had finished his readings.

"He's a very accomplished young man," Lyle said, impressed by Roderick's works. "I'm sure your brother has a great future in academia."

"He does love it so," Ellen told them. She turned her attention to Steve, thrilled to see him again. "What did you think?"

Steve had been so preoccupied with Julie's presence beside him that he'd paid scant attention to Roderick's ramblings. All of his attention had been on Julie and how right it felt to have her with him. He searched for a good answer for Ellen. "Your brother is quite a speaker."

"Did you enjoy the presentation?" Ellen pressed.

"Every minute," Steve answered honestly—and he *had* enjoyed every minute of it, because Julie had been by his side.

Ellen beamed at his response. She knew Steve wasn't just any run-of-the-mill gunslinger. He was an intelligent man. She wondered, if she told her brother Steve's opinion of him, whether Roderick would think any better of him. It was certainly worth a try.

"Let's go congratulate him, shall we?" Adele suggested.

Steve started to withdraw and go his own way, but Julie touched his arm.

"You'll come with us, won't you?" she invited.

"I won't be intruding?" He glanced toward the front of the room, where Roderick was surrounded by legions of women vying for his attention.

"Not at all," she answered, not wanting him to go.

They made their way toward Roderick.

"Well done, Roderick," Lyle told him.

"Thank you, sir."

"Will you be ready to leave in a few minutes?"

"Actually, you might as well go on. A Mr. Jackson from the *Weekly Star* wants to interview me for his next edition, so I need to stay here awhile longer, and Ellen can stay with me."

"You'll be all right getting back to your hotel?"

"We'll be fine. Thanks so much for picking us up tonight."

"We'll plan on seeing you sometime tomorrow then," Lyle said.

"That will be fine," Roderick answered, dismissing them as he turned his attention back to the women who were still gathered around him. He glanced toward Julie, expecting to find her looking quite disappointed, and was a bit shocked when he saw that she was walking away with Steve. He had expected that she would wait for him to do the interview. He almost called out to her, but was interrupted by another lady's question and could do nothing but let her leave.

As the Stevens family made their way toward the door, Lyle was stopped by a business acquaintance who invited him to a late dinner.

"Julie? Your father and I are going to dine with the Duttons. Would you care to join us?"

"No, I think I'll go on home, Mother."

"Let me speak to your father. We can drop you there on the way."

"Mrs. Stevens, there's no need. I'll be glad to walk Julie home," Steve said.

"Are you sure?" Julie looked up at him, a bit surprised, and very pleased, by his offer.

He nodded and waited to hear what her mother had to say.

Adele had had nothing but high regard for Steve since the day of the fire. "Why, thank you, Steve. That's very thoughtful of you. I don't imagine we'll be out very late, Julie, so we'll see you when we get home."

Adele moved off to join her husband and the Duttons, leaving Julie and Steve to their own devices.

Chapter Twenty-five

"Shall we go?" Steve asked.

Julie glanced back one last time toward Roderick, seeing how the women were fawning over him and how he was glorying in their adulation. She had thought him the perfect man, but she'd found she was mistaken. Roderick was sophisticated, true, but in being sophisticated, he also thought himself quite superior to others, and that type of arrogance was one trait that disgusted Julie. She never had been one to tolerate pompousness. She had always thought her dream man would be a solid, strong man—a dependable man, a man of character and decisiveness. Not a man who was primarily concerned about himself and how others perceived him, but a man who was brave enough to dare to stand for something.

"Yes, please, let's go." She was eager to get away from the sight of the crowd of adoring women encircling Roderick.

Steve was relieved by her answer. He'd noticed that she'd glanced back toward Roderick, and he'd feared for a moment that she wanted to be with him.

Julie felt almost lighthearted as Steve escorted her from the premises. When they stepped outside, she looked up at the sky and reveled in the majesty of its black velvet vastness. She took a deep breath of fresh air.

"I needed that," she told him with a grin.

"What?"

"A breath of fresh air. It got kind of stuffy in there." Her smile turned a tad wicked.

"You didn't enjoy the readings?" Steve was a bit surprised by her confession.

Julie looked thoughtful for a moment.

"I really had thought that I was going to find Roderick brilliant and interesting, but he lost me after the first twenty minutes. Everyday people living in a real world, dealing with real problems, don't have the time to concern themselves with the things that seem so important to Roderick." Even as she was speaking, Julie was surprising herself. All along she'd thought a man like Roderick was her heart's desire, but now she knew better.

"It is a hard world out there," Steve said, unable to keep all the bitterness out of his tone as they moved off down the street.

Julie heard the harshness in his tone, and it made her wonder how he had become the man he was.

"How did you . . ." Julie began, and then she paused, not quite sure how to ask him about his past.

"What do you want to know?" He looked down at her in the moonlight. Her pale hair gleamed in the soft light, and her complexion was flawless. She looked otherworldly, almost ethereal in her beauty, and he was mesmerized.

"How did you end up here in Durango?" She truly was curious.

Steve didn't say anything for a moment, not sure how much to tell her about his past. "It's a long story."

"It's a long walk," she returned. "But if you don't want to talk about it . . ."

"It doesn't matter. Talking about it won't change anything." He paused for a moment, and then decided to tell her the truth. "I came to Durango looking for revenge."

"Revenge?"

"There was only one thing I wanted when I rode into town, and that was to find the men responsible for sending to me prison."

"I didn't know you'd been in prison," she said quietly.

"I was finally released when the law in Arizona discovered I'd been wrongly convicted, but by then I'd already spent months locked up. I learned a lot during those months—and a lot of what I learned, I never wanted to know."

"That must have been terrible for you!" She looked up at him, shocked by his horrible revelation. "How did it happen?"

"I was framed by the men who really committed the robberies."

"How did you manage to prove your innocence?" She could well imagine the frustration he must have felt being convicted and sent to jail for a crime he'd hadn't committed.

"They finally caught one of the gang, who confessed that I'd never been involved. Only then did they let me go."

"And you believe the gang is here now?"

"I read a newspaper account about one of the stage robberies you'd had in the area and thought it might be the same gang. But I haven't seen any sign of the men I knew here in Durango."

"How did you get your reputation as a fast gun in the first place?"

"I was just a kid, barely sixteen. There was a shooting contest at a fair in our county, and I won it. I always did like to handle a gun, and I was naturally good at it. Later that night, the man I beat got one of his friends, and the two of them came after me. They beat me up pretty bad."

"Where was your family? Why didn't someone help you?"

"There was only me and my pa, and by sundown most nights he was already drunk and passed out."

"I'm sorry."

He shrugged indifferently. "The man I'd bested in the contest called me out. I guess he figured that if they'd beaten me up, I wouldn't be in any condition to draw on him."

Julie couldn't help herself. She reached out and took his hand in hers. She could just imagine the terror a sixteen-year-old boy would feel, being beaten and then forced to fight a real gunfight.

"It was a fair fight," he said tightly, "and I won

it." Steve suppressed a shudder at the memory of killing his first man. "His friend was so shocked that I'd killed him that he was ready to draw on me, too. I'd had enough by then. I turned on him and told him to get the hell off our land or he'd be dead along with his friend. He took the other man's body with him, and I rode straight in to the sheriff's office that night to tell him what had happened."

"That must have been terrible for you." She stopped walking to look up at him.

"It wasn't too long after that that the rumors started about what a fast gun I was. From then on, it was kill or be killed. I learned real fast what was important in life, and it's not what your boyfriend from back east was talking about. It's survival."

"Roderick's not my boyfriend," Julie protested quickly, suddenly finding the very idea abhorrent.

"But I thought . . ." Steve frowned.

Julie was glad that they were alone on the street when she looked up at him. "You thought wrong. He's only my friend Ellen's brother. He means nothing to me."

Steve was confused. "That night at Tessa's, though—"

"What night?" She didn't know what he was talking about.

He looked a bit uncomfortable. "When you came over for the dancing lessons. I heard you and Tessa talking about him when you were standing out on the porch. I didn't mean to eavesdrop, but you were talking right under my bedroom window. It sounded like you cared for him."

"At the time I thought I did, but I've learned a lot in these last few days. What I used to think was important, I've discovered doesn't matter quite so much."

"I don't understand."

Julie was frustrated, but excited as she gazed up at Steve. Her heart was beating a frantic rhythm as she decided to risk everything for love.

"Kiss me, Steve."

He needed no further invitation as he gathered her close and kissed her. He knew they were standing on the street, where anyone might happen by, but right then it didn't matter. All that mattered was that Julie had just asked him to kiss her. It was a request he couldn't—and didn't want to—refuse.

Their lips met, tentatively searching, then blending in a hungry exchange that expressed without words the depth of what they were both feeling.

When they broke apart, Julie gazed up at him. Her eyes were aglow with joy.

"Let's hurry," she whispered, taking his hand again and starting off down the street once more. She felt decidedly wild as she hurried toward her home. Her parents would be at dinner for a while, so she knew they would have the whole house to themselves.

Steve needed no further encouragement. He stayed with her every step of the way. The very idea of being alone with her was a dream come true for him.

When they reached the house, Julie unlocked the door and let them in. It was dark. She did not rush to light a lamp, but went straight into Steve's arms.

"Steve," she said in soft invitation as she looped her arms around his neck and drew him down to her for a kiss.

Steve groaned as his lips met hers. She was beauty and innocence and everything that was good about life, and he needed her. He crushed her to him, wanting to hold her close. The heat of his desire flared to life as he parted her lips and deepened the exchange.

Julie responded without reserve, kissing him back, moving against him, wanting him as he wanted her. When his hand sought the curve of her breast, she whimpered softly at the sensations his caress evoked. She did not try to stop him, but shifted in his arms to offer him more.

Her innocent invitation was almost his undoing. He went still, trying to slow his driving passion. He was no saint—Lord knew he wanted her—but he knew what could happen if he didn't leave her now. She was too much of a temptation for him.

"Julie," Steve said in a hoarse voice, "I'd better go."

She had been caught up in a sensual web that his kisses and caress had woven around her, and any semblance of sanity had vanished. She didn't want Steve to stop kissing her. She didn't want him to go.

"No," she whispered against his lips, teasing him, enticing him with small, soft kisses.

"No?" Steve was stunned. "But your parents—"

"Won't be back for ages."

She led him into the parlor and drew him down

on the sofa. Leaning back, she lifted her arms to him in invitation.

Steve told himself he should leave her right then. She was a virgin, unschooled in the ways of men. With his last shred of sanity, he cautioned himself to go while he still could, to protect her from himself. And then she touched him, running her hands up his chest, urging him down to her, and all reason was lost. It was only the two of them, alone in the darkness of the warm night.

They came together in a frenzy of desire. Each touch, each kiss, stoked the blaze of their need to a white-hot passion. He worked at the buttons at the bodice of her gown, then slipped her chemise from her shoulders, baring that sweet flesh to his kisses.

Julie gasped in delight and held him to her, reveling in the sensations the touch of his lips evoked. She had never known a man's touch or kiss could make her feel this way. But then she realized it wasn't just any man's caress that was thrilling her—it was Steve's. She shivered in excitement as she worked to unbutton his shirt.

Steve rose up over her and helped her free him from his shirt; then he bent to her, capturing her lips in a hungry exchange. The heat of his body seared her, and she wrapped her arms around him, caressing the sleek, hard-muscled width of his back. Instinctively Julie moved restlessly against him. Her body ached with an empty, driving need to get even closer to Steve.

Brushing her skirts aside, Steve fit himself more intimately against her. The contact was electric, and Julie arched up to him. She whimpered as her excitement built to a fever pitch.

"I want to love you," Julie told him, her gaze passion-dark as she looked up at him. "Love me, Steve."

"I do, Julie. I do."

He could no more have stopped loving her at that moment than he could have stopped breathing. He drew back only long enough to help her slip off her undergarment, then freed himself to take her.

Julie gasped as Steve sought the depths of her womanhood. Pressing forward, he pierced the proof of her innocence and claimed her as his own.

Steve had never known joy so sweet as that he found buried deep within the heat of her slender body. He continued to caress her and kiss her, wanting to tell her by his actions what she meant to him. He was not a man of words. He could only show her how much he cared.

With care and gentleness, he moved within her, introducing her to the joy of love. He kept his rhythm steady and arousing until he felt her matching him in his need.

Julie had known a little about the actual act of lovemaking, but the whispers she'd heard were nothing compared to the reality of being with Steve. Loving him was pure bliss. She was caught up in the excitement of Steve's loving. His every touch and kiss left her more and more breathless. An aching delight grew within her that left her clutching at him, wanting some mysterious release that only he could give her. And then it happened—the burning need within her crested in an explosion of ecstasy.

Steve had been holding himself back, wanting to please her. When he felt her reach love's peak, he quickened his own pace. He whispered her name as he, too, reached the heights of rapture. They clung to each other as they quietly marveled at the beauty they'd just experienced.

Enfolded in Julie's arms, Steve rested, knowing true peace for the first time in his life.

It was long moments later when their sanity returned. Steve finally tore himself away from the haven of Julie's embrace. He didn't want to leave her, but he had to. She was too tempting. Just being that close to her aroused him, and he had already put her at risk tonight.

"Julie, I'm—"

"You'd better not say you're sorry," she told him, her eyes aglow as she gazed up at him.

He leaned toward her and kissed her one last, passionate time. "I'll never be sorry for loving you."

"Oh, Steve." She reached for him, wanting him again.

He moved safely away.

"I'd better go," Steve said regretfully.

"Do you have to?" Julie wanted to hold him to her heart and keep him with her forever.

He grinned at her. "I don't think your father would be too pleased to find us like this."

"Then marry me," she said boldly. "Tonight. Right now. I don't care about a big, fancy wedding. We can go to the justice of the—"

"No, Julie."

His answer was so sternly spoken that she was startled by it. She looked up at him, shocked.

"But—"

"I can't even think of marrying you. Not until I've done what I came here to do."

Steve's expression turned grim as the reality of his life intruded into the loving haven they'd created. The need for revenge was too great within him to let it go. It had been driving him for months; he had to find the gang. Until they'd paid for what they'd done to him, he would have no rest.

"But I could help you. We all could," she insisted, devastated by what he was saying. "You can start a new life here. You can forget your past and—"

Steve pierced her with a cold glare. "There is no forgetting my past, Julie. Young fools like Avery Hanes won't let me forget it. I have to live with who I am every minute of every day, never knowing when someone might pull a gun on me." He realized in complete misery and fury that he'd been a fool to think he could fall in love with Julie and have any kind of future with her. But he had wanted her so badly, needed her so much.

The painful truth of Steve's words silenced her. She looked on as Steve straightened his own clothing. When he came to her wanting to help her with her clothing, she refused his help and quickly buttoned her own bodice. She stood up, wanting to go to him, to somehow reach him, but he moved away from her.

"Good night, Julie," he said.

Their gazes met for an instant as he stood by the door, and she could see even in the darkness the pain etched onto his handsome features. She said no more as he let himself out of the house.

Julie stood alone in the parlor staring after him. She was confused by what had happened. Steve had said that he loved her, but he'd refused to marry her. She bit her lip to fight back the tears as she ran upstairs to her room. She threw herself on the bed and cried until the tears would come no more. When at last she was quiet, she changed clothes, hiding the petticoat that showed the proof of her lost innocence. She knew she was going to have to sneak it out of the house somehow. She couldn't let her mother know what had happened.

When her parents returned home sometime later, and her mother opened her bedroom door to check on her, Julie feigned sleep.

Chapter Twenty-six

Tessa hadn't been able to get away from the Women's Solidarity meeting fast enough. She'd smiled at the few people who'd spoken to her as she was leaving, but she had not lingered and she had not looked back to see if anyone was coming after her. Judging from the way Melissa had been gazing up at Jared so adoringly, she doubted he would be in a hurry to leave her anytime soon.

When Tessa had reached the house, she'd gone inside and shut the door behind her. She was tempted to ignore the loud knock at the door when it came, and she did for a moment or two, but then Jared started calling out to her.

"Tessa, I know you're in there, and I want to talk to you."

She didn't respond.

"Tessa." His tone grew more stern. "You can

come out, or I can come in. I've broken this door down before. It won't bother me to do it again."

The last irritated her, and she all but stomped to the portal and threw it wide.

"Yes, Jared?"

"I need to talk to you."

"Why? Didn't you get much conversation out of Melissa?"

His gaze narrowed at her declaration, and then he smiled slightly. "You're jealous?"

"Of what?" She started to turn away.

"I need to talk to you—now." Jared was not a man used to having to beg for favors or explain himself to anyone. He was always honest and straightforward. He said what he thought whether people wanted to hear it or not. When it came to women, though, this one had the power to leave him sounding like a babbling idiot. He wasn't used to begging for things, and he damned well wasn't ready to start now.

"So talk." She turned back toward him and stood with her arms folded across her chest, regarding him with less than welcoming warmth.

"Come outside with me?" Jared held out his hand to her. "Please."

It was as close as he'd come to begging in years, and he found that with Tessa, somehow he didn't really mind.

"Why? Anything you have to say, you can say here."

Her stubbornness was testing him, but he told himself she was worth it.

He dropped his hand away. "Tessa, if I wanted

341

to be with Melissa, I'd be with her right now. I was planning to meet you earlier so we could go to the lecture together, but the Moore brothers caused some trouble and I ended up dealing with a couple of rowdy, not-too-happy cowboys. Believe me, I would rather have been with you." He lowered his voice as he said the last.

"I could tell," she replied coolly.

Not used to explaining himself, he went on in exasperation. "When I got to the hall, there were no seats by you. I was standing just inside the doorway and Melissa grabbed me and took me back to sit with her. There was no way to refuse without everyone noticing. I was trapped."

"Marshal Jared Trent trapped by a young woman?" she repeated, a bit disbelieving.

"Come outside with me. I want to talk to you now." His patience was at an end. He had tried to be reasonable, but it wasn't working.

"Jared, what a nice surprise. We missed you at the lecture tonight," Maggie said as she came up the sidewalk with Jim, Sludge and Henry.

"I was late," he explained, greeting them as politely as he could. He was irritated by the interruption. He wanted to talk to Tessa, but right now he could do nothing about that. "I had to make a couple of arrests." He cast a sidelong, taunting glance at Tessa.

Tessa's expression faltered a little as she imagined him "arresting" Melissa.

"Everything turned out all right?" Jim asked.

"Eventually, but by then Roderick had already started his readings."

"You didn't miss much," Sludge said with a grin.

Henry chuckled in agreement.

"It was . . . different," Maggie went on. "A little too dull for my tastes, but then how often do we get to hear a real, live author reading from his own works? It was a once-in-a-lifetime experience, and I'm glad we all went. Let's go inside and have a cool drink, shall we?"

"I'd love to, Miss Maggie, but first I have to talk to Tessa."

"Well, you two go right ahead. We'll be inside." Maggie bustled indoors with the others following her.

"Tessa?" Jared looked at her, his expression challenging.

Reluctantly she stepped out onto the porch, but she kept her distance from him. "Yes?"

Jared had been anticipating this moment all day. He'd practiced what he was going to say to her. He had been excited about seeing her tonight, just so he could propose—and he'd wanted to do it romantically. He'd wanted her to understand just how much he loved her. It had been a difficult thing for him to admit his feelings for her, but he was ready to declare himself. Yet here she was, frustrating him at every turn, and after the time he'd had with the Moore brothers and Melissa, that was dangerous.

"Damn it, woman, you're coming with me!" Marshal Jared Trent was tired of being ignored. He took Tessa by the arm and pulled her from the porch.

"What are you doing?" Tessa demanded.

"Taking you someplace where we can talk privately," he said in a growl, looking around for a nice, quiet, dark spot where he could have to her to himself. He spotted a wooden swing in the tree at the back of her yard. He stalked toward it, dragging her along with him.

"Where are we going?"

"Back here," he said as he pointed to the swing. "Sit down." His tone was imperious and brooked no argument.

Tessa was smart enough to do what he said.

"Steve made this for Clara and Mark," she told him, unable to resist swinging just a little bit.

"I didn't bring you back here to talk about Steve." He was standing over her, wondering how the situation had gotten so out of control. "I brought you back here because I wanted to have a moment alone with you, but if you keep resisting me, I may have to arrest you for interfering with a lawman trying to do his job."

"Your job?" She looked up at him as he loomed powerfully over her, so tall and broad shouldered and handsome. For all that he appeared angry, she felt no threat.

Jared was glaring down at her in the moonlight and all he wanted to do was kiss her. He was tired of verbally sparring with her. He just wanted to hold her and tell her that he loved her.

"Tessa, I've been waiting all day for this moment." His expression softened a little.

"You have?"

"Melissa means nothing to me. You, of all people, should know that. You're all I've been thinking about. There was nothing I wanted more than to be with you tonight, so I could tell you that I love you—and so I could ask you to marry me." Jared sounded very frustrated as he blurted out his proposal in a less-than-romantic manner.

Tears filled her eyes at his words. "You want to marry me?" she repeated in disbelief.

Jared's voice grew husky as he reached out to stop the swing's slight motion. "Very much."

He bent down to her and kissed her. Tessa met him in the kiss and delighted in it. She'd been holding on to the ropes of the swing, but let go to link her arms around his neck. He drew her up to him and held her close. She fit perfectly against him, and he never wanted to let her go.

"Marry me, Tessa." It was a command.

"Would you threaten to arrest me if I said no?" she asked.

He grinned at the teasing note in her voice. "I may threaten to arrest you if you say yes."

"Then yes, Jared. I'll marry you," she answered sweetly.

His mouth settled over hers in a possessive exchange that let her know she was his. Her response to him was eager.

"I liked the trespassing charge you brought against me last time," Tessa whispered as her lips left his to press kisses along the hard line of his jaw and then down his neck. She smiled to herself when she felt him shudder. It gave her a feeling of power to know that she could evoke such a reaction in him.

Jared needed no further encouragement. He began to caress her, his hands tracing arousing paths over her slender curves.

"Do you want to elope tonight?" he asked as

the idea came to him suddenly. He wanted her and didn't want to wait any longer. "We could find a justice of the peace to marry us right away, I'm sure. I do have a few connections around town."

Tessa looked up at him and smiled, thinking of her dream and knowing that she'd truly found her dream man. He wasn't faceless anymore. "I would love to marry you tonight, but I've always dreamed of having a real wedding."

Jared bit back a groan. "How long will it take?"

"I don't know. Let's go talk to my mother and tell her the good news. She'll know what to do." She started to move away from him.

"Wait."

Jared snared her wrist and pulled her back into his embrace. His mouth captured hers in one last, devastating kiss before he released her.

"Now let's go see your mother."

Tessa was almost laughing in delight as they headed, hand in hand, back to the house.

"Mother!"

"I'm in the parlor," Maggie called out.

They entered to find Maggie and Jim talking. The two looked up when Jared and Tessa stopped in the doorway.

"Mother, Jared and I have something to tell you." Tessa gazed up at the man who would soon be her husband. All the love she felt for him was shining in her eyes.

"What, dear?" Maggie asked; then, seeing her daughter's expression, she knew. She had never seen Tessa look at any man that way before. Though she had always thought Will would be the perfect man for her, she approved of Jared, too.

"Miss Maggie, Tessa and I are going to be married," Jared announced.

Maggie's smile was beautiful as she stood up and went to Jared. She had tears in her eyes when she kissed him on the cheek and then kissed Tessa.

"I couldn't be happier," she told them. She thought the world of Jared. For a fleeting moment she thought of Michael and was sorry that he wasn't there to share in the happy moment. "And I'm sure Michael would approve of your choice."

Jim congratulated them, too.

Tessa hugged her. "I'm going to need your help with planning the wedding, Mother."

"When do you want to start?"

"Now," they both replied.

"How soon do you want to have the ceremony?"

"How fast can we arrange it?" Jared asked, his gaze on Tessa.

She smiled, thrilled by his eagerness.

"I don't know. Let's get started," Maggie said, pleased by his desire to claim her daughter as his own. Jared certainly had good taste in women.

"I'm going to tell the boys," Jim said, and he hurried out into the hallway to call Sludge and Henry down to hear the news. Steve hadn't come home yet, so he'd have to tell him later.

By the time Jared and Tessa stood alone again on the porch, over an hour had passed. Tessa and her mother were to speak to the reverend in the morning, and if all went as they hoped, the wedding would take place in three weeks.

"When I was leaving the lecture hall, I never imagined that the night would end like this," Tessa said dreamily as she stood with her back against Jared's chest. His arms were wrapped securely around her, and she felt loved and cherished and protected.

"How did you think it was going to end?" he asked, brushing a soft kiss against the side of her neck.

"After seeing the way Melissa was looking at you when you were with her, I didn't think I would see you at all tonight. I thought you were going to spend the rest of the evening with her."

"Melissa is a nice person, and I know she would like for me to be romantically interested in her, but I'm not. You're the only woman I want. You're the only woman I need. You're the only woman I love."

Tessa turned in the circle of his arms and splayed her hands out on his chest as she gazed up at him, giving him a half smile. "You're not jealous of my boyfriends, are you?"

"How many are there?"

"I'm very fond of Sludge and Henry."

"I know they're very fond of you, too, but I don't think I have to be jealous of them. They had their chance, but I'm the one you agreed to marry."

She gave a throaty laugh. "And not a minute too soon, either."

Jared kissed her hungrily, parting her lips and delving within to taste her sweetness. Now that he'd found her, he never wanted to let her go. They stayed there in the shadows of the porch, stealing kisses and longing for the time when they could remain together.

"I'd better go now," Jared told her reluctantly. She was too tempting for his own good.

"Will I see you tomorrow?"

"I'll come by first chance I get."

"I'll be waiting for you."

They shared one last embrace, and then he left her.

Jared was in a very good mood as he made his way through town, and he decided to stop at the High Time and celebrate with a drink.

"Evening, Marshal," Dan greeted him.

"Dan," he said, smiling at him.

"The usual?"

He nodded.

"You're looking like you're in a good mood. Things must be quiet around town." He set his whiskey before him.

"I am in a good mood," he responded. "I just asked Tessa Sinclair to marry me, and she said yes."

"Damn!" Dan was impressed. "Congratulations! You are one lucky man."

"I know."

Suzie, one of the High Time's Saloon girls, saw the marshal come in, and hurried up to greet him. She'd long been sweet on Jared Trent, but had had no luck luring him to her bed. He was a challenge to her, and she never gave up trying to gain his interest.

"Good evening, Marshal Trent," Suzie said, posing next to him at the bar and smiling brightly up at him.

"Hello, Suzie."

"What are you doing out tonight?"

"I'm celebrating."

"Oooh, I'd love to help you celebrate," she said, her eyes rounding at the thought.

"I don't think the good marshal's wanting to celebrate that way, Suzie," Dan cautioned. "He's just gotten engaged."

"You have?" Her surprise was real. She looked at him, her eyes wide. "Who's the lucky gal?"

"Miss Tessa," Dan said before Jared could answer.

Suzie's expression reflected her disappointment. "Oh. Well, I'm real happy for you."

"Thank you, Suzie," Jared said. "I'm happy about it, too."

Steve had been sitting alone at a table in the back of the saloon doing some serious drinking when he'd seen Jared come in. He picked up his glass and went to join him.

"Must be a quiet night in town," Steve said with an easy grin.

Jared smiled in welcome. "I just came in to celebrate. Tessa and I are getting married."

"You've got good taste in women."

"Thanks."

Jared had come to respect Steve more and more as he watched him in the community. When he'd finished his drink, Jared was ready to call it a night.

Steve remained in the saloon. He was happy that things had worked out for Jared and Tessa.

He felt a stab of regret. As much as he loved Julie, he could never offer her what Jared could give Tessa—a safe and secure future. He lifted his drink in a silent toast to Jared as a vision of Julie swam before him.

Chapter Twenty-seven

"I think, sweet sister, that I'm going to pay Julie a visit this morning," Roderick announced at breakfast the following day.

He had been pleased with the way his readings had gone the night before and was feeling very good about himself. He knew they would be leaving Durango in another day, and he had little time to make a decision about Julie. Overnight, as he'd lain in bed thinking things over, he'd realized that Julie was a good marriage prospect. She was pretty and intelligent and had money. He wasn't concerned about love. He knew it was a highly overrated emotion. He was more concerned about his future at the university, and he believed Julie would be an asset to him. He planned to broach the subject with her today, but first he wanted to run it past his sister.

"For any special reason?" Ellen asked, pretending to be naive. She'd always known that Julie had feelings for Roderick. When they'd been in school, her friend had always asked her about him, and the few times Julie had seen Roderick, she'd seemed in awe of him. Ellen was pleased that her brother now seemed to return that interest. She secretly believed they would be a good match.

"Well, I've given it much thought, and, though I know we're supposed to be leaving tomorrow, I want to propose to Julie."

Ellen smiled broadly. "I always knew you were a smart man, Roderick. Julie is a wonderful woman."

"I believe we could be happy together."

"I think so, too, and I think she'd make a wonderful sister-in-law. Go see her right away! I can't wait to see what she has to say!"

Julie had finally fallen asleep, but had not slept soundly. She'd awakened numerous times, her thoughts on Steve and the pain she'd seen in his expression as he'd left her earlier that night.

When morning came, Julie lingered in bed, not eager to get up, not eager to face the new day. She was confused and unhappy, and wanted to talk to Steve again. Actually she wanted to do more than just talk to him. The thought of what she wanted to do with him brought a slight smile to her lips, but it immediately faded. She wondered when she would see him again, and what he would say to her when they did meet.

It was midmorning when she ventured downstairs. She knew she was due to have lunch with Ellen and Roderick and so had dressed accordingly, though her heart wasn't in the excursion. She realized she was looking forward to Saturday, when she would be putting them on a stage heading out of Durango.

It amazed Julie that she was feeling that way about Ellen and Roderick, considering how excited she'd been about their visit a mere week before their arrival. She'd learned a lot about herself during these last few days, though, and, as surprising as the revelations had been to her, she knew they were the truth. Julie was glad she'd come to understand the desires of her heart before it was too late.

The knock at the door was answered by her mother. Adele called out that Roderick was there for a visit. The news surprised Julie for they hadn't been due to meet until near noon.

"Why, Roderick, this is a pleasant surprise," Julie said as she went to join him in the parlor.

"You look lovely today." He was standing with her mother as she came in, and he smiled when he saw her.

"Thank you," she said demurely. "Did Ellen come with you?"

"No, we'll be meeting her at noon. I came early because I wanted to have the chance to talk with you for a while. Last night was so busy that I fear we didn't get to spend much time together."

Julie wasn't sorry at all that they hadn't been together last night, but she said nothing.

"I'll leave you two alone," Adele told them. "Roderick, it's always wonderful to see you."

"Thank you, ma'am."

"Do you want to sit in here or out on the porch?" Julie asked.

"This is fine." He went to her and took her hand, drawing her to the sofa.

They sat down, but he still didn't let go of her hand.

Julie's thoughts were on Steve and the memory of what had happened on that very sofa last night. She was hard-pressed to concentrate on what Roderick was saying.

"Julie, I've done some serious thinking these last several days, and I wanted to tell you that . . ." He paused, as if thoughtfully, then continued in earnest. "That I love you, and want you to marry me."

One week—a simple seven days before—those words would have left her ecstatic. She would have accepted his proposal without a thought. But she knew better now.

Julie knew her heart's desire now, and it wasn't Roderick.

It was Steve. No matter how difficult life might prove to be for them, she couldn't imagine an existence without him. She was willing to fight for Steve's love.

Roderick was waiting. He'd expected Julie to be delighted and to accept his proposal immediately. He was a bit put off when she remained so quiet.

"Julie, did you understand?" he ventured, prodding her, trying to hide his annoyance. No doubt, he reasoned, she was just overwhelmed by his proposal. That was why she was being so quiet.

"Roderick . . . you are a very nice man, and I

355

am honored that you have proposed to me, but I'm afraid I can't accept." She pulled her hand away from him and stood up.

"What?"

"I'm sorry, Roderick. I don't love you, and I don't want to marry you."

Anger flared in his eyes. This woman had the unmitigated gall to turn down his proposal of marriage? He was shocked and outraged. He had planned to take her back east and introduce her to polite society, but no more. "I see," he said tersely. "If you'll excuse me, then."

Roderick stood and strode from the house, his head held high, his posture rigid. He did not even bid her mother good-bye, so intent was he on returning to the hotel.

"Ellen," he called loudly as he pounded on her hotel room door.

"Yes, Rod? How did it . . . ?" Her voice trailed off as she saw his expression. "Oh, dear."

"Start packing. We're leaving on the next stage or train out of Durango."

"But I should go say good-bye to Julie."

The ferocious look he shot her ended any thought she had of seeing her friend again. When Roderick had left her, she quickly penned a note to Julie and left it on the dresser in the room.

They were on the noon stage out of town. Roderick hadn't cared about destination. He'd just wanted to leave.

When Julie went to meet them for lunch, she was shocked to learn that they had checked out and already left town. The maid who checked their rooms for them found the note and gave it to her. Julie took it and quickly read it. She returned home, her heart numb from all that had happened.

She longed to see Steve.

Tessa was not eager to make the trip to the mine. She wanted to stay in Durango to be close to Jared, but it was payday, and she knew Will would be expecting her. She and Jim headed out early that Saturday morning, but she detoured as they passed by the marshal's office.

"I have to make one short stop," Tessa told Jim with a conspiratorial smile.

"I think we can spare the time." He grinned back at her, completely understanding her need to see Jared before they left. They would be gone for close to four days, and that was a long time for these two young people to be apart, now that they'd discovered their love for one another.

Tessa reined in and quickly dismounted and tied up her horse. She was wearing her pants, and when Jared looked up as she entered the office, she could see the look of delight on his face.

"Woman, you do look good in those pants," Jared said, admiring her shapely form as she crossed the room to his desk. "Are you leaving already?"

"Jim and I wanted to get an early start, but I didn't want to leave without saying good-bye."

Jared was glad he was alone. He stood and motioned for her to follow him to the back. "I think I need at least one kiss before you leave."

"Only one?" Tessa asked archly as she went straight into his arms and kissed him warmly.

Jared hugged her close. "Hurry back."

Tessa drew away so she could look up at him. "Don't worry. I will. You're waiting here for me."

He tenderly touched her cheek. "That's right—I will be."

They walked back out to the front and he accompanied her outside.

"You take care of my woman for me, Jim," he told the older man.

"I'll keep an eye on her," he promised.

Jared helped her to mount and then let his hand linger on her leg just a moment longer. She was a sight in the pants, and he was thinking seriously of having her wear them all the time once they'd married. The idea held much appeal for him.

"I'll see you in a few days," Tessa said, giving him a look of longing.

Jared nodded and waved as they rode off. He wished he could have taken the time to go with them, but with that gold shipment going out shortly, he had to make sure everything was safe here in town.

Tessa had never before been so glad to reach the mine. The trek had seemed unusually long this time, and she knew it was only because she was already missing Jared. They rode in to find Will in the office and the others working the mine. Jim went to tend to their horses, while Tessa spoke with Will.

"Tessa, you are right on time. It's good to see you," Will said, sitting back down at his desk after offering her a chair before him. He was trying not to let the anger he was still feeling toward her show.

"It's good to see you, too, Will."

"How are things going in town?"

"Just fine." She filled him in on some of the town gossip and told him about Roderick's readings. She knew there was no avoiding telling him her big news. "There is one other thing I wanted to share with you."

"What?" He looked up, curious.

"Jared Trent and I are going to be married," she announced.

Will's expression didn't change, and he was proud of his ability to hide his true feelings. *She was going to marry the lawman?* The realization only increased his ire.

"I see," he ground out.

Will wanted to grab her and slap her for her stupidity. He clenched his hands into fists at his sides. It had been bad enough when she'd told him she thought of him only as a friend, but the news that she was planning to marry the stupid marshal left him almost in a rage. He'd show them! He'd show them both, and in just a few days!

At that moment, Zeke decided to come into the office, unannounced. Tessa was sitting with her back to the door.

"Will, I wanted to tell ya that—"

"Not now, Zeke!" Will snarled at the man, his anger showing.

"But—"

"I said *no!* Miss Tessa and Jim are here. We'll talk business later."

Will could never be sure what Zeke might say, and he didn't want to risk having him around Tessa and Jim.

Terror seized Tessa. She didn't know how she kept from bolting from her chair when Will responded to Zeke's interruption using the same words the outlaw leader had used during the stage robbery: "*I said* no!"

There was no mistaking their voices! There was no doubt in her mind!

Tessa supposed she hadn't noticed the similarity before because she'd been so distracted by Michael's death on her last visit. But now, not seeing Zeke but only hearing him, she was sure. Zeke Ferris and Will were two of the gang who'd robbed the stagecoach!

"I'm sorry if I'm interrupting your work," Tessa said sweetly, congratulating herself on her acting ability as she looked over her shoulder at Zeke.

"No, believe me, Tessa, we look forward to your visit every month," Will said, shooting Zeke a cold look.

The other man backed out of the office and shut the door as he went.

Will discussed how things were going at the mine with her for a while, and then Jim came to join them.

"Did you want to spend the night and head back to town tomorrow?"

Before Jim could say anything, Tessa spoke up. "We'll take you up on lunch, but I want to start back right away. I have a lot of things to get done before the wedding."

"Well, I'll rustle you up some lunch right now,"

Will said, leaving Tessa and Jim alone in the office.

When she was sure that they were alone, Tessa turned frightened eyes to Jim, who was confused by her eagerness to leave.

"Tessa? What's wrong?"

"We've got to get back to town as quickly as possible! I can't believe I didn't realize it before." Her expression was tormented.

"Realize what?"

"Jim, I know this will sound far-fetched, but I'm sure of it. Will and Zeke—they're part of the outlaw gang that robbed the stage I was on."

He looked totally confused. "I don't understand."

"I recognized their voices just now. Zeke came into the room behind me and I didn't see him when he spoke. He was the one who hit Doris and me!"

"You're sure?" Jim asked, looking grim.

"Positive. We've got to get to Jared and tell him, but you can't let on that you think anything suspicious is going on here, all right? I'm counting on you. Heaven only knows what they might do to us if they think we're on to them."

Jim nodded as Tessa started discreetly looking around the office for some clue that she was right, but she found nothing. A few minutes later, when Will brought them a simple lunch, they thanked him and ate hungrily.

Will did not question Tessa's hurry to return. He was glad that she was leaving. He wasn't sure he would have been able to keep his hands off of her—whether in passion or anger—that night if she'd decided to stay.

When they rode away later that afternoon, Tessa and Jim kept their pace normal until they were several miles from the mine. Then they put their heels to their horses' sides and rode as fast as they could. They rode long into the night, but finally had to make camp.

As Tessa lay by the fire, trying to get some sleep, her thoughts were haunted by memories of Michael's death and of Will bringing his body to town. She began to wonder in horror if his death had been an accident at all.

She wanted Jared with her.

Chapter Twenty-eight

Julie had tried to be patient as she'd waited for Steve to come back to her, but her patience ran out with the start of the new week. Determined to speak to him, she went to the Sinclairs' to seek him out. Maggie told her he was working around back, and she went after him.

"Steve."

Steve had been repairing one of the shutters, and he glanced up quickly at the sound of her voice. He had been fighting the good fight with himself. Any number of times he had almost thrown caution to the wind and gone to Julie, but he'd stopped himself each time. He had forced himself to stay away from her, but now she had come to him.

Steve swallowed tightly as he watched her walking toward him. She looked gorgeous. He wanted to go to her immediately and sweep her into his embrace, but he steeled himself against the need.

For days now, he'd been telling himself that he should leave Durango—that he should forget his revenge, forget Julie, and just go. But he couldn't. The need to find the gang was a driving force in his soul, and his love for Julie was his reason for breathing. She had become his whole world. He didn't know what he was going to do about it, but watching her move toward him now, he knew he didn't want to live without her.

"Hello, Julie," he said in a low, cautious voice.

"I've been missing you," she said, stopping a few feet away from him.

"Not as much as I've been missing you," he admitted.

She was heartened by his words, but didn't let the emotion show. "Roderick proposed to me."

Steve went still at this news. He was surprised by how much it hurt. Pain stabbed at his heart. He'd always known that Roderick was the man she wanted. Now he was certain that she would be marrying him and going back east to live just as she'd always wanted to.

"I turned him down," she went on when Steve didn't say anything.

"You turned him down?"

"I don't love him," Julie said simply. "I came here to see you, because I wanted you to know that I'll be waiting for you. I don't care if it takes a month or a year for you to find the men you're after. I love you, Steve Madison, and I will wait forever if I have to."

With that, she turned her back on him and walked away.

* * *

Steve stood unmoving, watching her go. He wanted to run to her and grab her and hold on to her forever, but he didn't. He held himself back. Only when she'd disappeared from sight did he turn back to his work and labor on, finishing the jobs Miss Maggie had given him.

It was after sundown when he decided to go to the High Time to have a drink. He was going to have to make some serious decisions about his life soon, but first he just wanted a shot of whiskey.

Steve had just come into the saloon and walked up to the bar when he heard the sound of raucous laughter coming from upstairs. He glanced up and caught a glimpse of one of the gang members he'd been hunting. The man was coming out of Suzie's room. She was clinging to him, and he was pawing her drunkenly.

"You!" Steve shouted, turning and going for his gun. "Hold it right there!"

Bob went stock-still. Will had sent him into town to see if he could learn anything new about the gold shipment, and he had gotten sidetracked by Suzie. He had been a long time without a woman, and it hadn't taken much for her to get him upstairs after a few drinks. He'd enjoyed having her and was ready to go downstairs to do some serious drinking again, when he heard the man's shout.

Bob looked down toward the bar, and he reacted instantly to the sight of Steve Madison. He remembered far too clearly that night in Arizona when Steve had played poker with him and Zeke in a bar for most of one night. He remembered laughing when he'd heard they'd thought of a way to frame Steve for the crime they were about to commit.

Knowing Steve was the kind of man who would want revenge, Bob panicked and turned back, running at top speed into Suzie's room. He locked the door behind him and all but dove out the window into the deserted alley below. Bob raced off into the night, stealing a horse and making good his getaway out of town.

Gun in hand, Steve ran up the steps, taking them two and three at a time. Suzie was not deliberately blocking his way, but her presence in the hall slowed him down. When he finally reached her room, he tried the door, but found it locked. Steve threw his full weight against it, and the door splintered as it flew open. He charged inside the room, ready for trouble, only to find that the room was empty. The window was open, so he leaned out to try to catch sight of the fleeing outlaw, but the alley was quiet.

Steve's expression was deadly as he came out of the room. Dan was on his way upstairs, carrying his shotgun, ready to help him.

"I'll pay for the repairs to the door," Steve told him. Looking at Suzie, he asked, "What name was that man going by? What do you know about him?"

"He said his name was Bob, and he told me he worked at one of the mines."

"Which mine?" he demanded.

"Miss Tessa's mine. Why?" Dan offered.

Steve holstered his gun as he started back

downstairs. "He's one of the gang that was robbing stagecoaches in Arizona Territory."

"He is?" Suzie was surprised. "Well, he sure paid me good enough."

"I have to find Jared." Steve stalked out of the saloon. There was no time to waste.

Jared was at the office, and Steve was relieved.

"Steve?" Jared saw the man's thunderous expression as he came into the room. "What's wrong?"

"I think I may have found the gang I've been looking for."

Jared frowned. This was the first he'd heard that Steve was searching for anyone. "What gang?"

"Back in Arizona, I spent some time in a saloon drinking and playing poker with two men I didn't know. The next day I was arrested and charged with being a part of their gang and robbing a stagecoach. Nobody believed I wasn't involved, and I went to jail for it."

"Who were they?" Jared was instantly aware that they could be the same men he was after.

"I never met the leader. I've learned since that he was known as Dave Turner in Arizona. Clark and Roberts were the two men I played cards with. Howard's in jail in Arizona, and I just saw Clark over at the High Time. I tried to catch him, but he got away. Dan says he's a miner who works at Tessa's mine, and Suzie says he's going by the name of Bob. We need to ride for the mine tonight."

Jared got up and grabbed his hat. Tessa was at the mine with only Jim to protect her. They had to ride out as soon as possible. "Let's go find Nathan."

"There's no time! We need to—"

Jared looked Steve straight in the eye. "I know you don't have a whole lot of love for lawmen, but right now, you need to trust me on this. There's more going on here than you know about."

Steve returned his regard and saw that he was serious. "All right, Jared, but whatever you do, I'm riding with you."

Jared paused for only an instant, then walked back to his desk. He opened a drawer. He took something out and tossed it to Steve. "Here, pin that on. You're with me now."

Steve stared down at the deputy's badge he held in his hand. "But I'm a—"

"You're a deputy," Jared cut him off. "Put on your badge, and let's go. We've got to catch us some bad guys." He led the way from the office.

Half an hour later they were back in the office, along with Nathan, Tom, and two other men who served as deputies when needed.

"Men, this is Steve Madison. I've just deputized him. He's riding with me tonight. Here's what we're dealing with."

He'd just started to explain the situation and his suspicions about the gold shipment when two horses came charging up before the marshal's office. He looked out to see Tessa and Jim dismount and come rushing inside.

"Jared! Thank heaven you're here!" Tessa said as she hurried to him. She noticed the grim looks on the faces of the men gathered there, and wondered at their presence.

Relief rushed through Jared at the sight of her, and he was hard-pressed not to grab her up in a protective embrace. He had been worried about her, fearing for her safety, and now she was here with him.

"You're safe," he said, allowing himself that much emotion before his men.

"Yes, but Durango might not be for long. It's them, Jared!" she related. "I don't know why I didn't realize it before, but Will and Zeke—I recognized their voices when Jim and I were up at the mine. They were two of the men who robbed the stage I was on!"

Jared looked up at Steve and nodded. "Steve just saw the man named Bob who works for you, and Steve believes he's part of the gang that was robbing stages in Arizona."

Tessa looked at Steve. "Bob was here? In town? When Jim and I were at the mine, they told us that he was working down in the shaft."

"So they are using aliases here," Steve said,

"Will Kenner, Bob Matlin, and Zeke Ferris," Tessa supplied.

"All right, men. We know what we have to do. Nathan, you and Tom meet with Lyle Stevens right away. The gold shipment is due to go out day after tomorrow. You make sure the stage runs, but that the gold is not on it. I want you two riding as passengers, and I want you armed and ready for trouble. This is going to be dangerous, so be sharp."

"What if there is no robbery attempt?" Tom asked.

"Then you'll be getting a free trip to Canyon Creek," Jared told him. "Steve and I will ride up to the mine to try to catch them before they attack the stage."

"I'm going along with you, Jared!" Tessa declared.

"No, Tessa. I want you to stay here in town, where I know you'll be safe," Jared said.

"Jared Trent," she said angrily, planting her hands on her hips. "This is my mine, and those men are working for me. I am going with you. Besides," she added slowly. "I was thinking about Michael on the ride back with Jim and wondering if his death was really an accident, as they said. What if he found out what they were doing and they killed him for it?"

Jared looked somber as he remembered how superficial Will's wounds had been, and yet the man had claimed to be in the same cave-in as Michael. "Tessa, I understand why you're concerned, but I'd feel better if you would stay here and let me handle it. This could get very dangerous."

"If you try to leave me behind, Jared, I will follow you. One way or the other, I am going after them. That is my mine and it was my brother who died. I'm involved in this."

Jared thought she looked magnificent as she stood up to him. Her eyes were sparkling with anger and fire as she faced the truth of what really might have happened to her brother.

"All right," Jared agreed. "How long will it take you to be ready to ride?"

"Fifteen minutes," she told him.

"Be back here then."

She nodded and left the marshal's office with Jim following her.

* * *

"Miss Tessa, do you think this is a good idea?" Jim asked, worrying about her.

"I have to do it, Jim—for Michael."

She swung up into her saddle and rode for home. She had to tell her mother what was happening. Then she would gather what she needed for long days on the trail, get a fresh mount, and meet Jared and Steve.

Once Tessa had gone, Jared put his other two deputies in charge of the town. He and Steve quickly gathered the rifles and ammunition and other supplies they'd need; then they saddled their horses. When Tessa returned from convincing her mother that this was something she had to do, they were ready to ride out.

As they rode out of town, they passed the Stevens' house. Steve was looking for Julie, but saw no sign of her. He glanced down and saw the badge pinned to his shirt. It felt different to be on this side of the law. Grim-faced, he concentrated on the quest ahead of them. He was ready to seek justice.

They traveled long into the night, and when they finally made camp, they were all exhausted. Tessa had matched Jared and Steve mile for mile and had never uttered a complaint. Jared saw to building the fire while Steve tended the horses. Tessa got her bedroll and was walking toward the fire with it.

"Put it right there," Jared directed, pointing to where he'd already laid out his own. He wanted her right next to him, so he could make sure she was safe and protected.

He hadn't said much to her since they'd left town, and she'd thought he was angry with her for insisting that he bring her along. She spread her bedroll on the ground next to his.

They didn't even bother about food. They were all too tired. Steve bedded down across the camp-fire from them. Both men kept their guns close at hand, knowing that trouble could come at any moment.

Tessa lay close beside Jared, staring up at the stars. It was a beautiful night, but she didn't notice. Her thoughts were dark and troubled.

"Do you think they killed Michael, Jared?" she asked him in a hushed, pained voice.

"We'll know more when we get to the mine, but thinking about how minor Will's injuries were compared to your brother's, I think there's a good chance."

Jared looked over at her and saw a lone tear trace a path down her cheek. He reached out to her and drew her near. She curled against him, her back to his chest. Holding her felt wonderful, but her pain was real to him. He did not try to kiss her. He wanted only to hold her close and keep her safe. They didn't speak again. There was nothing more to say.

When at long last Tessa slept, her dreams were troubled by visions of the outlaws at the stage robbery and Will riding into town with Michael's body.

Dawn found them riding out again. It was late afternoon when they neared the mine. Tessa had described the layout of the mine, and they were not going to take any chances riding in. Steve left his horse a distance away and moved silently on foot over the rocky terrain until he found a good position above the mine's entrance. He would be there, armed and ready, as Jared and Tessa rode in.

When all was ready, Jared and Tessa started toward the mine. Jared's hand was resting on his sidearm. He expected trouble and insisted Tessa ride some distance behind him.

The silence that greeted Jared worried him more than if Will Kenner had come out to meet them. Ever alert, he reined in before the mining office, dismounted and tried the door. It was unlocked. He shoved it open, staying back in case someone was hiding inside, but there was no sound or movement from within. Jared entered the building to find it deserted.

"Where would they keep their horses?" he asked Tessa as he came back outside.

"That's the stable over there."

"Stay right here," he ordered.

She wanted to go with him, but did as he'd told her. Jared strode to the stable and cautiously checked it out, too. A few moments later he returned to her.

"They're already gone," he said in disgust. He gave Steve the signal to join them.

"The one I saw in town must have hightailed it back here last night," Steve said as he stood with Jared and Tessa in the office.

"I want to look in that mine shaft where they said Michael was killed," Tessa said, wondering now why it had been boarded up.

Steve stayed outside to stand guard while Jared and Tessa took lanterns and a pick with them. She directed him toward the abandoned shaft.

"This is it," she said as they came to the turnoff. To her shock, the barricade had been torn down.

"I wonder why this is down?"

"I've got an idea," Jared said, realizing just how treacherous and conniving this gang was. He'd never heard of anyone doing anything like what he suspected, but it was brilliant. When they started down the shaft, his suspicions were confirmed.

"Tessa, look." Jared pointed to several gold coins on the ground. He bent to pick them up then continued on. A short distance later he found an empty chest on the floor. "That's what I thought."

"They were hiding the money here? In this shaft?" Tessa said, horrified at what had been going on at her mine.

"And look—there's no sign of any recent cave-ins." He was examining the support timbers.

"Michael must have found out what they were doing, and they killed him for it," Tessa said, lifting her tormented gaze to Jared as her worst imaginings were confirmed.

A muscle worked in Jared's jaw as he controlled his fury. He understood her helplessness and her horror. He opened his arms to her, and she went to him without speaking. The pain of discovering the truth was too great. She turned her face to his chest as sobs of anguish racked her. Jared knew there was nothing he could say that would make things better for her. He could only find the men who'd done this and bring them to justice.

And he would—for her.

Chapter Twenty-nine

Nathan and Tom remembered Jared's warning, and they were as ready as they could be when the shots rang out. Harley Jenkins, the stage driver, leaned low and urged the team to a faster pace, trying to escape the assault.

"Damn!" Nathan swore, glancing over at Tom as he grabbed his rifle. "I wonder what happened to Jared?"

"I don't know, and we don't have time to worry about it right now!" Tom replied.

Rifles in hand, they began to return fire out the windows of the stage.

Nathan and Tom's efforts did not deter their attackers, though. Will, Zeke, and Bob had planned a long time for this robbery. They were going to grab the gold and get out of Colorado while they could—especially now that they knew

Steve Madison was on to them. They'd picked this particular site for the robbery because just up ahead was an area where the hillsides were steep and rocky. They'd dislodged several large rocks and sent them tumbling to the road below. The stage might try to outrun them, but it wouldn't get far—and then the gold would be theirs.

Jared, Tessa, and Steve had been after the outlaws since leaving the mine. The miles had seemed endless over the rugged terrain, and tracking had been difficult, but this time Jared never lost the trail. It took him only half a day to realize where the gang was planning to rob the stage, and they had increased their pace, hoping to stop the gang before they could attempt the robbery.

They came close.

The sounds of shots being fired reached them as they rode across country, and Jared and Steve drew their guns.

"Tessa, stay back here!" Jared ordered.

Jared had already discussed with Tessa what he expected of her when this moment came, and she had agreed to stay out of harm's way and let him handle it. He had given her a handgun to protect herself, just in case one of the gang tried to make a run for it. So she was forced to stay behind as Jared and Steve spurred their horses to a dead run.

Will, Zeke, and Bob were all wearing their masks as they shouted down to the stage driver from their vantage points above.

"Throw down your weapons!" Will ordered. He'd been surprised that there had been return fire from the passengers, but then he'd realized this was a valuable shipment, and he should have expected guards to be riding with it.

Harley did as he was told.

"You passengers! I want to see your guns thrown out, too!" he shouted. "Or the driver's dead!"

From where he had positioned himself, Will could see two rifles tossed out the stagecoach window.

"That's better. Now, you passengers! Open that door real easy-like and climb out of there. Keep your hands up and nobody'll get hurt!"

Nathan and Tom shared a look.

"What do you think? We've still got our sidearms," Tom said hopefully.

"They won't do us much good, pinned down like we are. Where the hell is Jared?" Nathan said in growl. "He should have been here by now."

"You'd better take off your badge," Tom warned him.

Both men quickly put their deputy's badges in their pockets.

"You! In the stage! Get out now, or we start shooting again!"

Trapped, they swung the door open and slowly got out. They took care not to make any unexpected moves. They didn't want to give these men any reason to shoot. The gang was going to be angry enough as it was once they found out there was no gold in the strongbox.

* * *

"All right," Will said triumphantly as he saw the two men emerge. "Zeke, you and Bob go down there and get that strongbox."

Zeke was almost rabid in his excitement to get to the stage. The thought that this robbery would keep him from working for a very long time was a big incentive to him. He led the way down to the stranded stage. Reining in, he dismounted and climbed up on the driver's seat to grab the strongbox, while Bob rode over to keep an eye on the two passengers. He dismounted and collected their rifles off the ground.

"They were worried about this shipment!" Bob called out to Will as he eyed Nathan and Tom. He recognized them from town even without their badges on. "These two boys are deputies!"

Zeke didn't give the driver or the two men a thought as he dragged the strongbox from the boot. It was very heavy, so he let it drop to the ground, intending to scoop up the gold once he'd opened it.

"What the . . . ?" Zeke said in a stunned voice when he saw what spilled out on the ground—rocks, nothing but rocks.

"What is it?" Bob asked, staring in shock at the contents.

"Why, you—" Zeke turned on Nathan and Tom and raised his gun, ready to shoot them where they stood.

"What is it?" Will called down.

"There ain't no gold! It's all a hoax! There ain't nothing here worth anything at all!"

"What?" Will couldn't believe it. He'd heard about the shipment from the banker himself.

He emerged from his hiding place and started down toward the road, determined to find out what was going on. There were two deputies riding with the stage, yet there was no gold. Why?

The sudden realization that they might have been lured into a trap jarred Will.

"Boys, let's get the hell out of here!" Will shouted, wheeling his horse around. "Now!"

"Hold it right there, Will Kenner—or whatever your name is!" Jared shouted. He and Steve had maneuvered themselves into position above the road and had watched as Nathan and Tom were forced to climb out of the stage. "This is Jared Trent. You're all under arrest for attempted robbery. Drop your weapons and give yourselves up."

"The hell with you!" Will yelled back.

"We got you in our sights," Jared warned them. "You aren't going anywhere."

Will ignored him. Ripping off his mask, he urged his horse on, desperate to escape. When a shot exploded in front of him, though, the horse shied and reared. Will drew his handgun and fired back at Jared as he fought to keep his seat and control his mount. His shots went wild.

As the shooting began, Nathan and Tom both dove for cover, and so did Harley. The deputies drew their sidearms and began to fire at Zeke and Bob as the driver crouched behind them.

The two outlaws tore off their masks and raced for their horses. They paused only long enough to return fire. One of Zeke's rounds wounded Nathan in the shoulder, but Bob screamed and collapsed in the dirt when Tom got off a clean shot at him.

"You all right?" Tom called over to Nathan.

"I'll live," he said with a groan.

Zeke kept firing at them to discourage them from coming after him, as he successfully managed to get on his horse and ride out.

Steve was in a perfect position to deal with any fleeing outlaws. He took careful aim at Zeke and fired once. His aim was true and deadly.

Zeke shrieked in agony as the bullet tore into his chest. He fell from his horse and was dead before he hit the ground.

Will was leaning low over his horse's neck and trying to make a run for it. He'd witnessed the carnage below and realized he was running for his life. The horse charged on as best it could on the rocky terrain.

Jared was already giving chase, taking what shots he could at Will as he closed the distance between them. This was the leader of the gang that had been robbing stages in his town and had been behind Michael's death. He was not going to get away from Jared. Will Kenner was his.

Tessa had heard all the vicious gunfire and began to fear for Jared's and Steve's safety. She knew Jared had told her to stay where he'd left her, but she couldn't wait there any longer. She had to be sure he was safe.

The chase didn't last long. Will made it to the road ahead of the stage and paused to get a shot off at Jared, but he never got the chance. His stopping gave Jared the opportunity he needed. With careful aim and deliberation, he fired at Will. The outlaw leader screamed in pain and fell from his horse.

Steve had ridden after Jared to help him. He

reined in beside Jared, who now stood over Will, where he lay facedown in the dirt. The bullet had struck him in the back, but he was still breathing. Jared had his gun in hand, and his expression was stony.

"He dead?" Steve asked, coming to stand with him.

"No," Jared said tersely. He kicked the gun from Will's grip, not trusting him no matter how serious his wound, and then rolled him over.

Will groaned and opened his eyes. He glared up at Jared and Steve, hatred plain in his expression. "You thought you were so damned smart," he said with a sneer and gave a strangled laugh. "You ain't nothing but a fool: All that time you were searching for the robbers, and I was right there. You didn't even know it." His eyes closed again.

The sound of a horse coming at top speed caused Jared to look up, and he saw Tessa galloping toward them.

Tessa had ridden down to the stage, searching for Jared, and Tom had told her the direction in which he and Steve had gone. Frantic, she'd followed them, giving no thought to her own safety. Finding Jared and Steve standing over Will, she reined in and dismounted. She ran to Jared's side and immediately wrapped her arms around his waist.

"You're all right?"

"I'm fine."

Will opened his eyes again at the sound of Tessa's voice. What he saw infuriated him. Tessa was hugging the lawman! He found strength enough to lever himself up a bit on one elbow.

"You bitch!" he managed in a hate-filled voice. "You ruined everything! You and your stupid brother!"

"Will!" she gasped and looked down at him. The malevolent look on his face frightened her. She had never seen such open hostility in anyone before.

"I'm glad I killed your precious brother! I'm glad!" Will said, laughing crazily.

Jared tightened his arm protectively around Tessa when he felt her stiffen and then begin to tremble at Will's confession. Their worst fears had been confirmed. Michael's death had been no accident. He had been murdered.

"I could have had you, Tessa. I was going to have you. You were mine." Will's gaze was feverish as he stared at her. The sight of Tessa in Jared's arms represented everything that had gone wrong in Durango. He'd planned everything perfectly and now . . . Mindless anger filled him. He wanted to get even with them.

"Jared, go on. Get Tessa out of here." Steve gestured toward the horses. "I'll take care of him."

Jared holstered his gun and started to walk away with Tessa. She was clinging to him, needing his strength and his support.

Mad with pain and fury, Will saw his gun lying in the dirt a few feet away, where Jared had kicked it earlier. With what little strength he had left, Will made a lunge for the weapon as he screamed Tessa's name.

Steve reacted instinctively. He had been watching Jared and Tessa, wanting to make sure she was going to be all right, but when Will made his move, Steve turned and fired before the outlaw could get off a shot.

Steve's aim was unerring and true.

Will Kenner would never hurt anyone again.

Epilogue

The church was aglow with candlelight, and the heavenly scent of flowers filled the air as Tessa slowly made her way down the aisle. The full skirt of her lace and satin bridal gown swayed gracefully about her hips as she moved ever forward.

She was getting married.

At last, she was getting married.

All around her were her friends and family. They were smiling as she passed them, their gazes warm and approving upon her as they whispered among themselves.

"She looks so lovely."

"I always knew she'd make a beautiful bride."

Tessa lifted her gaze to the altar. She could see the reverend waiting for her, Bible in hand. At the end of the aisle and off to the side, with his back to her, stood her future husband.

Tessa smiled. Her mother had been urging her to find a good man and settle down for several years now, and it seemed the time had finally come. Getting married to the man she loved was every woman's dream, and her groom was her dream man. He was tall and dark and handsome and . . .

Her heartbeat quickened as she reached the end of the aisle. Anticipation quivered through her.

This was her wedding day. She was going to live happily ever after.

Tessa stopped before the minister, who was gazing down at her, his expression serious. The moment had come. She was to be married.

The minister began the ceremony, "Dearly beloved, we are gathered here today . . ."

Tessa started to turn, to look up at her future husband as the minister went on. She wanted to gaze into her beloved's eyes and let him know without words just how much she loved him.

". . . to join in holy matrimony . . ."

This was the man she had dreamed of. This was the man she'd been waiting for. This was the man she wanted to spend the rest of her life with.

"Tessa Sinclair and . . ."

Tessa's gaze met Jared's and she smiled serenely. He was so handsome, so strong and powerful—and he was hers.

"Jared Trent," the minister said.

Tessa's heart was pounding a frantic rhythm and her pulse was racing, but it had nothing to do with fear. It had everything to do with love. No longer was her dream man a faceless phantom. Jared was real. Jared was her love.

They repeated their vows, each word heartfelt, as they pledged themselves to each other.

"I now pronounce you man and wife," the minister announced. "You may kiss your bride."

Jared stared down at Tessa and thought she had never looked more beautiful than she did now in her bridal gown. With utmost care and tenderness, he gathered her close and kissed her. His lips moved over hers in a cherishing exchange that sealed the vow he'd just made. Tessa had never known such happiness.

"I love you, Jared," she whispered when he released her.

He smiled down at her. "I love you, too."

The music started up then. Tessa took Jared's arm, and he walked her down the aisle. They looked blissfully happy, and all who'd gathered for the wedding were delighted at the match.

Jared glanced down at his bride as they emerged from the church into the sunlight. He had not known that he could ever be this happy. In the inside pocket of his jacket, he carried his father's Bible. The weight of it so near to his heart reminded him that there was no greater gift than to love and be loved.

Steve looked down at Julie as Jared and Tessa passed by their pew.

"You aren't sorry we didn't have a big wedding like this, are you?" he asked, frowning slightly, worried.

Julie gazed up at her husband and smiled. "Not at all. A wedding was never important to me. What was important to me was marrying the man I love—and I did."

Her words touched him deeply, and right there in front of everybody, Steve bent to her and gave her a sweet kiss. The day they'd returned to town from tracking the outlaws, he hadn't even bothered to stop at the boardinghouse and get cleaned up. He had ridden straight to Julie's house to propose. She'd accepted and had insisted that they go find a justice of the peace right then. Steve had never regretted their haste, and he knew he never would.

"I didn't know life could be this wonderful," he told her seriously.

For years before he'd gone to prison, he'd moved from town to town, never staying in one place long enough to make any friends. Now he had Julie, her parents had accepted him without reserve, and Jared had given him the deputy's job permanently. They would have a good life together. He was going to see to it.

Trace and Elise had looked on in delight as they'd listened to Jared and Tessa exchange their vows.

"Thinking of another wedding, love?" Trace asked.

"I was thinking of several weddings," she told him, slanting him a conspiratorial smile. She remembered how she'd first met Trace and how she'd bribed him to "marry" her so she could finish investigating the story she'd been writing for the newspaper. "I liked our second wedding the best."

"So did I," he agreed.

"Do I get to tell Jared that I told him so?" Elise asked as she watched the couple walk down the aisle on their way out of the church.

"There's no need. They've found each other, and they're happy. That's all that matters."

They started to file from the pew to congratulate the newlyweds.

Della Emerson attended the wedding and watched with pure love in her heart as Tessa and Jared were married. She had never known two more wonderful people. She thanked God for Jared's and Tessa's help in her time of trouble and prayed that their life together would be blessed.

It was after dark when Jared and Tessa finally escaped from the reception given by her mother. The house had been crowded with well-wishers, and they'd had a wonderful time enjoying the delicious food and friendship. But they had also been eagerly awaiting the moment when they could escape and be alone together. Any number of times, their gazes had met across the room, and they'd both known that soon, very soon, they would be man and wife in all ways.

"We could go to the jail," Jared suggested as he drove the carriage to his house.

"Don't tempt me," Tessa replied, giving him a very suggestive smile. "I want to disturb your peace tonight, and I'm definitely looking forward to doing some trespassing."

"So am I," he said, his voice husky with emotion.

"Can you go a little faster?" Tessa asked, resting her hand on his thigh and smiling when she felt him tense beneath her touch.

Jared just slanted her a devilish grin and slapped the reins on the horse's back. When they drew to a stop before the house, he climbed down and tied the horse up, then came back to help her out of the carriage. Tessa leaned forward and braced her hands on Jared's broad shoulders, giving him an unrestricted, enticing view of her bodice. Her breasts swelled temptingly before him, and her body made contact with his as he lifted her down.

Heat jolted through Jared and settled low in his body. Excitement pulsed to life within him at the thought that soon—very soon—she would be his in all ways. He wanted to kiss her right then and there, but he feared that if he did, he wouldn't be able to control his desire for her until they got inside. She was just too irresistible.

They made their way to the porch, and without saying a word, he scooped her up into his arms and carried her over the threshold.

"Welcome home, Mrs. Trent," he told her as he kicked the door shut behind them and locked it.

Slowly Jared lowered her to her feet and pulled her to him. His mouth claimed hers in a passionate kiss that spoke of love and need and burning desire. Tessa met him eagerly in that exchange, wanting him to know that she needed him as much as he needed her.

"I love you, Jared," she whispered when they finally ended the kiss.

Jared's eyes had darkened with the power of his emotions. He slipped out of his jacket and tie and began to unbutton his shirt. He did not want to waste any time. They had waited long enough for this moment.

Tessa felt decidedly brazen. She went to him and brushed his hands aside, finishing the buttons for him and then caressing the hard, golden width of his chest. He started to grab her and kiss her, but she gave a low laugh and took his hand to lead him toward the bedroom.

She was smiling, for nothing was going to interrupt them this time. Steve and Tom were in charge of things around town tonight. Jared was hers, alone.

"I need your help," she said softly as she went to the bed and then turned back to face him, leaning slightly against it. She gave him a sensuous look as she lifted her skirts to give him a view of her legs. "Can you slip my garter off?"

Jared was staring at the beauty of her legs, bared to him for the first time. He'd always known they would be attractive, but he hadn't dreamed they would be this beautiful. He went to her and knelt before her. He ran one hand up her thigh, caressing the silken length, then paused to toy with the garter. He lifted his gaze to hers, and she could see the fiery passion burning there. Ever so slowly he slipped the garter lower and lower. His hands trailed fire upon her willing flesh, and she gasped at the erotic sensation. When at last he'd slipped the garter from her leg, she shivered in anticipation of what was to come.

"Was I trespassing?" he asked, rising to stand before her.

"No, you have my full permission," she said with a smile as she reached out to help him slip his shirt off.

Jared stood still, letting Tessa have her way with him. She drew back and reached up to take off her veil. He took her by the shoulders and turned her so he could help remove the hairpins that held the veil in place in back. When she'd set it aside, he began to work at the buttons at the back of her gown.

Tessa waited in breathless anticipation as Jared unfastened the gown, and she gasped as it fell from her shoulders. She stood before him clad only in her chemise and petticoats. Turning to face him, she could see the hunger in his expression. She slowly and deliberately slipped off her voluminous petticoats and then went to him, not wanting to wait any longer to love him.

Jared gave a low growl as he lifted her in his arms and carried her to the bed. He lay with her upon the welcoming softness, savoring her nearness. All thoughts of reality vanished as they were caught up in a world of love.

They came together in a rush of desire—wanting, needing, loving. Each caress, each kiss took them closer and closer to the sweetness of love's perfection.

Tessa was an innocent, and Jared knew he had to be gentle with her. With the utmost care, he taught her the beauty of loving and introduced her to the ecstasy that would be theirs forever. She proved an apt and eager pupil, responding to him fully and without reserve.

When the last of their clothing had, at long last, been stripped away, Jared moved to make her his own. Tessa cried out her love for him and trembled with the force of the emotions that filled her as his body joined with hers.

They were one.

A long time later, they lay together enjoying the peace and beauty of the moment.

"Are you sorry we had the big wedding, Jared?" Tessa asked as she raised herself up on one elbow to look at him so she could read his expression. "I know you wanted to elope."

"I only wanted to elope so I could make love to you sooner," he told her with a sensual smile.

"If I had known what I was missing a few weeks ago, I would have agreed to elope with you in a minute."

Jared gazed at her lovingly. He lifted one hand to gently touch her cheek. "Every time I think about what you've suffered . . ."

"It's over now," she said softly, thinking of Michael and missing him. "You were wonderful, Jared. You caught Will and his gang. They'll never hurt anyone else, thanks to you, and you saved me from Boyd, too. Sometimes I think you're my guardian angel."

He smiled up at her. "I think I like being your husband better."

Jared drew her down to him and kissed her. They loved long into the night, sharing the exquisite beauty of their passion and desire.

Dawn found them wrapped in each other's arms, watching the sun rise. The eastern horizon was a breathtaking rainbow of pink and gold and glowing vibrant light, and they knew their future together would be as beautiful as the beginning of this new day.

They would live happily ever after.

BRIDES OF DURANGO: ELISE
BOBBI SMITH

Elise Martin will do anything for a story—even stage a fake marriage to catch a thief. Dressed in a white lace gown, she looks every bit the bride, but when her "fiancé" fails to show, she offers ten dollars to the handsome gentleman who just stepped off the stage to pose as the groom. As a fake fiancé, he is all right, but when he turns out to be Gabriel West, the new owner of her paper, the *Durango Star*, Elise wants to turn tail and run. But she can't forget the passion his unexpected kiss at their "wedding" aroused, and she starts to wonder if there is more to Gabriel West than meets the eye. For the more time they spend together, the more Elise wonders if the next time she says, "I do" she just might mean it.

___4575-3 $5.99 US/$6.99 CAN

Dorchester Publishing Co., Inc.
P.O. Box 6640
Wayne, PA 19087-8640

Please add $1.75 for shipping and handling for the first book and $.50 for each book thereafter. NY, NYC, and PA residents, please add appropriate sales tax. No cash, stamps, or C.O.D.s. All orders shipped within 6 weeks via postal service book rate. Canadian orders require $2.00 extra postage and must be paid in U.S. dollars through a U.S. banking facility.

Name_____
Address_____
City_____ State_____ Zip_____
I have enclosed $_____ in payment for the checked book(s).
Payment <u>must</u> accompany all orders. ❑ Please send a free catalog.
    CHECK OUT OUR WEBSITE! www.dorchesterpub.com

BOBBI SMITH

THE LADY & THE TEXAN

"A fine storyteller!"—*Romantic Times*

A firebrand since the day she was born, Amanda Taylor always stands up for what she believes in. She won't let any man control her—especially a man like gunslinger Jack Logan. Even though Jack knows Amanda is trouble, her defiant spirit only spurs his hunger for her. He discovers that keeping the dark-haired tigress at bay is a lot harder than outsmarting the outlaws after his hide—and surrendering to her sweet fury is a heck of a lot riskier.

___4319-X $5.99 US/$6.99 CAN

HALF-BREED'S

Lady

BOBBI SMITH

To artist Glynna Williams, Texas is a land of wild beauty, carved by God's hand, untouched as yet by man's. And the most exciting part of it is the fierce, bare-chested half-breed who saves her from a rampaging bull. As she spends the days sketching his magnificent body, she dreams of spending the nights in his arms.

___4436-6 $5.99 US/$6.99 CAN

Dorchester Publishing Co., Inc.
P.O. Box 6640
Wayne, PA 19087-8640

Please add $1.75 for shipping and handling for the first book and $.50 for each book thereafter. NY, NYC, and PA residents, please add appropriate sales tax. No cash, stamps, or C.O.D.s. All orders shipped within 6 weeks via postal service book rate. Canadian orders require $2.00 extra postage and must be paid in U.S. dollars through a U.S. banking facility.

Name_____
Address_____
City_____ State_____ Zip_____
I have enclosed $_____ in payment for the checked book(s).
Payment <u>must</u> accompany all orders. ❏ Please send a free catalog.
CHECK OUT OUR WEBSITE! www.dorchesterpub.com

WESTON'S *Lady*
BOBBI SMITH

There are Cowboys and Indians, trick riding, thrills and excitement for everyone. And if Liberty Jones has anything to say about it, she will be a part of the Wild West show, too. She has demonstrated her expertise with a gun by shooting a card out of Reed Weston's hand at thirty paces, but the arrogant owner of the Stampede won't even give her a chance. Disguising herself as a boy, Libby wangles herself a job with the show, and before she knows it Reed is firing at her—in front of an audience. It seems an emotional showdown is inevitable whenever they come together, but Libby has set her sights on Reed's heart and she vows she will prove her love is every bit as true as her aim.

___4512-5 $5.99 US/$6.99 CAN

Dorchester Publishing Co., Inc.
P.O. Box 6640
Wayne, PA 19087-8640

Please add $1.75 for shipping and handling for the first book and $.50 for each book thereafter. NY, NYC, and PA residents, please add appropriate sales tax. No cash, stamps, or C.O.D.s. All orders shipped within 6 weeks via postal service book rate. Canadian orders require $2.00 extra postage and must be paid in U.S. dollars through a U.S. banking facility.

Name_____
Address_____
City_____State_____Zip_____
I have enclosed $_____ in payment for the checked book(s).
Payment <u>must</u> accompany all orders. ❑ Please send a free catalog.
    CHECK OUT OUR WEBSITE! www.dorchesterpub.com

A FAERIE TALE ROMANCE

VICTORIA ALEXANDER

Ophelia Kendrake has barely finished conning the coat off a cardsharp's back when she stumbles into Dead End, Wyoming. Mistaken for the Countess of Bridgewater, Ophelia sees no reason to reveal herself until she has stripped the hamlet of its fortunes and escaped into the sunset. But the free-spirited beauty almost swallows her script when she meets Tyler, the town's virile young mayor. When Tyler Matthews returns from an Ivy League college, he simply wants to settle down and enjoy the simplicity of ranching. But his aunt and uncle are set on making a silk purse out of Dead End, and Tyler is going to be the new mayor. It's a job he takes with little relish—until he catches a glimpse of the village's newest visitor.

_52159-8 $5.50 US/$6.50 CAN

The Snow Queen

Anne Avery

When Boston-bred Hetty Malone arrives at the Colorado Springs train station, she is full of hope that she will soon marry her childhood sweetheart and live happily ever after. Yet life amid the ice-capped Rockies has changed Michael Ryan. No longer the hot-blooded suitor Hetty remembers, the young doctor has grown as cold and distant as the snowy mountain peaks. Determined to revive Michael's passionate longing, Hetty quickly realizes that no modern medicine can cure what ails him. But in the enchanted splendor of her new home, she dares to administer the only remedy that might melt his frozen heart: a dose of good old-fashioned loving.

__52151-2 $5.99 US/$6.99 CAN

ATTENTION ROMANCE CUSTOMERS!

SPECIAL TOLL-FREE NUMBER
1-800-481-9191

Call Monday through Friday
10 a.m. to 9 p.m.
Eastern Time
Get a free catalogue,
join the Romance Book Club,
and order books using your
Visa, MasterCard,
or Discover®

Leisure
Books